"This vivid historical novel of 1840s Medicine Bow Indian Territory graphically depicts cross-cultural stresses through several generations. . . . An historical romance infused with Indian lore and Western color."

—*Publishers Weekly*

"Lambert has written a powerful story of the Plains Indians. . . . She has packed it with facts about Indian life and customs and tempered it with love and family loyalty."

—*Library Journal*

"Lambert gives soul and life to her characters in this touching tale of transition from girl to woman."

—Wichita Falls *Times Record News*

"Shi_____
hear_____
strin_____

"Lar_____
histo_____
such_____

SHIFTING STARS

STARS

A NOVEL OF THE WEST

PAGE LAMBERT

A TOM DOHERTY ASSOCIATES BOOK
NEW YORK

6-07
6-

This is a work of fiction. All the characters and events portrayed in this book are either products of the author's imagination or are used fictitiously.

SHIFTING STARS

"October Song" used by permission of the author, Elizabeth Canfield. "Song for the Sky" used by permission of the author, Gwen Morgan-Jones.

A Forge Book
Published by Tom Doherty Associates, Inc.
175 Fifth Avenue
New York, NY 10010

Forge® is a registered trademark of Tom Doherty Associates, Inc.

ISBN: 0-812-57149-5
Library of Congress Catalog Card Number: 96-53930

First edition: June 1997
First mass market edition: February 1999

Printed in the United States of America

0 9 8 7 6 5 4 3 2 1

In honor of my paternal grandmother, Helen Denishia Terry Dunton, born in the Choctaw Nation, Oklahoma Territory, November 11, 1894, and my maternal grandmother, Effie Tom Payne Corum, born in Bolivar, Missouri, October 15, 1887, and in honor of all who seek to know their lost ancestors.

Grandmothers of long ago—silent, gentle warriors—hear us. Know that we care. Tell us your stories—for we are, at last, ready to listen. Teach us, honored grandparents, the eternal truths that only the past remembers, so that we may open our hearts to the promise of tomorrow.

Acknowledgments

Once again, I want to thank Michael and Kathleen O'Neal Gear for their unselfish and unfailing encouragement. To my dear friends at Bearlodge Writers, my utmost gratitude for the endless hours of insightful critiquing. To my agent, Matt Bialer, gratitude for your faith and growing friendship.

I owe a tremendous debt to Dr. R. D. (Ronnie) Theisz at Black Hills State University in South Dakota for his help with the Lakota language and, also, to Calvin Jumping Bull at the Oglala Lakota College in Kyle, South Dakota. Any inaccuracies in the use of Lakota are certainly not due to errors on their part, but to misunderstandings on mine.

Norman Zollinger, you have been my mentor and my friend. Denise Chavez, your spirit is the epitome of a good woman's—strong yet gentle, loving yet fierce. Thank you both.

Dee Brown, I thank you for awakening in me, twenty years ago, a cultural conscience, and for encouraging me, now, to write about Wyoming.

And to my supreme editor, Harriet McDougal, my paramount thanks for letting this story truly find a place within your heart.

My father, Loren Dunton, taught me that to write is to dream. My mother, Jane Dunton, taught me that to dream is to become. And you, Brooke, esteemed sister, remind me always that reality is spirit.

Mark, thank you for your patience and your steadfastness. No wife could ask for more. You truly are *the Man*. And may you, Matt and Sarah, my beloved children, find a bit of yourselves within the pages of this book.

OCTOBER SONG

by Elizabeth Canfield

*Even after dark, my machine-stitched moccasins
know well the toeholds on this trail.*

*tonight I walk where once
Lakota people walked—at least I've found
their spearheads here—and ghosts
of other faded summers come slipping
down smoke-smothered rays from blood-red glow
of this October moon*

*canapekasna wi
(cha-NAH-peh-ka-SHAH-wee)
the moon that shakes off leaves*

*At the rim, the wind
that always meets me here
has not yet come; it's moving—
a relentless giant whisper
pushing against thick black pines
at the far end of the great divide*

*I see shallow, rock-bottomed hollows
that have trapped the last rains of the year—*

buffalo wallows, old timers say
their water glistens eerily
under the restless moon,
begins to ripple under the rising wind

the lost buffalo
the lost people

I merge with pulsing spirits,
mourn with gut-deep loss and sorrow

My heart echoes old Lakota drums
I feel the coming winter moons
the long Lakota hunger moons.

Contents

SHIFTING
STARS

Prologue

THE SHINING MOUNTAINS, CIRCA 1816

"When you step on the badger's back," Turtle Woman said, "be like the flick of a rattlesnake's tongue. If you are too slow, the striped-faced one will flip himself over, and tear your feet to pieces! *Waste*, good! Like that!"

The Hewaktoka slave girl jumped on the folded hide, landing quick and hard. The stick hidden beneath the leather snapped with a loud crack, like a spine breaking in two.

"*Han*, yes," said Turtle Woman. "Soon you will be faster even than the warriors of my own Lakota camp, as quick as the striped-faced one himself. Then maybe our Kangi captors will call you Little Badger, instead of slave girl."

"Soon I shall be fast enough to outrun their beatings! Then they shall call me Gone!"

Turtle Woman laughed, despite the bruises on her own flesh. Maybe *she* should rename her Little Badger. The young Hewaktoka had a strong, stubborn spirit and was easy to like, even if she did come from an enemy tribe. Turtle Woman watched as the girl drew the broken stick from beneath the leather and replaced it with a new, stouter branch taken from the pile of firewood Turtle Woman was supposed to be gathering.

"You have really killed a badger," the girl asked her, "by breaking his back?"

"*Han*. Once. Many moons ago, before my husband's seed grew

within me." Turtle Woman patted her rounded belly. "Now, I am not so nimble."

"Do you miss him?"

Did she miss Sunstone, her forever-mate? Like the heavens would miss the stars. "No more than you must miss your own people," she answered, drawing a shield around her heart.

Nearly two moons had passed since the Kangis had raided the Oglala Lakota camp of the Standing People. Sunstone did not yet even know their first child grew within her, but Turtle Woman had great faith in his love for her. She expected him to ride into the enemy camp leading a war party any day, any moment.

Two moons ago the Kangis had also brought the young Hewaktoka into the mountain camp, high in the Shining Mountains. The friendship between the two captives had blossomed quickly; they put salve on each other's bruises, and strengthened each other's spirits.

Little Badger jerked her head up, then snatched the leather from the ground. "Turtle Woman, quick," the girl warned, "gather your wood. Wasp Man approaches, and he looks angry."

Turtle Woman grabbed at the deadfall, clutching the branches to her chest. "Go," she whispered, "go back to your lodge."

Heavy footsteps neared and a dark shadow fell upon the ground in front of Turtle Woman. She busied herself with her task, keeping her eyes to the ground. The first kick came so rapidly she had no time to duck, no time to protect herself. The second kick knocked the branches from her grasp, and sent her reeling to the ground. The third kick sank deep into her abdomen.

"Remember that, woman of the Titonwan, next time you choose to laze around like a dog." Wasp Man's heavy footsteps retreated, leaving her to lie in pain, clutching her stomach. A cramping came to her, an ache deep inside her womb. She tried to will the pain away. She lay on the Earth Mother, dug her fingers into the dark fertile soil, felt the ground yield beneath her. She willed herself to think only of a fully formed child, a newborn suckling at her breast. But the agony within her womb worsened, the cramps like vicious teeth gnawing at her insides. And then she knew, when she felt the warmth seep from between her legs, when her blood, *her child*, spilled onto the ground, then she knew.

She held the fistful of soil to her breast, letting her tears moisten the earth. She lay there while the sun slipped from the sky, while the stars pricked the darkness with their light, letting the Earth Mother cradle them both beneath the vastness of Father Sky.

This new mountain, where the Kangi shaman had led the people only last night, had two faces—like Anog Ite of creation days, Turtle Woman thought to herself. Beautiful on one side, with gently sloping hills and smooth-needled trees. Harsh and unforgiving on the other side, where the flesh of the mountain had worn away, exposing the skeleton beneath, treacherous crags that jutted away from the side like broken bones.

The people had followed the Kangi shaman to the barren plateau of this strange, two-sided mountain. An ancient medicine wheel, built of stones laid upon the earth, spread before them. The Kangi women tied prayer bundles and left them upon the piles of stones that joined the twenty-eight spokes to the heart of the wheel, while the men placed the skull of a sacrificial buffalo atop the center cairn and lit the sacred pipe.

The people danced and prayed, yet Turtle Woman and Little Badger could not participate, but were forced to haul wood from the smooth-needled trees up the well-worn path to where the ceremonial fires burned. The mountain was *wakan*, a sacred place, and Turtle Woman ached for the songs and prayers of her own people.

The Kangi women in the lodge where Little Badger now lived refrained from beating the young Hewaktoka during these ceremonies, and even Wasp Man kept his distance from Turtle Woman. Then, early the second morning, the holy man came to Turtle Woman and, taking her arm, led her to the dangerous side of the mountain. *A-i-i-i.* She sucked in her breath. *Does he intend to push me off the edge? I will be crushed, like the shell of a winged one falling from the nest.* But instead they climbed down the rocks like mountain sheep, clinging to a narrow path that skirted the limestone crags until, finally, he stopped.

"You wear the Kangi mark of the Shooting Star," he said, pointing to her quilled moccasins. She knew the design well—a five-pointed star with a comet shooting through its center. Most Lakota women used only the cross with trail lines leading from it to signify the comet. But the five-pointed star made this design unique. It had been passed down to her by her own mother of the Standing People band of Oglala Lakotas. Their band was named for the cottonwood and for the sacred star hidden within the wood of the rustling-leaf tree that reminded the people of their origins in heaven.

The shaman gestured to the side of the jagged rock wall and pointed at an etching deep in the limestone—an etching that matched the heirloom design on her moccasins.

"The rock, too, wears this special mark of the Shooting Star," he said. "It is the mark of a Kangi woman, a grandmother who came here many, many winters past."

A Kangi woman? It cannot be. She shook her head. "This design belonged to my mother, Shifting Star of the Standing People."

"And how did she come by her name?" he asked.

"On the night of her birth a great comet shot across the sky. This is why she was called Shifting Star."

"Ah," he said, scratching his chin. A long silence followed. "The mark is Kangi," he finally said. "Your mother had Kangi blood."

His words sank into her heart like a hot stone tossed into a cooking paunch. Kangi? They were *tokas*—enemies. She had no *toka* blood in her! The shaman lied. She rubbed her fingers across the etching and felt the bile rise to her throat.

That night the shaman called Turtle Woman forth and made her stand beside him as he spoke of her to the crowd. Little Badger listened from just beyond the throng.

"A person who catches his first breath on a night the stars move around," the shaman said, "that person will be born with warrior power. And here, at the Medicine Wheel, that person's ability, especially the power of prayer, will be seven times a holy man's. Even the prayers of that person's offspring will have great force."

Little Badger looked at Turtle Woman with awe, as did the others. Then the shaman walked to the heart of the sacred wheel and began to pray. From dusk until the sky turned red with daybreak, he prayed. When he finished, he came to Turtle Woman and Little Badger, and he brought with him a prophecy.

"A great woman warrior will be conceived within the womb of the Titonwan," he said. "She will spill from the heavens like a thousand stars."

"Will be conceived?" Did he speak of her ill-born child, or a child yet to come? Turtle Woman turned the shaman's words over and over in her mind. But the etching on the rock filled her with dread. Kangi blood? What would Sunstone think? He must never know. It would shame him, bring dishonor down upon them all.

That night, Turtle Woman dreamt of a comet streaking across the night sky while a baby girl, still covered in birthing blood, gave forth her first newborn cry. The marks of a medicine wheel were tattooed upon her tiny wrists, but she held in her hand the knife of a Kangi warrior. Turtle Woman awoke drenched in sweat.

"Remember," the shaman told her the next day as the gathering left the high plateau to return to their summer camp, "the prayers of one born beneath the shifting stars have the power to change destiny—to alter that which has been preordained."

Later, Little Badger came to her, fresh welts upon her young skin. The shaman's prophecy had brought to the people a new respect for the slave woman. "Pray for me," Little Badger pleaded, unaware of Turtle Woman's anguish, "pray that when I grow, I, too, shall become a great warrior. Then no one will ever take me captive again!"

In the days to come, Turtle Woman prayed often for the young Hewaktokta, and she prayed for the moment when she would see Sunstone ride into the enemy camp. Hope became her strongest ally, and she taught the girl what she knew of warrior ways.

"Remember," she instructed Little Badger one day, "you must

take within you the living power of the weapon—the strength of the rooted-people from whom the bow was carved, the speed of the antlered-people from whom the knife was formed."

Little Badger shook her head. "I will never be as quick as you."

"Your muscles are alive with quickness. Just have faith. This time, before you throw the knife, feel the earth beneath your feet. Let your thoughts flow from the earth, through your fingertips, into the weapon. Let them form a trail to the heart of the *toka*."

Little Badger squared her shoulders and lifted the butchering knife to eye level. She held the knife by the tip, then bent her elbow and snapped her wrist. The knife flew through the air and embedded itself, chest-high, in the bark of a pine.

"*Han!*" Turtle Woman exclaimed. "With warrior speed!" She plucked a ragged turkey feather from the ground and poked the quill into Little Badger's braid. "Warrior speed!"

Suddenly, a loud and vehement war whoop cut through the day. The camp erupted. Women ran for their lodges, snatching young children up beneath their arms. Men sprinted about, retrieving their hanging weapons and shields from their tripods, grabbing at their tethered war ponies.

Turtle Woman smiled, hope exploding into joy. She knew that voice, had heard that war whoop in her dreams. Her eyes scanned the mayhem, found High Bear and Dark Cloud among the Lakota warriors surging into the Kangi camp. Fear and excitement swelled her heart. There—his hair flowing long and loose behind him, his fastest war pony spinning beneath him—her husband!

"*Hokahe!*" yelled Sunstone, raising his bow to the sky. "I have come to rip the *toka*'s heart from his chest! I have come for my forever-wife!"

A triumphant trilling burst from Turtle Woman's lungs, traveling across the panicked camp.

"*Hokahe!*" Sunstone's strong voice called out and she answered him again, her trilling like the call of an eagle. He sped toward her, shooting arrows into the flesh of the unprepared Kangi warriors. She ran to him and leaped onto the back of his horse, her own victory song piercing the thin resolve of the enemy.

Wasp Man rushed toward them, pushing the young Hewaktoka to the ground, trampling the turkey feather in the dirt. Keeping one arm around Sunstone's waist, Turtle Woman kicked the war pony forward. She grabbed her husband's stone-headed club and swung it in a circle over her head. With one swift blow, she crushed Wasp Man's oily skull.

"For my earth-child!" she yelled, her blood hot with vengeance. "And for the slave girl!"

They spun away. Her eyes searched the chaos, jumping from lodge to lodge, from woman to woman, but Little Badger had disappeared.

A lone figure stepped from behind a tipi. Sunstone raised his bow, an arrow nocked and ready. The figure turned, and Turtle Woman gasped. The shaman faced them, unprotected, unarmed.

"*An he!*" Sunstone yelled, drawing his arrow back.

"*Hiya!* No!" The cry came unbidden from Turtle Woman's throat.

"But he is Kangi!"

Her heart shriveled at the hatred in Sunstone's voice. Kangi. Kangi blood. *How could she ever tell him?* Her cheeks reddened with shame.

The pony lunged forward.

"*An he!*" Sunstone yelled again, but he lowered his bow and, with arrow in hand, he raced by the shaman, touching the holy man's shoulder with the tip of his arrow.

"*An he!*" A great coup!

Turtle Woman saw no fear in the shaman's eyes as they flew past. Only a knowing look. She tightened her hold on Sunstone's bare waist. His flesh was warm, his scent familiar. He was her forever-husband. She was his one-only-one-wife.

Not all truths needed the light of day. Some were meant to live in darkness. She turned her gaze toward the crest of the hill as the other Lakota war ponies fell in behind Sunstone's, leaving the camp in a whirlwind of dust.

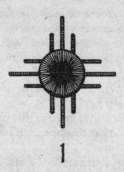

1

MEDICINE BOW MOUNTAINS, INDIAN TERRITORY, 1841

The rank odor—a pungent reminder of the vicious blow dealt her by the enraged humpback grizzly—clung to the cougar for days. The pain lingered even longer. A dozen times, the half-bitten moon hovered in the night sky like the eye of an owl; a dozen times, the bloodred sun rose from the bowels of the earth. The pain crippled her; the fear infuriated her. Fear belonged to the weak—to the fleeing black-tailed antlered-ones and the slow-moving, spiny tree-eaters. Fear had never before belonged to her.

She rubbed up against the rough bark of a pine, trying to rub the pain from her shoulder, then lay in the crystal-cold waters that flowed down from the snow-covered peak. As she stretched her long, lithe body along the frozen shore of the creek, the beast of hunger gnawed at her insides, twisting her shrunken belly. Food. The few tree-eaters whose bellies she had torn open provided barely enough meat for her yowling cubs, let alone her. She needed the flesh of an antlered-one.

Shifting her weight, she felt a stab of pain travel from her shoulder to the thick pad of her clawed foot. The pain reminded her of the humpback's huge claws, and as she stood, a snarl, like distant thunder, rumbled from her throat. She lifted her broad, tawny nose into the wind, and caught the oily scent of the two-leggeds who had invaded her territory several winters past. The smoke from their early morning fire spiraled upward from the mountain meadow, thinning as the sharp needles of the pine trees cut the smoke into a thousand wisps.

The cougar's snarl became less like thunder and more like lightning, a screaming bolt of frustration piercing the dawn. Rage—at the hump-back, at the two-leggeds, at the beast of hunger in her belly. Her high-pitched yowl sliced through daybreak and cut like a sword into the cabin of the two-leggeds.

The hair on the back of Breathcatcher's neck rose, a delicate ridge of uneasiness. A shiver traveled down her spine. Shuddering, she turned on her moccasined feet and closed the heavy hand-hewn door behind her, shutting out the frigid wind and the eerie cry of the great cat. *Igmu'tanka—whose haunting howl pierces the heavens like a woman's grief-stricken wail.*

She shook the echo from her mind and, letting the warmth of the cabin settle around her, turned to face her husband.

"I shall return with a fine stag for ye," he said, putting his grandmother's beloved book of verse back on the table. He lifted Breathcatcher's arms to his neck, then placed his broad hands on her waist. She stroked his hair.

"Naked Warrior may hunt like the fierce mountain lion," he whispered into her ear, "but when I return, I shall be like the *hehaka*, snorting and tossing my great antlers to impress you."

She smiled. Naked Warrior. A fitting name to call him for many reasons.

Breathcatcher lowered her arms. Even now, after nearly seven winters of marriage, her own desires embarrassed her, especially in front of their daughter. The Lakota way was to save the touching for the privacy of the robes.

She glanced at Skye. The child stood beside the rough-cut table, a pensive expression upon her face. She had pushed up the sleeves of her leather dress and appeared to be examining her own, paler skin. A handful of turkey feathers jutted up from her braid. The word *half-blood* came unbidden to Breathcatcher and a twinge of guilt grabbed at her.

"Our little one has antlers of her own," she said, brushing a few stray breakfast crumbs from Gregory's beard and buckskin shirt. Skye plucked a pretend coup feather from her hair and blew on it.

"Have your skinning knife sharpened, woman," Gregory said, picking up his pewter mug and draining the last bit of brew from it. "The luck of me kinsmen will be with this old hoss today!"

Breathcatcher wished that she had the dried dung of the shaggy *pte* to scatter on the fire to send the spirit-filled smoke to Wakan Tanka, that her husband's hunt might be blessed.

Instead, she would burn the sweetgrass when he left, inhale the sacred scent of Wohpe, beautiful patron of harmony and pleasure, Shooting Star who fell from the heavens in the long-ago days of creation. She would smoke the pipe and pray to Wakan Tanka, pray in the old Lakota way.

Gregory jostled her affectionately. "Breathcatcher, stop your daydreaming and finish me possibles bag."

She put a handful of pemmican on top of the leftover acorn bread, closed the leather haversack, and held it out to him. He tied the bag onto his wide belt, then reached up and touched the *hehaka* antlers hanging over the door to the cabin.

" 'Tis an irony," he said, more to himself than to her or Skye, "these forked branches cradle the very rifle that caused their death." Taking down the brass-mounted plains rifle, he oiled the barrel and checked his powder horn.

"Mind yourself while I'm gone," he said, tugging on Breath-catcher's long braids. He gave her a swat on her rear, and the trade bells hanging from the fringes of her doeskin dress jingled.

"Come over here to your father, lass. Send me off with a squeeze, now." Skye stuck the feather in his hat, then ran laughing and hid in Breathcatcher's skirt. Gregory pushed open the door and strode away.

A crisp wind assaulted the cabin. Breathcatcher's sense of foreboding returned.

Here at the base of the mountain lodgepole pines stretched straight trunks into thin air, and during the moons of summer, the saplings of cottonwood and ash, no longer gnawed by the disappearing beaver, grew thick like willow brush. Breathcatcher missed the pools of still water that had swelled the mountain streams where the beavers used to build their lodges.

The wind penetrated her skin. She wrapped her arms around Skye as the haunting call of *igmu'tanka* echoed in her mind. Much snow already covered the ground, more than usual for the Moon of Falling Leaves, the time of change, when *pte* calves grew hair to protect them from Yata's bitter breath. The snow would cause hunger to come early to the bellies of the four-leggeds.

Her husband headed out, past the rough-barked corral by the shed, across the edge of the meadow, and into the bare-branched thickets. Her mind wandered as she watched him leave, back to the winter she first saw him, the gaily dressed *wasicu* who came from across the great waters, from a place called the Highlands of Scotland.

He had come upon her and her mother, Turtle Woman, in the woods, barging through the shaggy-leaf trees like a long-legged moose—a burly bearded stranger wearing a striped blanket-skirt around his waist, a bearskin hat upon his head, and high black boots upon his feet. In his hand he grasped a long-knife, and hanging from his waist, with black swaying tassels, dangled a white fur pouch.

She had never before seen such a long-knife, never before seen such a man.

A swift shadow of sadness darkened Breathcatcher's heart. She longed to hear her own native tongue—the warriors as they lifted their voices and sang their brave-heart battle songs, her own mother's songs of prayer. *My child has no grandparents from whom to learn the sacred ways.*

Another gust of wind assaulted the cabin. Her husband's footsteps had long since faded into the dawning day, and her daughter had long ago wriggled free from her arms.

"Ina," Skye's voice came from inside, "Ate did not take his long-knife with him."

Breathcatcher closed the door and turned to face her daughter. *"Hinu!"* she gasped, seeing her daughter standing with Gregory's unsheathed double-edged sword clutched in her small hands. "You know you are not permitted to take your *ate*'s long-knife from the wooden trunk."

She took the heavy sword from Skye. The girl's eyes had opened wide in a mixture of fear and fearlessness. Leaning the sword against the large, wooden box, Breathcatcher lifted the trunk's metal clasp and slowly raised the lid. "The blanket-skirt," she whispered to herself, stroking the kilt with her awl-toughened fingers. *Worn by my husband only once every twelve moons, when the call of the Highlanders strikes his homesick soul.*

Homesick. She knew the feeling well; it swelled within her at times like a never-to-be-born child. Her own *ate*'s gentle deep-set eyes and craggy features came to mind. *Naked Warrior,* he had been the first to call her husband, *the one who fights like the wolverine, and roars like the bear.*

They had not visited her own tribe for three winters, not since the Standing People's band of the Oglala Lakota had moved to the Shell River valley country to the east. Her people had left the Medicine Bows, gone to raid the river tribes and hunt the shaggy *pte* on the plains.

She picked up the leather sheath of the long-knife and carefully slid it down over the double-edged blade, the feel of the hard metal sending a chill down her back. Once again, the hairs on the nape of her neck rose as they had when the great cat's eerie yowl pierced the dawn.

Was the long-knife a wotawe? A wakan *thing with supernatural power? A-i-i-i!* Quickly, she laid the sword on top of the woolen kilt. The trunk should not have been opened!

She lowered the lid and secured the metal clasp. But foreboding would not leave her; it clung to her like lodge-fire smoke.

Gregory cursed at the snow, trying to shake the evil feeling. He'd had his mind set on a fine-antlered stag, but nary a creature had shown itself. Finally, on his way back to the cabin, and with dark nearly upon him, he'd downed this yearling. Och! And a doe at that. He flipped her over, letting her bleed out. He'd gut her at home.

The wintry autumn day had started out well enough—that is, till his packhorse commenced to acting squirrelly, spooking at the stump by the shed as if it were haunted, then shying away from the stand of willows by the creek, refusing to go any nearer. After a spell, and after a little coaxing, ye might say, they'd made for timber, Gregory reading sign as they went. Only he'd been so busy looking for meat that he'd ignored the real signs—signs no Highlander, brought up to fear the ways of the Otherworld, ought to ignore.

The evil time of the ancient fall feast of Samhuin had come, he could feel it in his bones—that awesome eve when the powers of the Otherworld stalked the woods, when maidens were sacrificed and spells were cast. He thought back to that morning—Breathcatcher's moodiness, the blackened stone that fell from the fire and landed at her feet—the pair of ravens perched on the cabin as he was leaving. He'd thought nothing of it then, had even let the scavenging birds alone, ignoring them. But they were sure signs of evil doings. *Signs of death*, his graunie Maggie would say.

Aye, she would blame it on the Droch Shuil, the evil eye. "Beware the eve of Samhuin," she had always warned, " 'tis the night of black art." If he didn't know better, he would say a witch had cast a spell on him, or worse, put the eye on Breathcatcher.

Gregory scooped up a handful of the bloody snow and sprinkled a bit on his buckskins, hoping to change his luck. "Not quite me colors," he mumbled, "but it'll have to do."

Graunie Maggie had loved the old ways; he reckoned she still did. And Grandfather Macdonald surely had. He'd been the town's *seanachaidh*, the teller of tales. Every year the clan had gathered in the *tigh-cheilidh* and listened to him recite the ancient ballads, knowing he would finish with the tragic story of Glencoe.

He shuddered. Seemed as if the old ways were dying, the real men and women, the hard cases, nearly dead and gone. The old trappers forced out.

What was the verse by Scott he had read this morning? Written in Graunie Maggie's journal? *But search the land of living men, Where wilt thou find their like agen?* Gregory slung the doe's carcass across his horse's back and began the short trek home. *Where wilt thou find their like agen?* Perhaps, with a bit of luck, around the campfires of the Sioux, or the Cheyenne, or the Arapaho. But not for long.

2

PREY

Skye touched the front hoof of the deer, which moved loosely, not yet stiff with death. Though Father had come back with meat, he had left his good mood up the mountain.

"I wear out me legs hiking the ridges," he grumbled, "then find fresh meat nearly at me own front door."

Father pulled the deer's severed heart from the bloody chest cavity and handed it to her. Despite Ate's poor mood, the touch of it thrilled her, caused her own blood to race and heart to pound. Life and death—like different sides of the same leaf.

Lingering warmth radiated from the heart. Skye imagined the heart still pulsating, still throbbing. Blood, redder than the Indian paintbrush flowers that dotted the meadow, formed webs between her fingers. Someday she, too, would hunt the antlered-ones. "Why," she had once asked her grandmother long ago, before her grandmother went away, "why do the four-legged people allow us to kill them?"

"Ehaaaaanni," Unci had answered, "once, in the long-ago days, there was Tokahe, First Man. He, and the others, had nothing to eat. A vision came to him, a snowbird who would lead them to food and clothing. The trickster, Iktomi, convinced the Real People to follow the magpie instead. But First Man followed the snowbird to a cave, which sheltered him from Yata, the cold north wind, and there he found four-leggeds gathered at a watering

hole. The animals gave of their lives so that he might have food for his belly and robes for his nakedness. But those who followed the magpie found, instead, only hard paths and hungry bellies."

"Well, ye gonna stand there gawking all day, or are ye gonna go tell your mother there'll be fresh meat for supper?"

Skye jumped at the sound of Ate's voice. "I wasn't gawking," she argued as she stood up, "just remembering."

"Well, do your daydreaming on your feet, lass. You'll earn no coup feathers setting on your rear end." He plucked the feather from her hair and tossed it to the ground.

Someday, I will earn real coup feathers—feathers from the cloud-bird who soars above the meadow. Like Little Badger. Like Unci. She turned to go and caught her skirt on the rifle that leaned against the side of the shed. Setting the heart down on the tree stump where Father sat to smoke his morning pipe, she jerked the hem loose.

"Go and fetch Ina's skinning knife," he called after her. "I want ye to help me butcher the deer." *Help butcher? Han!* Yes! Ignoring her father's bad mood, she broke stride and skipped down the snow-covered path, leaving the forgotten heart on the stump, bloody and lifeless.

Breathcatcher sighed. Her husband had not returned from his hunt snorting and tossing his antlers, as he had promised. Perhaps she should call him Grumbly Bear instead of Naked Warrior. She added another log to the fire, poking at the embers with the fire iron.

Gregory settled down in the rocker, the small journal, old and tattered, in his hands. Thoughts captured on paper. *Spirit words,* she called them. He had told her once that, long ago, his grandmother Maggie had drawn the spirit words into the little book, like the winter-counts painted by the tribe's keeper-of-memories. Breathcatcher shook her head at its mystery and, moving aside a rock from her husband's collection, settled down with her quillwork, awl and sinew in hand.

"Please read a bit, Ate?" Skye pulled on his sleeve.

"Lass, ye act like an impudent pup. Bring me me pipe first."

Skye handed Gregory his pipe, then climbed bravely onto his lap. He reminded Breathcatcher of an old *tatanka*, allowing a young spike-horn to steal his wallowing hole. Skye burrowed into his fringed shirt, nestling into his broad chest, his reddish-blond beard brushing against her forehead. Hairy-faced ones, Breathcatcher's mother, Turtle Woman, had called the *wasiculas*.

A new coup feather, from the round-eyed night-bird, sprouted from Skye's disheveled auburn braids. The rocking chair, fashioned from stout green saplings, groaned in quiet protest.

"Read here." Skye opened the journal and pointed her finger at a random line of faded writing. Gregory began:

> "Where shall the lover rest
>   Whom the fates sever
>   From his true maiden's breast,
>   Parted forever?"

Breathcatcher looked up from her sewing and glanced at Gregory. Their eyes met. *Parted forever?* She shook the solemn thought from her mind and returned to her quilling, listening to her husband drawing on his pipe, the sound of burning *cansasa*, her daughter's restless breathing.

"Not that one," Skye demanded, pointing again. "This one."

Breathcatcher winced at her daughter's impetuousness, but Gregory allowed it. He switched his gaze to the new verse. " 'Old times were changed, old manners gone . . .' "

Impatient with the poetry, Skye interrupted him again, flipping the pages and pointing at yet another verse.

"Lass, either let me finish or let me be." He began anew.

> "They bore within their breasts the grief
>   That fame can never heal—
>   The deep, unutterable woe
>   Which none save exiles feel."

His voice grew hard, like stone. The room grew quiet, except for the wood crackling in the fire and the porcupine quills being drawn, soft and moist, from between Breathcatcher's teeth. She put her awl down and looked up. Gregory stared at her, his eyes a disturbed lichen-green. Then he shut the book, stood, pushed Skye from his lap, and opened the door of the cabin, disappearing into the darkness. Skye started to follow but Breathcatcher halted her with a stern *"Hiya."*

Old times were changed, old manners gone? Gregory kicked at the snow. Little did Breathcatcher know how much the fate of her people—aye, the fate of all the Indians—reminded him of the tragic fate of the Macdonalds. Indeed, of all the Highlanders. It didna' take a seer to look into the future. Just as the land-thirsty Argyles and the bloody landlords had forced the clansmen from the Highlands—burning their crofts, killing their women and children, selling their young folk off as slaves—so were the Lakotas being forced from their land. It grieved him. Nay, it angered him!

He could see it coming. Just as the Highlanders had been murdered for wearing their kilts, or playing their pipes, so the red man would see his life disappear before him. They may not have the tartan to lose, but just as surely as the flesh of the buffalo rotted on the prairie, so would the hearts of the Lakotas rot if they were forced to live a white man's life. Sunstone, Turtle Woman, Wolf-skin Necklace. Aye. All of them. Good as dead and buried. *And where*, he asked himself, *does that leave me daughter?*

The red embers in his pipe faded, then nearly died. He leaned against the cabin and drew on his pipe until, from deep within the bowl, a red glow appeared. He had never told Skye, or Breathcatcher for that matter, the whole tale of the Macdonald massacre at Glencoe. Perhaps it was time he did. He shivered, trying to shed the dread from his bones like a snake ridding itself of unwanted skin.

The door closed loudly as Gregory entered the cabin—an angry mood or an angry wind, Breathcatcher could not tell which. She held her finger to her lips and silenced Skye. *The moods control the man. Yet doors do not slam in a lodge made of hides.* She took a deep breath to ease the small ache inside. Gregory lowered his bulk back into the rocker.

"Ye know," he said, looking at her again, "the day we met, 'twas one hundred and forty-nine winters to be exact since the Macdonald massacre, when the Campbells shucked their ruse as friends, and slaughtered me sleeping kinsmen. Men, women, lads, and lassies."

He motioned for Skye to return to his lap, then said nothing for many long moments. Breathcatcher waited. A storyteller must be allowed to tell his story, for a story untold is like a stillborn child—breathless, lifeless. Finally, he continued.

"Aye, many a Highlander lost his kin on that brutal day. *Glencoe.*" He whispered the name. "The Glen of Weeping. 'Twas the beginning of the end for the Highlanders . . ."

Breathcatcher had never heard so many words come from her husband's mouth—*hiya*, from his heart. Did Skye understand all the words her *ate* spoke? It was good, Breathcatcher supposed, for her daughter to hear the Scottish stories, to set her moccasins upon the path of her ancestors from across the great waters. She sighed, her heart torn, only half-believing the truth of her own thoughts. What of the stories of the Oglalas?

Gregory eased back into the chair and patted Skye on the knee, seeming to force a new mood upon himself. He took the feather from her hair and smoothed its edges, then tucked it back into her braid.

"Course, ye know," he said, changing the subject, "I would never have met your *ina* had I not traveled across the sea. I figure I owe a debt to that miserly, no-account Governor Simpson. Had to have a bagpiper along in his canoe, he did, so as to announce his arrival at every post! Damn greenhand fool, wanted to do away with the beaver so there wouldn't be any left for the Americans! Might never've met your *ina* otherwise, though.

"Course, he was right about the new land. I decided to go it alone, ye know, be a free trapper, long afore I came across your *ina* slipping, doelike, through the woods. But no matter where I be, nor what I be doing, I never forget the anniversary of the Macdonald massacre. For one hundred and forty-nine years now me kinsmen have donned their tartans and played their pipes in remembrance of the day."

He drew on the stem of his pipe and the smoldering *cansasa* hissed, smoke rising from the hot, reddened embers. Easing his back deeper into the willow chair, he let a smile come to his face.

"Why, can ye only guess what she thought, seeing me standing there in the middle of the woods, dressed in me kilt and saffron shirt, with me fancy heather brooch—and what with me grandfather's claymore strapped on and me bearskin hat upon me head?" A boisterous laugh, perhaps too loud, filled the small cabin.

Breathcatcher allowed herself to smile at the memory, especially the blanket-skirt. Gregory drew on his pipe again, the smoke sifting slowly out of his mouth. He stroked his beard and gazed at her.

"Ah, me Breathcatcher." She shivered at the gentleness now in his voice. "You did indeed catch me breath, standing there boldly, flashing your dark eyes at me. Aye, you had beauty enough to catch a man's heart, as well as his breath. And still enough grit to catch me all o'er again, ye know!"

"Hoh!" Breathcatcher lifted a hand to her face, covering her mouth. *Now he causes me to blush like a young* wikoskala, *making me think womanly thoughts, feel womanly things. His moods are like the wind, tossing us both about like leaves in a storm.*

"Then what happened, Ate?" Skye tugged at his beard.

"Why, I put me rifle down and introduced meself to the young lass. Then your grandmother pops out of the thicket and stands herself between us. Oh, but she was a fierce one at first! Till we backtracked to where me horses were tied and I showed her me foofaraw. Then I followed them back to camp—admiring your *ina* as we went, of course!

"Ye can imagine the commotion when we arrived. Dogs yipping, womenfolk ducking out of their tipis, warriors gathering by the council lodge, their weapons readied. But I kept me claymore sheathed and me rifle lowered. 'Twas a friendly mission I was on, and I came escorted by a lovely young lass and her fine mother. 'Twas not long before the others lowered their weapons as well."

"There was one, my husband, who kept his bow taut and his arrow ready." Breathcatcher pulled her shawl up, draping it across her shoulders. *Caws Like Magpie was not one to give up easily.*

"Aye, that there was. That cocky, skinny Caws Like Magpie never has lowered his bow."

"He was not so skinny. He hoped I had decided during my thought-gathering time in the woods to share his blanket. He did not like this *wasicu* who strutted like a prairie rooster into camp."

"Ha! A strutting rooster? 'Twas more like a bull elk! But you're right, I had come to take his bride, and well he knew it!"

"I was not his bride."

"Well, lucky for me, Turtle Woman and Sunstone had not taken a shine to Caws Like Magpie. Lucky for me, ye did not like him, either. But if Sunstone had favored him, all the fine plews in the Medicine Bows would not have been enough. As 'twas, I gave a whole cache of tobacco to your *ate* anyway."

Wakan Tanka, onsimala ye! she had prayed. *Great Spirit, pity me!* She did not want to pitch a lodge for Caws Like Magpie, to make children with this man from the Muddy Water camp who chased her through the prairie grasses like a clinging spider.

Breathcatcher held her quilling up to the fire and inspected the star-shaped design in the dim light, a design passed down to her by Turtle Woman. *She had not wanted a man with a mother who dreamed of the evil Anog Ite.*

"Do ye remember when I played the Scottish Ceol Mor on me pipes? Why, when I filled that camp with the booming bass notes, they all went crazy. I showed them the way the Scottish warriors trip their toes and soon they were all dancing about—all except Caws Like Magpie. I learned not to turn me back on that one."

"When did you marry Ina?" Skye interrupted, her eyes barely open.

"Why, not till I had given Turtle Woman many hides and carved many walking sticks for Sunstone. I brought four horses to camp, one of them the same red roan mare your grandmother rode when she left—ye know, the one whose foot turned in as she grew? That, along with enough beads and vermilion for the whole tribe, soon won the lot of them over to me side.

"Your *ina* just sat there, like she's doing now, sewing on the soft hides and pretending not to notice. I would catch 'er looking, though, and would see the twinkle in her eyes. I knew, sooner or later, I would win meself a bride."

"And I a strutting rooster!" Breathcatcher teased back.

"A bull elk! Better a bull elk, or even a strutting rooster, than a cawing magpie!"

"Yes, you were better than a magpie. But the magpie swore to the thunder and lightning that he would seek vengeance."

"Aye, that he did. But they've been gone over three winters now, and there's been nary a word from Caws Like Magpie, or his band."

"Magpies do not always make noise. Sometimes they appear without notice, like Yata, bringing the early blizzard."

Breathcatcher's words settled on the three of them, like drifting flecks of cooled ash blown from the fire. Once again, the mood shifted. Gregory eased Skye off his lap, emptying his pipe in the coals. "Toss on another log, Skye, afore ye crawl into your bed robe."

"The moon has climbed high into the night sky, little warrior-girl," Breathcatcher said, smoothing the owl feather in her daughter's hair. "You must sleep while the night-bird hunts."

Breathcatcher set her quilling on top of the wooden trunk and pulled her shawl around her; she would cleanse herself in the creek before crawling beneath her own robe, go to her husband smelling of the night. She lifted a soft rabbit hide from the nail where it hung, then opened the cabin door. A draft of frigid air entered the room. Perhaps it had been the wind earlier, after all, slamming the door.

"Sleep well, my daughter, sleep well," she said.

"Do ye need to be washing up this eve?" Gregory's question surprised her. She went down to the willow creek every evening.

"The lights of the Star Council People will light my way."

Gregory gave her a worried look as she closed the door behind her. She stepped into the darkness, away from the faint light of the cabin, and, inhaling deeply, stared into the sky at the milky Ghost Road, pathway to the Land of Many Lodges. Stars shone brightly.

The night held its breath—the wind withdrew from the meadow and whistled quietly through the shaggy branches of the mountain pines, the wandering-dogs no longer called to their mates from the ridgetops. Breathcatcher sensed the sudden stillness, wondered at its meaning. *Are the moods of nature as changeable as the moods of man?* Then a shadow of movement by the shed turned into a snarling yowl, and Breathcatcher's heart leapt with fear. She tried to flee, pivoting away, but was pulled, instead, from her own past into her daughter's uncertain future.

Skye slipped off her moccasins and held them in her hands, caressing the blue and yellow quillwork sewn long ago by her *unci*. She tried to remember their camp—the tipis silhouetted against the setting sun, the red roan mare grazing just beyond the lodge. She tried to picture Turtle Woman's face but remembered only her long gray braids and the elk-teeth dress she wore the day they said good-bye.

"Daughter of the Sky, I must leave you. But do not forget me." Her strong gnarled fingers had placed the polished shell of a tiny turtle in Skye's hand.

"There is power in the mixing of your blood, my *takoja*. The night you were born, a flash of light pierced the darkness. A great star lit the heavens. You will be like the turtle, strong with long life. But you have much to learn. It is the turtle's slow pace which allows him to see all. My heart will be like the turtle's heart—in you it will keep beating long after I have left the flesh."

The moccasins, now too little, cramped Skye's feet but she wore them anyway. She tucked them safely under her robes and closed her eyes. "Dear Lord," she whispered, "Wakan Tanka, I pray for my grandparents, for my *unci* and my *tunkasila*. Bring them back," she pleaded, "bring them back." Then the shadow of sleep overcame her.

Skye woke to the sound of Ate taking his gun off the antler rack. She jumped up and tiptoed out behind him. The deep, throaty growl of an *igmu'tanka* assaulted her, then a scuffling sound, then the *"Yun! Yun! Yun!"* of Ina's scream echoed through the thin, cold air, traveling up the snow-covered mountain and into the darkness.

The cougar fled at Ate's approach. Skye searched the shadows of the nearby pine trees, afraid she would see the animal crouching, *watching*.

Ina lay facedown in the snow. "Ina, Ina," Skye whispered as Ate slowly turned her over.

Blood seeped out of a jagged wound at her throat. Even in the weak light of the moon, Skye could see the large circle of red that stained the snow. Ate knelt, pulling the limp body to him.

"Breathcatcher." He spoke the word as if it were holy. "Ah, me Breathcatcher . . ."

Numbness crept from the frozen snow into Skye's bare feet. She hugged her shivering arms to her chest and stared at Mother, lying so still in Ate's arms. Ina. Her feet began to retreat, inch by inch, from the horrible scene. An owl screeched. Ina's name rose from Ate—"Breathcatcher!"—an anguished cry, piercing the dark night like an arrow shot into the very heart of heaven.

Skye could stand it no longer. She turned and ran, back to the cabin. Anger pounded at her with each set of tracks she passed— the *igmu'tanka*'s, Ina's, Ate's, her own. Her heart shrank and forced her grief downward, deep into her soul. The tears would not flow. Reaching the shed, she slowed her pace, not ready to go back to the cabin, to the emptiness. She sat on the stump and stared at the half-bitten moon.

Pale light fell on the ground at Skye's feet, and at a dark object which lay in the snow beside her. She picked it up.

It was the heart of the deer—the blood-scented, half-eaten

heart which she had left, forgotten, on the stump, the stump surrounded by *igmu'tanka* tracks.

Ate carried Ina into the cabin.

"Move the lamp from the table, Skye." The movement of the oil lamp caused shadows to flicker across the room.

"Now, get ye the bearskin rug and put it upon the table, lass."

Skye could not lift the great weight of the rug, but dragged and pulled at it until the thick brown fur slid over the top of the hand-hewn table. She looked at Ina's body draped across Ate's strong arms and felt her own muscles ache from exertion, her own heart press like a leaden weight against her breast.

She yearned to ask: *Is she dead?* But she did not, could not. The burning question seeped like pungent smoke into the room, enveloping them in terrible clinging reality.

An unnatural twist in Ina's neck forced her head backward, as if she were looking over her shoulder. Ate slowly passed his hand in front of her face, sealing her dark eyes closed, easing her head around.

"Set ye some water on the coals to warm and fetch me a clean bit of broadcloth out of your mother's sewing basket. Then sit ye down and warm yourself by the fire."

Skye sat in the bent-willow rocking chair, the unyielding wood pressing into her back. *Ina, how I long for your lap, your words, your hand upon my cheek.* Silence answered her, the only sound the back-and-forth rhythm of the rocker, the sound of Ate's buckskins as he moved, the sound of him wiping the blood from Ina's torn throat. Skye did not have to hide her emptiness from Ate, for his grief had blinded him to hers.

He loosened Breathcatcher's waist-long braids, carefully removing the yellow cloth which encased their tips. With her porcupine-quill hairbrush, stroke after stroke, never speaking, he smoothed her hair until it draped her body like a silken shawl. Then he separated a strand at her forehead and, taking his knife, cut it off.

Opening the wooden trunk, he cut a square of plaid wool from his kilt. He gently wrapped the wool around the lock of hair and placed it in the trunk. Then he got their whitest-tanned doe hide and tenderly turned Ina's body until the doeskin lay beneath her. He adjusted the medicine bag which hung from her throat so that it rested between her breasts. As he pulled the ends of the doeskin over her, a deep shudder escaped him.

"Ina," Skye whispered. All that she could see of her now were the tips of her moccasins and the top of her dark, silken head. She wanted to leap out of the chair and pull the doeskin off, rouse her, shake her awake, be told that it was all a bad dream which had escaped the webbing of her dreamcatcher. She wanted them to sew on new leather thongs for the good dreams to slide down upon, wanted Ina to mend this jagged hole where the happiness had been torn from her life. But Skye could not move, could not talk, could barely even breathe.

Ate went and stood by the window. Skye rose and eased up next to him. The tops of the pine trees stood black against the pale moonlight. The stars of Ina's ancestors had faded from the sky, their presence darkened by the cruelty of the night. All was silent. The moment became an eternity, the harsh finality of Ina's death stretching into forever.

Until a high-pitched scream pierced the night air, shattering the silence.

The eerie, human-sounding yowl traveled down the mountain and across the meadow, penetrating the thick log walls of the cabin—Ina's death cry all over again, the sound of life challenging the power of death.

The next morning, Ate took all of Ina's things—her elk-teeth wedding dress, her wedding moccasins, her porcupine-quill hairbrush, her lizard amulet, even her unfinished beadwork and quilling—all that Breathcatcher had brought with her from the camp of the Standing People. These things he set aside, out of reach. Then he took away Skye's moccasins and snatched the feather from her hair.

"Never," he ordered, his green eyes hard and impenetrable,

"do I want to see a feather in your hair again!"

"Ate," she implored, "no, Ate."

"The Lakota burial ways are different than ours," he said impassively. "We will wait their four days, then we will place her up high, close to her Great Spirit. By then, I will have rid the mountain of the bloody painter."

Four days? Alone with Ina's doeskin-wrapped body while Ate hunts the cougar? Ey-ee! An eternity! But I am a warrior child. I must do it.

Though the shroud of white leather covered Ina's body, it could not hide her image from Skye's mind—the bloodied throat, the lifeless gaze. She remembered how gently Ate had loosened Ina's braids, had tenderly combed her dark hair, never speaking, lost in his own memories. The doeskin shroud could not veil these things from her mind's eye.

She studied the rocks that Ate had collected, images of sea creatures and animals carved into them, creatures, he said, no one had ever seen in this part of the world. Shells and winged lizards and creatures dead and gone, their stories written in stone. She held one in her hands and tried to grasp this creature called death. She saw these things with the eye of her heart, but she did not understand.

Each evening, Ate returned empty-handed, having found no enemy at whom to strike, no pelt of the *igmu'tanka* on which to cushion his grief.

Gregory, exhausted, came back to the cabin on the afternoon of the fourth day, put wood on the ill-tended fire, and coaxed it back to life. *Your child needs ye. Lay your grief aside, man, and tend to your flesh and blood, for one evening at least.* He waited until the flames grew large enough to cast a warm, golden glow upon the table where his wife lay, then dimmed the oil lamp and motioned to Skye.

He handed her a strand of braided sweetgrass and loose leaves of silver sage. They sprinkled the sage on the fire and held the tip of the sweetgrass to a burning ember, inhaling the pungent aroma that filled the cabin. He reached out to Skye, pulling her to him, and for the first time in these four days sat with her in the willow rocker. Her tears finally flowed, and he felt the tenseness leave her small body.

He remembered the keening and pipe playing at his grandfather's funeral, remembered what it was like to be a child coping with death. The words from a Scottish lullaby, meant for an infant chief, floated through his mind. *O hush thee, my babie, thy sire was a knight, Thy mother a lady, both lovely and bright.* But talking did not come easily. He held his daughter, let the enveloping warmth of the fire say what he could not. He became lost in the hypnotic rhythm of the flames, the sounds of the fire like language, like primeval worship. He imagined himself, not at his grandfather's wake, but in his mother-in-law's lodge, sacred smoke rising from a sacred pipe. *"Breathcatcher,"* he heard the flames whisper. *"Breathcatcher."*

The sound drifted upward with the vapors of the sweetgrass and silver sage. The orange flames turned yellow, then white, and suddenly a vivid blue—the color of turquoise—entered the fire. The blue lasted only a heartbeat, then the flames became orange again and the wood popped and crackled. *Tonwan. Sacred essence. Eye of the eagle.* The strange thought pierced his consciousness like a shooting star.

He stared, dry-eyed, at his wife's wrapped body. The ethereal moment dissolved, leaving him with his grief, leaving his soul still imprisoned. He put Skye on her feet, rose, exhausted from his days of tracking, and walked to the table, reaching beneath the buffalo robe on which Breathcatcher rested.

"Skye, bring a bit of jerked meat with ye and a small piece of cloth."

He picked his wife up and, turning sideways, carried her outdoors, checking to make sure that Skye had gathered the meat and cloth. They moved away from the cabin, south, down the path that led to the creek. When he came to a tall, broad-limbed cottonwood, he stopped, leaning against the trunk of the tree, still holding her in his aching arms. He allowed himself a moment of rest. Then, as he lifted Breathcatcher into the crook of the tree, the bells on the hem of her dress tinkled faintly. *How many times has that sound warmed me heart?*

Beads of sweat ran down his face to freeze into small icicles in his beard. The bearskin robe had fallen open and clung to the bark of the tree. He straightened his wife's legs, still wrapped in the doeskin, and heard the haunting bells again. Finally, he pulled the bearskin over her.

"Skye, dig yourself a small hole, here at the base of the tree."

She knelt and began digging in the frozen dirt with her hands, her fingers white with cold. He watched but did not help.

"That'll do. Now bury the jerky. Wrap it up good in the broadcloth. That's a lass, cover it up now."

She did as he said, burying the blue bundle of jerky, covering the spirit food with a small, curved mound of dirt and sodden leaves. Tears fell from her eyes, moistening the earth. He reached down and put his hand on her shoulder.

" 'Tis time we be saying a farewell prayer, lass."

Skye stood, shaking the dirt from her skirt.

"Yea, though I walk in death's dark vale," he began, then stopped, a shudder shaking his broad chest. The Twenty-third Psalm was his daughter's favorite. He began again, "The Lord's my shepherd, I'll not want . . ." But the rest of the words would not come.

They stood there, father and daughter, under the spreading moonlight, and listened to the night sounds. Snow drifted over their tracks and a light dusting filtered through the barren limbs of the tree, covering the buffalo robe in a gossamer veil of white.

Slowly, Skye walked back up the path with Ate. *Yea, though I walk in death's dark vale, yet will I fear none ill . . .* The words ran through her stunned mind, over and over. *Oh, how I want to hear Ina's moccasins upon the trail, feel my hand in hers.* She wiped a tear from her eye, forcing herself to think about the snow, or the cold, anything but Ina.

Once inside, Ate relit the oil lamp and put another log on the

fire. Then he took the elk-hide bundle of Ina's things and raised
the lid to the wooden trunk. He took the lock of hair and placed
it inside the bundle. With a thin strip of leather, he secured the elk
hide, pulling the knot tight, then placed the bundle inside the
trunk, on top of his kilt, his pipes, and his grandfather's claymore.
Closing the lid, he took a metal key out of the pocket of his buckskin shirt, lowered the clasp, and turned the key in the lock.

Skye wanted to cry out, "Don't lock her away!" but she could
not, for he was locking her heart away, as well.

She slept that night clutching the turtle shell which Unci had
given her. In the morning, she strung it on a slender thong and
wore it hidden beneath her dress. Once again, Ate left early to
hunt the *igmu'tanka*. She watched him from the window as he
headed out, shifting the rifle in his hand and moving at a fast pace
up the ridge into the pine trees. Pulling a robe over her shoulders,
she opened the door and went outside.

She followed the trail south, to the cottonwood tree. Her feet,
clad now in bearskin boots, left no moccasin tracks on the fresh
snow. Many times she had walked this path. Always before, Ina's
quiet footsteps had led the way. Now she walked alone.

The dark shroud of the buffalo robe rested in the arms of the
tree, stiff and frozen. A breeze ruffled the fur. The loose trilling
song of a lone snowbird broke the silence.

Skye knelt at the side of the tree and picked up a handful of
snow. The wet coldness eased the raw stinging in her fingers, still
sore from burying the jerked meat—the spirit food which would
help Ina's departing spirit return to the Ikce Oyate, the Real People.

Turning toward where she had left the spirit food, she started
to add the handful of snow. Then she jerked her hand away, jumping to her feet. Her eyes watered from the cold. She blinked and
looked again.

Nothing remained but a dirty hole, freshly dug, and the paw
prints of *igmu'tanka*.

3

THE COUGAR

Hunger gnawed Gregory's shrunken gut. Little food had passed his throat in over a week, not since that damnable night. He fought to concentrate on revenge. The painter must die, as had Breathcatcher. What he wouldn't give to come face to face with the killing beast, to toss his lightning stock aside and grab ahold of the huge cat by the throat—to tear the life from her as she had torn his life asunder when she ripped her claws into the soft skin of his wife. *Damn the Evil Eye. This would be* his *day of wrath!*

He shifted his rifle into his left hand and adjusted the pouch of gunpowder which hung from his shoulder. No acorn bread filled his waist pouch, no fresh johnnycakes. No meal had simmered on the cook fire for four days now. Skye had scrounged for food from the remnants in the larder, but he, he hadn't the stomach for any of it. *Skye. I can barely dare to look at ye, so like your* ina *ye are. Aye, maybe your dark eyes are flecked with gold, and your long hair a tint of auburn, like a nut-colored doe, not the deep, rich tones of freshly turned earth. But ye move like your* ina, *gliding along with barely a sound, and ye talk like Breathcatcher; your words soft yet carefully chosen, words a body should heed . . .*

Pangs of guilt tugged at Gregory as he thought of Skye. He knew he should stay with her, console his child. But instead, he pushed on, his own grief twisted and bent until it smelled and reeked only of anger—passion turned to hate.

The west slope of the mountain steepened. Gregory paused and looked back down the trail, marked with occasional week-old droppings of wild sheep. Below, cradled in an ancient glacier pocket, a small alpine lake reflected the gathering storm clouds. He pulled his striped capote around his broad torso, overlapping the thick wool and shutting out the thin, cold air. Winter's frigid breath had already forced autumn to retreat from the twelve-thousand-foot mountain. A delicate border of icy lacework fringed the small lake, crystalline fingers glittering toward the center of the water every time a wintry wind rippled the surface.

Today he hunted the mountain's uplifted south spine. He walked with head bent, picking at the fragments of sandstone and slate that littered the trail. He started to kick at an oblong-shaped rock that stood upended, then realized that four more stood upright beside it. They pointed toward the sky like miniature versions of the Standing Stones of Callanish. A small shiver traveled down his spine. Some claimed the Callanish stones marked the rising and setting of the moon. *And what do these stones mark? Has some evil witch of the Otherworld set them here to ward me off?* He kicked at the stones, sending one flying into a stand of old-growth spruce.

He strode on. More mountain-sheep dung. Surely he would find lion sign today. The she-cat had not left the mountain. Of this he was sure. He could feel her, sense her.

Wind shook the tops of the spruce and the crowns of the straight lodgepole pines. The whooshing sound echoed through the forest, filtering down through the branches of the trees. Dawn had come and gone, short-lived in this mountainous terrain. Sunlight appeared briefly through the cracks in the building clouds, then remained aloof and hidden. The majority of the forest birds had already begun their journey south, though the brazen blue jays still filled the air with their raucous cawing, mimicking the sharp-beaked hawks soaring above the pines. He saw no ravens, no birds of the black art.

Gregory trudged on, his breath forming clouds that quickly dissipated into the chilled air. He headed toward an outcrop of rocks protruding from the escarpment. From there he would be

able to see north to the peak, and to the south, across the breadth
of the small valley where the hills formed a saddle. He had hunted
all the other ridges and faceted slopes, the caves and hidden recesses where a cougar might bed down or drag a kill to feast upon
the carcass. But they had all proved empty of fresh sign—deserted.
Still, the great boulders that jutted into the horizon at the end of
the path might yield a bounty. Perhaps this would be the day he
would make the painter come . . .

Keeerrr, keeerrr . . . A high-pitched call penetrated the echoing
wind, spiraling down to the steep path where Gregory trudged.
Keerr, keerr. He raised his eyes from the rock-strewn path. A red-
tailed hawk perched upon the most prominent rock, silhouetted
against the gray sky. The screech was a warning call that man had
entered the forest domain. The hawk pushed off the rock with his
strong talons, stepping into thin air. His wings spread to their full
width of over two feet, his angular body rising as he caught an updraft. The raptor flew in a circle, going higher and higher until he
became a disappearing speck.

A lone rock skittered down from somewhere in the boulders.
Gregory jerked his gaze away from the hawk and caught a dark
flash of movement. As quickly as the hawk had taken flight, the tip
of a long, tawny tail flicked against the horizon and disappeared
down the other side.

*The painter. Finally! It will be a cold day in hell when I let go the
likes of her.* "I'll be graining your damned skin afore ye know it!"
The bitter wind pummeled his lungs.

Gregory switched the rifle into his right hand and began running up the steep, frozen path, grabbing at low-growing scrub oak
and boughs of scrawny junipers as he scrambled upward. *Damn ye,
painter! Streak it, ye bloody cat. Ye won't get away this time!*

He scaled the broad scree ledge. Panting, he walked around
the outcropping, his boots dangerously close to the unstable edge.
He looked to the north, to the east and west. No cougar. She was
gone, like an apparition, like a figment of his imagination. Had he
really seen the flick of a tail? Did his obsession so addle his brain
that he saw movement where there was none? Was it the work of
the Droch Shuil? *Damn ye, painter!*

Disappointment washed over him. So close! He turned away, afraid that there would be no tracks to find, no sign to follow—for apparitions left no mark. He kicked at the scree, his mind so focused on revenge that he failed to see what lay before him. He knelt and picked up a rock, intending to hurl it over the precipice.

Had the pile of bones been a coiled snake, he would have felt the piercing sting of poisoned fangs. *Wagh!* Fresh porcupine bones—bare of flesh, cracked open and the marrow sucked out—scraped and gathered into a pile, all but the prickly hide.

He peered closely, brushing aside the loose quills. He searched the bare rock surface for tracks, knowing that he would not find them where the wind had swept the rocks clean, where there was too little soil for even the most spindly of trees to grow. He jumped over the pile of bones and, moving at a near-run, bounded down the far side of the scree after the disappearing tail, deep into the heat of the chase once again. *Evil Eye or no, I'll be coming after ye!*

The rocky mountaintop succumbed to tenacious bushes and altitude-dwarfed pines, forcing Gregory to slow his pace. The hard ground gave little sign. He stooped, searching for a broken twig, a displaced stone, any indication of passage. But the inhospitable earth offered no clue. He would have to slow down, be cautious. He must not overlook anything.

He crawled at an agonizing snail's pace for the next fifty feet. Every muscle in his body, every drop of racing blood, wanted to burst forth—to attack the mountain, to cry out a challenge to the cougar. *Here I am! Come at me, as ye came at Breathcatcher! Show yourself!* But the mountain remained still, the jays silent, the hawk gone.

He descended another hundred feet. Ponderosas and occasional white pines stretched upward, their height increasing as the air became less rarefied. He ran his hand down the length of his beard and gulped at the air, then knelt and examined a barren area beneath a gnarled spruce. Dried needles had been scraped into a small pile, and sharp claw marks had furrowed into the compacted soil. *A lion scrape. Aye, the painter has been here, spent time here.*

Enough time to call the territory her own, to leave her mark.

Gregory kicked at the pile of needles with his boot, scattering them across the ground. The corner of what appeared to be a piece of blue cloth fluttered in the midst of the needles. He bent over and took the exposed triangle of cloth between his fingers, shaking the debris from the material. Blue broadcloth. The same cloth Skye had taken from Breathcatcher's sewing box. *The same cloth in which they had buried the spirit food the day he lifted Breath-catcher into the limbs of the cottonwood* . . .

He straightened, held the cloth to his nose, and sniffed, un-consciously wanting it to be scented with his wife's familiar, sub-tle femininity. It smelled, instead, of cougar—of the strong urine odor of lion. As if bitten, he jerked the cloth away from his nose and shoved it between the lapels of his capote, then turned back to the trail.

A deep instinct, as ancient as the Stones of Callanish, as an-cient as prey and predator, made him look up—into the deep green shadowed depths of the gnarled pine. And just as he raised his Hawken to shoulder level and pulled the hammer, just as the gunpowder ignited and the ball sped toward the cougar, she jumped.

She landed on Gregory's broad back, digging her claws into the heavy wool, through the buckskin shirt, into his flesh. An en-raged cry surged through Gregory, all the pent-up grief hurling forth in a tidal wave of fury. The cougar's claws tore the flesh from his shoulder blade—but it was Breathcatcher's blood that he smelled, the memory of her torn throat that assaulted him. He screamed, his cry curdling the turbulent air.

A guttural snarl curled the cougar's lips, baring four daggerlike canine teeth, each nearly an inch long. The tremendous force of her onslaught could have broken his neck, her teeth could have found their mark in the jugular vein at his throat had the rifle ball not raked across her temple, ripping flesh from bone and tearing open an artery. Blood gushed from the wound, temporarily blind-ing her left eye. Her claws dug into Gregory for balance; her snarl turned into an eerie, high-pitched yowl that pierced the forested walls, and, like a bolt of lightning, rebounded from the mountaintop.

The cougar's blood spurted on Gregory's woolen coat as she sprang from his back. He staggered and fell, striking his head against a jagged chunk of quartz jutting up from the needle-strewn ground. The earth vibrated beneath him, his fall like the rumbling of an embryonic quake. The clouds closed over him, shutting off the last bit of dim sunlight that filtered through the trees. The sky grayed and thickened. The wind blew, freezing the clouds into millions of crystallized flakes of ice.

Gregory awoke three hours later. He sat up, then rose slowly on stiff, aching legs. The joints of his feet, arthritic from years of wading in cold beaver streams, groaned in protest. He rubbed dried blood from the swollen gouge on his head and gingerly touched his injured shoulder. Wincing in pain, he shook fresh snow from his capote and stamped his boots to force the blood back into his feet. Shuffling through the snow to the gnarled spruce, he brushed the snow from the bark, then blew on his hands to warm them. There were claw marks in the tree. Fifteen feet away he found tracks where the cougar had landed after pummeling him into the ground. He scraped up a fistful of wet, snow-covered dirt, and his hands, white with cold, turned reddish-brown with cougar blood. He inhaled the mineral and metallic odor. On bent knees he began to crawl along the obscured bloody trail. As the snow deepened, and with each running stride the cat had forced from her weakening body, the trail grew fainter and fainter.

Heavy snow continued to fall from the dingy sky, covering the rocky abutment and layering itself upon the branches of the spruce and lodgepoles. Patches of white grew like fungus on the gangly limbs of the ponderosas, and Gregory cursed his throbbing head as the snow fell hard and fast. He squinted to clear his vision. The wind whipped the whiteness from the ground, hurling it into serpentine drifts. The winter storm breathed down his neck, filling the tracks of the fugitive cougar. *Damn ye, painter! Ye got a tough bark! But surely ye'll not be tough enough to survive that lead ball.*

May your death come slow and cold . . . Then dizziness overcame him and he staggered, pitching head first into a drift.

Death would come to the cougar, but it would not come that day, or that night, or the next. The snow obliterated her tracks, but she did not stop to rest until she was far from the oily smell of the two-legged. Winded, her lungs aching, she finally rested. She tried to shake the pain from her forehead, then lay on her side, letting the cold snow soothe the muscles injured by the humpback. Soon, she moved on, not resting again nor cleaning her wounds until she finally reached the deserted den of her kittenhood.

She crawled into the dank cave and a deep shudder shook the snow from her tawny coat. She opened her parched mouth and made a feeble attempt to lick her paw and rub the six-inch gash in her forehead. Belly dragging, she crawled back to the cave opening and buried her fangs in the wet snow, sucking the moisture through her teeth. Then she returned, pulling herself deeper into the recessed shadows of the cave. She licked at her stomach, her rough tongue scraping her dry teats, a low rumble vibrating her chest as she remembered her cubs. None had survived the hunger. Finally, she sank into bone-weary sleep, her feet twitching as if they were running, as if she were being chased.

Ten miles south, Gregory roused himself from brief unconsciousness. The snow continued to fall fast and hard; he was forced to give up the hunt. He pictured a pack of hungry mountain wolves tearing into the wounded cougar's murderous flesh. An eye for an eye. No pity rose from his grieving heart. The penetrating cold numbed his aching body as he headed back down the mountain, back to the lonely, gloomy cabin where his daughter waited.

4

WINTER CAMP OF THE STANDING PEOPLE, 1841

Far To The Southeast

Howling winds tore at the brittle stalks of the prairie grasses, leaving them bent and bruised as if trod upon by the hooves of a thousand blackhorns. Among the wiry little bluestem and the densely matted buffalo grass, a shining sumac bush, the purple faded from its autumn leaves, leaned into the hillside, frozen roots clinging stubbornly to soil mixed with sandstone, limestone, and shale. Three feet beneath the dormant sod, above the stable bedrock, stretched a layer of hardened salts. Nearby a well-used buffalo wallow had hollowed out the earth, nearly exposing the white sheeting of mineral. This land of mixed prairie, land of the enemy Liar People, the Scilis, would soon be the new home of the Standing People band of the Oglala Lakotas.

Yata, firstborn of the Four Winds, took a deep breath, and for a moment the incessant howling ceased. Turtle Woman listened. The stillness allowed her husband's low voice to filter in through the hide walls of their tipi as he spoke with their second son, Wolf-skin Necklace.

"Our people are truly scattered now," Sunstone said. "Bull Bear's death at the hand of Smoke's people has split the Oglalas in two as surely as the wolverine tears the innards from his prey."

"*Hecetu yelo*, it is true." Sadness stretched the voice of Wolfskin

Necklace into thin whispers. "Our people divide themselves, as when the deep angry rumbling of our Earth Mother rips raw chasms into her own flesh."

"The Smoke People are not our enemies. They are kin. Our true *toka* is the *wasicu* water which burns the bellies of the warriors. They awake from their drunkenness to find that the enemy has robbed them of their souls."

"*Hoye, hoye.*" Turtle Woman could not see the men nod their heads in sorrowful agreement, but she knew her husband's mannerisms, and Wolfskin Necklace's gestures, as intimately as she knew her own. Although not their birth son, Wolfskin Necklace had chosen them as his second parents, and they had contributed much to his upbringing. Was he not already a Naca, one of the youngest Big Bellies ever chosen? To have such responsibility was a great honor. He might even, someday, be a Shirt Wearer like Sunstone. This was their hope, their dream.

The voices outside became muffled again as Yata exhaled, hurling his cruel breath against the lodges of the Oglalas. Turtle Woman thought about Wolfskin Necklace, glad that he had chosen her to be his second mother. When she looked at the old mourning scars upon her arms and remembered the baby that Wasp Man had kicked from her belly, the son lost to her husband, she knew that the tradition was good. Breathcatcher, their only daughter, was lost to their ways, living in a white man's cabin instead of the sacred, circular tipi of her people. It was a good thing to have this man to call son. Without him, the spirit would be gone from Sunstone, leaving him a sad and withered man, like the lone plum which hangs too long upon the branch.

Turtle Woman heard the wind-borne nicker of her roan mare who grazed, untethered, just beyond the edges of camp. Turtle Woman's long graying hair, loosened from its confining daytime braids, glistened in the light of the fire. She took her butchering knife from the thong which belted her elk-skin tunic and flicked a vagrant coal back into the dwindling fire. Then, with the knife point, she began scratching a medicine wheel into the compacted soil.

A withered plum. No daughter to keep her company during the long Moon of the Hairless Calves, only the shadow of a grand-daughter to cheer her when the frost in the tipi grew thick and the sound of popping trees could be heard at dawn—like a withered plum whose seed has fallen upon frozen ground.

Three winters had passed since she had last seen their daughter—three summers of camp circles and celebrations, of watching the ear-piercings of other women's *takojas*—too many seasons since she had seen Skye run like a colt through the tall grass. Would Skye remember the teachings of her elders? Would she remember the hearty laugh of her *tunkasila*, her grandfather, as she tugged on the otter-skin wrappings of his braids?

"Hoye," Wolfskin Necklace again grumbled in agreement with Sunstone's murmurings outside the tipi. Turtle Woman added another spoke to the wheel.

"The Smoke People travel to the forks of the Shell," Wolfskin Necklace said. "They prefer to pitch their tipis near the land of the enemy Scilis. Others lead their families west, camping within the arc of Susuni arrows."

"Han, even within the arc of the arrows of the Kangis," said Sunstone. "Did you not hear of the Kangi woman warrior who raided the Oglala lodges less than three sleeps away, during the Moon When All Things Ripen?"

"I heard. The Kangis leave the protection of the Shining Mountains to move the arrows against our people."

"Yet even as the enemy spills the Lakota blood of the Oglalas, so does the Oglala spill the blood of his brothers. In my dreams, I hear the mournful voices of our grandfathers as they watch the blood of our own people stain the earth red."

The men's voices faded into low tones of somber agreement. Turtle Woman nodded, carving the final spoke of the wheel into the dirt. She, too, grieved at this fighting among the Oglalas. All Lakotas should stand as one.

Sunstone spoke again. "We are like orphaned coyote pups, snarling over their mother's carcass. Travel east with us, my son. We will camp near the waters of the Smoky Hill Fork. We will fight the Scili and snarl over their carcasses, not our own. Come. There is much *wasna,* enough for all to eat. . . ."

The wind, howling again like an angry spirit, stole the voices of the men, carrying their murmurs out across the prairie. *A Kangi woman warrior? Could it be Little Badger grown?* Turtle Woman lifted the knife point and considered her drawing. Twenty-eight spokes radiated from the center cairn. She retraced the easterly pointing spoke, deepening the thin furrow in the dirt. Her brow wrinkled as she thought of the few moons she had spent captive among the northern Kangis. The shaman's words still echoed in her mind.

"*A great woman warrior will be conceived within the womb of the Standing People. She will spill from the heavens like a thousand stars, and the power of her prayers, and those of her blood, will be seven times a holy man's.*"

The night her *takoja* was born, a great comet had streaked across the sky, as it had the night her own mother was born, nearly ninety winters past. Two women, within one family, born beneath a shifting star. *E-i-i-i*, what was the meaning of all this? Yet, had the shaman been wrong? Had Little Badger been destined to become the woman warrior? A slave girl turned Kangi? Not a woman of the Standing People?

Turtle Woman lifted her knife from the dirt and poked at the dying fire. She added two small branches of dried wood. Replenished, the fire crackled and flared.

The scattered sage of this Shell River country did little to stop the cruel north wind which swept its way across the prairie. *Yata, you do not frighten me, any more than do the Scilis or the Kangis.*

Though the wind howled like an angry spirit, it brought no early snow. She pulled her robe over her shoulders and shivered. She, too, missed the sheltered valley camps of the Black Hills, missed their cool streams and the songs of the mountain birds. She did not want to venture east. She wished to return home to the sacred hills. She wished to see the poles of their lodges silhouetted against the tips of the pines. *I wish to grow old among the memories of my family.* But first, a thought she had never dared to share with Sunstone, first she wished to return to the Medicine Wheel. She wished to touch the face of the rock where the shaman had shown her the five-pointed star. Did such a drawing really exist? Many winters had passed. Perhaps she had only imagined it. Perhaps there had been no Kangi grandmother.

Family. Turtle Woman shivered again, digging her callused fingers more tightly into the buffalo robe. Not all of their tribe would journey east. Some preferred to stay. Some did not want to journey to a new camp, not when the cottonwoods along the river's edge would soon. pop and snap as coldness filled their wooden limbs.

Turtle Woman did not fear the Scilis or the Kangis or the Susunis. No premonition of danger had come to her in her dreams, no warning of mishap—only the sorrow that hung heavy upon her heart when she thought of Breathcatcher and Skye. But sorrow alone would not prevent the journey east, would not slow the steady progress of the horses, who were in good flesh, fat after a summer of ripe, lush grass. Even her roan mare still had sound and sturdy legs, despite her turned-in foot, though they were both becoming long of tooth and short of breath.

It would be good to sit upon the back of the red roan again. *The red roan. Given to me by the Scottish man who shares Breathcatcher's blanket. Much as I dislike Caws Like Magpie, at least he would not have taken my daughter from me.*

The wind shifted, and a sudden gust blew down the smoke hole. A few cinders, caught in the updraft, flew into Turtle Woman's face. Dropping her knife, she rubbed her watery eyes, soothing the grainy itch.

When she opened her eyes, flames from the fire cast flickering shadows across the walls of the tipi. The smell of sage and sweetgrass wafted up from the flames. She rubbed her eyes again. *This old body deceives me. I burn no sage, no sweetgrass—nothing but gnarled wood.*

She stared into the fire. The pungent odor of sage and the purifying aroma of burning sweetgrass filled the tipi. She gazed at her drawing in the dirt and thought of the cliff high in the Shining Mountains. A child had, indeed, been born. A girl child, just as the shaman had predicted. But no comet had shot across the sky the night of Breathcatcher's birth; it was not until the birth of her *takoja* that the stars shifted in the heavens. And now this grandchild, and her only daughter, lived far away, with a man whose ancestors were born across the great waters.

The scents of sage and sweetgrass grew stronger, almost overpowering her. She rubbed her eyes again, then opened them and stared into the fire. *Ah, the power of the stars, is that what this is? Does the legacy of the Standing People come to me once again? Am I to be shown a* wakan *thing? Or is it only the trick of a body growing old and tired?*

The flames grew higher. Turtle Woman's eyes cleared. She tucked her heels beneath her legs and began to rock back and forth. The fire gave birth to fluid, moving shapes. A sleek tawny cat, an elusive *igmu'tanka*, crouched before her, a bloody scar upon her forehead. Steady amber eyes stared at her—eyes sharpened with hunger, quick with cunning. The muscles of the animal grew hard and taut as she sprang at Turtle Woman's throat. Instinctively, Turtle Woman threw her scarred arms in front of her grimacing face. A terrible cry of *Yun! Yun! Yun!* filled the tipi, but the cry did not come from her.

As quickly as the cougar had materialized in the orange flames, the vision disappeared. Turtle Woman stared into the depths of the fire, rubbing the leathery folds of thinning skin at her throat. A new image began to form in the flames, a woman fluid and beautiful, young and dark-haired. Turtle Woman could not deny the sound that now filled the tipi—a wail that rose from the heart of a stricken *wasicu* like an arrow piercing the very heart of heaven. As the grief-stricken cry disappeared up the smoke hole, taking the scent of sage and sweetgrass with it, the flames of the fire turned yellow, then white, then suddenly a vivid turquoise blue.

Breathcatcher, Breathcatcher.

Turtle Woman grew still, rigid. Her butchering knife lay near the stones which circled the fire. She bent to pick it up and the robe fell from her shoulders. She held the knife before her and raised it to the sky, then lowered it toward the earthen floor. She offered the knife to the Four Winds, then with slow deliberate motions placed her left hand upon one of the warm stones by the fire. The flames' reflection flashed off the blade of the knife, which she grasped in her right hand. One swift cut severed the first joint of the little finger from her left hand.

Blood gushed onto the rock and seeped into the dirt. Shudders shook her body. She picked up the severed joint and tossed the offering into the fire, then fled from the tipi, almost knocking the startled men from their feet. Into the cold dark night she ran, her anguished keening trailing behind her like a lost spirit.

The roan mare lifted her muzzle from the dormant winter grass and nickered softly. Turtle Woman reached the horse and flung her arms around the gracefully arched neck. Still holding the butcher knife in her right hand, she grabbed the mare's dark mane and pulled herself up onto the horse's back. Blood dripped from the injured finger onto the dark mane. With one slice, Turtle Woman cut through the handful of blood-matted hair. She kicked the roan mare in the sides, urging her forward. With her hands raised to the starless night sky, one holding the knife and the other the bloodied strands of mane, she rode away from camp and into the cruel, dark wind—into the very breath of the vengeful Yata.

5

TEN YEARS THENCE, 1851

Skye set the steaming mug of hot tea on top of the wooden trunk, next to where Father sat rummaging through his collection of rocks. She was in no mood to put up with his irascibility; she was feeling a bit touchy herself. The cold night wind that swept down from the mountain irritated her, for the summer months had arrived and she expected balmy, starlit evenings.

Father set the stones down with a thud.

"Haste ye back to Scotland," he said.

"What did you say, Father?"

"Haste ye back to Scotland. That's what they said—there at the harbor." He lifted the mug to his lips. "Och, what I wouldn't give for a cup of honest-to-goodness black tea."

"I thought you liked my strawberry-leaf tea."

"Ye make the finest cup of berry tea I've ever drunk. It isn't your fault if berry's all we've got. Just don't expect me to drink that damn kinnikinnick tea again. Smoke it, aye. But drink the bitter stuff, child? I thought ye were trying to put me under!"

"I'm not a child anymore, Father. Haven't been for quite some time."

She was not surprised when he didn't answer her, almost glad, actually. She had grown accustomed to his smoking his pipe in silence while she tried, with little skill, to sew with bone awl and sinew. Usually the silence was soothing, but sometimes, like this evening, it seemed simply a prelude to a litany of self-pity.

The cabin rarely housed laughter, her own or Father's. She preferred the woods, where the breeze caressed the leaves of the cottonwoods with invisible fingers, eliciting faint lonely melodies, where her feelings were overwhelmed by the grandeur of nature.

Her attempts to please Father with Highland dishes—sausagelike haggis, Scotch broth or cock-a-leekie soup, even the make-do scones—more often than not ended in unpalatable failures. It seemed the only thing she could do fairly well was steep him a mug of tea.

Skye had not seen Father don his kilt or heard the notes of the bagpipes since Mother's death, ten years past. The wooden trunk remained closed, locked.

"Ye've never seen a tam-o'-shanter, have ye, girl?"

"A tam-o'-shanter? No. What is it?"

"Aye, that's what I thought. And what about a stone springhouse filled with crocks of fresh milk and cream. Have I ever taken ye to see that?"

"You know you haven't."

"Your grandmother would be appalled."

Skye felt her jaws tighten. "Which grandmother?" she asked, not caring if the question riled him. She meant it to rile him. It wasn't her fault that she didn't know these things, that she couldn't bake a decent scone or sew a decent pair of moccasins.

"And I suppose I've never taken ye to see the mist-covered floor of the Great Glen. Or the steep mountains rising from the glacier-carved valleys? Why, I'll bet me last plew I've never even played the Highland Muster Roll for ye!"

"Father, stop it! You know you haven't." She pushed a strand of loose hair out of her eyes. "Why don't you get out your bagpipes and play it for me, then?" she demanded, her blood quickening at her own boldness. "Teach me the damn Muster Roll!" *Aye, open the trunk! Let me hold my mother's things! Let me put on her doeskin dress and feel her brush smooth my tangled hair once again.*

She had gone too far. Father glared at her for a split second with narrowed green eyes, the color of lichen clinging to shadowed stone. Then he looked away, not speaking for several minutes.

"Did I ever tell ye the story of Jamie Macpherson?" he finally asked in a soft voice. Without waiting for an answer, he went on.

"Jamie Macpherson was a fiddler. Best fiddler in the Highlands." Skye tucked her long skirt beneath her and sat cross-legged on the floor, regretting her earlier rash behavior.

"Trouble was, Macpherson had been caught stealing cattle. Caught and convicted. He stood with the rope taut about his neck, clutching his fiddle. Then he shouted, in a voice which bellowed across the crowd, 'No one else shall ever play Jamie Macpherson's fiddle!' And before anyone could stop him, he shattered his famous fiddle over his knee, and sprang to his death!"

A deep sigh came from Father's broad chest, making Skye wish that she were small enough to once again curl up on his lap, in the safe grip of his strong arms. He sighed again and then began puffing on his pipe. The smoke drifted upward in thin, spiraling wisps. She knew his moodiness was only temporary. She should have waited it out, said nothing. Mother would have known how to gently crack Father's hard shell, but Skye's bungled attempts only maddened him.

Once in a rare while, some comical situation would soften Father. A spontaneous laugh would erupt from his broad chest and Skye would remember her younger days, when Mother's rich doe-brown eyes sparkled and Father's affectionate bear hug warmed her heart.

Were it not for the dog-eared volume of verse from which Father had taught her to read, she might almost have believed that his tough exterior went soul-deep.

"Your great-grandmother Maggie," he had once told her, "now, she was the real poet. Not only did she recite it, word for word, but she used to write it as well. Your grandmother Iona has some of her poetry ferreted away somewhere—unless she's given it to me sister Katie."

His sister Katie? He rarely spoke of any of them. Oh, how she would love to see them—from a distance, at least. But to meet them in person? The thought panicked her. No, she had no desire to go anywhere. She *was* grateful for the journal of Scottish verse, though. It helped her to imagine the Highlands, and often stirred Father's dormant laughter, especially when he imbibed "a wee dram of the rosy god" and felt the urge to put a tune to one of the lighter verses, such as Sir Walter Scott's:

> "Oh, young Lochinvar is come out of the West,
> Through all the wide Border his steed was the best.
> So faithful in love, and so dauntless in war,
> There never was knight like the young Lochinvar!"

The singing would last for as long as the memory of Mother's death remained sequestered, never more than an evening or two.

Had Father returned that long-ago day with the skin of the cougar, perhaps things would have been different. Though he spoke as if the beast were dead, a faraway look entered his eyes whenever he stared up into the mountain's rocky abutments or high trails. The doubt tormented him; the tracks that had circled the tree beneath Mother's robe-covered body were a shadowed question.

Oddly, the very memory which haunted him was a source of

comfort to Skye. The tree beckoned her and she often found herself sitting in its cool shade. A sudden gust of wind might stir Mother's death shroud, and the bells tied to the fringes of her dress, a few of which had escaped the taut folds of the buffalo robe, would whisper soft chiming sounds.

Near the cottonwood tree, the waters of the creek tumbled over rocks and stones. Feeding trout hid in pockets beneath small rapids of foaming white water. The creek's music washed over her, easing her into accepting the unalterable. Destiny, she now realized, had played a greater part in Mother's death than had the cougar.

Father cleared his throat and held his pipe at arm's length, running his stout fingers through his rusty-blond beard.

" 'Tis time ye started behaving like a proper lass," he said, "and that is something I surely canna teach ye. Ye should be setting in some fine parlor sipping from china, not cussing and moping around a worn-out trapper the likes of me."

Months ago, he had spoken of taking her back east. Terrified, she had refused to go. She liked "moping" around him, didn't want to leave. Only once had they saddled the horses and left the Bows, heading west, not east. They had followed the Cherokee Trail across the Continental Divide and into a great expanse of high desert plains: sand and sage flanked by ancient granite thrusts. The desert, awash in subtle color and vast undulations, had mesmerized her. But Fort Bridger, crawling with rude unkempt men whose cruel tongues cut into her like knives, still made the hair on the back of her neck rise.

"By beaver, there's a good-lookin' breed," they had jeered. "Bring the young squaw back in a year or two!" The lechers had heckled Father, "Play you a quick hand of euchre for a roll in the hay with the little *femme du pays*." Oh, how she had wished Father had brought the claymore along. She would have unsheathed it herself!

The path to the cottonwood and the banks of the mountain stream were well trodden and bare of undergrowth. This sheltered spot, with the only horizon the tops of forest trees, satisfied all Skye's needs. She loved the waving grasses of the high meadows, the challenge of helping Father track the regal elk or keen-eyed mountain sheep. She desired no other teacher. The wildflowers taught her all she wished to know of art—the lyrical mountain stream, the loose trill of the snowbird all she cared to know of music. She needed no stranger to stare at her rudely, condemning her coppery skin and golden eyes.

Only at night, when evening closed in around the cabin like a dim reminder, did she allow herself to miss Mother. Then she would draw the turtle shell from beneath her bodice and hold the polished amulet in her hand, permitting her grandmother's words to echo in her.

"You, Daughter of the Sky, are like the blue above, the meeting of east and west. In you, there is hope. In your veins flows the blood of the great Lakota people. In your veins, also, flows the blood of the Highlanders. The two mix. Like the river that joins the ocean, there is a moment of turbulence. But there is also a calm, a stretch of shallow water which smooths the sand. You are like this blending."

But the past was gone. Death would never loosen his eternal grip. The few memories left to her formed a frail legacy. Adrift, like a leaf which must go the way of the current, she bided her time.

6

THE STORM GATHERS

Duncan, Skye's bay horse, whinnied from the rough-barked corral. Skye looked up, expecting to see Father riding in on the sorrel, Roy. What she saw instead caused her to drop the bucket, and creek water sloshed over the edges, splashing the front of her cal-

ico skirt and spattering mud on her bare feet. She raced to the
cabin and grabbed the old Hawken off the antler gun rack above
the door, then stepped back outside.

Three men mounted on piebald geldings rode up to the cabin.
They reined in their horses just three feet from where Skye stood,
rifle in hand, heart pounding. Oglala Lakotas, she ventured to
guess, slightly relieved.

The first man, about Father's age, wore large shell earrings
and several coup feathers. Silver trade discs, also attached to his
scalp lock, trailed down his back. A black stripe had been painted
on his right cheek and ran from the outer corner of his eye to the
angle of his jaw. Fringes and elaborate quillwork decorated his
yoked buckskin shirt and leggings; an ornate belt encircled his
midsection. From a string of trade beads dangled two blackish, iridescent feathers. The two other men dressed simply by compari-
son, except for an impressive bear-claw necklace on one of them.

The leader spoke. "We will talk with Gregory Macdonald."
His eyes took in the scene as he spoke, surveying the cabin, the
shed, the corral where Duncan stood alone. Did he really think
that Skye would have been the one holding the Hawken had Father been home? She said nothing.

The man swung a long, spidery leg over the horse's hind end
and dismounted. "There is no woman here either?" he insinuated.
Skye did not like this man's harsh black eyes or his manner. She
took a step back and held the rifle in front of her. Undaunted, he
looked at her mud-spattered feet.

"You think you are a little woman chief, pointing your long
gun? Chiefs do not play in the river," he said, his voice heavy with
sarcasm.

The tone of his voice brought back memories of Fort Bridger.
Playing? She was not a child!

"If you were bathing at the river, you did not do such a good
job!" He laughed loudly at his own joke.

"I expect my father to return any moment," Skye retaliated,
forcing a rough confidence into her voice. She stiffened her
spine and stood up straight, pulling her shoulders back. One of
the other riders, the youngest, with the bear-claw necklace,

nudged his tobiano paint forward, listening intently.

The gaudy one spoke. *"Waste,"* he said, fingering one of the hanging feathers. "Good. We will talk with him."

His birdlike eyes appraised Skye—from her muddy feet, up the calico cloth of her threadbare skirt, to her pale yellow bodice. Pausing, he lifted a feather to his craggy nose and scratched the side of a large nostril.

"You want me to help with your bathing? Ha!" Probing, insinuating words.

"I want nothing," she retorted, angered and confused by his boldness. She fought the urge to turn on bare heels and run like a frightened deer into the woods.

"Has your father's *wasicu* blood colored your manners white? You do not offer your guests anything to eat? We have traveled many sleeps. Our bellies grumble and dust clings to our throats. Have you no black medicine to drink in your square lodge?"

The youngest man, who had edged his mount even closer, slid from his horse in one fluid motion, causing the older man to step awkwardly to the side. A thin ridge of scar tissue, almost identical in location to the black stripe worn by the older man, marked his face. He stood six feet tall, naked but for a plain breechcloth, moccasins, a leg ornament of furred otter skin, and a quilled armlet on his upper right arm. Around his neck, resting on a well-muscled chest scarred in two places, hung the superb bear-claw necklace. An assortment of feathers, their significance lost on Skye, hung from his scalp lock. His lips parted, revealing straight white teeth.

"The biting wind of the north should not expect a warm welcome," he said to the older man. Dark almond eyes seemed to flash a warning.

The two men exchanged hot looks. Anger blazed between them. The gaudy one shifted his weight, his spindly legs jutting out beneath his short-waisted torso. He continued toying with the dangling feathers, moving his cracked tongue across dried lips.

"Mahto, your words are like sparks. One day they will start a fire you cannot put out." Skye had seen antlered bucks during the rut behave like that, bluffing while backing down.

This young Mahto did not appear to be bluffing. Long braids

draped over the bear-claw necklace. Well-muscled legs, spread slightly apart, stood poised for action. Skye's gaze traveled back up the warrior's sleek figure. Their eyes met and she realized he had been watching her stare. Embarrassed by her boldness, her pulse raced, fueled by a new and confusing brand of fire. She looked away awkwardly before speaking.

"There is jerked meat, and johnnycake from this morning. You'll have to drink your coffee cold." Intending to bring the food out, she hurried inside, reaching behind her to close the heavy wooden door, but a gaudily clad arm pushed the door open, thwarting her efforts. So close did the arrogant stranger follow that she could feel his dank breath on the nape of her neck.

Setting the flat bread and jerky on the rough-hewn table, she turned and headed for the open door, almost colliding with the other two Indians who stood at the entrance. *I may have to feed them, but I will not stay inside with this stranger who handles his hanging feathers like fangs and has the breath of a beast!* Skye picked up the overturned bucket and, half-running, headed for the seclusion of the stream.

Skye listened as low arguing voices, punctuated by moments of silence, leaked from the log walls of the cabin. Then a louder, bolder *"Hiya!"* More disagreement. Then the sound of something heavy being dragged across the floor, and perhaps lifted, set upon the table. Duncan whinnied, racing with short quick strides up and down the length of the corral fence. The three riderless, ground-tied horses lifted their heads, ears perked forward, and stared across the meadow at a rapidly approaching horse and rider. 'Twas Father, hell-bent for leather, Roy's hooves pounding the meadow turf in full stretch.

Skye put the bucket down and stood so that Father could see her, waving her right arm. The gesture, meant to ease his mind, apparently only spurred him on. Even at a distance, he could spy the strange horses.

Roy, with sides heaving, tucked his haunches under and dug his hooves in. Pistol in hand, Father leapt from his back, vaulted to the cabin, and pushed the heavy door open, all in one blur of motion.

Skye rushed in after him. The wooden trunk rested upon the hand-hewn table and the gaudily dressed Oglala stood over it with head bent, shell earrings dangling. He held the fire iron poised over his head for a downward blow against the brass lock of the trunk.

The stranger jerked himself upright at Father's abrupt entrance. The young one, the one called Mahto, stood in a corner with arms folded in displeasure. The third man stood by his side, a half-eaten crust in his hand and a dark scowl upon his face. Father's eyes, their verdant green turned cold and calculating, surveyed the scene. Then his deep voice filled the crowded cabin.

"Caws Like Magpie!!"

Was this stranger he? The man whose name had caused Mother's face to turn to stone, who had sworn to the thunder and lightning that he would seek vengeance upon Father? Skye's eyes darted from man to man. Her skin prickled as electricity filled the charged air.

Father's voice softened, but his words were as deadly as poison. "Strike that trunk, and I swear I'll kill ye."

Caws Like Magpie hesitated, the fire iron still upraised. Skye searched his beady eyes; a hint of cowardice, well hidden beneath his arrogance, floated to the surface like a piece of rubbish. She stared at Father's poised pistol, his thumb on the hammer of the single-shot weapon. Would he pull the trigger?

"Mac-don-ald," Caws Like Magpie finally said, the word stretched thin. A nervous sneer crept across his face. "We await your return," he said, lowering the fire iron.

Father kept the pistol raised. "The trunk belongs in the corner. Ye'll be putting it back." It was not a question, but an order.

The third stranger stepped forward out of the shadows. "*Hau*, Macdonald." he said, lifting the trunk. "I bring you big-hearted words from Sunstone."

All eyes followed the wooden box as he carried it to the corner. Then he turned and strode toward Father, an open palm raised to shoulder level. Father lowered his weapon. Caws Like

Magpie swaggered away from the table and leaned the fire iron against the hearth.

"Wolfskin Necklace," Father said, his voice warming. "I did not recognize ye. Ye have wintered well these many years. Why do ye travel with the people of the Muddy Water camp?" Father looked disparagingly toward Caws Like Magpie.

Wolfskin Necklace. The adopted son of my grandparents?

"A handful of warriors go to the medicine woods to gather the *wakan* branches for our bow making. A few Kiyuksas from the Bear Den camp"—he glanced at Mahto—"a few Standing People, a few of Muddy Water camp. Sunstone grows too old to make another long journey so soon. He asks me to come in his place."

"Sunstone—he fares well? And his wife?" Father took off his broad-brimmed hat and wiped his forehead with the back of his sleeve.

"*Han*, the old woman still lets him throw his robe in her tipi." A touch of affection warmed his words. "He sends greetings to his special *kola*, Naked Warrior.

"He also sends word that the camp of the Standing People is no longer in the Smoky Hill country far to the east. We camp near the Shell River, where the waters of Bitter Cottonwood begin to flow down from the big peak. They say their hearts will soar like the *wanbli* if you bring their *takoja*, their only grandchild, to visit them."

All eyes turned in Skye's direction. A flush crept up her neck as her eyes met Mahto's. Flustered, she averted her gaze.

Caws Like Magpie, scratching his nostril with a feather while eyeing Skye lewdly, said, "Too bad so much *wasicu* blood colors her looks. But the little warrior-girl would keep a man warm when the cold moons come. She's too mouthy for much else. Ha!"

Rage once again twisted Father's features. He lifted the muzzle of his pistol and stepped back. Mahto, quiet until now, moved forward with lightning speed, placing himself between Father and Caws Like Magpie. With his back to Father he stared, unblinking, into Magpie's small black eyes.

"You shoot words like a bickering hag," he said contemptuously. "A true warrior fights with bow and arrow."

The young Lakota's unmistakable challenge hung in the tense air.

"Lad, move yourself out of the way. 'Tis time that surly bastard and I settled this thing!"

Mahto did not move. Nor did Wolfskin Necklace, who stood solidly, his legs spread slightly apart. Magpie appraised his two challengers, then addressed Mahto.

"Scout, you push me too far. The meager coup feathers which hang from your scalp give you big visions. But a pup does not grow into a wolf in one sleep."

Caws Like Magpie held his craggy nose in the air, taunting, daring. The muscles in Mahto's face quivered; the thin line of scar hardened. The silence held Skye captive, as if caught on a high ridge during a lightning storm, waiting for the sky to explode, with no shelter in sight. Then, almost in slow motion, Wolfskin Necklace moved his oaklike body in front of the one called Mahto and she was able to breathe again.

Wolfskin Necklace began to speak slowly and with great control, looking directly at Mahto with eyes that had seen many battles, seen the fires of many council lodges. "In Sunstone's absence, this Wicasa Itacan asks of you a favor. Hanging from my saddle is a gift. Leave your anger, and bring the gift to me."

The young scout clenched and unclenched his fists. His lips parted slightly, as if he were about to speak. Then, staring back into the eyes of his friend, he gritted his white teeth and turned away.

Father looked at Skye, but he stood poised and ready, waiting for the winds to shift, for the inevitable storm. As Skye started to move away from the door to let the young warrior pass, their arms brushed against each other, like branches caught in a whirlwind. The warm feel of his tautly muscled arm stirred Skye root-deep, filling her with a new, puzzling kind of tension. Glad to leave the stifling cabin, she followed him outside.

The ponies stamped their unshod feet and whisked their tails through the hot air, their slick, shiny coats glistening in the light of the high sun. Skye watched Mahto undo the clasp of the fringed parfleche hanging from Wolfskin Necklace's saddle and remove a bundle wrapped in soft, finely tanned leather. She stepped aside to allow him to pass, only then realizing that the others had come outside. Caws Like Magpie walked to his impatient horse and slid, spiderlike, onto his back. Father stood, pistol still in hand, glaring at Caws Like Magpie. Mahto, too, shot a hot look at the mounted man as he handed the neatly wrapped gift to Wolfskin Necklace.

Expecting Wolfskin Necklace to pass the gift to Father, Skye edged closer, anxious to see what the bundle held. Instead, the Lakota turned to her, shading his face from the bright sun. The hint of a smile graced his broad features.

"Since last we met, you have sprouted from a seedling into a blossoming tree. Your *unci*, Turtle Woman," he said, holding the gift out to her, "wishes you to have this. She also sends these words, 'Tell my *takoja* that my heart beats in rhythm with hers. Soon, our paths will join.'"

Skye took the bundle from him, his words slowly seeping into her. *For me? From my grandmother—our hearts beating in rhythm?*

With trembling fingers she loosened the leather thong that bound the gift, carefully folding back the soft hide to reveal a small, rectangular case. Fine quillwork adorned the bag: a comet, in red, shooting through the middle of a five-pointed star embroidered in vivid blue. Diamond-shaped patterns of yellow and green filled in the background. Delicate fringe edged the entire case. Skye stood transfixed, her finger gently tracing the bag's exquisite stitchery. A vague image floated by—a woman, head bent, awl and sinew in hand, drawing a flattened quill from between straight teeth—*Grandmother. Unci.*

"It is a foolish gift for a white girl!" Caws Like Magpie spat the vindictive words into the hot air, and they landed like lead upon Skye, and upon the beautifully quilled bag. "The *wasicu* has no use for a quilling case!"

His words entered Skye's heart as surely as would have a bullet from Father's pistol. They dug beneath her skin, spiraling toward the sacred place where Mother's memory hid, the place where shame resided. *Wasicu? White girl? Half-breed? Squaw?* Did she belong nowhere? Was her blood considered tainted in both worlds? She wanted to lash out, to strike him with her hunting knife!

"No wonder your name caused my mother to bristle with hatred. Ye are a horrible man!" Forcing her tears back, she jutted her chin into the air, defying him to speak again.

Father's words rolled forth. "Let this be a warning to ye, Magpie. The next time ye loose your tongue upon my ears, I shall take me claymore to it!"

Magpie spun his horse around, at the same time pulling an arrow from the quiver on his saddle. He raised the arrow, attacking the sky with his defiant gesture, then dug his feet into the gelding's flanks and, pulling on the single rope looped over the horse's lower jaw, spun him around. Another jab of his bony heels into the animal's flanks, with arrow still raised to the sky, and the pony lunged forward. Father's sorrel, Roy, caught off guard, did not shy away in time. Magpie struck the unsuspecting horse between the ears with the arrow; the stout wooden shaft shattered. The disengaged arrowhead hurled through the air, impaling itself in the dirt at Skye's feet. Roy reared backward and a warlike caw erupted from Magpie's throat:

"Aaaaaggg!!"

Dirt flew in her face as he spun his horse around again and, gripping the broken arrow shaft like a lance, thundered away across the meadow yelling the Lakota war cry, *"An he!!! An he!!!"*

Skye fled, her eyes burning with tears and her heart aching as surely as if the arrowhead had pierced her flesh. She fled to the sheltering cottonwood by the water's edge. Cradled beneath the overhanging branches which still held Mother's bones, she watched a gnarled piece of driftwood float downstream. *A foolish gift for a white girl!* Would she always feel this way? Halved? Severed from both worlds?

The mountain stream moved on, full of purpose, secure in its destination. She gazed after the disappearing driftwood, listening to the melody of water rippling over rocks and the vibrations of insects hovering above the ever-changing surface of the creek. Soft as the breast feathers of a snowbird, words wavered in the barely moving air. *"There is power in the mixing of your blood."*

The words floated above the water; they filtered down through the leaves of the cottonwood; they started deep within Skye and worked their way through her memory, through the pores of her skin, to the depth of her soul. *"There is power in the mixing of your blood."* Words spoken by Unci the day they said good-bye. But why had she looked away when she spoke them? What power did she mean? Lakota blood? Scottish blood? The blood of Shifting Star and Sun Dog? The blood of the Highlander, and of Graunie Maggie, red-haired lover of verse? Who were these people? How did their lives, most long since spent, empower hers? Would they always be mere whispers in her life, casting lonesome shadows where she walked? Leaving no footprints along the path?

"Aye, daughter. I thought I would find ye here." Skye jumped at the sound of Father's voice, so lost in melancholy that she had not heard his heavy step upon the trail. He was scowling.

"Come, Skye. We must make ready for a journey. 'Tis time I be taking ye to visit your grandparents."

She unfolded her legs, shaking the folds of her calico skirt as she rose. Father, in an uncommon gesture, reached for her hand. His clasp, strong yet gentle, eased her past the tree. As they walked in silence his grip suddenly tightened. Her hand, enclosed within his, was the only thing that prevented his hand from forming a fist. Skye shuddered, knowing that the storm continued to gather, knowing that Father had another, more urgent reason for the journey to the camp circle of the Oglalas. Their travels would take them east, but a foreboding told her that it would be the biting wind of the north which would bring the thunder and lightning.

7

SACRED WATERS

Alone but for his horse, for many sleeps Mahto had been following the yellow circle of sun as it journeyed across the open sky, traveling within the great arc of the Shell River that ringed the northern Medicine Bows. He glanced down at the hard ground and the half-circle prints left by his horse's strong hooves. *The curved bed of the Shell leaves a similar mark upon the land, like a new moon hanging alone in the darkness of night.* The southwestern tip of the river, where the peaks and folds of the mountains smoothed themselves into desert grassland, was a very short ride away.

A tall birch tree, ten feet from the path, caught Mahto's eye in the early morning light. He put away the cedar flute he had been playing and reined his tobiano gelding off the path and into the small grove, pulling the paint horse within an arm's length of the tree. Bare white wood, where the bark had been peeled back from the tree, revealed the carved hieroglyphic of a Kangi warrior: *I, enemy of the Titonwan, have invaded your territory!*

Had the carving been fresh, Mahto would have been tempted to head north and track the invader, but the symbol was more than a season old. Like the dried dung of a fleshless mountain sheep, the trail was not worth following. There were enemies enough in his own camp without worrying about the Kangis.

"Come, painted one, we will not let the enemy divert us from our purpose." The tobiano turned back onto the path and they continued on their way, an irritating grumble rising from Mahto's fasting belly.

"You whine like a neglected pup," he said aloud. The tobiano flicked his ears backward at the familiar voice. "Not you, my friend. You are tireless and brave. You carry me upon your back without a single, complaining snort."

Mahto tried to ignore the hunger pains that had been plaguing him since yesterday's sun rose in the eastern sky. Out of respect and in preparation, he had not allowed even the smallest of berries to pass his lips. The first few days of going without food were always the hardest. Grateful, he reminded himself that this would be a short fast. Quickly he chastised himself. *I am a whining pup. My father would never have had such a thought.*

Soon, a pungent, mineral odor tainted the dry air, and Mahto knew that he had entered the neutral ground of the sacred waters. He dismounted, led the tobiano to the edge of the spring, then knelt and held his hand in the hot vapors which rose like fog from the pool. He swirled his finger, agitating the hot sulphurous water until it spun like a small whirlwind upon the dusty plains. *It is good that I have come. Here, I can gather strength, purify my unworthy thoughts . . .*

He removed the bridle rope from his horse's lower jaw and wrapped a pair of leather hobbles around the front feet. Then he stooped and unlaced his moccasins and loosened the leg ornament of furred otter skin, setting them on a nearby rock. He slid the quilled armlet from his upper right arm, removed his leggings and the plain breechcloth. The bear-claw necklace, a gift from his father, remained, as did the two white, black-tipped feathers and lock of horse hair which hung from his scalp lock. Only good scouts, those keen and quick, were permitted to wear the small eagle-wing quills.

He scooped a handful of water from the spring and, raising his hands, offered it to Sky above and Earth below and to the Four Directions.

"Tunkasila," he said, "Grandfather, I am not worthy. My heart is full of anger for many wrong reasons. *Onsimalaye*, pity me. May the big medicine of these waters purify me. *Hye*, Tunkasila, thank you, Grandfather."

Mahto lowered himself into the near-scalding spring, sliding his lanky frame cautiously into the steaming heat. He scooped more water into his hands and splashed his face, letting the drops travel the path of the scar, across the corners of his eyes and down his cheekbones. The penetrating heat eased the tension in his chest. Stretching his long legs in front of him, he let the water caress the tired muscles of his thighs.

Just as the water swirled at his touch, so did many thoughts swirl within his mind. They had gathered much medicine wood—mountain mahogany and white mountain cedar—for the making of bows. Two weeks had passed since they had visited the cabin of Macdonald, two weeks since he had first seen the granddaughter of Turtle Woman and Sunstone.

He had known the Standing People had had a daughter who lived far away, for Wolfskin Necklace had told him of the sadness that gripped Sunstone's heart and caused Turtle Woman to grow old before her time. But he had not expected the granddaughter to be grown into the plumage of a woman. Nothing had readied him for the strong, stubborn girl with hair the color of ripening chokecherries and eyes as bright as the swiftest fox's.

Caws Like Magpie's crude talk still made his blood run hot. He had felt this rage before—six winters ago, when he was but fourteen, and his father had said he would not take him along with the many warriors who would go to move the arrows against their enemy, the Susunis. And when the warriors did not return, *when his father did not return*, their winter camp was filled with the mournful keening of the women. Rage seethed within him. Then the Susunis returned the scalp of the brave warrior Male Crow to Male Crow's father, Whirlwind. The gesture did little to appease Whirlwind's grief, or Mahto's, and the war pipe circled the camps of the Oglalas, even as far away as the camps on the Big Muddy—the Missouri, the *wasicus* called it.

"*An he!*" Mahto startled himself with his own outburst. He had not meant to speak aloud. He had been thinking of the first blow he had finally struck against the enemy who killed his father, thinking at the same time of the blow he would like to strike against Caws Like Magpie.

His harsh battle cry was out of place in these sacred waters. Remorse settled on him at this violent thought against one of his own tribe.

He stood, rising from the thermal waters, and shook the moisture from his flushed skin into the relatively cool air. He thought of the high-spirited *wikoskala*, with the flashing eyes of a fox and the gentle curves of a woman, and he lowered himself slowly, inch by inch, back into the steaming waters of the spring.

Perhaps the blood that grew hot within his veins, and the stirring within his heart, should not be blamed on rage alone. Perhaps it would take more than cool air to soothe his rising temperature . . .

8

MOVING ON

A gentle, late-morning breeze cooled the perspiration that glistened on Skye's tanned throat. She watched as Father leaned over a rawhide pannier, packing a bundle of jerked deer meat next to a small bag of flour. A second, empty rawhide pannier rested on the ground next to the first.

"Go and fetch the mugs, Skye. Ye'll be glad for a bit of comfort on the trail." Father straightened, placing his hands on the small of his back, then arched backward into a stretch.

" 'Tis a pity," he moaned, "that just about the time a person gets used to his bloody body, it starts wearing out on him."

She smiled. Father was still as stout as a grizzly and just as ornery.

"Looks like you'll be the one wanting a bit of comfort," she teased.

She headed into the shadowed cabin to get the two pewter mugs, which sat on the hand-hewn table just within the door. A third, tucked behind an empty tin of saleratus and a few of Father's rocks, gathered dust on a shelf by the window. Her gaze lingered on the third pewter mug, tarnished by time, dulled from lack of use. She took a deep breath, exhaling with an unsettled forcefulness. A vision of her grandmother, pulling awl through softened leather, came to mind. Confusing anxiety filled her with uneasiness. She picked up the third mug and took it with her.

Back outside, Duncan, her bay gelding, and Roy, the sorrel, waited patiently beneath their high-bowed mountain saddles, tightly rolled blankets, and heavy saddlebags. They carried only a part of the journey's load, however. A young mule, recently bartered for and just yesterday broke to lead, would be carrying the panniers.

She nestled the mugs between the flour and jerked meat, being careful not to disturb an assortment of small gifts—ready, if necessary, to appease the unfriendly Crows or Snakes or Utes who might wander onto their path.

But it was not the people of the Crow nation whom Sky feared most, nor the fierce Utes or dangerous Snakes. Leaving their cabin to travel through the Medicine Bows did indeed cause her stomach to tighten. But this fear she could calm. The fear which she could not calm caused her heart to quicken and her palms to grow moist.

Ever since I was a little girl, since Grandmother's quilled moccasins became too small for my feet, I have dreamt of seeing Turtle Woman and Sunstone again. Why now, when I am finally able to go to my grandparents, does it frighten me so?

"The look on your face would wither the heather off a hillside. You're a touchy lass, Skye. Your moods sway like an aspen caught in a windstorm." Father turned toward the green-broke mule and began whistling a Highland tune. Skye couldn't help but laugh at the irony of what he said. *My moods sway like an aspen? Ha!*

He unfastened a strap on the mule's sawbuck packsaddle and loosened the breeching, lowering it further down on the mule's haunches. The animal stood nervously, still wary of Father's touch, ready to pivot away at the slightest warning.

"Aye, but you're a skittish one too. No doubt a few uphill miles will take the vinegar out of ye." He refastened the strap and stepped back. The second pannier, still empty, rested on the ground next to the first. Father had yet to load a single thing into it.

The pannier gaped open, seeming to mouth the question that Skye, in ten long years, had not dared to ask. The unspoken words swirled within her. *What of your bagpipes and your claymore, the kilt and saffron shirt, the heirloom brooch? What of Mother's things? Are they to remain forever in that wooden box?*

As if in answer, Father stopped whistling, turned, and entered the dark cabin. The morning fire had grown cold, breakfast long since eaten. Skye followed quietly, the late morning sun warming her back and casting her shadow across the open doorway.

He walked over to the corner of the one-room cabin and knelt by the wooden trunk, stroking his reddish-blond beard and running his fingers through his unkempt hair. He reached into the pocket of his buckskin shirt and removed a rusty metal key. Lost in thought, he held the key in his broad hand for a moment, rubbing it gently between his fingers. Finally, when it seemed that moments had stretched into hours, Skye heard the sound of metal turning metal.

Father raised the lid slowly. The hinges creaked and groaned from lack of use—from a decade of shutting away memories and hiding grief. He reached inside and tenderly removed Mother's elk-skin bundle. He cradled it in his strong arms, his touch almost a caress. But suddenly, perhaps to prevent the memories coming to life, the deep wound penetrating the surface, he pushed the bundle away from him and held it out to Skye.

"Take this outside and put it in the pannier."

Lost in her thoughts, she jumped at the sound of his voice, skittish as the new mule. She took the bundle from him and stood staring at it, the leather cool against her bare arms. Many times she had wished to hold Mother's belongings, to hope someday to wear the sunburst hair ties, the elk-teeth wedding dress, the finely crafted wedding moccasins.

"I said to ye, go put it in the pannier." Father's mood shifted *like an aspen* as he repeated his order. Skye's temper flashed but she silenced her tongue, for the harshness in Father's voice did little to hide his sad eyes. Would grief forever cling to them both, like lichen upon the dark side of a pine, hidden from the healing sun? She turned and walked softly out of the cabin, her calico skirt brushing against him as he knelt, alone, by the open trunk.

Father had not worn his kilt or played the pipes since Mother's death. Skye could remember a different father, one who danced gaily about the cabin with the bearskin hat atop his head and his feet dancing a Highland jig, pulling Mother from where she sat, shyly hiding her mirth behind a graceful hand. His booming voice and Gaelic spirit filled the cabin with song until Skye, too, was swept up by his bear hug into the middle of the room. Those were different days, days belonging to a child whom she only remembered in brief stolen moments. Even the anniversary of the Macdonald massacre no longer tempted him to play his Highland bagpipes. Why, now, had he decided to take them along? Would the pannier only serve as another burial cache?

Skye lowered the elk-skin bundle into the empty pannier. Father came out shortly carrying his Scottish regalia—the bagpipes, kilt, and sheathed claymore. All but the claymore fit securely within the pannier. Father lifted first one load, then the other, testing for an equal distribution of weight. Satisfied, he picked up the sword.

"Skye, bring the mule here beside me."

She walked over to where Duncan and Roy stood, swishing the summer flies with their long tails. Taking both sets of reins in hand, she collected the mule's lead rope and led all three animals to where Father waited. He checked the packsaddle, then lifted the pannier that held most of the edibles and the gifts, and started to settle the half-load cautiously on the sawbuck.

The mule pinned his ears back. He flinched as the weight of

the pannier pulled on the cinches which girthed his belly. With a
quick sidestep, he tried to move away from the frightening pressure. But the pressure did not lessen. He spun, colliding with Roy,
forcing the other animal to back up. The tangle of fast-moving
legs caused Skye to lose her balance. Roy, resenting the long-
eared newcomer's brashness, bared his teeth and with a quick,
painful nip reminded the mule of his place in the pecking order.
The wide-eyed mule snorted, pivoted away from the pain, and
pulled his lead rope from Skye's hand. The end of the rope
whipped through the air and caught the mule on the tip of his sen-
sitive nose. This final insult undid what little training he cared to
remember. The mule had had enough.

He spun around and bolted past Father, past the shed, and out
into the open meadow, the lead rope streaming out behind him,
the sword hanging for a split second in midair, the half-loaded
sawbuck bouncing up and down on his striped back.

"Why did I let go of that infernal rope!" Skye chastised herself, regaining her balance.

Father, who had miraculously caught the claymore, grabbed
Roy's reins and, cursing "Damn ye!" at the mule, leapt on the startled horse and went pounding after the pack animal. Skye glanced
down at the remaining pannier, still resting upon the ground. Father's regalia and Mother's elk-skin bundle were undisturbed.

Streaking across the meadow, the mule headed straight for the
creek and the safety of the timber. The open pannier bounced up
and down on his back, pulling the breeching across his buttocks
and rubbing the rear cinch across his flanks. With each bounce,
the mule brayed and bellowed, his protests echoing off the mountain. Rawhide parcels of jerky flew through the air. Pewter mugs
ricocheted off the sawbuck's rigging. A length of blue trade cloth
unraveled itself and, catching on the cantle of the saddle, waved in
the wind like a high lord's banner.

Notwithstanding the solemnity of the journey's beginning and
her frustration at losing the lead rope, Skye could not help grinning. With a hurried leap, despite her long skirt, she mounted
Duncan and loped off across the meadow, following the trail of
scattered objects. Ahead, Father, his sword-carrying hand raised

high and legs flailing against Roy's sides to urge him onward, pursued the ornery mule, who looked as if he might run clear across the Medicine Bows and on to the Platte River. She contemplated pressing Duncan forward to join the race, but decided the fun was in the watching, not the pursuing.

Father's loaded saddlebags bobbed up and down in rhythm with the sorrel's stride. The gap between the two animals narrowed. Roy responded by lengthening his stride. The creek stretched in front of the mule. The mule took one look at the noisy, fast-moving mountain stream and came to a sudden, decisive stop. The sorrel, not as agile nor as surefooted, did not stop, but instead made a ninety-degree turn along the rocky banks of the creek. Father, unseated by the lightning change of direction, flew through the air and landed with a splash in the cold current.

By the time Skye caught up with them, Father stood on the banks of the creek, sword still in hand, water dripping from his beard and buckskins. The mule quivered near the edge of the stream, his sides heaving nervously, his uneven and greatly lightened load perched precariously atop the sawbuck.

Father stepped toward the mule. The mule stepped back. Father stepped forward again. The mule moved back another step. Skye braved a laugh.

"Father, he'll never come to you while you're holding that sword. It looks as if you're wanting to cleave him in two!"

Just as the packsaddle threatened to go one way or the other, Father's mood swayed between anger and laughter until the ridiculous situation finally won him over. He began to laugh. The laugh, born of a reluctant smile, finally grew and spread until his entire stout frame shook, from the broad brim of his hat to the wet fringes of his buckskin shirt clear to the tips of his boots.

Skye dismounted and walked slowly toward the mule to retrieve the lead rope. "You know, Father, he might behave better if we gave him a name. What do you suppose we should call him?"

"Call him? Aye, you're right. The creature needs a name. Fact of the matter is, I've already called him several. 'Tis a pity none of them are fit for ye to hear."

The morning's tension drained away as they laughed together

near the banks of the creek. The sun, by now, hung high in the clear June sky. The mountains stretched up, pulling away from the meadow, their lodgepole pines and mountain birch trees hidden in the deep green shadows of their peaks.

"Let's call him Quickstop, Father, for he surely is good at that!"

"Aye, Quickstop it is, then!" He chuckled as he tied the claymore to Roy's saddle and cautiously took the retrieved lead rope from Skye's outstretched hand. "Quickstop it is."

They returned to the cabin, retracing the chase across the meadow and reclaiming the scattered objects. Once again, Father attempted to hang the two panniers from the sawbuck.

"Will ye do me a small favor this time, and don't be letting go of the lead rope?"

"I'll hold on to it with my teeth if need be!"

The mule, his adrenaline spent, stood quietly. After draping a neatly folded bundle of hides and robes across the panniers, Father secured the load with a loop and a half-hitch, drawing the rope into a gooseneck with just enough tension to stabilize the pack without rubbing the mule's withers.

Skye, catching sight of their wood ax protruding from the stump of a pine, walked over and jerked the ax loose. She attached it to her saddle, then turned back to the open door of the cabin. Sunlight spilled inside, coming to rest on the empty wooden trunk. The rusty hinge, which still carried scars of Caws Like Magpie's attempt with the fire iron, glowed softly in the rays of sun.

Will I ever return here? Will I ever sit beneath the cottonwoods by the willow creek again? Who will pluck the wild bird-foot violets and lay them beneath mother's shroud? Must we really go?

She shook these thoughts away and forced herself to focus on the journey ahead. The earlier feeling of uneasiness gave way to a restless desire to move on, a need to see new country.

Father is right. The time has come for me to visit the camp of the Standing People. I cannot allow the past to hold me captive, as it does him. I must not fear it any longer, any more than I should fear the future . . .

On a shelf just above the trunk lay Graunie Maggie's well-worn volume of verse, veinlike creases marking its leather cover. Skye's footsteps echoed as she crossed the room. Opening the cover, she turned the thin pages. A small square of blue broadcloth, perhaps a bookmark, fell from the volume and fluttered to her feet. Her eyes skimmed the marked page. Then she saw it, the stanza which surely must have riveted Father, a poem by Scott about two lovers torn by death from one another, a poem vaguely familiar.

> "Where shall the lover rest,
>   Whom the fates sever
> From his true maiden's breast,
>   Parted for ever?
> Where, through groves deep and high,
>   Sounds the far billow,
> Where early violets die,
>   Under the willow."

Oh, there was so much about him she did not understand. All these years, no flowers would he allow in the cabin; never once did he go to the creek with her. And all the while he was torturing himself!

She stooped and picked up the blue cloth. A faint musky odor, one she could not identify, emanated from it. She placed it gently back in the book. Graunie's volume of verse would fit in her saddlebag. Perhaps she could find a different verse to ease Father's loneliness, perhaps one to soothe both their souls. She took a last look around. There was nothing else to take with them.

Skye pulled the heavy wooden door closed behind her, narrowing the beam of sunlight which spilled in through the cabin's entryway until it gave way to near darkness. As she turned on her heels, her back to the closed, but unlatched door, the sunlight caught her full in the face. With a strong, tanned finger, she flicked the straying strands of auburn hair from her shoulder and strode with determined steps toward the bay gelding. Sliding the slender book in her saddlebag, she looped the reins over the horse's neck, hiked up her skirt, lifted her left foot into the stirrup, and swung her right leg over the saddle.

"Father," she said, forcing a lighthearted lilt to her voice, "if ye and Quickstop be through with your shenanigans, what say ye we be off?"

The two-leggeds were gone. Their strong, oily scent no longer tainted the meadow. The old cat walked the perimeter of the upland pasture, stopping every few strides to lift her broad dark nose to the wind. Her nostrils twitched and flared at the stale scent of horse manure. A scarred tongue slid over worn, dulling teeth and licked the heart-shaped nose, moistening the tender nostrils.

She moved on, her large, thickly padded paws scarcely disturbing the tufted fescue that grew on the edges of the meadow, where the forest thinned. She stopped beneath a solitary lodgepole pine and rubbed her angular shoulder against the rough bark; then she turned her face toward the tree and, pushing her forehead into the unbending trunk, scratched her scarred temple. A black-capped chickadee whistled a warning and flew from one of the lodgepole's lower branches. The cat shook her head and snapped at a large bee fly which hovered just beyond reach.

She proceeded on, stepping from the shade of the lone tree into the sunlit meadow. A willowy young racer, reddish-brown splotches coloring his serpentine back, slithered from beneath the unbranched leafy stem of a blue flax. The cat, undaunted, strode across the meadow, the pollen from a stand of purple lupine dusting her tawny belly. Finally, she reached the far side of the meadow.

She paused, testing the wind again. Her ears pricked. No noise came from the deserted den of the two-leggeds. A striped ground squirrel skittered beneath the sun-bleached corral fence, and a lone, yellow-flowered arrowleaf balsam sprouted from the barren ground in front of the cabin, near the door, which hung askew.

The cat circled the cabin, sniffing the weathered logs and cracked chinking. She halted at the door, one paw raised, one eye cocked. The sun caught her black-lined eyes and flashed in the amber orbs. The dark pupils narrowed to pinheads, then widened as she entered the dimly lit room. The heel pads of her paws left the print of three distinct lobes and two indentations on the dust-covered floor. Four widely spaced teardrop shapes marked where her toes touched the planking.

She sniffed the bent-willow rocker, her needlelike whiskers twitching from the end of a whitened muzzle. She lowered her haunches to the floor, sitting upright and staring through the open door. She swept her tail across the floor, all thirty inches of it, and as she did so the darkened tip of the muscled appendage slid between the floor and rocker and lodged itself. The lion twisted her sleek torso around and batted the chair with her massive paw. The rocking chair began swaying; the dry, neglected wood groaned and creaked. She jumped at the sound, pulling her tail free, and faced the imaginary foe with bared teeth. The rocking chair continued swaying, melancholy moans echoing from the wooden floor.

No odor of flesh and blood came from the moving chair. Barely a whisper of stale, oily scent tainted her nostrils. She turned and headed for the sunlight, stopping to peer into the open trunk as she passed by. The dark turreted eyes of a long-legged spider peered back.

The cat moved away from the deserted den without a backward glance and loped across the upland pasture. Stopping only once to lap cool water from the creek, she entered the forested slope of mountain and moved easily up the incline, leaping over rocks and deadfall. Several miles farther on, near her old cave, she paused again. Lifting her nose to the wind, she caught the scent of the young female cougar who had crowded into her territory. A low, gut-deep growl vibrated the painter's lungs. Lowering her chest to the cool earth, she laid her head upon her front legs and rested until the sun began its westward curve. Revived, she moved on.

Her travels led her north, toward more alpine meadows and the white ridges of the snowy range. A mysterious pull urged her on; a restless instinct drew her from the land of her youth, the land where she had suckled her own young. She would behave like a wandering male, seek a new domain, claim a new territory—no matter how far she must go. Even if she must travel across the high plains desert to the next ridge of mountains, or the ridge beyond that. Even if she was forced to travel clear to the summits of the Shining Mountains . . .

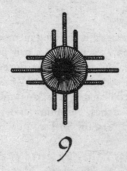

9

THROUGH THE MEDICINE BOWS AND BEYOND

Macdonald led the mule up the steep path. Behind them, the snowy range looked down upon the tableland. Ahead of them, at an altitude of nine thousand feet, lay an alpine meadow, a vast, open plateau. And beyond that, rising up from the glacial basins at the base of the range, rose Elk Mountain's timber-covered peak.

Gregory turned and looked at Skye, who sat astride Duncan a few feet behind the heavily laden mule. Her calico dress covered her saddle and the tops of the clumsy, too-large boots that she wore. A leather hat shaded her eyes and long silken hair. A shawl of homespun rested on the saddle's cantle.

Gregory suddenly wished that they pointed their mounts west, where the Rocky Mountains stretched along the Continental Divide, the mountain creeks and streams flowing into the Green, and from there into the Pacific.

The trail widened and Skye urged her horse forward until he caught up. "Do you want me to lead Quickstop for a while, Father?"

"No need."

A billowy cloud passed beneath the sun, darkening the trail

and softening the sharp edges of the trees and bushes. Then the cloud moved on, and sunlight reached once again into the shadowed tunnels and densely needled pines.

"Remember the Green?" Gregory asked, speaking more to himself than to Skye.

"The green what?"

"Now there's a river with trapping memories," he continued, ignoring her question. "Pack mules, a pair per trapper, an extra halter for the horse, and more than a dozen feet of rein." He sounded as if he were taking inventory. "Wooden stakes with iron-socketed ends; striped blankets; bearskins and buffalo robes; critter traps and plew caches; vermilion and seed beads; trading knives for buffalo tongues; the Snakes, the Crows . . ."

"And Lakotas."

"Aye, and Lakotas." Gregory stared at the path in front of them. "The Green. The Sweetwater. I knew their deep pockets and shallow waters like I know the swells and valleys of the Medicine Bows."

He knew the sound of a hungry mountain bear as well as he knew the rustle of a rattlesnake slithering along a rugged red sandstone cliff. He could see the rolling plains of sage and rabbitbrush, the bare granite rocks and red horizons. These memories rose up before him as real as the trail they now trod. The ghosts of other trapper friends, long since dead, whispered to him of the old days. Their bones were scattered from snowcapped Bridger Peak to the crystalline Snowy Range—old Henry Fraeb and others like him. *Damn, they could read sign!*

Overhead, from the stately upper branches of a ponderosa pine, a finely furred red squirrel scolded the small traveling party as they passed by. She scurried down the gangly length of branch, her tail pumping up and down. Gregory reached for the single-shot pistol in his saddlebag. He had a dogged itch to cut shine, raise a little hell.

"The mule may have settled down a mite, Father, but I wonder what he'd think of the sound of a pistol firing in his ear?"

"No doubt it would set him off again. But ye must admit, roast squirrel is a tempting thought." He aimed the pistol and pretended to fire, then lowered the weapon and returned it to his saddlebag.

"Ye know, Skye, your father used to have the hair of the bear in him. He ain't such a hard case anymore."

"Aye, he's worse!" She laughed.

Och, if she could've seen him back then, the man her mother fell in love with.

He took hold of his wide-brimmed hat, wiping the sweat from his brow with the leather sleeve of his shirt. The June mountain air, though cooler than the valley floor, still carried the sun's heat—even to the needle-strewn depths of the forest's undergrowth.

A queersome feeling nagged at Gregory. He had foolishly expected to feel the same carefree exhilaration, the same excitement, that used to spur him on when he headed out for the spring hunt. But this was not a jump-off into rich trapping grounds, a rendezvous with old coons, free trappers like himself. The reunion that awaited him at the end of this trail would bring recollections, to be sure, but most of them would be hard and painful.

The corners of his rusty mustache curled up slightly, changing his grimace to a partial smile. Twenty-five years had passed since his first rendezvous at Cache Valley.

"Wagh!" he grunted, "those fandangos were something." *You should've been there,* he started to say to Skye, glad in an instant that she hadn't been. Most hard cases, himself included, had had but one thing on their minds when it came to women.

"Fandango?"

"Aye, the rendezvous—where not an honest tale was told, nor an honest swap was made." *Nor a brown-skin woman was safe.* "We bartered and bullied till dawn, then started the doin's all over again."

He tightened his grip on the mule's lead rope, and his smile slid back into a grimace.

"Did I ever tell ye about the night when that cursed Scotsman, Campbell, threatened to pilfer me bagpipes?"

"You always said you would just as soon skin a Campbell as look at one."

"Aye. Never had any use for 'em. Never will. That night, the men sweet-talked me into getting out me pipes, and a finer version of the Scottish Ghillie Callum I had never played. Why, I had some of them old coons dancing the fling! Along comes Campbell, telling me to put away me pipes. But I was beholden to no man, and I'd be damned if I'd let that cocky upstart tell me when to play me pipes! To hell if Campbell was a lieutenant in charge of one of the fur brigades! He still were a traitorous Campbell; he couldn't escape the fact that it were his clansmen who did the butchering that fateful night at Glencoe. *In the middle of the night, when all were sleeping!* Damn the Campbells! Backstabbers they were—not fit to be called Highlanders!"

"Father, that happened over a hundred and fifty years ago. Will ye never let it go?"

"Aye, that it did. And it was almost three hundred years ago that the MacLeods murdered three hundred and fifty Macdonalds by suffocating them in a cave. Men, women, and wee lads and lassies, too! Are we to be forgetting them as well? They're still finding the bones of those poor souls in that blasted cave. Shall we just forget it ever happened?"

Gregory could hear his grandfather's fine Scottish brogue echoing the old familiar tales; he could almost feel the wooden floor of their thatched stone house shake beneath him as his grandfather marched up and down in his tartans, waving his double-edged claymore in the air, his grandmother right behind waving her cooking knife.

" 'Long live the Macdonalds!' your great-grandfather used to shout. 'Your ancestors captured the whole of the Hebrides from the seafaring Norse! Ye have Highland blood in your veins! You're a crofting Gael and don't ye be forgetting!' Why, if only ye could have heard him."

Aye, Grandfather remained fiercely loyal, despite the godawful clearances—wretched chiefs banishing the Highlanders from their crofts to make room for the bloody sheep, thousands of kinsmen herded onto ships for indentured service in the New World. Had it not been for his mother making sure he learned the pipes, he, too, might have been one of them. And now, here, he saw it happening all over again—the Indians being pulled and pushed, till they'd no place left to go.

He looked at Skye, noticing all of a sudden how much her eyes, despite their darkness, resembled his mother's. When she got riled, their golden specks flashed like so many stars in the night sky. They had the same keenness as his grandfather's, the same passion as his Graunie Maggie's. A savvy graced Skye, though, a wise gentleness that his grandfather had lacked. Not even his grandmother, God bless her, had had the same look.

He wished Skye could get to know the sweet-smelling, heather-covered hills the way he had. But too much, now, had changed. The world of the Highlanders, like the world of the Lakotas, would never be the same.

He shook the melancholy from his heart. " 'Twas your great-grandmother, ye remember, who used to read poetry to me. She expected me to commit it to memory, line for line." He grew quiet for a moment, listening to the rhythm of the horses' hooves. Had Graunie, he wondered, ever gotten the letter he'd written to her, and the wee river stone he'd put inside the letter? Though he'd posted it nearly seventeen years ago, he remembered every word of it, for 'twas the only letter he'd ever written, and it had taken him days to do so. *Last night, ye became a great-grandmother, for me wife (didna' I tell ye I'm married now?) gave birth to a baby girl on the shores of this very creek. Let this stone plucked from the waters remind ye of her, for she's as spunky as the river, yet like her mother, as gentle as the curves of this stone. We've named her Skye, after your beloved island . . .*

The pace of the horses had turned into a slow plod. He pressed his heels lightly against Roy's sides. "Your great-grandmother," he said to Skye, "once told me that a man with poetry in his heart would never die a lonely soul." Then, in a voice too soft to be heard, he added, "she wasn't right, though, ye know."

"So you memorized it?"

"Aye. Graunie Maggie wasn't a woman to be denied."

"Then recite something for me. You haven't for so long. Let me hear your favorite."

His favorite? Was there such a thing—anymore?

"It has been a long, long time, lass."

"Not so long ago, Father."

"More than a lifetime, Skye." He shook his head. *Coward.*

"Then I'll read a poem, if you're too stubborn to recite one."

He watched as Skye reached behind her and opened one of her saddlebags, rummaging around until she pulled out the small volume. *Confounded lass! Can't she leave things well enough alone?* With her reins tucked in one hand, she flipped through the pages, ignoring the scowl on his face.

"Here's a good one of Scott's, Father. See if you remember this:

> "Come fill up my cup, come fill up my cann,
>   Come saddle my horses, and call up my man;
>   Come open your gates, and let me gae free,
>   I daurna stay langer in bonny Dundee."

"Girl, ye never let up on a man, do ye? Aye, I surely do remember that one." Perhaps his grandmother had been partly right—poetry in the heart at least brought the homeland a little closer. Maybe it were a good thing, after all, that Skye had brought along the dog-eared volume. Many a lonesome night he'd been grateful to his grandmother for that gift of verse. He looked at his daughter's hopeful, expectant face and softened.

"Seems like only yesterday that ye were sitting on your mother's lap, listening to me read. Now you're doing the reading, and this old hoss is doing the listening."

Ahead, Douglas firs, ponderosas, and a few spruce cast elongated shadows upon the winding path. The sun, far to the west now, no longer warmed their trail. The temperature dropped a quick ten degrees, and the horses, invigorated, stepped up their pace. Darkness always arrived early in the mountains—and with the darkness, the night hunters of the Otherworld. They should make camp soon.

Gregory extended his stiff legs, pushing his boots against the saddle's oxbow stirrups. His muscles were cramped from the tedious hours horseback. They ached to straighten and stretch.

They had covered a lot of ground in three days, more than

Gregory had expected with Skye along. She had said little, complained not at all. He glanced at her. What had made her think to bring along Graunie's journal? She seemed to be deep in thought. That was his fault, too, he knew. He brooded and moped about, leaving her to fend for herself. 'Twas a good thing the girl had grit.

"You've had a rough time of things, living in the backwoods with an old coon like me." He stopped Roy and waited for her on a wide swath of trail. "Being raised up with no other children about, no women to talk with." He hadn't realized how grown-up she had become, how much the blush of womanhood was upon her, until Wolfskin Necklace and Caws Like Magpie had come visiting. *Caws Like Magpie.* The name soured his tongue. The lecherous scamp eyed Skye like an old rooster. 'Twas bad enough that he had tried to force himself upon Breathcatcher—but now his daughter as well!

"What was that young scout called?" He knew bloody well the name of the young Lakota, and he was sure she did, as well.

"What young scout?" Skye's voice was pitched just a hair too high.

"Surely ye know who I mean—the Kiyuksa, the one who came calling with Wolfskin Necklace and that tail-tying Magpie."

"Mahto, I think they called him." He saw a flicker of excitement in Skye's eyes. Mahto? At least the young warrior had made an effort to avert his gaze from Skye in the presence of her father.

Gregory had recognized the flush of admiration in the scout's face, though. And he was sure Skye had noticed it, too. Women did notice these things. The hang-about-the-fort women who begged for firewater at the trading posts had often pretended to see the look of desire in his eyes—offering their pitiful flesh, no hope left in their dead eyes. Once, he might have wanted it—but now the thought turned his blood cold.

Did visions of the young warrior fill Skye's thoughts? Do they even now, as we trek through the Bows? Or does she think solely of Turtle Woman and Sunstone?

"Ye know, I never asked if ye wanted to go visit your grandparents' camp." He had figured she would be eager to go. Any reluctance, he had also figured, would be his own.

She lifted the homespun shawl lying on the cantle of her saddle and pulled it up over her shoulders.

"Would my answer have mattered?"

"The time has come for ye to be with other people, with family."

Gregory had nothing left to offer her, only worn-out memories. And he'd be damned if he'd live to see that same empty look haunt his own daughter's eyes. Wagh! *But be straight with yourself, man. Ye'll never take her to meet her Scottish relatives.* Much as it shamed him to do so, he admitted it. He didn't have the courage to present her to his family. What would they think of this dark-skinned, golden-eyed, auburn-haired blood kin? What would they think of him, after these many years? And would there even be a Highlands to go home to, after the clearances? What would his father say about a half-caste granddaughter? *Half-caste. Half-breed. Either way, it's a hell of a thing to call your own kin. Hell of a thing to call me own daughter—Breathcatcher's child.*

"Father, you're looking at me as if I were a ghost. What do you mean, *be with family?*" Skye flicked the ends of her reins and it seemed to Gregory that her hands had never before looked so Indian. "From what I saw of people at Fort Bridger," she said, her jaws clenched, "I don't much care to be around them."

"Those were strangers. I'm talking ye to family. Ye aren't a child any longer, ye know."

The arrogant, sweaty face of that hovering Magpie had proven as much. Womanhood had slung a shapely lasso around Skye and captured her restless youth. He'd rather tangle with a wolverine than try to wrestle with the wants of a ripening lass.

"Ye need another woman to teach ye now."

"I'll not be able to learn much in just one visit, Father. Besides, I'm doing fine. You've taught me all I need to know."

"Oh, how I wish it were that simple, lass. You don't know much more than a pup. And besides, lately I'm always at a loss as to what to do with ye, never knowing the right thing to say. Seems clear as powder horn to me that ye need to be around another female."

Something else had finally become clear as powder horn to him—as obvious as a vulture perched on a bloody corpse. *He had a score to settle, a score long overdue. It was time to cut some shine.*

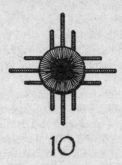

10

PEAKS AND VALLEYS

Sheer cliffs marked the descent down the east face of the Bows. The alpine tundra receded, replaced by sparse lodgepole pines clinging to rocky soil. At seventy-five hundred feet, the scarred skin of the earth smoothed into a broad expanse of high plains.

Gone were the mountains of Skye's childhood. Ahead lay a strange vista—an expanse of antelope-rich basin leading to a new ridge of mountains, and a massive peak that jutted into the eastern skyline. The thrill of this exciting openness quelled Skye's homesickness and made her eager to move on.

"Chunk up that fire a mite, afore ye go scare us up some breakfast." Father bent to repack the panniers, which had become unsettled after yesterday's long ride down the steep eastern slope.

"I scrounged up supper," Skye teased, shaking out her boots before pulling them on. "You were supposed to scare up breakfast."

"Aye, that ye did." Father's mustache curled up in a wry smile. "If ye call cactus mush supper. I call it poor bull."

"I could have left the thorns in, saved you having to pick your teeth."

"My, but you're getting to be a sassy lass. My paunch is growling like Old Ephraim himself. 'Give me meat!' it's bellyaching."

Skye stood, straightened out the folds of her dress, and picked up the old brass-mounted rifle.

"I'll shoot you one of those tender young jackass rabbits you like so much," she offered, heading out toward a flat open area dotted with scattered rabbitbrush and sage. Then she added, enjoying his unusual cheerfulness, "If you'll get the horses saddled, that is."

"Wagh! Ye can saddle your own mount, girl!" he shouted after her, exaggerating his lilting brogue—a sure sign of good humor.

The bunch grasses crackled beneath her feet. No rain had blessed the basin in at least a fortnight, maybe longer. The sun, just beginning to crest the Black Mountains to the east—Father said folks now called them the Laramie Range—already warmed the arid plains.

Morning. Her favorite time of day—a whispered promise in every sunrise, in every meadowlark's song. She smiled to herself as the sound of Father's deep Gaelic voice echoed within her. She was searching the brush as she walked, looking for the least sign of movement, the slightest flick of a furred ear.

She liked carrying the rifle, the feeling it gave her. When she was younger, she had pretended to be a warrior, like Little Badger. "Teach me, Unci," she had begged her grandmother after hearing the slave girl's story, "teach me to throw the knife!"

"You are too young, *takoja*," her grandmother had laughed, "barely four winters." Then her eyes had grown serious. "If you wish to learn, Daughter of the Sky, I will teach you."

Feel the earth beneath your feet. Let your thoughts flow from the earth, through your fingertips, into the weapon. She had never forgotten her grandmother's lessons.

Fifty feet ahead a sage plant sprang to life. Skye had flushed a hare out of hiding. She jerked the cocked rifle to her shoulder, aimed, and pulled the trigger. BOOM! The rifle's retort echoed across the sage-covered prairie.

The animal jumped, then collapsed in a sudden spasm of death. Lowering her rifle, Skye leapt over the low-growing bushes, cussing her awkward skirt. She followed the bullet's path, challenging herself to fly just as straight, just as sure.

The gray hare lay beneath a silverish clump of sage, hidden but for large furred feet that spanned the full length of Skye's hand. She gripped the feet and slid the creature out into the open, placing a finger on the animal's small jugular vein. No pulse. No life. *Morning. A whispered promise in every sunrise.*

Grasping one of the sage plant's woody stems and pulling upward, she stripped the fuzzy, wedge-shaped leaves from their stalk. Then, flipping the hare over, belly up, she laid it down on the rocky soil. Telltale patches of bare skin revealed that the hare, a female, had used her own chest fur to line a nest hollow. *A mother, with a litter of young.* Swollen pink nipples, surrounded by small matted circles of buff-colored fur, showed recent signs of suckling. Somewhere nearby, a nest of fully furred, wide-eyed baby hares awaited the doe's return. They would, no doubt, starve to death. Or they would wander from the nest, driven by thirst and hunger, only to end up as some coyote's supper. A coyote who perhaps also had a litter of young. *So it is. So it has to be.*

Skye rubbed the sage leaves between her work-toughened palms, squatted on her heels, held the crushed leaves to her nose, and inhaled deeply. The pungent plant released its fragrance into the cool morning air. More distant memories rose from her childhood. Ina, sage leaves in hand, kneeling over an outstretched rabbit, a porcupine, a motionless fox, praying to the spirits.

"Grandmother Earth, hear me! You have made us a gift of this four-legged. *Hye!* May we learn to be as quiet and humble as the long-eared *mastincala*, as patient as the quilled *pahin*, as gentle as the red *tokala. Hye!*"

The ancient ritual, like her grandmother's words, had taken root in Skye's heart like a lone sapling.

She stayed squatting for several minutes, listening to the unusual overhead call of an airborne longbill: *"cur-lee, cur-lee . . ."* She glanced upward, searching for the cinnamon wing linings of the shorebird. A great expanse of cloudless sky, dawn's blush gone, stared back. The bird, more than likely en route to one of the more than eighty lakes in the Medicine Bows, remained invisible.

Returning to the task at hand, Skye sprinkled the crushed sage leaves over the soft belly of the rabbit. Beginning with the broad nose and slender whiskers, and carefully avoiding the bloody bullet wound betwen the long translucent ears, she pressed her palms against the animal's thinning summer coat and drew them down the nearly two-foot-long body. She paused as her fingers slid over the swollen nipples.

"Babies," she muttered. "A whole passel of babies." She shook the vivid picture from her mind, hesitated for a moment, then decided to repeat the ritualistic stroking.

Not many things are able to call forth your memory, Ina, so young was I. The ritual is my own, but the sage . . . the sage is for you. She lifted her hands to her face and inhaled the plant's fragrance. It never failed to remind her of Mother. The memory brought a smile. She was grateful to the wild sage for this gift of scent, this gift of fleeting childhood.

Skye fixed her eyes on the dead animal in front of her. Leaning forward on her knees, she gathered the folds of her calico skirt and tucked them beneath her. *'Twas a foolish woman who invented the skirt, if you ask me. One of these days I'm going to defy Father and stitch me a pair of homespun britches—or better yet, a pair of stout buckskins, fringes and all!*

With exaggerated bravado, intended to strengthen herself for the unpleasant task, she picked up the limp rabbit. Taking the hare's head in her hand, she gave it two quick twists. The vertebrae cracked easily, and one yank tore the delicate skin that joined head to torso. She placed the animal's head in the shade of the nearby sagebrush. Grasping the loose hide dangling from the rabbit's neck, she pulled downward, removing most of the sage-scented fur in one sleevelike piece. Setting the fur aside, she removed her skinning knife from its brass-studded sheath at her belt. With the point of the knife, she pierced the tender flesh just above the anus and began gliding the sharp knife up the animal's belly, stopping just below the rib cage. With a practiced hand and a deft twist of the cutting edge, she carefully pierced the abdominal cavity, careful not to cut through the intestines, and jerked the hare's innards out, tossing them into the grass.

The scent of sage mingled with the metallic odor of blood. Skye found herself salivating.

"Roasted rabbit and biscuits will make a fine breakfast. I hope Father has the horses saddled!"

She rose, gutted carcass and curled hide in hand, and began walking back to camp. Thirty strides away, she paused at another clump of sagebrush. A tuft of buff-colored fur clung to one of the bottom branches. Shallow scrapes marked the grainy soil. She resisted the urge to hunt for the nest of newborn rabbits—tender meat, to be sure. *Coward*, she thought as she moved on. She didn't notice that her fingers, on their own, caressed the furred hide that she held in her hand, hair so soft it was almost feathery to the touch—almost as elusive as the cry of the long-billed curlew.

Elk Mountain lay behind them, two days' ride to the west—two days of hot sun and little shade, across the sandy floor of a wide valley that gave off as much heat as the rainless, cloudless sky. Only once, when they journeyed to Fort Bridger, had Skye been out of the mountains before, away from the inspiring heights of the Bows and the sheltering shade of her forests. A naked, exposed feeling made her pull her hat more tightly over her brow. Instinctively, she reached for the polished turtle shell that hung from its leather thong about her neck.

They had followed the old Cherokee Trail east for half a day before angling northeast, toward the Black Mountains. One day's ride beyond the eastern slope, according to Wolfskin Necklace, they would find the Standing People camped on Bitter Cottonwood.

"Father," asked Skye, riding abreast, "what are we going to do once we get there?"

"Do? Why, I don't suppose we'll *do* anything. Don't figure we'll make it in time for the Sun Dance. 'Tis a pity. It's some sight. Might still be a camp circle, though. Probably find more than your grandparents' band camped on the creek—more than likely there'll be a few still gathered for a small hunt."

*More than one band . . . Caws Like Magpie's band? Perhaps even
some of the Kiyuksa band, Mahto's people?* The young warrior's image
made Skye blush. She could still feel the lightning as his arm
brushed up against her, could still feel the confusing rush of blood.

"Will you be glad to see Sunstone, Father?"

"Aye, I'll be glad. Your grandfather is quite a man, ye know. A
leader, a great Shirt Wearer. And before his council days, he was a
great warrior. I've seen him in action meself."

"In action? When?"

"Back in '23, long afore ye made it into this world. On the
upper Missouri, fighting the Arikaras. Fur trader named Ashley
had his men camped near the mouth of the Bad River, the country
that birthed your grandmother. I'd been trapping with a chap
name of Pilcher. Might ought to say I'd drunk a wee dram of the
rosy god, as well. 'Tis a confusing story. Seems the Arikaras—
those the pox hadn't killed off—were in a fighting mood, killing
some of Ashley's men. The military joined the skirmish, along with
a few Sioux—Yanktons and Lakotas. Sunstone was among them."

"How did you meet him? Did you know him before?"

"No, 'twas the first time we'd met. I was, ye might say, feeling
me oats. They'd called on us trappers to help fight off the Arikaras.
And like a true Scottish warrior, I was preparing meself for battle!"
Father laughed, stroking his reddish-blond beard. The horses
plodded on, veering occasionally to avoid rocks and solitary thrusts
of yucca. In the distance, a herd of pronghorns raised their heads
as a hot breeze carried the small party's scent to them. The mule
followed along placidly, efficiently trained by the arduous miles.

"I was, ye might say, in a bit of a compromising position when
Sunstone happened upon me. Naked, I was! Standing knee-deep
in the river with a flask of whiskey in me hand!"

"Father!"

"Had this old hoss been merely drinking the whiskey, your
grandfather would have had no cause to carry on so. But he about
split a gut laughing! I reminded him afterwards that the Sioux
have some mighty strange traditions of their own!"

"Traditions?"

"Aye. 'Tis a traditional thing for a Highland warrior, when making ready for battle, to bathe in an ice-cold stream and rub whiskey on his naked flesh. Toughens a man, they say. I meself didn't see the humor in the situation—unless of course it was because I wasn't *quite* naked . . ."

"What do you mean, 'not quite naked'?"

"Well," Father said, beginning to laugh at his own recollection, "ye see, I was wearing me bearskin hat and me tasseled kilt garters!"

Father slapped his thigh with his free hand and burst into a roar, a laugh as loud as Skye had ever heard. He howled, his ruddy face becoming as red as jasper. It didn't take Skye long to join in.

At the sound of Father's hand striking his buckskins, Roy broke stride and began trotting across the hard, rock-strewn ground. Duncan followed suit, despite the heat. The mule had little choice but to keep up with the horses. Father's mood invigorated them all, and before the laughter settled into relaxed grins, a mile of grassland had passed beneath the rhythmic hooves of the geldings. But the sun now demanded its toll: Sweat glistened from the horses' necks, turning to dusty beads that dripped from the cinches of their saddles.

"Och, lass," Father said as they slowed to a walk, "ye know, there's a touch of Highland grandeur in the peaks and glens of the Bows."

"Reminds you of your homeland?"

"Aye, it does a wee bit. Though 'tis hard enough for me to remember the way it was—the smell of a peat fire smoldering in the hearth, the way a Highland night barely begins to darken afore the pink light of dawn spreads over the craggy hilltops. Why, girl, ye've never seen such a sight as a herd of longhaired Highland cattle grazing the soft, peaty soils of Glencoe."

"Like summer, when the buffalo bring their calves to the high country?"

"Aye, a bit like that, only now there's more sheep than cattle. But I'll wager it won't be long afore there's as many crofts spoiling the Medicine Bows as there are castles marring the open moors of Scotland."

Behind them, the sun began its evening descent, casting its last rays upon the unseen face of Elk Mountain. Rising five thousand feet from the high plains, the mountain threw its shadow across the valley floor. Ahead of the small traveling party, the level prairie gradually gave way to rocky, half-bare hillocks, the precursors of the next uplift of mountains. Gnarled limber pine and lodgepole pines dotted the undulating foothills. Less than a mile away, Skye saw the upper branches of willow and cottonwood, standing no doubt along the banks of a creek.

A wave of homesickness swept over Skye—for their cabin in the woods, for the deer and their young grazing in the meadow. She thought of the willow rocker, unused, and the empty wooden trunk. And Mother's shroud—now only a bone-filled, stiff buffalo robe in the limbs of the cottonwood.

Peering across the plains and into the depths of the foothills, she took her feet from the stirrups and stretched them out before her, squeezing the stiffness from her muscles, hoping to force out the uneasiness that began to fill her.

"I suppose," Father said, breaking the silence, "instead of jawing about my homeland, I ought to let ye get used to the idea of being with your mother's people. Ye might find a bit of comfort in their lodges, ye know—a welcome change from living with this old coon."

"What do you mean, 'a welcome change'? I thought this was to be only a visit." Skye's pulse quickened, the uneasiness turning to anxiety. Her palms began to sweat and the reins became damp in her clammy hands. She took a deep breath. "What do you mean?" she repeated, trying to pin him down. She hated losing control.

"I only mean that ye need to spend a little time visiting with your mother's people. Their ways may be strange to ye, but ye'll get used to them."

"Used to them? And how long will that take? And do you suppose they'll get used to me, as well? You're taking a hell of a lot for granted, if ye ask me!" The curse word flew hotly from her young mouth as she brushed unruly hair from her reddened face. *How dare he!*

Jamming her feet back into the stirrups, she tightened her thighs, tucked her hips into the cantle of her saddle, and kicked Duncan into a lope, and then a gallop, pulling away in a burst of anger.

A trail of dust rose behind Skye as she headed for the creek and the distant grove of trees at the base of the Black Mountains. A big peak rose before her like a beacon—warning her of the future, daring her to return to the past.

11

THE EAGLE

Wisps of morning smoke from the many cook fires of the Oglala camp spiraled into the hot, motionless air. A few women wandered away from the bend of the creek where the bands had pitched their tipis; some searched for late-ripening gooseberries; some gathered firewood, breaking dead, brittle branches from the cottonwoods that fringed the creek. Pebbles of flint and jasper lay scattered across the stream's white sand bed, interrupting the smooth flow of the clear water. The rippling sound eased its way into the circle of tipis, a melodious background to the day's activities.

Turtle Woman straightened from the staked elk hide over which she knelt, rubbing the small of her aching back with arthritic fingers.

"Why is there no younger wife to help tan the hide of this tough *hehaka?*" she muttered to herself, knowing full well the reason. Many times, when they were young and strong, Turtle Woman had suggested to Sunstone that he take another wife— marry this one, or that one. It would have been good to have had another woman's help with the cooking and sewing, to gather firewood, to give Sunstone another child . . . Ha! Many times, when they lay beneath the thick robes in the privacy of their tipi, she had suggested it. Each time he responded with a playful caress, brushing aside her long loose hair to kiss the tender nape of her neck. Only once did he answer seriously.

"Many moons ago, when I went with High Bear and Dark Cloud and the others to capture you back from the Kangis, I knew that I would warm myself by the light of your fire alone, knew that only one woman would share my robe."

Elk Man . . . her private name for him, whispered from breathless lips during intimate moments. The passing of many winters had not stilled his need for her—the old bull! Numerous nights, in younger times, the flames of their winter fires had grown dim because they were busy fanning their own flames beneath the buffalo robe.

She stared across the stretched hide, past the Standing Peoples' lodges to the tipis of the Muddy Water camp. Two women stood there talking and cackling, discordant voices disturbing the quiet. Her thoughts wandered back to Sunstone, back to the old days when their lifeblood ran hot with hopes and dreams. She pictured him in his warrior days, remembering each coup feather he had added to his scalp lock, each new warhorse he staked beside their lodge. Even now, the soulful brave-heart song which he used to sing before battle echoed within her, bringing the familiar mixture of fear and pride. Ha! But their reunions were sweet! As the nectar of the flower awaits the bee, so often had she awaited his return.

"What a fool I am! With no more flesh left on my aging bones than this tough *hehaka* hide. Yet I behave like a heat-struck cow during the rutting moon!"

Turtle Woman leaned back, settling her weight on the heels of her feet. The high-pitched voices of the two women irritated her. She wiped the bloody tangle of tissue from the scraping edge of her elk-horn flesher and flicked it from her callused finger. Scores of black dots decorated the flesher, one for every skin tanned. On the other side, red dots boasted of every ten skins tanned. A circle incised at the base of the handle indicated that she had more than one hundred hides to her credit. This flesher, one of the most highly decorated in the tribe, denoted Turtle Woman's high status—as did her membership in the One-Only-Ones society for older women. She touched the red dots with a soiled finger, caressing the circular shapes.

"One man, one lodge," she whispered to herself. A respected achievement, this lifetime of fidelity. "Easy to be faithful to an honorable man. I deserve little credit," she said under her breath. A twinge of guilt surfaced as she remembered the only secret she had ever kept from Sunstone. *Kangi blood. Someday I will return to the Medicine Wheel and face this secret.*

The cackling grew louder as the two Muddy Water women moved away from their tipis and headed in her direction. Turtle Woman raised her left hand to her forehead, shading her eyes. A knot of scar tissue covered the knuckle where, ten winters ago, the upper joint of her small finger had been. She squinted into the descending afternoon sun. One woman, she saw now, was Black Tail, a Kiyuksa. The other, a member of the Muddy Water camp, was Doublewoman Dreamer, the mother of Caws Like Magpie. Turtle Woman liked the crude woman barely more than she liked the pompous son. *A family of scavengers . . . landing on the nearest corpse.*

Turtle Woman leaned forward, kneeling over the staked *hehaka* hide, and busied herself to avoid the approaching women, who weaved boisterously toward her within the edge of the camp circle. Her long gray braids swung forward, rubbing against her scarred forearms. Gripping the flesher in her right hand, she moved it to the center of the hide and then pulled it toward her.

As the women drew nearer, Doublewoman Dreamer's words could be distinguished from the cackling laughter.

"Someone is meeting me here," she sang saucily amidst the laughter. "He is the one!"

Turtle Woman did not look up to see which unfortunate man was the target, but continued her scraping.

"He is the one!" Doublewoman Dreamer sang out raucously. The laughter of the two women shattered the afternoon's peacefulness. They were both *witko*, yet their craziness had an aura of *wakan*—of the Great Mystery. They were as vain and untrustworthy as Anog Ite, the two-faced woman from the long-ago days of creation. Men feared their laughter, feared they would become possessed by the dreamers. The promiscuity and vulgar mannerisms of the women only made their presence more awesome.

The two women had tied themselves together with a horsehair rope. They gaped spitefully at her. Painted designs of fork-tailed swallows decorated their elk-skin tunics. A small bundle, intended to imitate a baby, hung from the center of the rope. Doublewoman Dreamer's face carried the pockmarks of the *wasicu* sickness that, two winters ago, had taken scores of their people to the Land of Many Lodges. Tangled gray hair, sheared to shoulder length because of the recent death of Magpie's father, framed her diminutive black eyes. Perched precariously on her scrawny shoulder, a tethered raven-black crow teetered back and forth, flapping his wings and digging his claws into her flesh to regain his balance.

"Black bag of feathers," she swore at the bird. *"Itka sapa!"*

"See who scrapes!" Black Tail said, sneering at Turtle Woman.

"See who adds another mark to her flesher. Where's your man?" Doublewoman Dreamer asked sarcastically. "He is the one, you know! Ha! He is the one!" Both women pointed to the imaginary baby.

The ruse of avoidance had not worked. Turtle Woman thought of the Medicine Wheel, and of Little Badger. "Not all who will challenge you," she had taught the young Hewaktoka, "will be worthy of your courage." Worthy or not, some challenges must be met.

She leaned back, balanced her weight on the balls of her feet, and in one smooth movement—ignoring her stiff spine and aching muscles—straightened her tall frame to a standing position.

"You have the tongue of a vulture," she said to Doublewoman Dreamer, staring into the dark orbs which were the *witko* woman's eyes.

"It is the vulture's beak which tears the flesh, not his tongue," Doublewoman retaliated.

Turtle Woman slowly slid her butchering knife from the sheath at her waist and ran its blade across the edge of her bloody scraper. She balanced the knife in her hand and wondered, only for a moment, if she could still throw with her old deadly accuracy.

"The wise rattlesnake," she warned the dreaming woman, "sheds many skins, lives many winters, because he does not waste his venom. *That does not mean he will not strike.*"

Their eyes locked—and held. For a brief moment Doublewoman's crazed facade slipped, leaving a cold and haughty expression on her face. Then the mask returned. She forced a cackle from her dry, cracked lips and swore again at the bird.

"Black bag of feathers! *Itka sapa!* Sit still or I'll toss you to the old woman to put in her meager pot! Ha! He's the one!"

Turtle Woman sheathed her knife and averted her eyes, dismissing the two women. She had not asked to be an enemy of Caws Like Magpie's mother, any more than a she-wolf asks to fight the hump-backed bear. Some things just happened. Some things were meant to be.

The women's occasional outbursts of *witko* behavior did not last; they tired easily of their taunting game, unless of course some inexperienced young man happened to cross their path. Then they rankled and taunted the poor thing with lewd language and insinuations.

They moved on, dancing lewdly from side to side while pointing their crooked fingers toward an invisible apparition in the sky. Doublewoman Dreamer could not resist one final taunt.

"The vulture's beak is sharp," she yelled out, "sharper than its tongue. Ha!"

They began singing once again, the sound of their shrill voices growing fainter and fainter.

"Someone is meeting me here! It is he! It is he!"

Father avoided the better-known trails which crisscrossed the Black Mountains, preferring instead paths devoid of wandering soldiers and scouting parties. Occasional yucca plants dotted the low-flying flatlands between ridges. Black and brown western rattlers slithered through prairie dog towns and between lichen-covered rocks, while gangly ponderosas and large, singular boulders stood like sentinels guarding the wind-eroded landscape. An immature turkey vulture, his naked black head just beginning to turn bloodred, feasted on the decaying flesh of a porcupine.

On the east slope, red willow and wild plum sprouted beside small creeks that meandered through deep ravines carved into gentle foothills. Shallow hollows, abounding with herbs and cactus, weaved their curves between tall, chalk-white cliffs. Cottonwoods and ash, their widespread roots hidden beneath the soil, held their voluminous green branches up to the sky. A few more miles of country rich in wildlife and wild ways, and they would be at the Oglala camp, where the Standing People had pitched their tipis.

"Perhaps, Father," Skye said, not yet ready to come face to face with her relatives, "we should let the horses rest here for the night. Then we could arrive first thing in the morning."

"No need for that, lass. Why, ye can almost smell their cook fires from here. We've but a few miles left to go."

She reached up to her bodice and absentmindedly took the polished turtle shell in her fingers. *There is power in the mixing of your blood, takoja. The night you were born a flash of light pierced the darkness and a great star lit the heavens. You will be like the turtle, strong with long life. My heart will be like the turtle's—in you it will keep beating long after I have left the flesh* . . . The memory of these words had comforted her during many lonely nights. Why did the prophecy now seem ominous?

"Do you think they'll remember me?"

"Sure as me rifle shoots center."

"But it's been ten years. What if they don't want to see me?"

"Didn't your grandmother send ye a gift? She wouldn't have sewn ye such a fine quilling case if she didn't remember ye. Why else do ye think Wolfskin Necklace came calling, anyway?"

"You're right, I know. It's just that . . ." Skye let the sentence fade away, dropping the shell.

Fear was making a coward of her. What was there to fear anyway? Nothing! She straightened her spine and shifted her shoulders back, pushing away the feeling.

Rays of late afternoon sun bounced off the chalk-white cliffs. A flash of movement on an overhanging ledge caught Skye's eye, then disappeared.

"Did you see that, Father?" she asked, pointing toward the cliff.

"See what?"

"Something moved on that ledge up there."

"A mountain sheep?"

"No, I don't think so. More like a coyote maybe."

"Odd place for a coyote to be."

As she stared at the rocky outcropping, a winged shadow moved across the face of the cliff below the ledge. The shadow grew broader. She looked skyward, her eyes following the invisible cord that linked shadow to feathered flesh. High above, a golden eagle soared and circled, his dark underside silhouetted against the cloudless sky.

"An eagle," Father said. "A good sign. See, ye have nothing to fret about."

The dark bird of prey soared, flat-winged and silent, above the steep cliffs. His presence gave her courage. She thought of her mother, the image as fleeting as the eagle's shadow; faint memories slid across her consciousness—a gentle touch upon her cheek, the feel of the porcupine hairbrush smoothing her hair.

"I suppose you're right. These are Mother's people, after all. My people, as well—at least, half my people." She forced bravado into her words, but the effect was less than convincing. "And it is just a visit!"

She had been apart from them for so long, too long perhaps—long enough to feel severed in half, belonging to both worlds but at home in neither. *Could a person cloven in such a way ever become whole again?*

Turtle Woman returned from the creek carrying a buffalo paunch swollen with cool water and sprigs of fresh pungent mint. The *hehaka* hide, thoroughly cleansed with the soap of the yucca plant, had already been laid in the open to dry. A pot of fragrant berry soup simmered over the hot coals of the cook fire.

Wi, the sun, traveled his afternoon path to the land of the thunder-beings—the Winged Gods. Turtle Woman peered questioningly into the western sky, sensing a change. The yelping *kya kya*, of a golden eagle answered her, the aerial call spiraling toward earth. The great bird circled, his dark wings spanning a distance wider than the tallest Lakota warrior.

"Ah, *wanbli*, my silent friend. Your call does not usually grace the ears of my people. Why do you choose to speak? What news do you bring?"

She watched the eagle fly, the radius of his circle growing smaller and smaller as he came closer and closer. Below him, climbing through the air in elliptical glides, rose a cliff swallow. Suddenly, the little bird began beating her wings frantically, an alarmed *keer! keer!* piercing the air. The golden eagle pulled his dark wings into a gliding position and dove with talons extended.

One moment the swallow lived—the next moment, she died. Gone. The only trace lone feathers drifting toward earth.

"This thing you show me, Tunkasila, it is good. *Li'la waste.* A cloud-bird does not usually bother with a swallow."

Turning away, Turtle Woman bent over as she entered the tipi, being careful not to let the waterskin drag in the dirt. She hung the paunch on a tipi pole by the door, then dropped a sprig of mint through the small wooden hoop that held the mouth of the bag open. Lifting a second green stalk to her nose, she inhaled the refreshing aroma before pulling three lancehead-shaped leaves from the square stem and plopping them into her mouth. She walked to the back of the tipi, her moccasined feet soft upon the hide-covered floor, and placed a sprig of mint on Sunstone's embroidered buckskin pillow.

"For dreams as sweet as this old woman's breath. Ha!" She laughed at her own joke. Taking two quilled pillows from a handsomely painted rawhide box, she positioned them on top of the buffalo robes skirting the tipi's inner circle, carefully placing a stalk of mint on each pillow.

"So, *wanbli*, my friend. We are to have company. For this I have waited many winters."

Turtle Woman withdrew her ceremonial dress from the rawhide box. Rows of elk teeth and meticulously quilled stars embellished the soft doeskin. Quickly, she slipped from her everyday leathers. Then, raising her scarred and thin-skinned arms, she slid the ceremonial dress over her head.

By the time the scroungy camp dogs' high-pitched yips began warning of approaching strangers, Turtle Woman, in all her finery, waited outside her tipi. She sat astride the red roan mare, her regal torso stretched tall. A saddle blanket, richly embellished in blues and reds, decorated the horse's back. Three coveted white feathers from the tail of a trumpeter swan hung from the mare's dark mane.

"So, *maske*," she said, stroking the mare's neck, "once again, friend, I sit upon your back. But this time, we have only to wait." The mare stomped the ground with her turned-in foot, leaving a telltale print in the earth.

Turtle Woman lifted her chin and angled her head to the west. Fiery red colored the horizon as the sun lowered himself from the sky, like molten lava spewing forth from the earth.

Red. A sacred color. To a woman, the color of birth and renewal, the color of death and rebirth. With the passing of each new moon, a woman's birthing power tied her to the earth. What was it, then, that tied her to the sky?

Perhaps dusk would bring the answer.

12

MUDDY WATER CAMP

Leaning against the tautly staked tipi, Caws Like Magpie pulled his long, grasshopperlike legs out of the hot sun, bending his knees into his bare chest. Once beside his own lodge, his vanity had succumbed to the overbearing heat and he had reluctantly removed his ornate Naca shirt. But he did not remove the gaudy leggings, nor the broad, heavily quilled belt that encircled his thick waist. Nor did he unclasp the dangling shell earrings or the heavy silver trade discs that hung in a trail down his back.

He watched as Doublewoman Dreamer gave a scrap of deer meat to his pet crow, which stood on a forked perch of upright cottonwood. The tethered bird paced back and forth, gulping the chunk of meat with one quick extension of his black throat. Doublewoman shuffled a few steps farther, toward a small doghouse erected behind the tipi. Stretching her spidery arm out to a slick-coated black and white dog, she offered the female a choice morsel of tenderloin.

"*Wey, wey,* come, my scruffy friend, I have a treat for you." The dog pulled back her lips and snatched the tidbit from the woman's awl-toughened fingers.

"You feed that *sunka* better than your own son. Must this Naca beg like a bitch in heat for a few meager ribs?" Caws Like Magpie complained, resting a pointed chin on his knobby knees.

A musty, sour smell emanated from the dog's cavelike

dwelling, a sod-covered structure much like the wigwams of a cen-
tury earlier, when the Lakotas had been mound-building corn
farmers. Magpie's people had retained their camp name, the
Muddy Water People, even after they followed the Standing Peo-
ple to the shores of the Big Muddy, and from there to the Bad
River. In Magpie's lifetime alone, they had migrated to this Shell
River country, and before that, they had lived in the rugged Bad
Lands to the north.

"Wey! Wey!" the crow mimicked in a high-pitched nasal
voice, a perfect imitation of Doublewoman calling her dog. *That
feathered scavenger is good for something!* Magpie's fleshy lips curled
into a brief, uncomfortable smile.

The dog raised her muzzle from the tender chunk of meat and
cocked her head. She looked from the old woman to the crow, trying to decide which one had beckoned her, then, not really caring,
returned her attention to the fleshy scrap. Two fattened puppies,
born three moons past, waddled out from the dark entrance of the
wigwam into the bright light. They squinted their slate-gray eyes
and, following their twitching noses, sniffed out their mother's
juicy tidbit. She lifted one whiskered and bloody lip and snarled a
warning at the whining pups. Dissuaded, they attached themselves
instead to her sagging, near-empty teats.

"Why do you allow those leeches to still suck, heh, *maske?*"
Doublewoman Dreamer asked rhetorically, leaning over to pat
the dog's head. "You fatten them for the celebration pot, ha!"
Pointing to Caws Like Magpie with a wiry, callused finger, she
criticized, "You do the work of only half a warrior, yet you eat like
two!"

"Your tongue is as sharp as the burnt end of a lance," Caws
Like Magpie said in irritation, speaking but one of the bitter
thoughts in his mind. Her nagging ways suffocated him, just as his
first wife's nagging ways had goaded him to find a second wife. But
he had found no peace in either lodge. The tipis of both squab-
bling wives had closed in around him like a death robe. He willed
away the thought, pushed aside the image of their fevered, dying
bodies—pushed aside the image of his father's burial scaffolding
silhouetted against the horizon. He hated looking at his mother's

pockmarked face, hated the sickening stench of memories. *Hated the* wasicus *who had brought the disease.* These unworthy thoughts remained unspoken, festering within him, further tainting his attachment to her, a twisted bond that neither one had outgrown.

Others noticed the stunted relationship, snickering behind upraised palms, ridiculing in low whispers as he passed by: *"Little husband, little husband . . ."* None dared to speak aloud, to use the derogatory expression in front of the woman dreamer. Few cared to subject themselves to her wicked tongue, and all feared her *wakan* status. And no one doubted the strength of *his* lance-throwing arm.

Magpie absently toyed with two iridescent, greenish-black feathers that hung from his necklace. Lifting one of the feathers, he scratched his right cheek, being careful not to smear the black *akicita* stripe which, despite his elevated Naca status, he still painted on at the beginning of each day.

To his left, nearest to the creek and just north of the circle's east entrance, were the orderly tipis of the Standing People. A scowl darkened his face. *Sunstone. Robbing me of the honor I deserve. Always a coup ahead . . .* Magpie collected the saliva in his mouth and, lifting his chin slightly, forced the spit from his pursed lips. A thin stream of spittle lingered on his chin. The ejection landed with a splat on the bitch's black-and-white head. She lifted her muzzle slightly and gave an almost imperceptible growl. The tethered crow flapped his scraggly wings, cawing hoarsely.

"Sst, sst," Doublewoman hissed at both dog and bird through worn-down teeth, mere stubs from years of quillwork. Turning to face Caws Like Magpie, she shook her finger at him. "You were born with a frozen heart!"

So the winter-count painting shows. During the Moon of the Terrible, when Yata blew so fiercely that the starving crows, huddled in the trees, froze and fell like dung upon your birthing tipi . . . Many times she had rubbed this story into him—the pain he had caused her, his wickedness in choosing to come during the Moon of the Terrible. A good child would be born during the Moon of Shedding Ponies, or when the calls of wild geese once again filled the air.

"Ey-ee!" she would cry, "you have a wicked, frozen heart!"

The seed of your womb.

He enjoyed taunting her, testing her loyalty. He had never known it to fail—no matter how thinly stretched the allegiance. It was the most honorable thing about her. The only honorable thing about her.

Across the camp circle, Sunstone stood near the shade of a chokecherry bush talking with that condescending Wolfskin Necklace. Occasionally his arms rose and fell as he spoke. An old woman, one of the Standing People, struggled with the weight of a wet hide, then stood and stretched. Caws Like Magpie squinted his coal-black eyes against the high sun. Sunstone's woman. She strolled down to the creek, returning with a paunch of fresh water. Her lodge, pitched in the place of honor, was but a few strides from the stream. Her long-toothed roan mare grazed near the water.

"Your walk to the creek," he said, not bothering to look at his mother, "is at least twice the distance of hers. As far as the cast of one well-drawn arrow." The *wasicu*'s sickness had passed over the lodges of the Standing People like a harmless breeze. Their escape galled him.

"What are you mumbling about?"

"The mother of Caws Like Magpie should not bear twice the burden. You are the mother of a Naca!"

Doublewoman straightened her spine and lifted her chin to the air, like a prairie chicken preening her feathers. "It is a good son who worries about his mother," she said.

Fool. Her walk to the creek didn't concern him. It was Sunstone's respected position that angered him! What had he done to deserve the honor? Nothing! Besides marry into Turtle Woman's Ghost Heart band.

Magpie had never believed the gossip that surrounded Turtle Woman. A holy woman with the power to see into the future? *Hiya!* He doubted it! Many winters ago, further back than the winter counts went, her family had stolen the legend of the cottonwood tree and claimed it for their own. The only thing desirable about her had been her daughter, Breathcatcher, and they had foolishly let the *wasicu* steal her! Caws Like Magpie gathered more saliva and shot it into the stifling air. A small puff of dust rose where the spittle landed. Doublewoman Dreamer glared at him through slitted eyes, then returned to butchering the deer, her own mood changing as abruptly as her son's.

"*Wasicus,*" he muttered bitterly. They took and took. They took the best women. They took the fat of the land. They brought the disease that killed the Lakotas. They ripped the tongue and hide from the buffalo and left a stench of rotting meat in their wake.

"Someday I will count coup on the *wasicus,* instead of our old *tokas.*" Many times his mother had danced through camp waving the black wavy scalps of the Kangis or Scilis. "One day, soon, I will bring you another scalp. Only this time, the color will not be black. The scalp will be colored like the tail feathers of the red hawk. And I will pluck it slowly and painfully . . ."

"Ha! My son the warrior speaks bravely. I will dance the scalp dance for you! I will hold the lance high and wave a *wasicu's* scalp for all to see!" Doublewoman lifted her arm to the sky, dangling a piece of raw, bloody meat from her gnarled fingers. "For all to see!"

Magpie shook his head at her bragging words, then shifted his gaze. To the south, in the direction of the Kiyuksa lodges, children skittered about oblivious to the heat, chasing each other through the tangle of meat racks and staked hides. A few low shelters made of bent willow and covered with blankets were pitched near the larger tipis. Inside these wickiups rested the bedrolls of lone young warriors. Mahto, the cocky scout who had ridden with him to gather the medicine wood, stood next to his wickiup. He held a bow between his legs, tapering the ends and grip to suit his needs. Occasionally he bent the carved bow over his knee, testing the weapon's strength and resilience.

The scout acted like a young bull in rut, ready to take the place of the old bulls. But this old bull still had a few seasons left in him! He would not let the young, mouthy scout embarrass him again. "*The biting wind of the north,*" Mahto had called him. What else had Mahto said that day at the *wasicu's* cabin, in front of the young, but old enough, *wikoskala?* "*A true warrior fights with bow and arrow. You shoot words like a bickering hag . . .*" He would not allow him to speak with such disrespect to this Naca again!

This old bull could still bend the bow, could even show the *wikoskala* a thing or two about the rut—teach her to enjoy the prod of an old bull!

Sunstone's woman huddled over her cook fire, dropping something into the rising steam. Then she straightened and, holding her hand to her eyes, stared in the direction of the no-longer-arcing sun.

"What does the old woman stare at?" he asked, aiming his words toward Doublewoman Dreamer.

"Who?" she questioned, looking up from the deer. "What woman?"

"Who do you think I've been talking about? The old wife of Sunstone. There," he said, pointing a gnarly finger, "by her fire."

"The old hag stares at nothing. She's had her head stuck in the clouds for so long, her nose juts forever into the air!"

"No. She watches something. See, there—above the cliffs?"

Doublewoman squinted her eyes into narrow slits, deepening the creases in her pockmarked temples.

"Wanbli," she murmured, nodding her head. "The golden eagle. Look, he dives at another bird. His aim is true. Feathers fall from the sky." She combed her blood-encrusted fingers through her chin-length graying hair, pondering the significance of this death in the sky. A *wanbli* was very *wakan*—everything one did carried great meaning.

A sudden whirlwind disturbed the hot, still air, and dust spiraled into the stagnant sky. The feathers from the eagle's prey became caught in the twirling whirlwind, spinning in narrowing circles until they hovered above the woman dreamer's tipi. As suddenly as the whirlwind began, its strength ebbed. The feathers floated softly to the ground, landing at her feet. She picked them up, inspecting them.

"Swallow feathers," she said in almost a whisper. She knelt, seeming to wither.

"A few feathers make you cringe?" Magpie asked disparagingly, barely understanding her mumbled whisper. He followed the trail his mother's eyes cut through the still air to the painted swallows that adorned the sides of her tipi.

"Ey-ee," she cried, covering her face with her dirty hands, the swallow feathers sticking up through her bloody fingers like lances poised for war.

"Yip! Yip! Yip!" High-pitched barking pierced the camp. The black-and-white bitch lunged to the end of her rope, sending the pups tumbling. The crow paced his perch, straining his ebony neck against the taut rope tethering his foot.

Magpie swung his head to the east, his eyes suddenly alert and wary. He saw nothing suspicious, nothing to cause the camp dogs' warning. Looking north, he saw Sunstone's woman lead her horse beside her lodge. She pulled herself astride the horse's back.

"Why does Sunstone's woman dress her old mare in a ceremonial blanket?" he wondered aloud.

Doublewoman Dreamer lowered her bloody fingers, leaving red streaks across her cheeks. "She stares into the distance like an old fool."

"Look," he said. "She cloaks herself in a ceremonial dress as well."

"And fancy moccasins."

"Foolish old woman." Magpie spat again into the dirt. "No celebrations are planned. Too many winters rob her of her senses."

He stood, straightening his stiff legs from their lounging position, and saw the travelers winding their way down the foothill trail west of camp.

"*Wasicus,*" he whispered, "two, with a pack animal." His stomach knotted up like a clenching fist: the lead rider's reddish hair glistened in the heat.

He wet his large fleshy lips, sliding a cracked tongue over their film of dust. Then, reaching for his Naca shirt, he slithered his sweaty arms into the sleeves of the painted buckskin, taking great care not to smudge the black stripe that lined his clenched jaw.

Two—one colored like the tail feathers of a red hawk, the other soft-hued as the downy feathers of a fledgling.

13

THE REUNION

The big cat stretched her muscles, parting her jaws in a yawn. She rose from beneath the overhanging slab of granite where she had bedded down for the day and began heading east, away from the rays of the descending sun. She glided noiselessly down through the limber pines and Douglas fir, following a narrow deer path which crisscrossed the steep eastern slope.

Her smooth strides had carried her across the great expanse of sage-covered, low-lying basin, up the gentle western slope, and to the summit of this low-profiled mountain range. But still she found no safe ground, no unclaimed territory to call her own.

The deer path widened, intersected by a trail marked with the half-circle tracks of horses. The fresh scent of two-leggeds tainted the alpine air. Oily ones. Alert and cautious, the big cat tightened her stride. She stopped to sniff the remains of a dead porcupine. The animal's soft underbelly had been devoured; all that remained were picked-over bones and the bristly, needle-sharp hide.

The cougar lifted her broad, tawny head, nostrils flaring as she inhaled the thin air. Two-leggeds. Pine pitch. Vulture droppings. *Another lion's day-old urine.* The ridge of hair along her spine rose, beginning at her scarred forehead and traveling down the cord of muscles that flanked her vertebrae. The dark tip of her muscled tail flicked nervously and a low, guttural growl emanated from her throat.

She pushed on, stopping to drink from a nearby creek. The stream water slithered into the cat's empty paunch, and her gaunt belly rumbled. Tonight she would hunt. She would feed on the fleshy carcass of a big-eared deer. She would eat the still-warm heart and liver, lapping at the blood that pooled in the animal's ravaged, empty cavity. Prey. She would gorge herself, strengthen her weary bones with a long-overdue feast.

The scent of pine gave way to the chalky smell of white cliffs. An eastern breeze carried the scent of willows and cotton-woods. The cat loped down the trail, invigorated by the change in terrain. The rocky ground leveled, easing into liebacks and over-hangs that formed the plateau of a steep rock face. She did not break stride until she was nearly at the edge of the plateau. With an agile twist, she dug her rear claws into the earth and lowered her haunches, slowing to a walk. She eased up to the edge of the lime-stone outcropping. The tumbling sound of a dislodged rock on the trail below echoed up the face of the cliff. Two-leggeds. The cougar crouched, lowering her belly to the ground. Amber eyes flashed.

Motionless, she watched the descent of the two-leggeds, mounted on clumsy, plodding horses. The large, tamed beasts trudged on, unaware.

The big cat lifted her nose to the hot, eastern breeze that rose from the valley floor. The acrid, smoky odor of campfires tainted the sweet fragrance of the willows and cottonwoods. She wrinkled her broad nose at the unpleasantly pungent air.

A winged shadow darkened the ledge, moving across the cat's tawny back. Then the shadow floated across the face of the cliff. The cat angled her head upward, following the flight of the golden eagle as the bird circled above the bluffs. She tossed her scarred head and rippled her skin, trying to shake off the odors of the two-leggeds. Still wary, she rose and exhaled deeply, purging her lungs. With a flick of her tail, the big cat turned and headed north.

The deep creases framing Sunstone's wide-set eyes curled as he smiled. He placed his arms lightly on Macdonald's shoulders and, with eyes respectfully downcast and in a low-key voice, greeted his old friend.

"*Hau, kola.*"

"By beaver!" Gregory returned Sunstone's affectionate but traditionally reserved greeting, placing his broad hands on his father-in-law's shoulders. "You're a sight for sore eyes, old hoss! How do ye come on?"

"My friend, Naked Warrior!" Sunstone allowed enthusiasm to color his voice. He lifted his dark eyes and gripped Gregory with his strong, bent hands. "You have wintered well these many seasons."

"Aye, and it appears that ye've been keeping that meatbag of yours full as well!" Gregory gave his own broad stomach a hearty pat. He glanced toward Turtle Woman, who sat astride an old horse standing several feet behind Sunstone. In the few split seconds of looking that strict tribal tradition allowed, Gregory noticed many things about his mother-in-law. Age had draped a wrinkled cloak of gray upon her, though her erect shoulders carried the burden well. *An impressive woman, after all these years. With enough grit left in her to cut plenty of shine. And still riding that old roan.* His green eyes appraised the fancy saddle blanket, the ceremonial dress, the fine moccasins quilled with a comet shooting through a five-pointed star. His breath caught in his throat at the familiar design. For what special occasion was she dressed? The Sun Dance ceremonies were two weeks past, at least.

Ah. He had always underestimated her. Her uncanny ability to foresee. *She knew we were coming, knew we were coming this very day.* The woman stared past him to her granddaughter, her gaze cutting across the distance like the first strong beam of daybreak.

"Skye, get yourself down from there and say hello to your grandparents!"

Sunstone's dark eyes, beginning to cloud with age, shone with pride as he beheld his granddaughter. The warmth, tinged with sadness, transformed his craggy features. He moved toward Skye, his feet treading so gently that they raised no dust.

"*Mitakoja,* my grandchild. Wolfskin Necklace tells me you

have sprouted like a willow. He speaks truly. You sit tall upon your horse."

"Skye, come down from there," Gregory repeated. "Give your grandparents a proper greeting."

A breeze blew into the circle of tipis, ruffling the three white swan feathers that hung from the mane of the red roan. Turtle Woman slid from the mare and moved noiselessly toward Skye. Skye sat her saddle, seemingly rooted, and watched her grand-mother approach.

The contrast between the two, yet at the same time the like-ness, caused Gregory to suck in his breath. Skye's clumsy boots made her feet look nearly as large as his. The homespun shawl and ragged skirt contrasted sharply with Turtle Woman's white doe-skin dress, embellished with elk teeth and quilled stars. Skye had pulled her well-worn leather hat down over her forehead, almost hiding her dark golden eyes and disheveled auburn hair. Turtle Woman's silvery gray hair hung in neat braids, the tips of which were enclosed in little sacks of bright yellow trade cloth. *Just like me Breathcatcher used to wear.* Pain gripped Gregory's chest as an image of his wife flashed before him: kneeling beside him in the softness of night, loosening her braids, combing slender, graceful fingers through dark strands that cascaded down naked, bronzed breasts, like the sweet water of the Green running pure and straight over smooth beds of sand. *Get aholt of yourself, man!* Greg-ory shook his burly head and turned toward his father-in-law.

"We broke camp afore dawn this morning," he said brusquely to Sunstone in a voice too loud, as if hoping to scare away the painful memories. "I durst say we're both feeling a mite wolfish."

"Come," Sunstone replied. "You know you are welcome in our lodge. We will eat, then smoke and rest. Then we will talk—make jokes about the old days, tell big lies, *han!* Seeing my old *kola,* Naked Warrior, makes me feel like a spiked-horn again!"

Sunstone took Roy's reins and the mule's lead rope from Greg-ory and handed them to Turtle Woman. He raised his hand to her braid, cupping the yellow trade cloth in his palm, then touched her lightly on the cheek. He spoke, his voice barely aud-ible.

"*Mitawicu*, my wife. Finally, we can celebrate. I will take care of our guest while you and our *takoja* take the four-leggeds to drink. Perhaps the running waters will help wash away the many lonely winters between you."

Lonely winters? Aye, they surely had been that. With more hours in the days—nay, in the nights—than stars in the sky. Gregory turned away from the women and bent to pick up a small, shiny black sliver of stone. The flake of an old spearpoint. Then, together, the two men ducked inside the tipi, Sunstone holding the decorated door flap open for his son-in-law. Once inside, Gregory paused, listening to the tipi's dewclaw dangles rattle as Sunstone closed the flap, listening vainly for the voices of the women, absently rubbing the flake between his fingers. He waited for Sunstone to walk to the rear of the lodge. Then, being careful not to step on the small square altar of bare earth, he sat down next to his host on a heavily furred robe and leaned against a wide willow-rod backrest, painted and adorned with tassels. A finely quilled pillow rested on the robe next to the backrest.

"We're like a couple of old, rangy buffalo bulls," he said, shifting his saddle-sore bones, "more than a mite grateful for a patch of soft prairie."

"*You* may be old and rangy, but this warrior still has the Moon of the Rut in his heart," said Sunstone, laughing.

"Aye. But the heart's wishing ain't always the body's doing. The bones I hear a-groaning ain't all mine." Gregory forced a laugh, tried to lead his mind elsewhere. He tossed the flake onto the robe and picked up the pillow, not noticing the wilted green sprig until it rolled off the pillow onto the robe. He raised the stalk to his nose and sniffed. Mint. A sign of welcome—from a woman to whom protocol would not allow him to speak. Sunstone seemed to read his thoughts.

"Turtle Woman's greetings. To freshen your trail-parched throat."

"She has aged." *She reminds me too much of Breathcatcher.*

"The winters have been hard. A dark cloud shades my people from the warmth of the sun. All have aged."

"I heard Smoke's people fled north, back to the White Earth

River country, trying to outrun the sickness. Suspected you might have headed north, too."

"Many thought we could escape the cramping sickness if we returned to the Black Hills, the land of our grandfathers. But none wanted to follow the Smoke People."

"Wolfskin Necklace spoke of a white man's council, to be held afore winter sets in."

"The big issue. A few moons ago, when the red grass poked up through the earth and the ponies began to shed their winter coats, the *wasicu* chief sent men up the rivers—up the Big Muddy, the Shell, and Elk River. The men carried word of a great council to be held on the Shell during the Moon of Yellow Leaves."

"This fall? And do your people plan on going to this big palaver?"

"Some do. Some do not. The people of the Muddy Water camp want to fight." Sunstone made a cutting motion through the air with his fist, like a swinging war club. "Some Kiyuksas of the Bear Den People want to fight as well. The Standing People have not decided. No one trusts the words of the *wasicus.*"

"Aye. And I reckon there are some who don't take to the idea of ye sharing your tipi with this *wasicu* either." Gregory thought of Caws Like Magpie with renewed hatred. *Damn brown-skin!*

Sunstone stared at Gregory, his craggy, dark eyes peering deep into his son-in-law's green Gaelic eyes. For a moment the distance between them gaped like a chasm and Gregory feared that the wise old man had read his thoughts. But if he had, he gave no indication.

"The door of our lodge is always open to Naked Warrior," Sunstone said. "From your loins sprang the seed of our granddaughter. You are one of the Standing People. You are welcome at our fire."

The old familiar sound of Turtle Woman's deep and throaty voice finally filtered in through the tipi's smoke hole. Skye's response was hesitant, her usual vigor no doubt tempered by the strange surroundings. *Ye'll get used to being one of the Standing People, lass. Ye'll get used to it.*

"I am glad you have come for many reasons, my son. You told

me once, long ago, the story of your tribe, but my old and feeble mind forgets many things. It seems there are lessons for us to learn from your stories—lessons that may help with our decision about this great council. After we smoke, then we talk, *han?*"

Gregory picked up the flake of black rock again. The story of his tribe? Aye. The cursed red-coated soldiers forcing his kinsmen to leave their beloved lochs and moors, their rugged Highland crofts. The English lords demanding money—rent they'd called it—from land the Highlanders had lived on since time immemorial. And yet none of the Highlanders had deeds to prove it! He'd not been the only one to escape starvation and brave the ocean for the new land across the sea.

He rubbed the rock between his fingers. After the Saxons had outlawed their kilts and pipes, Graunie Maggie had sewn them anyway, working by the light of a single candle, fearing for the lives of her family. It broke his heart.

Could he tell Sunstone what he really thought? What he really feared would happen?

He glanced around the inside of the tipi. Turtle Woman's touch was everywhere—in the painted parfleches, the willow backrests, the quilled pillows. To outlaw all of this? Aye, maybe 'twas a good thing Breathcatcher had not lived to see these lands crawling with desperate immigrants.

Breathcatcher. His wife kneeling beside him, her loosened hair cascading across bare breasts. *How many times could a man's heart be broken?*

The image, like a trickster, turned on him—Breathcatcher's bare breasts now red with the blood streaming from a torn and fragile throat. He shook his head, trying to rid himself of the death, only to hear dark words echo in his mind. *And come he slow, or come he fast, It is but death who comes at last.*

Angry, he tossed the flake of black stone back onto the robe. Was there no escaping these memories? Raising his eyes toward the triangular patch of sky visible through the smoke hole, he stared into the small opening.

Bloodred dusk stared back.

14

SACRED FIRES

Gray hair. Leathery, wrinkled skin. Hands bent with age. Twisted, lumpy fingers, once long and graceful. *Could this old woman truly be my grandmother?*

Still mounted on her horse, Skye averted her rude stare, forcing herself to look at the ground beneath Duncan. Father had warned her that her grandparents would look aged, different than she remembered. Still. *So old?*

"*Takoja*, grandchild. We have both grown older, *han?*"

The same deep, throaty voice. Both grown older? Did the woman read her mind? Her very thoughts?

"Your journey was a long one. You have been gone many sleeps, *han?* You had no trouble with the *wasicus?*"

Skye shook her head, noticing that the yipping of the camp dogs had ceased. She and Father had encountered no one else on their journey. No Crows. No Shoshones. No Lakotas. No other white men. She lifted her gaze back to the old woman's face. Brown eyes, as dark as the floral center of a prairie star, stared back. Sun-deep creases defined the woman's weathered skin, but the eyes, the eyes seemed ageless, as if defying time. There was something familiar about them, something . . . Skye struggled, her mind denying what her heart already knew . . . *Mother's eyes.*

Roy and Quickstop, restless with hunger and thirst, strained against the reins and lead rope that Turtle Woman held. She soothed the animals with a few soft words of Lakota and ran a tanned, leathery hand down the mule's sweaty neck.

"Long-eared one, you carry a heavy load, *han?*"

The roan mare, standing untethered beside the tipi, answered the familiar voice with a soft nicker. Skye smiled. It was good to see the horse, old as she was.

Duncan stretched his nose into the air, and a few inches of rein slid through Skye's slack grip. Father and Sunstone had disappeared into the tipi. Her shoulders ached with stiffness, and twinges pulled at her weary calf muscles. Putting her left hand on the saddle horn, she balanced her weight in the left stirrup, stepped from the horse, turned, and faced her grandmother. Sharp pains, like pinpricks, stabbed her numb feet.

"Hello, Grandmother."

"Welcome, *mitakoja.*"

The words hung between them, heavy with meaning, yet as weightless as hope itself. An instinct, long subdued, long quelled, like a deep hunger that one must forever ignore, rose suddenly to the surface, and Skye felt the urge to reach for her grandmother's hand as she had so often when she was a child. But her grandmother's hand was ugly, gnarled and maimed, the little finger missing a joint. Skye reached, instead, for the turtle-shell necklace suspended from her neck.

Turtle Woman's lips curved slowly, like the arcing sky, into a gentle smile.

"You have not outgrown the shell, I see."

Skye's hand dropped to her side. The heat of embarrassment rose to color her neck and cheeks. She dug the toe of her boot into the dirt and traced a dusty half-circle.

Her grandmother spoke, the words low and earthy. "Many winters have passed. Many things have changed. I am honored that you still have the shell."

Skye straightened her shoulders and lifted her chin, fixing her gaze straight ahead. "It is the *only* thing I still have."

A quizzical look shadowed Turtle Woman's countenance, and Skye regretted her reply. Her slender grandmother stood half a hand taller than Skye. The yoke of the doeskin dress, quilled in ra-

diant yellows and reds, shone in the late afternoon sun. Polished
elk teeth, sewn in graceful curves, further embellished the tunic.
High-topped moccasins, embroidered in vivid hues, completed
the ensemble. Worked into the intricate stitchery was a comet
shooting through the center of a five-pointed star. The same design as on the quilling case. *The quilling case.* Her bent and callused
fingers must have toiled hour after hour. Takoja *she called me—
grandchild.*

"I am like a stranger to you, *han?* Yes?" Turtle Woman asked.

"Strange, perhaps. But a stranger? No."

The words, not intended to offend, seemed harsh, and once
again she regretted her abruptness. She wanted to thank her
grandmother for the quilling case, to tell her how she had gently
caressed the stitchery. But the words became tangled in her throat,
and what she finally uttered seemed woefully inadequate.

"Your dress is beautiful."

"An important occasion deserves an important dress. Come,"
Turtle Woman said, ending the awkward moment, "we must
water the four-leggeds."

Skye followed behind Turtle Woman, her clumsy boots landing heavily in her grandmother's tracks, the threadbare calico skirt
swishing around her tired legs. They led the horses behind the
tipi, where a small spread of cropped grass stretched between the
camp circle and the cottonwoods that lined the creek. The red
roan mare trailed after them, the red-and-blue blanket shifting
gently back and forth on her swayed back.

"We will leave the saddles there," said Turtle Woman, pointing toward the base of the tipi.

Skye let Duncan's reins drop to the ground and hurried over
to help her grandmother lift the heavy panniers from the mule's
sawbuck. The woman's gnarled hands worked deftly. This time,
Skye tried not to stare at the knot of tangled scar tissue that covered the joint of her left little finger. Together, they loosened the
rope that tied the bundle of ropes and hides to the packsaddle. As
they lifted the panniers, Skye pretended not to notice when her
grandmother faltered under their weight. How old had Father

said she was? Sixty-five? Seventy? The woman wore her years well. They settled the panniers next to the tipi. The mule breathed a deep, audible sigh.

Skye unfastened the mule's breast collar while Turtle Woman undid the breeching; then they unfastened the cinches and slid the sawbuck from the mule's sweaty back. The mule pawed at the ground, wanting to roll in the dirt. Skye unsaddled Duncan, flinging the pair of saddlebags over her shoulder. Both geldings shook their weary bodies, the shudders beginning with their well-muscled necks and traveling clear to their unshod feet, vibrating every inch of hide.

"Feels good, hey, Duncan?" Skye rubbed the horse's stomach where a band of sweat had been left by the girth.

"The sacred-dog is good to us. He carries us upon his back and asks nothing in return. When my *ina* was born, the women still did the carrying."

"Where was your mother born?"

"Your great-*unci*? Between the river of the Dakotah and the great bend of the Big Muddy."

"And your father?"

"He was born into the camp of the Strong-Backed Women, also near the Muddy Waters."

Long ago, Mother had spoken briefly of her grandfather Sun Dog, and her grandmother Shifting Star, who had died on the long journey south to the Shell River country. Sun Dog had always blamed himself for her death, Breathcatcher had told her, for Shifting Star had longed to remain in the sacred Black Hills and did not want to heed the white traders who urged them away. "I was nineteen winters old when my *unci* Shifting Star went the way of all flesh and began to walk the *nagi* trail." Mother had told her of the spirit trail leading to the Land of Many Lodges, but had said little else, for the departed were rarely spoken of.

And now, no one speaks of Mother.

The air was still. No gusts ruffled the white swan feathers that hung from the old mare's mane. No whirlwinds kicked up powdery dust. The hot red sky had faded to a tepid dusky rose.

"Follow me," Turtle Woman said. "We must let our four-legged friends drink from the creek."

The horses' hooves flushed a red-winged blackbird from the grass. The bird flew toward the creek, landing on the tip of a cattail that sprouted from one of the stream's rare swampy overflows, while the high-trilled rasping call of a nocturnal male frog bounced through the air, urging the night along.

The animals buried their muzzles in the water, their hooves deep in the stream's muddy bank; thirsty sucking noises rose from the creek. Skye stood next to Turtle Woman, neither one speaking. Once the animals had quenched their thirst and lifted their heads to look around, Turtle Woman spoke.

"The water flows on, giving life to everything in her path. So it is with women."

Skye turned the strange statement over in her mind. She knew the nature of water well, but women? Her thought came out unbidden.

"Women frighten me."

"These waters," said her grandmother, seeming to ignore Skye's comment, "these waters have known the cold of many winters since last we camped together on her banks."

"Together? I was here as a child?"

"No. Only as a vision. But it was here, when the lodges of the Standing People were pitched along these same waters, that your *ina* decided to marry the *wasicula*."

The wasicula? An odd way to refer to Father. Skye squatted and rolled up the winged sleeves of her dress. Scooping water, she rubbed the dusty trail grime from her forearms, then closed her eyes and splashed cold water on her face, letting the liquid trickle down her neck. Had she been at home, in the seclusion of their meadowed valley, she would have stripped off her soiled dress, slid out of her shift, and waded eagerly into the stream. But she was not at home. And there was no seclusion for another hundred yards. Behind her, more than thirty tipis pointed conical tips toward the graying sky.

The sounds of camp life filtered down to the creek, penetrating Skye's awareness. As if suddenly waking from a dream, she realized the true import of her surroundings. She was in the camp of the Oglalas!

Duncan flicked his ears forward, then stretched his bay neck, flared his nostrils, and whinnied. On the far side of the creek, in a broad clearing populated by tall stands of prairie cordgrass, grazed a large herd of horses. This was the camp of her grandparents! The high-pitched voices of curious children and gossiping women could be heard above the lower mutterings of the men. Skye had no trouble guessing at the meaning of their words.

"Wasicus! The granddaughter of Sunstone and Turtle Woman! The Scotsman is back!" Would they be welcomed? Would the handsome young scout be here? Her grandmother's voice pulled her from her reverie.

"Women should not frighten you."

"I am not like other women. Sometimes I think I am more like Father."

"You are what Wakan Tanka meant for you to be."

"Perhaps God made a mistake."

Turtle Woman sucked in her breath. "Ahh-h! You do not know of what you speak."

Her grandmother stared across the rippling surface of water. The red-winged blackbird spread his wings, lifted from his cattail perch, and flew from the swampy bank to the graceful branch of a red willow. Skye silently cursed herself, knowing that this time she had truly given offense.

Turtle Woman gave Skye an admonishing look. "You carry the Standing People's legacy of the five-pointed star. You carry the prophecy of the Kangi holy man. You carry the blood of the great Lakota nation. Your words do not honor this blood, nor Wakan Tanka."

Skye struggled to say she was sorry, searching her buried childhood for a Lakota phrase asking forgiveness. The Lakota words that she finally uttered, so strange and foreign to her tongue, yet so familiar and soothing to her heart, stirred the long forbidden.

"Unci," she faltered, "respected Grandmother, *winyan wicasa okinihan* . . ." The Lakota words twisted her rusty tongue into silence. "I am sorry," she finished in English, but the clumsy attempt brought warmth to her grandmother's eyes. The old woman's face softened, the anger gone.

"We both lost a worthy thing. Still, the *wanbli* must learn to fly no matter how he is urged from the nest. It is good you have come. My heart swells with happiness."

Skye searched her grandmother's dark, ageless eyes. From deep within, rising from the depths of buried dreams and a forgotten childhood, more memories stirred. She heard the rich throaty voice of long ago. She saw the warm flames of the old lodge fire and felt the strength of her grandmother's arms surround her small body in the privacy of her grandparents' tipi. The voice, called forth from earthbound memories, had begun to tell a mythical story of times past: *"Ehaaaaanni."* The ghostly memory of her grandmother's voice stretched out the significant word, emphasizing the importance of the tale about to be told. "Long, long, long ago . . ." But that was all Skye could remember—a thin, lonesome word. The tales themselves were hidden in shrouds of pain.

Now, the same throaty voice spoke again. Skye again reached up for the polished turtle shell, caressing the smooth surface with the tips of her damp fingers.

"The sacred fire of our people has burned for generations. The *Peta-oihankesni.* Fire without end. The embers, never allowed to grow cold, are always coaxed into flame." Turtle Woman looked at the turtle shell in Skye's hand. "Be patient with yourself, *mitakoja.* Be patient with both of us."

"Cahr! Cahr! Cahr!" Startled, Skye almost dropped Duncan's reins at the harsh cawing sound and stared in disbelief at the two women coming down the path. An ebony-black crow perched on the lead woman's shoulder. The woman's gnarled, blood-encrusted hand held the end of a frayed tether. Both women wore elk-skin tunics with fork-tailed birds painted on the leather. The leader's diminutive black eyes stared at Skye. Tangled gray hair, sheared to shoulder level, framed a pockmarked face. She had seen

such scarred faces at Fort Bridger, heard about the diseases that the whites had brought to the Indians. Had wondered if she, too, were especially susceptible.

As the strange pair halted before them, the crow took a strand of the woman's oily hair in his beak and tugged. The old woman kept her eyes pinned on Skye.

"So," the woman said, "the *takoja* returns, no longer a child." Skye forced herself not to squirm under the woman's scrutiny.

Turtle Woman stepped forward, leading the mule and Roy behind her, and said, "Your eyes do not fail you, Doublewoman Dreamer."

"Ha! They cloud with age, just as yours do, Turtle Woman. But they show me all that this old body needs to see. Do you dress this day for your burial?"

"Do you come to greet my *takoja?*"

"I come to wash the butchering blood from my hands and to water this pathetic black bag of feathers! My son is a fool to keep such a bird."

Skye's grandmother did not argue with the statement.

"Cahr! Cahr!" the bird squawked again, still tugging on the old woman's hair.

"Itka sapa!" she cursed at the crow, flicking a sharp, jagged fingernail at the bird's black beak until he released the oily strand. A chortling sound came from the other woman.

"It would seem the bird keeps you," Turtle Woman said dryly, a satirical smile curling her lips. Her eyes flashed. She appeared to be enjoying herself.

"Ha! The bird keeps you!" the other woman repeated, laughing.

"Hold your tongue, Black Tail," ordered Doublewoman. "And did your old man tell you," she said to Turtle Woman, changing the subject, "that the Nacas will meet in the Red Council Lodge when the sun next rises in the sky?"

"The Big Bellies will meet in the council lodge," Turtle Woman reiterated for Skye's benefit, "to decide about the great council of the *wasicus.*"

"To be held during the Moon of the Yellow Leaves!" the other woman, Black Tail, interjected, not heeding Doublewoman's warning to hold her tongue.

"Who has time for a *wasicu*'s council? There is much work to be done." Doublewoman spat. "Will they feed our bellies during the Moon of Bitter Cold? When watery broth is all that remains? *Hiya!* They will not. The only thing they will give us are more *wasicu* babies!"

Doublewoman turned her head and stared at Skye with her small rodentlike eyes. The pointed slur met its mark. Skye forced back the stinging tears brought on by the woman's intended cruelty. Turtle Woman tugged on the lead rope, urging the mule and Roy forward.

"When you wash the filth from your hands, old Dreamer, take care that the cleansing waters of the stream do not wash you away as well. Take care that you do not wash away both faces, Anog Ite." Her grandmother pushed past the two women, forcing them to step off the path and onto the soggy bank of the creek.

Anog Ite? A memory floated to the surface. The creation tale of the woman who gave birth to the Four Winds—a woman who turned vain and promiscuous and whose fifth son was thus born a cripple. They named this fifth son Whirlwind. Fallen from grace, Anog Ite was given two faces, one beautiful, one ugly. *White-man babies, Doublewoman had said?* Angered, Skye slipped a rein around the far side of Duncan's neck, slid onto his back, and prodded his sides with her heels. Duncan trotted past the two old women, his hooves flinging mud behind him. For a moment, the slimy pellets of muck hung suspended in the hot, pregnant air, then fell, spattering ooze on the invisible cackles that rose from the throats of the two laughing dreamers.

Turtle Woman ladled more steaming stew into the small buffalo-horn bowls, and, ignoring the pain in her stiffened fingers, collected the remains of the gnawed-on ribs. The men hungrily slurped the fragrant, rich berry soup.

Tomorrow she would trade for a young pup from that jealous

dreaming woman who reminded her of Anog Ite. *The old hag's words may be foul, but the meat of her dogs is sweet!* Too bad that long ago, when Winyan Numpa, Double Woman, came to the Muddy Water woman in her dreams, telling her to choose between two paths, she chose the way of the *witko* woman instead of the path of an honorable woman. Too bad for everyone.

But the arrival of their *takoja* was, indeed, cause for celebration! They would feast upon delicacies and give gifts to all of the Standing People. Turtle Woman's weary heart pounded. It was too much, almost, for an old woman to bear.

An evening breeze blew in through the raised side of the tipi, cooling the hot still air within the lodge. She refilled empty bowls until all stomachs were full, then smiled across the tipi at Sunstone. Their eyes met. Together, their gazes traveled to the quiet form of their *takoja*, whose weary body had nearly succumbed to sleep. Sunstone returned her smile, his lips thin with age.

As usual, he sat bare-chested on his buffalo robe with legs crossed. A small white pouch hung from a leather thong around his neck. Small pebbles, streaked with gold, filled the pouch—stones found by Sunstone when he was seven winters old. Born to a Brulé mother and an Oglala father, he grew into Lakota manhood in the country east of the Black Hills. The pouch had much medicine, given *wotawe* status after a Brulé shaman had consecrated it:

"*Inyan.* Stone. All Father. Wi, Sun, has left his sacred mark upon these pebbles. But help this warrior boy to learn that *all* stones are sacred, all rocks hold within them the Great Mystery."

The stones gave to him his name, his power, his medicine. He never removed them. Not even when the two of them hid beneath the robes and played the *hehaka* game! Even then, the golden nuggets hung between them, swaying back and forth like a fresh Scili scalp dangling from a war lance.

Turtle Woman glanced furtively at her son-in-law, lowering her gaze quickly so that their eyes would not meet. He, too, had aged. Could it be that grief had once gripped his heart as well? Did he grieve even now?

Sunstone removed his long wooden pipe from its fringed

buckskin bag. A narrow band of beadwork and patterned burn marks decorated the sumac pipestem. The red stone bowl, though skillfully carved, lacked the ornateness of Sunstone's ceremonial calumet.

"Naked Warrior," said Sunstone, the bowl resting in the palm of his hand, "you have filled your meatbag with hot soup and fat ribs. Now we smoke. Then you tell me big lies and I pretend to believe them! Ha! *Han?*"

"Me life has been a dull one since last we met. I've nary a tale to tell." Macdonald stretched out first one leg, then the other, before gathering them back into him and leaning his bearlike body deeper into the slanting willow backrest.

"No stories? No more fights with the fur-man, Campbell, to talk about?"

"Your memory is mighty good for an old bull, but I've no more trapping yarns to swap. I've been spending me time dusting the dirt off rocks and such. This old hoss was hoping that ye would bend his ear with a story or two."

"Many things have happened in the camp of the Standing People since last we smoked together. But first, we smoke. Then, maybe I bend both your ears!"

Sunstone reached his fingers into a pocket sewn into the buckskin pipe bag. Turtle Woman knew the routine, the gestures, as intimately as she knew every scar, every wrinkle, of her husband's tough old body. He took a deep, almost inaudible breath. The smile lines in his face straightened and his expression became solemn. He took a pinch of *cansasa* between his thumb and forefinger and raised it to the sky and earth and the four sacred directions. His strong aged hands shook with the slight tremor that had plagued him since the season, nearly ten winters ago, of Bull Bear's death.

He sprinkled a small amount of the *cansasa* on the altar of bare ground before placing a pinch into the red bowl and lighting it. But he did not speak of the *Peta-oihankesni*—the Fire Without End. Those sacred words would be saved for the ceremonial lodge.

Smoke drifted from the pipe, engulfing his creased face and

deep-set eyes in a cloud of blue. The breath of Wakan Tanka. Reaching across the thick *pte* robe, Sunstone handed the pipe to their son-in-law.

Macdonald took the pipe, then smoothed the reddish-blond hairs of his mustache, running his fingers over his beard. Turtle Woman glanced at her husband and tried to imagine a whiskered face, chuckling to herself at the ludicrous image. *Wasicus*. Short pants and hairy faces.

Macdonald drew on the pipestem and the burning tobacco glowed red in the dimming light. Carefully, he passed the pipe, stem first, back to Sunstone.

"Why does Naked Warrior spend his time dusting the dirt from rocks?" Sunstone asked, pointing to a black flake of rock that lay on one of the robes. Turtle Woman did not remember seeing the chip earlier.

"It came no doubt from a spear," Macdonald said. "But do ye never wonder about the man who fashioned it?"

"My grandfather used the black rock to make his spears and knives," said Sunstone. "And before that, my grandfather's grand-father."

"Aye. The art of making blades from stones. But what of the black art? Do ye have none of that?"

"Black art?"

"Aye. Witches and elfins and such. Ye know, the powers of good and evil."

"These things exist in all men."

"But I'm speaking of things existing *outside* of men. Mysterious things, like huge stones standing on end, as if they were uprooted from the earth by a giant creature from the Otherworld. Things no mortal could do. Like the pictures ye find carved in rocks— pictures strange as ye could ever imagine."

Turtle Woman smiled. Her son-in-law looked as puzzled as the pup of a wandering-dog contemplating its own reflection in the water. Surely he knew nothing of the five-pointed star carved into the rock wall at the Medicine Wheel.

"Pictures?" Sunstone asked.

"Aye. Etchings. I've seen a stone what had a winged lizard

etched into the face of it, with a snout like a pelican and wings like a bat. Now, have ye ever seen a creature the likes of that afore?"

Sunstone laughed, then drew on the pipe. "Relax, my son. We two-leggeds are not meant to understand all the mysteries of Wakan Tanka."

"I've me own theory," Macdonald said, taking the pipe. He drew long and hard, then exhaled and leaned forward. Turtle Woman kept her head turned away, but listened intently.

" 'Tis the work of the fairies."

She lifted her head and looked quickly at her son-in-law. His face was somber. *Fairies?*

Sunstone voiced her question. "Fairies?"

"Aye. Fairies. Spirits of the dead. The ones who snatch babes from their cribs and steal milk straight from the udder. Fairies. Elfins."

"Fairies." Sunstone shook his head.

"Methinks the etchings are like your people's winter counts. Telling stories of the fairies' lives. Only I've yet to piece together the whole of a tale."

"Ah," said Sunstone, pretending to be serious. Turtle Woman could tell he was up to no good. "Now, winter counts I under-stand. Iron Shell of the Brulés keeps good winter counts—keeps track of everything important—paints good pictures. Like the winter the trader, Peeler, froze his leg. That happened just a few winters after my uncle, Ties His Penis in a Knot, died. How the women hated to see him go! And you should have seen the picture Iron Shell drew for that!"

Ha! What a tease he had suddenly become! The men laughed, holding their full bellies with their hands. Turtle Woman hid her own smile, then turned her gaze to their *takoja*. Skye lay curled on a soft robe, fighting to keep the weight of sleep from her eyes. A smile lit her face, too, then faded as she gave in to drowsiness.

Earlier, the girl had sat with legs crossed while eating. Turtle Woman had noticed that Sunstone had ignored their *takoja*'s im-modest pose. *She has much to learn*, thought Turtle Woman. *Lakota blood flows beneath her skin and shapes her bones, but the Lakota ways lie in her as dormant as pte grass during the Moon of Frost.*

Turtle Woman's eyes began to water as she stared, unblinking, at Skye. The men's laughter turned back to conversation that droned on, like the hum of unseen honeybees. Her granddaughter's long auburn hair faded into the shadows, the golden flecks in her brown eyes turning to stars as bright as those that lit the *nagi* trail.

Turtle Woman had dreamt of the *nagi* trail once, long ago. Four nights after the *igmu'tanka*, and then her daughter, had appeared in the flames, and the aroma of burning sage and sweetgrass had scented the air.

"I am Hinhan Kaga," she had said to Breathcatcher in her dream. "I examine every wandering *nagi* to make sure the skin of the body bears the necessary tattoo."

Her daughter had approached, holding her hands before her. Turtle Woman took her daughter's hands and gently turned them over, palms upward.

"Your hands carry the sign of a medicine wheel, no larger than the eye of a newborn fox." Indeed, tattoos etched the transparent skin of each slender wrist. They smiled at one another. She whispered her daughter's name.

"Breathcatcher, Breathcatcher . . ."

"Mother," her daughter answered, but it was a foreign word that fell from her lips, a Kangi word. Then she walked on, up the trail toward the seven stars, into the breath of the wind—to be carried like a fallen leaf into the very heart of Skan.

"Many a night"—Macdonald's rumbling brogue broke through Turtle Woman's thoughts—"I've sat beneath the flickering stars, mindin' the old times." He spoke with both voice and hands, gesticulating key words.

She closed her watery eyes again. Gone was the image of her daughter floating up the spirit trail. A different woman stood before her. A Hewaktoka, with an arrow-filled quiver and bow slung over her back, and fresh hides hanging from her belt. Little Badger grown. A voice called out, *"Woman Chief, Woman Chief,"* and then she was gone.

Turtle Woman opened her eyes. The young woman asleep before her now, with tattered dress and unkempt hair, bore no tattoos on her wrists, no mark on her forehead, spoke no Kangi. She had declared no allegiance to the Lakotas. Nor were her ears pierced in the tradition of her ancestors. No elder had performed the ear-piercing ceremony, vowing to raise the girl to honor the ways of the Lakotas.

"*Hinu!*" The sorrowful whisper escaped Turtle Woman's throat and Sunstone looked at her in concern. She lowered her head in embarrassment, her long gray braids almost skimming the floor of the lodge. Why had the Standing People followed the Kiyuksas to the Smoky Hill country? Why had she left her only daughter behind? Suddenly tormented by guilt and overwhelmed by loneliness, she wanted to claw at the scars on her arms, to make a flesh offering of appeasement—but to do so now, at this moment? *Hiya.* Her outburst had been enough.

Macdonald reached for his sweat-stained hat, removed it from his ruddy head, and took his own small, well-worn pipe in the palm of his broad hand.

"Me graunie Maggie used to smoke a pipe," he said, turning the pipe over, then tucking it back beneath the beaded hatband. He set the hat aside and leaned back into the willow backrest. "Gave me grandfather fits. She claimed it calmed her soul and soothed a sinful nature. He claimed 'twas the only thing which kept her quiet, so he let her keep on with it!" He held his hand to his full belly again and stifled a laugh.

Sunstone smiled, deepening the craggy lines in his face. "Our *takoja* Skye is not like her Scottish grandmother in this way. She has grown to be more like the voiceless one, the prairie rabbit who never speaks."

"Voiceless? Ye haven't seen her riled. The girl's got me temper, I'm afraid, and her red-haired grandmother's way of showing it. Ye would have taken a shine to Graunie Maggie, though many folks thought she weren't quite proper. They used to call her the 'red-haired rebel.'"

Turtle Woman shook the daydreams from her mind and listened to the men with lowered eyes. She could feel Macdonald's gaze pass over her.

"But then, some of us like our lasses strong-willed, with a wee bit of the rebel in them, don't we." His voice toyed playfully with the words and she felt a blush begin to heat her throat. Sunstone's voice, too, skipped lightly across his words.

"A wise husband is not bothered that his wife stands tall. It is the foolish husband who shrinks when standing in the shadow of a good woman. As for me?" Sunstone paused for a moment. "I like *mitawicu* any way, standing, or lying down . . ."

The blush rushed from Turtle Woman's neck to her cheeks. The old *hehaka*! To tease her in front of her son-in-law, when she could say nothing in return! Standing or lying down! Ha! The words praised her; still, for this she would get even. Perhaps she would challenge the old bull to try once again to play the *hehaka* game with her while standing. That would put an end to his boasting!

At least her son-in-law had the manners to pretend to ignore Sunstone's comment, though she had no doubt that a barely contained smirk hid beneath his hairiness. She glanced at Skye, whose eyes fluttered with dreams. Macdonald spoke again, this time more softly.

"Grandfather used to say that me grandmother's orneriness was caused by the stars."

"The stars?" Sunstone cocked one eyebrow.

"Aye, the stars. The night she was born, a great comet went shooting across the sky."

"What is this thing, *comet?*" asked Sunstone, starting to slip the cooled pipe into its fringed buckskin bag.

"A great star, streaking across the sky. With a tail as long as the heavens. Well, ye know, like on the night Skye was born. In the old country, some say the comet 'tis a bad omen."

Turtle Woman felt the blood drain from her face. A great star? *Does he speak of the Shifting Star?* She looked at Sunstone. He held the pipe motionless, half in, half out of the bag. Before she could stop herself from breaking tradition, the question in her mind burst forth.

"This red-haired grandmother of Skye's, this *wasicu* woman, she was also born on the night stars-move-around?"

Immediately ashamed, she hung her head, not wanting to look

at Sunstone. Never before had she spoken directly to her son-in-law. Sunstone atoned for her breach by repeating the question himself.

"Your grandmother was born under this comet?"

"Aye. I don't reckon I've ever told the story to Skye." Macdonald ran his fingers through his reddish-blond hair. "The High-lander, me great-grandfather, used to say that during the dark of night, when me great-grandmother was deep in the throes of childbirth, a sudden flash of brilliant white pierced the blackness. 'Twas at that exact moment the girl child came into the world and gave her newborn cry."

Two great-grandmothers born beneath a shifting star?

"Haun-n-n-n," Turtle Woman sighed, hunting for thoughts, hunting for answers. *What is the meaning of this* wakan *thing?* Not only her own mother, Shifting Star, but Macdonald's grand-mother as well? And what of the Kangi grandmother? The prophecy of the holy man proved even more mysterious than she realized. *A great woman warrior will be conceived within the womb of the Standing People. She will spill from the heavens like a thousand stars.*

But the prophecy had been incomplete. Or at least Turtle Woman's understanding had been incomplete—for the blood which gave life to Skye did not belong to the Standing People alone, nor to the Kangis, but to the Scottish *wasicu* who lived be-yond the great waters as well. She had always known that she had to share Skye with the Highland clan, but did she now, also, have to share this sacred prophecy? And what of this Kangi blood?

The voices of the men droned on, their conversation traveling far from Turtle Woman's whirling thoughts. She stared at her *takoja*, beginning to stir from sleep. The girl turned over on her side, tossing a strand of disheveled hair, the color of reddened earth, across her cheek. She would awaken soon.

Turtle Woman leaned into her backrest and straightened the creaking bones of her legs out before her. Discreetly crossing one moccasin over the other, she began loosening the small sacks of yellow trade cloth tied to the ends of her braids. She combed bent fingers through the woven strands of hair, working her way up the length of braid until her gray hair draped loosely across her breasts. She thought of Skye's red-haired great-grandmother across the big waters, and of the secret she had always kept from Sunstone, and felt the barbs of jealousy, and guilt, stab at her heart.

Sunstone's voice grew boisterous. Skye opened her eyes, yawned, and stretched her slender torso, arching her back like a tuft-eared cat rising from a sunbath. Sitting up, legs crossed immodestly, she looked about her and smiled shyly at her grandmother. Sunstone glanced at his granddaughter's inappropriate pose before continuing to talk with Macdonald.

"You were a hairless pup when we first met on the shores of the Big Muddy! A pup who fought every *sunka* in the village! I should have called you Wolverine!"

"Aye, those were shinin' times, they were. 'Twere only a few minor scuffles, though. Nothing like a wolverine tangle!"

"Minor? Many winters ago, your deeds had wings. News of the Naked Warrior traveled fast."

"Well, 'tweren't always me doing! I'd have been content to drink a wee bit o' the rosie and play a few notes on me pipes."

"Ha!" Sunstone grunted good-naturedly. "This old crackedhorn knows better. You still paw the ground like a young *tatanka*. A bull is always a bull."

Turtle Woman reached into the rawhide case for her porcupine-quill hairbrush and began pulling it through her slick, wavy hair. Skye sat only a few feet away. Her unkempt hair hung down her back in snarled waves. The sight angered Turtle Woman. *She wears her hair like a* wasicu. *A young Lakota girl would know better.*

But then a giggle came forth from Skye as she listened to the men, and the golden flecks in her dark eyes began to sparkle. Turtle Woman regretted her anger. *You feel sorry for yourself, old woman.*

"Tell me again about the talk of this big council," Macdonald asked, curling his fingers into loose fists while placing the knuckles of his hands together and moving them up and down—signing the word *council* as he spoke.

"The *wasicu* chief sends messengers up Elk River, up the Shell, even the Big Muddy. They ask all tribes to gather on the banks of Horse Creek for this big council. Even the Kangis! There is much division among us . . ."

She feared that nothing good would come of this big council. She spread her scarred hands before her. Her own feelings frightened her. *For as many winters as I have fingers, I have prayed to Wakan Tanka to return my Lakota granddaughter. She returns, but she returns as a* wasicu. She stared at Skye, wishing for darker hair, darker eyes, darker skin. Wishing for Breathcatcher. *Ahh-h!* Must the lessons of Wakan Tanka always be so painful? Would the true nature of Taku Skanskan always be just beyond her grasp? Oh, what a foolish woman she was!

She had been trying to walk the path of the long-ago past. *It is not good to set one's moccasins upon this path, for it will bring only heartache. Does the sun not always move forward? Begin each day anew? Life and death circle our lives like the sacred sun. Your* takoja *returns to you. Teach her. Set her feet upon the good road. Help her to learn the sacred ways. Her presence warms this lodge like new blades of grass on the winter-worn prairie. Do not turn away from her.*

Turtle Woman ached to reach out and gather Skye's mane of unruly hair in her hand, easing the snarls into silken strands as she had so often when Breathcatcher was a child. Did she dare? Would the gesture offend the young woman?

Skye turned to look at her. Turtle Woman cleared her throat and sucked in her breath. She wrapped her gnarled fingers slowly around the handle of the porcupine-quill hairbrush and she held it up, offering it to her granddaughter.

Skye stretched out her arm and reached tentatively toward her grandmother, their hands almost touching—one light and smooth, the other dark and bent. The brush passed between them, like a fragile bridge stretching across the great chasm of time, across the deep abyss of heartache and sorrow.

15

THE STALLION

Skye slipped from beneath the summer bedrobe and quietly lifted the tipi's door flap, easing through the opening without disturbing Father's sleeping figure, nor those of her grandparents. She moved with the quiet grace of a young doe, tiptoeing barefoot between the circular lodges toward the creek. The horses nickered softly.

"Shh," she whispered, stopping to stroke the neck of the old roan mare, "you must be quiet."

Following yesterday's path, she walked past the cattails downstream to where wet sand and small stones formed a beach on the bank of deepening waters. A quilt of predawn gray still covered the slumbering morning; no cook fires yet burned, and the camp dogs whimpered in their sleep. Not even the meadowlarks had begun to stir.

Here dense gooseberry bushes and stands of leafy red willows edged the water, providing solitude. Tall cottonwoods separated the creek bed from the circle of tipis, providing even more seclusion. The cool damp smell of night clung to the earth, and dewdrops poised precariously on the leaf blades of razor-sharp canary grass. Flowing eastward, the creek, unusually high, tumbled over rounded rocks, lapping its wet tongue at curved sandbars and overhanging willows.

Looking over her shoulder one last time, Skye undid the clasps of her faded calico dress and eased the bodice down over her shoulders. Many days of trail dust and salty sweat clung to her skin. The dress slid easily past her small waist but caught on the curves of her maturing hips. She lifted one hip, then the other, wriggling her way out. The dress crumpled in a threadbare heap at her feet. Slipping out of her shift, she piled it on top of the dress, then dipped her naked toes into the creek water. "Oh," she whispered to herself, "what I wouldn't give for a washtub full of hot suds." She recoiled from the water's cold, wet touch.

Her body tensed as she waded in knee-deep, then thigh-deep, then deeper still. The current, strong from the melting of exceptionally heavy winter snows, pushed against her body, forcing her to lean into it and brace her feet against the hard slippery rocks of the creek bed. As the water lapped at her bare skin, she inhaled sharply, filling her lungs with air, then pushed off with her feet and felt her body float to the rippling surface.

Flipping onto her back, she let the stream lift and carry her. The waters caressed her limbs, splashing across her breasts. *Embraced by water, kissed by air. Is this how it feels to be a piece of driftwood? Pulled along, out of control? Destiny nothing more than a fickle whim of nature?*

Her thoughts turned to the mysterious young scout. Was this how it would feel to be caressed by a man, to be carried away in a passionate embrace?

Embarrassed, she rolled over onto her belly and put her face into the water. She shook the confusing but pleasing thoughts from her mind and began swimming, her strong arms cutting through the turbulent water and pulling her toward the opposite bank, her legs cleaving long swaths through the current.

The rough streambed scraped her fingers and toes as she dug into the sandy bottom and stood up, regaining her footing. The clinging creek waters loosened their grip and slid dripping from her skin, lapping hungrily at her calves. The sudden noise disturbed a red-barred turtle dozing on a nearby rock.

"Did I wake you, wise one?" Skye asked, gathering strands of her wet hair into a ponytail and squeezing the moisture from it. The turtle blinked her eyes, watching Skye.

"Turtle, is it true what they say? Does your heart really go on beating even after you're dead?" Stretching out her striped yellow neck, the turtle crawled to the edge of the rock.

"You, at least, have a shell to protect you from the frigid waters—while here I stand, like a featherless hatchling fallen from the nest." Skye ran her hands down her arms, then across her chest and down her hips, wiping the water from her skin. As she flicked her fingers the turtle dipped her head and slid noiselessly into the creek.

She stepped onto the dry shore and faced the faint rays of the rising sun. She inspected her two-toned skin—tanned a golden bronze where the hot summer sun could reach, remaining a translucent pinkish hue where it could not. She felt the invigorated beat of her own heart as it pounded in her chest. *A shell to protect the heart . . . My pale skin is like the tender skin beneath a turtle's shell—vulnerable, an easy mark for a cruel barb.* She thought of Caws Like Magpie, and the memory created a rancid taste in her mouth.

Cautiously she eased down a deer path that wove in and out of the willows, then paused to feed on a bush of ripe gooseberries, ridding her mouth of the bitterness. The undergrowth thinned and tall cottonwoods stretched stout trunks into the still-gray sky, a gentle breeze rustling their coarse-toothed leaves.

She paused at the clearing and leaned against a young cottonwood, shielding her body from the breeze. A small band of horses that had wandered from the rest lounged in the open area. Some grazed; others stood sleepily awaiting the warming rays of morning. No boys guarded the strays. On the horizon, where the clearing rose to a crest, a lone iron-gray horse stood silhouetted against the dawn. He had a thickly arched neck, finely formed withers, and a broad back with strong loins leading to narrow hips and powerful, angular hind legs.

"What a fine specimen you are," she whispered to the distant stallion, "like a king with his harem." The majesty of the scene caused Skye's skin to tingle, and she took a deep breath.

She eased around the tree and lowered her body slowly against the deeply furrowed bark, settling her bare rump onto the soft damp grass under the cottonwood. Leaning into the live wood, downwind of the horses, she watched.

A mare grazed nervously in a tall stand of prairie cordgrass a short distance from the stallion. She held her tail high and lifted her head to the breeze, flicking her ears back and forth. The stallion nickered and moved closer, flexing his neck and stomping the ground. The mare pivoted and turned away, lowering her head to graze, then lifting it again to look at the stallion. Neither saw Skye.

The stallion whinnied, flaring his nostrils, then pranced back and forth, working his way closer. The mare dug her hooves into the soft dirt and ran to the far end of the clearing, holding her tail like a flag in challenge. He reared and chased after her. The other horses watched with little interest, except for a few colts who tried clumsily to mimic the herd stallion. The stallion, ignoring the colts, pursued the mare until suddenly she pivoted and turned to face him. He snorted and approached her.

Creek water from Skye's wet hair dripped down her bare back, forming little rivulets over the swells of her gently curved hips. Shivering, she pulled her knees up to her chest and wrapped her arms around them. A movement in the trees that flanked the far end of the clearing caught her eye, but she saw nothing more. She turned and looked behind her. The tips of the camp's lodgepoles were barely visible in the gray dawn. No fresh smoke rose from early cook fires; no women yet wandered down to the water's edge to fill their buffalo paunches. She breathed a sigh of relief, hoping for another hour of privacy, yet wishing at the same time that she had a patch of noonday sun in which to lie down.

The two horses continued their mating dance, fascinating Skye. Yet despite the stallion's bravado, snorting and pawing the earth, sending clouds of dust into the air, his every movement was a reaction to the mare's subtle teasing. The bucks and does in the meadow back home behaved much the same way. Even the birds, with their aerial acrobatics, did the same dance. *And people? What do I know of men and women?*

Skye let her arms fall to her side and stretched her legs out before her, crossing one ankle over the other.

She looked critically down the length of her two-toned body. Only half a specimen. Neither half a match for the other. Yet, her father and mother had been well matched, despite their differences. She began to softly hum a bit of Scott.

> "Oh, River Spirit,
> Tell me, thou who view'st the stars . . .
> What shall be the maiden's fate?
> Who shall be the maiden's mate?"

The sheer strength of the stallion, the mass of throbbing muscle, mesmerized her. She stopped humming, holding her breath. How could such a creature balance on just two legs? The horse's hindquarters bulged, so tightly were the muscles flexed, his front legs flailing the air as he sought to reposition his weight. The wavy mane on his massive neck rippled as he hovered over the squealing mare and bared his teeth, biting the mare's withers.

Skye stood and turned away, overcome by the physical passion of the act. To see such a thing was to witness one's own mortality, one's own frantic grasp for life. The moment should be private, held in high regard. Even the other animals seemed to lower their gazes. *Was this an integral part of living, this submission to one's own passions?*

Suddenly, her nakedness embarrassed her. The grayness of predawn had succumbed to the pink blush of sunrise, and now, even the blush was about to melt from the morning sky. Her seclusion could no longer be assured.

She looked nervously about her as another flash of movement caught her eye. More aware than ever of her nakedness, she began to panic. She reached instinctively for her skinning knife but found only bare flesh. "Cursed fool, alone with not a stitch of clothes on, and your only weapon back at the river. You're not at home!"

Moving quickly through the trees, down the deer path, in and out of the gooseberries, ignoring the sharp nettles which scratched her skin, she reached the sandbar where the turtle had been, saw her footprints in the damp sand, then heard a stomping sound and the far-off whinny of a horse. Glancing behind her, she saw no movement, no immediate danger. Had the noise come from the stallion?

Following the creek upstream until she spied her pile of clothes on the opposite bank, she moved a little farther on, knowing that the current would carry her downstream. Then, finding a suitable place, she waded in, gritted her teeth against the cold wetness, and with strong capable strokes forged through the stream.

She hauled herself up onto the sandbank and shook the water from her skin, then walked a few yards upstream to her clothes. Shaking the dust from her shift, she began patting dry her bare neck and shoulders. Bare? The realization hit her like a blow to the gut. *The polished turtle shell! It's gone!*

Grabbing her dress, she shook out the folds of faded material, hoping the keepsake would tumble from the crumpled skirt. She pulled the threadbare dress over her head, then eased her figure into the bodice, the full skirt settling gently over her hips. Clutching her shift to her, with her knife gripped in her hand, she searched the sandbar, walking up and down the bank of the creek. There! She stooped and fingered a wet, glistening pebble. Nothing! The shell was gone. Floating downstream, most likely, never to be seen again.

"How could I have been so careless?" she cried out in despair. "How could I not have noticed?" Then a flicker of hope: perhaps the shell had torn loose as she fled through the undergrowth, or fallen perhaps beneath the cottonwood? She would return that very morning to look for it.

She squeezed the moisture from her long hair, then rinsed the shift in the creek and wrung the moisture from it. She tucked it beneath her arm and hurried back onto the path that bordered the stream, heading toward the circle of tipis that were finally coming to life.

A young fox, flushed from the woods, bounded toward the water on the far side of the creek. He stopped at the brink and paced quickly back and forth, then looked over his shoulder, his ears pricked. He turned and ran downstream along the cluttered bank. Skye peered across the water, searching the slender willows and cottonwood trunks for something out of place, something to flush a fox from the trees.

Her eyes followed the invisible path of the fleeing fox, cutting a trail in reverse. There! A mounted horseman slid through the woods just this side of the clearing. At such a distance, Skye could barely discern the color of the horse, let alone the features of the rider. It was a man, though, of this she was sure. An Oglala, for he wore no shirt nor leggings, and she could make out a few feathers dangling from his scalp lock.

Had he seen her? Had the flash of movement among the trees, there in the clearing, been he? Oh, what a rotten way to begin her first day. She was a fool to have swum in the creek. These meadows offered no sanctuary, no peace. She would urge Father to return home soon, to tarry only long enough for a proper visit. She winced as a sharp stone cut into her foot and red willow branches snagged her skirt, reaching out to scratch her bare throat.

She would make him promise. A short visit—no more than a fortnight.

16

THE NECKLACE

"Pilamaya, **thank you,** my shelled friend," Mahto whispered as he slipped the leather-thonged necklace over his head. His lips parted in a half-smile, revealing even, white teeth.

The polished turtle shell came to rest between two slightly yellowed bear claws. Its delicacy, entwined with the claws of the great and ferocious grizzly, pleased him. The memory of Turtle Woman's granddaughter in the water, and leaning naked against the rough bark of the cottonwood, also pleased him. She had cut through the swift current with forceful strokes, like a falling star shooting through the night sky.

"Do not worry," he addressed the empty turtle shell, "I will return you to the Light-skinned One soon. I will even be so brave as to hand you to her myself. But first, first I will enjoy the light touch of the leather around my neck and the coolness of your shell upon my breast."

Mahto nudged his pale tobiano horse forward. The creek water swirled around the horse's legs, wetting Mahto's calves and the band of furred otter skin that he wore on his ankle.

The turtle. Of the earth and of the water. A feminine force—guardian of life, controller of accidents. The turtle is wise, hearing many things yet saying nothing. Protected by a shell which even an arrow cannot pierce.

Mahto believed these things. Everybody knew that they lived on the back of a great turtle who had risen from the depths of the vast waters to create an island, a sprawling world of immense plains and snow-covered peaks. *The shelled one. With a heart which continues to beat even after the spirit has left the flesh.*

More than once, Mahto had seen Turtle Woman assist the medicine man, High Bear, grinding up the dried heart of a turtle, mixing it with water purified by the smoke of sweetgrass.

He had seen wounded warriors drink this powder and rise to fight again. "*Hye, hye,* Tunkasilas," High Bear had often prayed in thankfulness. "We are grateful that our grandfathers hear the pleas of the Ikce Oyate, the Red Sun People." He had even dreamed that the medicine man had poured this healing liquid down the parched throat of his dying father. In the dream, his father's wounds, inflicted by the enemy Susuni People, grew whole again. In the dream, his father returned with the scalps of many warriors tied to his lance, and the Bear People danced and feasted through the night. Whirlwind passed the pipe to his son, Male Crow, and Mahto celebrated with his own father. In his dream, the medicine worked.

But his father had not returned from the raid against the Susu-nis. No one had returned. The prayers of the Ikce Oyate had gone unanswered, the winter-count paintings of the tribes' historian re-minding them all of their dead kinsmen. The Susuni warriors re-turned Male Crow's scalp as an act of peacemaking, but when Whirlwind held his son's shriveled scalp in his hands, vengeance ran like hot blood from his hardened heart. *"Hoppo!* Let us go!" the men had shouted when Whirlwind sent the war pipe circling all of the Oglala camps.

Six winters had passed since then. And for six winters now the bear-claw necklace of his father had hung heavy upon his muscled chest, rubbing against the tender scars of his first Sun Dance, re-fusing to let the inner wounds heal.

He urged the tobiano through the deep water and up the far bank of the creek. Water slid from the horse's back and cas-caded down his sides, while warm rays of sun fell upon Mahto's shoulders. Behind them, from the clearing in the trees where the cordgrass grew tall, the call of the iron-gray stallion pierced the morning air. The tobiano snorted in response and shook his head. Mahto tightened his grip on the wet bridle rope.

"You envy the life of the seed-horse, my friend? A little jeal-ous? Wishing you had earned the right to father many foals? Ha! Is it not every man's dream?"

Mahto's thoughts returned to the *wikoskala.* The faint impres-sion of her body had lingered on the grass beneath the tall cot-tonwood tree; a few radiant reddish-brown hairs had clung to the tree's rough bark. He had even imagined that he could still smell her lingering scent. He had found the turtle-shell necklace nearby, clinging to a gooseberry bush. He had not meant to intrude upon the Light-skinned One's time of aloneness, for he, too, had been seeking solitude, yet he, too, had found himself entranced by the stallion and the mare.

And by the Light-skinned One.

Has someone cast a spell on you, that you behave like a heat-struck elk with no sense at all? Ha! On the other hand, a man would have to be lying on his death scaffold not to be aroused.

He nudged the tender flanks of the tobiano with his moccasins and the horse moved into an easy trot, sliding through the willows and thick undergrowth. As he did so, a red fox darted across the path in front of them, then disappeared into the trees.

"Do the spirits send a sign," he wondered, "that a fox should cross my path now?"

Mahto belonged to the Tokala, the Kit Fox Society for warriors. In fact, he was one of four lance owners, a prestigious position. For him to disregard this visit would have been unthinkable.

He pulled his horse to a stop. Why had the fox chosen to run across his path? What message did he carry? Did the *wasicu* girl bring danger? He chanted the Tokala song in his mind. *I am a fox. I am supposed to die. If there is anything difficult, if there is anything dangerous, that is mine to do.* No, the fox did not warn him about danger, for danger did not frighten him. He did not fear fighting, or letting the arrows fly. What did he fear, then?

The answer came to him the moment the image of the Light-skinned One came back to mind. *His passion—he feared his passion*, feared that if let loose, this rousing fervor would find its way straight to her. *A-i-i-i*, he must be careful!

A frown flickered across Mahto's face. His dark eyes narrowed and the thin scar that ran across the corner of his brow bent slightly. Maybe returning the necklace was not a good idea? Maybe it was a foolish thought put into his head by the Bone Keepers. Their medicine was bad, not to be trusted. Maybe the *wasicu* girl would be like the two-faced Anog Ite, the deceiver of men; maybe he had only seen one side of her nakedness—the side of temptation and deception.

He rode on, slowing as he approached the camp circle, and frowned when he approached his wickiup. He had lived in small low shelters of bent willows and *pte* robes for over two winters. Always before he had found their compact shapes comforting. Now he stared at the lodge with distaste. *I am no longer a young colt running with the band. I should be throwing my robe within the circle of a tall tipi, next to the robe of a warm woman, not bending to sleep like a dog in a cave.*

He slid his long-limbed body from the tobiano and glanced across the stirring camp to the tipis of the Standing People. At the same time the Light-skinned One, clothed, hurried up the path from the creek.

"I preferred her naked," he whispered to himself.

The nagging doubts retreated as he watched Skye advance up the path, and a new thought entered his mind. Maybe the doubts themselves were bad medicine? Maybe the doubts were not to be trusted? A sly trick of the two-faced?

"*A-i-i-i!*" he exclaimed, reaching for the turtle shell that hung between the bear claws. "I will have to be careful, for nothing is as it seems . . ."

17

SPIDER MAN

"**The pretty *wikoskala*** had never been with a man before," Doublewoman Dreamer said, interrupting the lewd folktale midsentence to scratch her scalp with the sharpened end of her digging stick, "and Iktomi, Spider Man, was hungry to sleep with her. So he hid his hairy body in the dress of an old woman and went in search of the girl."

The other woman listened to Doublewoman with restrained grins on their faces, all except Black Tail, who cackled loudly. Turtle Woman knew that the others were uncomfortable in the presence of her foreign-acting *takoja*, for they bent their heads to the tedious tasks of root digging and berry picking, despite keeping their ears tuned to the unfolding of the tale. Turtle Woman watched Skye, wondering how much she understood. *She is unused to the talk of women, even though she is old enough for the ways of a man.*

"Iktomi," continued Doublewoman, digging another prairie turnip, "found the *wikoskala* wading on the shores of the creek. '*Hau maske*, how are you, friend?' he asked. 'Let's cross the water together.' So they raised the hems of their dresses and walked into the water. The girl did not want to be rude, but the old woman's legs were very ugly. 'Your legs are covered with hair,' she said to Iktomi. Iktomi answered her with sly words. 'When you get older, you will have hairy legs, too.' " Doublewoman Dreamer put down her digging stick and wiped the sweat from her upper lip. "Not this old woman," she cackled, lifting up her own dress to reveal shrunken, hairless thighs. "Ha!"

Turtle Woman chuckled, shaking her head at the lewd behavior, then forced herself to straighten the lines of her mouth, sobering her expression. But her eyes gave her away. She glanced at Skye, who prodded the ground with a sharp stick, trying to loosen the roots of a prairie turnip. The sun cast a graceful shadow of the girl upon the earth, and the image caught Turtle Woman unguarded. *So like Breathcatcher. How many times did your* ina *and I dig the wild* tinpsilas *together? Does the sacred circle now come around, once again?*

"As the creek water grew deeper," the woman dreamer continued, "they lifted their robes up past their hips. 'You have a very hairy backside,' said the *wikoskala* to Iktomi. Spider Man nodded as they waded in deeper yet. 'What is that thing between your legs?' asked the girl, for she had never before seen a naked man . . ."

Turtle Woman had heard this ribald tale many times. She let her mind wander, thinking of the celebration that night. The young *wikoskalas* would wear their finest clothes—quilled and beaded dresses, their best moccasins. She watched Skye, who still knelt by the half-buried turnip, her bare feet peeking out from beneath the hem of her worn calico dress. She had rolled up the wide-winged sleeves and had tied her hair at the nape of her neck with a strip of leather. The shell necklace, Turtle Woman noticed, was gone.

Crude cackles of laughter slithered over Doublewoman's worn-down teeth. She squinted and gripped the digging stick suggestively. " 'How I wish to be rid of this thing!' said Iktomi. 'But just when I think the growth is shrinking, it gets large again. There is only one way to get rid of it. You are kind to help me, *wikoskala*. But we must get out of the water and go over where the grass is soft.' "

Skye put down her digging stick, straightened her spine, and sat back on her haunches, listening curiously now to Doublewoman Dreamer. She reached for her throat, as if to fondle the missing necklace, then let her hand fall to her side. Doublewoman's beady eyes did not miss the gesture as she rattled on. She hobbled over to Skye, letting the last suggestive line settle on the working women, and more pointedly on the young half-blood. " 'Elder sister,' said the naive *wikoskala*, 'you are right. The growth keeps coming back—this truly *is* hard work.' Ha!" Doublewoman's cackles splintered the still, afternoon air, like shards of broken glass. Black Tail laughed, revealing worn teeth yellow with age.

Giggling, restrained only by the presence of Skye, rippled from the other women. They glanced discreetly at the young girl, appraising her reaction.

"You do not work so hard, eh, *wasicu?*" Doublewoman Dreamer said, pointing her digging stick at Skye. "Or maybe you work better when there's a man around? Ha! Like the *wikoskala*. *Han!*" She laughed crudely.

"Old woman, you have made enough jokes for one day," said Turtle Woman. "Be careful, or Iktomi will make a joke of you."

"Has the girl lost her tongue? Must you always put words in her mouth?"

"I have not lost my tongue," Skye said, standing to face Doublewoman.

"She speaks!"

"I speak. I hunt. I trap. And sometimes, like you, I even dig in the dirt."

Turtle Woman hid the grin on her face with her hand. Her *takoja*, it appeared, had had enough.

"You do not dig very well," taunted Doublewoman. "You behave like a foolish boy! Has no one taught you the ways of a woman?"

Turtle Woman took a deep breath, and stood, unbending her stiff knees while brushing the prairie dirt from the fringed hem of her elk-skin dress.

"You are the foolish one," she said. "Not content unless you are causing trouble. You remind me of a mushroom sprouting from dung. Come, *takoja*, there is much to do before the celebration."

Skye tucked her basket of turnips beneath her arm and met the cold hard stare of the woman dreamer with a narrowing gaze of her own.

"I am coming, Unci," she said, emphasizing the familial term while turning away.

Several of the other women stretched their legs and, gathering their filled baskets, followed Turtle Woman and Skye across the open prairie and back toward the circle of tipis, leaving Caws Like Magpie's mother standing alone on the hill with Black Tail.

"I hear there will be a Night Dance tonight," she yelled after them, "and maybe a knife-biting ceremony. Make sure your granddaughter is there. I will butcher a puppy to honor her arrival!"

"A puppy? What does she mean?" Skye asked, turning toward her grandmother. "And what is a knife-biting ceremony?"

"It is a foolish woman's idea of trouble," Turtle Woman muttered, shifting the weight of her heavy basket. "Nothing but trouble." She shook her head and her long braids swayed across her aging breasts, like silver sage bending before the prairie wind.

The council lodge stood in the center of the circle of pitched tipis. Its door opened to the east, looking past the entrance of the camp to the plains beyond. The large interior of the lodge accommodated many warriors, many Big Bellies, shamans, and Wicasa Itacans. No robes covered the bare floor of the lodge. A sacred altar of earth and a small spirit fire were its only furnishings.

At least forty buffalo hides had been used to make the lodge, Gregory guessed, maybe more, and eight, even nine half-stocked Hawken rifles could have been laid end to end across the floor. He followed Sunstone inside, noticing that his father-in-law took a place of honor to the west of the altar. Wolfskin Necklace sat to Sunstone's left.

"Naked Warrior should also sit on the heart-side," Sunstone said, motioning for Gregory to sit to the left as well.

The old man looked regal in his ceremonial shirt. The deer hide had been altered only where necessary; the animal's shape could still be seen, his power still felt. The leather was dyed sky-blue on the upper half, and sun-yellow on the lower half. Hair locks representing the people of the tribe fringed the sleeves, and meticulous bands of quilling decorated the arms, shoulders, and yoke. A beaded choker encircled the deep, leathery creases of Sunstone's neck, and his braids, wrapped in otter skin, hung to his waist. Six eagle feathers, attached to his scalp lock, jutted off to the right.

How long had it been since he and Gregory had fought side-by-side against the Arikaras? Twenty-five years? Aye, at least. Maybe thirty. 'Twas twenty-two years exactly since they met up again on the south fork of the Cheyenne River, at the Oglala trading post. Sunstone had had his family with him then. Turtle Woman, tall and elegant, and Breathcatcher, a tempting lass just beginning to grow the curves of a woman. The sight of her standing there, long legs and black silken hair, those bonnie doe eyes peering at him—the memory of her had haunted him for the next five years, till he finally had gumption enough to make her his bride.

But those days were gone. Over and done with. His father-in-law was no longer a big man. Next to Wolfskin Necklace's broad, oaklike torso he appeared shrunken, withered. But his presence still commanded the attention of everyone entering the lodge. What the old man lacked in strength, he made up for in wisdom. Gregory was beginning to feel the ravages of time himself; his joints ached day and night, and he had begun to curse his trapping days spent wading waist-deep in frigid rivers.

Twenty men now sat inside the tipi. Sunstone straightened his spine and pulled his shoulders erect.

"The Ones Who Decide have gathered. It has been said that a people without history is like wind on the buffalo grass. This will be a day of decision for our people, a day of history for the scattered ones."

Gregory shifted his weight from one hipbone to the other, easing his crossed legs. He had gone soft these last few years, too used to setting his carcass on a bent-willow rocker instead of hard ground. He twisted the ends of his mustache and combed his fingers through his beard, watching as Sunstone pulled an ornately carved pipe from the fringed pipe bag that he held balanced across his lap. Eagle feathers decorated the carved stem of the pipe, along with strands of horsehair and strips of fur. The pipe measured the full span of Sunstone's arms. He held it over the thin wisp of smoking incense that wafted up from the altar, purifying it in the pungent fumes.

"From this Square of Mellowed Earth, we offer prayers to the Ones Above. The stem of the pipe is strong, like the backs of the scattered ones. The bowl of the pipe is red, like the blood of the prairie people. Hear us, Wakan Tanka, Onsimala Ye! *Hye*."

Sunstone took a pinch of *cansasa* and scattered it on the altar. Then he filled the stone bowl and, holding the pipe sideways, lifted it to the Sky, then lowered it to the Earth, and finally to the Four Winds. The men in the tipi were silent. Gregory looked around for Caws Like Magpie. The lecher had not shown his face.

Sunstone used a hot coal from the spirit fire to light the *cansasa*. "*Peta-oihankesni*, flame of our grandfathers, flame of our grandchildren. *Hye!*" After taking a long draw on the pipe he passed it, stem first, to Wolfskin Necklace. His adopted son, probably five winters shy of Gregory's near-fifty years, inhaled the pipe's sacred smoke, then passed it on to Gregory.

No one stirred in the big lodge. No one spoke. Gregory held the pipe to his mouth and inhaled. The smoke filled his throat and his lungs sucked it hungrily downward. His breath seemed to bellow loudly in the solemn stillness and he suddenly became fearful of committing some unknown sacrilege—like when he was a wee lad in the kirk. Lordy, he must be going daft, thinking of a thing like that at a time like this.

At least he knew to pass the pipe to his left. It hadn't been that many years since last he palavered with the Sioux. He exhaled the pungent smoke and was offering the pipe to the man sitting next to him, a tall wiry fellow, when Caws Like Magpie barged through the oval door flap of the tipi and yelled, "The *wasicu* does not belong in the Red Council Lodge!"

The words seared the solemn lodge like molten lava as Magpie, forced to bend over at his thick waist, charged in. Large dentalium-shell earrings swung forward, framing his angry face. The black stripe painted on his right cheek was wider and darker than normal, and, for a split second, he reminded Gregory of a giant jumping spider about to leap.

"The pipe travels the sacred circle," Wolfskin Necklace said quietly. "Those within the circle are brothers."

Gregory cursed Magpie silently. He didn't dare fight him here, now. *The cowardly brown-skin had better watch the day when I black me own face against him. What I wouldn't give to wade into his liver with me claymore, drive it clear up to the Green!*

"It is an insult to the Lakotas to call *wasicus* brothers." Caws Like Magpie spat the words out as he straightened his bony frame, pointing at Gregory with a skeletal hand. The dried skin of an old crow, attached to his wrist as a *wotawe*, a warrior society badge, dangled in the air. His wide, ornately decorated belt appeared to cut him in half, separating the two black, fanglike feathers hanging around his neck from his gaudily quilled and fringed leggings.

The man seated next to Gregory took the pipe and forced himself to inhale slowly. Magpie squatted down near the door flap, in the only available space. Deeply inset eyes stared at Gregory across the breadth of the tipi. Gregory returned the challenging stare. Magpie looked away, feigning a glance toward the circulating pipe.

"One winter ago," Sunstone said, "during the Moon of Making Fat, when the Juneberries ripened like a woman with child, we met as one great Lakota nation. A great nation!"

"Hoye," the men muttered in agreement, nodding their heads.

"Our camp circles covered the earth like stars gathered in the heavens."

"Yelo," the men said. "It is so."

Sunstone raised a bent, leathery finger to scratch the side of his wide nose. "A winter ago, the whole nation gathered in celebration. Many warriors danced beneath the sacred tree, dragging the sacred *tatanka* skulls. Many voices sang the great songs, raising their voices in prayer."

Gregory turned his head slightly, watching as the pipe was passed to Magpie. Magpie closed yellowed teeth over the buffalo hide that covered the mouth of the stem, and the burning tobacco hissed and reddened. A serpentine wisp of gray smoke rose from the bowl.

"Now, the Great Chief of the *wasicus* wants us to gather. He sends Broken Hand with word of a great powwow to be held on Horse Creek."

Broken Hand. Gregory knew him as Fitzpatrick. Thomas Fitzpatrick. A trapper who sure as hell knew fat cow from poor bull. He'd rendezvoused with him at Cache Valley back in '26, before Fitzpatrick was assigned able lieutenant of one of the fur brigades. Last time he'd seen him was in '34, when he heard Sunstone's band had moved south and was camped on Bitter Cottonwood. Heard the old trapper'd become an Indian agent, had a hand in turning the old trading post on Laramie Fork into an army fort.

"Broken Hand sends messengers up the waters of the Shell, the Elk River, even the Big Muddy. Word travels to all the Lakotas—to all the tribes. Our friends, the Sahiyelas, and the Mahpiyatos. Even the Susunis, the Palanis, and the Hewaktokas."

"Hiya!" Caws Like Magpie spat into the dirt. "It is said some of the Kangis will send Woman Chief. *Hoh!* A woman! The Kangis are *tokas.* The Palanis. The Susunis. All, *tokas!*"

The man seated to Gregory's left spoke up. "It is true. We have always moved the arrows against these tribes. My grandfather counted coup against these warriors. My great-grandfather counted coup, even his great-grandfather. But now an enemy invades our territory who knows nothing of our ways."

"*Hoye*. Dark Cloud is right," some of the men muttered in agreement.

"The *wasicus* crawl across our hunting grounds like ants," said Magpie, fingering his dangling feathers. The shells of his long earrings clicked together as he shook his head.

"Do the ants worry about the pesky lizard when the great rains flood their hills?" asked Wolfskin Necklace.

Aye, no sense in fighting with other brown-skins when the real enemy was white. 'Twas clear as powder horn, what Wolfskin said. Money-hungry men heading for California had flooded the plains like hordes of locusts, their eyes bright with the promise of gold, their hearts filled with greed for the mother lode. Thousands of white men. Killing the grass they trod on. Leaving cholera and the pox in their wake. Gregory doubted the Oglalas realized how many had already passed.

"Our hunters must go farther and farther to find meat for their families. Dead *pte* rot on the prairie, slaughtered by the *wasicus*," the man sitting next to Magpie said, nodding at Caws Like Magpie in agreement.

"It is said that even some of our own Oglalas, desperate for *wasicu*'s liquor, slaughter the *pte*," said a man across the fire.

"*Hosti*." The men shook their heads, regretful of this sorrowful thing.

"Broken Hand calls us together," said Sunstone, "because he knows these things are bad. He asks the Great White Chief to compensate us for this damage. He asks us to lay down our bows and make peace with one another."

"The *wasicus* do not understand peace," said Caws Like Magpie. The words pelleted across the tipi like hail falling on hard ground. Gregory felt his jaws tighten, his teeth clench.

"Peace," said Sunstone, looking directly at Magpie, "is harder for some of us to understand than others." The double meaning of his words drifted through the circle of men.

"If we are to go to this great powwow on Horse Creek," asked Dark Cloud, "how can we trust our enemies to respect the *wasicus*' council? It would be a dangerous place to take our women and children."

"*Han,*" agreed several men. "A foolish place."

"And if we don't go?" asked Wolfskin Necklace.

"Broken Hand sends word that the great council will not be held until the Moon of Yellow Leaves," said Sunstone, receiving the pipe, which had completed its circle. He held the pipe out to an elder shaman sitting quietly, a man who as of yet had said nothing. "Tell us, High Bear," Sunstone said, "what are the holy man's thoughts?"

The man called High Bear rubbed his chin, then took the pipe. "Two moons will pass before the hair on the *pte* calves grows thick." He paused. The crowd listened patiently, even Magpie. "The *pte* do not push away their suckling young; they know it takes more than a few moons for their young to grow strong and wise. We must not rush our decision."

He raised the ceremonial pipe toward the center of the circle. "We smoke the sacred pipe, like infants suckling at our mothers' breasts. Our Earth Mother nourishes us. Father Sky guides us. The great Skan gives motion to the two-leggeds and the four-leggeds. Skan will lead us."

"*Hye,*" said the men in low, guttural voices. "We thank the spirits."

"*Mitakuye oyasin,*" Sunstone said, his deep voice rising above the murmurings of the men.

We are all related Gregory knew it meant.

"*Mitakuye oyasin,*" nodded the men in unison. The traditional prayerful ending resonated in the round lodge. Gregory looked at Caws Like Magpie, who sat silent, his fleshy mouth clenched shut, a scowl darkening his shadowy face.

Like a spider about to leap, thought Gregory. Related? Like hell! Not by a long chalk!

The door flap of the tipi was lifted, and a shaft of sunlight entered the lodge, catching Gregory full in the face. He narrowed his eyes against the glare and stared through the opening to the camp circle beyond.

Coming down the path that led into the village from the outlying prairie, Turtle Woman and Skye, with baskets tucked beneath their arms, were walking side by side. Their shoulders almost touched. They walked with heads bent, as if sharing some womanly confidence. *Mitakuye oyasin.* Sunstone's words echoed ominously. All related? Perhaps, more than Gregory cared to believe . . .

18

THE SACRIFICE

Caws Like Magpie puckered his fleshy lips and collected saliva, cradling it in the hollow of his tongue. He forced the spittle from his mouth and hurled it into the trodden grass near the edge of the tipi. It landed on a large slab of quartz which had been baking in the scorching sun since daybreak, and sizzled on the hot rock.

"The *wikoskala* asks for trouble. She wanders away alone, then returns carrying half her clothing." He had also seen Mahto, riding stealthily into camp in the early dawn. "The cocky scout. They both ask for trouble."

"*Wey, wey,*" whined Doublewoman Dreamer. She was calling her fleabag of a dog.

"Do you not hear me, woman?"

"Here, *sunka.* Good girl," she said, ignoring her son's disgruntled mutterings. The black-and-white bitch answered the call and emerged from the shadowed entrance of her small, cavelike wigwam, bringing a sour smell with her into the open air.

"Yes, I hear you," Doublewoman Dreamer said finally. "But I grow tired of your complaining." The dog wagged her tail submissively, keeping it half tucked. Magpie lifted his arm in a threatening manner, as if to strike, and a pitiful whine came from the cowering animal.

"Magpie, you behave like the son of a wolverine! Leave the *sunka* alone," snarled his mother, narrowing her rodentlike eyes into dark slits.

"*Your* son, Mother—the son of a *witko* woman." Truly, the offspring of a wolverine, he thought to himself.

"Ha! *Han!* What other woman would have endured so much pain to birth an ungrateful son? *Ey-ee*, why am I being punished with such a son?"

"You whine like your *sunka*. Have you no honor? You are the mother of a Naca. And do not forget, your quilling marks fill the lining of the Red Council Lodge as well. You could have been the best quiller in the tribe, better even than Sunstone's woman. But you chose to spend your time chasing the men instead. Now she is the one who walks like a lizard, her pointed nose leading the way."

A bead of sweat dripped down Magpie's temple, smearing the black stripe which cut from the corner of his eye to his bony jaw. Another bead of sweat formed on his generous upper lip, which was incongrously fleshy compared to his long spiny neck.

"The red-haired *wasicu* was in the council lodge," he said.

"In the council lodge?" asked Doublewoman Dreamer.

"*Han.* He was permitted to smoke the sacred pipe."

"*Hiya!* The sacred pipe?"

"Took a seat of honor, too."

"*Hiya!* A seat of honor?"

"You sound like that black bag of feathers, repeating everything I say. *Han!* Seated in a place of honor in the council lodge, smoking the sacred pipe." Caws Like Magpie glanced from his mother to the pet crow and shook his head. He was fed up with her—fed up with everyone, especially the tribal elders. They were fools, all of them.

"I thought you were butchering those pups today?" he asked her.

"I am," she answered, affectionately rubbing the black-and-white bitch behind the ears. "No more pups hanging on your *azes*, heh, girl? You will thank me."

Only two pups remained from a litter of five. The people had feasted on the others during the celebration of the Sun Dance. Magpie watched as the two fat animals staggered from the doghouse out into the bright sun.

"Well, then. Get it done," he snapped at her.

Casting him an embittered look, which he ignored, she grabbed one of the sleek fat puppies by the nape of the neck and carried it over to a pile of dried fuel. The mother dog followed her, whining.

"Your belly is already swollen with young *sunkas*," she said to the bitch. "You'll be glad to be rid of these leeches."

She retrieved a few cottonwood branches from the wood pile and tossed them into the fire. The flames flared up, snatching at the air with arms of hot orange and fiery red. The captured puppy struggled in the woman's strong grasp and the crow, tethered to his perch, strained against the leather thong and choked forth a feeble *caw, caw.*

Magpie licked his dry lips. He walked to the entrance of the tipi, entered, and helped himself to a drink from the water paunch hanging just inside the door.

"This water tastes like gut slime. Why do you not hang it in the shade outside, where the breeze can cool it?" The muttered complaint did not penetrate the thick hide walls of the tipi. He stooped and went back out into the glaring sun. His mother's only friend, Black Tail, had appeared out of nowhere. She looked as bedraggled as his mother.

"Here," she said to Doublewoman Dreamer as she slipped the nooses from two long cords over the puppy's head, "I have brought the ropes."

Doublewoman set the puppy down next to its sibling, and Magpie watched as the snared pup scurried toward his mother. "You will not get away, little *sunka*," he said under his breath. The pup's escape efforts ended abruptly as the two women tightened their ropes, each pulling from opposite directions until no slack

remained, pulling until the nooses tightened. The puppy's sniveling ceased as the breath was slowly squeezed from him. Caws Like
Magpie found he could not watch. *They enjoy it. The two witko
women enjoy it.* He looked away. Tradition demanded that the
blood of a sacrificial dog not be spilled while the animal remained
alive. Still. He pretended to sharpen his knife as the two women
repeated the procedure with the second pup.

By the time he turned back, Doublewoman Dreamer was
kneeling near the two limp bodies, feeding more kindling onto the
growing fire. The black-and-white bitch sniffed at her dead offspring. Magpie noticed that Black Tail had disappeared.

"Did your friend disappear into the lodge of the *sunka?*" he
taunted, laughing at his own joke. At the sound of Magpie's voice,
the black-and-white dog lifted her head, and a low, almost imperceptible growl came from her throat.

"Joke too much, my son, and you could feel the noose around
your scrawny neck."

Magpie ignored her and watched the fire send red sparks high
into the hot, still air. White-tipped flames licked at the sky, as if
kin to the white-hot sun. Doublewoman picked up a puppy with
each hand and, holding them by their soft-boned back feet, tossed
them quickly onto the burning cottonwood. The flames soon engulfed their lifeless bodies, the fire singeing the short black-and-
white hairs from their bodies. Magpie twitched his nose at the
pungent, sickening smoke that billowed from the blaze.

"You hate Turtle Woman. Why do you make a gift of boiled
puppy?"

"Ha! You forget. I dream of the Double Woman."

"You may have dreamed of the Double Woman long ago,
when there was still flesh on your bones, but you look like Anog
Ite."

"You, my ungrateful son, see only the ugly face, marked with
the *wasicu*'s sickness. But I, like Anog Ite, have two faces. To some,
I choose to show the face of generosity."

"Generosity? You fool yourself, old woman."

"I fool others."

"You fool no one. They call you *witko.*"

Reaching across the flames with a forked stick, Doublewoman Dreamer retrieved the singed bodies of the pups. "I am *witko*. Crazy as a red-haired *wasicu* who enters the camp of his enemies."

Caws Like Magpie smiled. His mother's occasional barbed wit entertained him. He reached a curved and yellowed fingernail up to his scalp and scratched his scalp lock, causing the silver trade discs that trailed down his back to clank.

"You have more wisdom than the Ones Who Decide," he said to her. "Maybe next time, I'll take you to the Red Council Lodge. Ha! That would give the Big Bellies something to talk about."

"We women send you Big Bellies to the council lodge to get you out of our way," she retorted, setting the singed bodies on a large, flat rock. "The real decisions are made around the cook fires of the women."

In less time than it would have taken a warrior to black his face for war, his mother chopped the charred bodies into cooking-size pieces, then placed them into a large kettle of water to boil. As the liquid began to simmer, the dismembered heads bobbed to the surface.

"The choicest portion," she said to him, pointing a bloody finger at the flesh-covered skulls.

"To be served by the choicest *wikoskala*," Caws Like Magpie said for her, insinuation tainting his words.

"To the first-chosen warrior," she finished, turning to face him, her suspicious eyes making it clear that she understood the wickedness of his thoughts.

Bitterness festered in him like an abscess. Never had he been the first-chosen. His was a life of scraps—meager tidbits to be scavenged for, like a buzzard picking at decaying flesh. Once, only once in a long life of many winters, had he had a chance for the choicest morsel, and he had let it pass him by.

But now a second chance had fallen into his lap like a ripe plum. This opportunity would not pass him by. He intended to have his fill.

19

THE OVERTURE

A celebration? Gregory was in no mood for it. He had half a mind to shake the dust from his kilt, don his Highland regalia, unsheath his claymore, and finish this damnable thing with Caws Like Magpie once and for all—have his own bloody fandango!

But one look at his comely daughter, and at the joy on her grandmother's face, and he couldn't bring himself to spoil their fun. He leaned into the willow backrest, stretched his legs out onto the hide-covered floor of the tipi, and listened.

"Oh, no, Grandmother," Skye said, shaking a head of unruly hair at Turtle Woman, who stood holding an ornately embroidered elk-teeth dress up to Skye. "I couldn't wear it. It's much too fine."

"I have told you: tonight there will be a ceremony—dancing and feasting. You are the *takoja* of the great Shirt Wearer Sunstone. A too-small dress, torn and soiled, does not honor the occasion."

"But then you would have nothing to wear." Skye stared into the near-empty parfleche from which Turtle Woman had just taken the ceremonial dress. "And are you not the wife of the great Shirt Wearer? For you to wear your root-digging, hide-scraping dress would not honor the occasion either." She gave her grandfather a smile, then winked at him mischievously. *A wink?* thought Gregory. *The lass is making herself at home.*

"*Mitawicu*, our *takoja* has outwitted you, like a fox toying with a prairie mouse," Sunstone said, a smile softening the deep, craggy features of his weathered face. "She is right. It is you who should wear the elk teeth."

Gregory shifted his weight. It had been so long since he had said *mitawicu*. Wife.

"*E-i-i-i!* What am I to do—I am no match for the two of you." Turtle Woman's voice was harsh, but a furtive glance at her moist eyes told Gregory of her true emotions. She had waited many long years, he knew, to have her granddaughter stand before her.

"It will be all right, Grandmother. I will gather purple asters from the field, braid them into necklaces. I'll wash my dress and let down the hem. Perhaps I will ask you to adorn my hair—in proper Lakota fashion." Skye's voice grew quiet as she lowered her gaze to the floor. "I will not shame you, Unci. I promise."

Gregory watched the two women from the corner of his eye, buried feelings of pain and anguish hurling headlong into guilt and remorse. *He* knew where there was another elk-teeth dress. And he knew, staring at his daughter's maturing figure, that the dress would fit like a glove. Aye, the lass would look as lovely in the wedding dress as had her mother. Durst he open the bundle? Had he the courage?

"Naked Warrior," Sunstone interrupted his thoughts.

He turned to his father-in-law.

"Our women's problem," said Sunstone, "is not so serious that it should hover over you like a thundercloud—not as serious as the decisions that face the Shirt Wearers of the council lodge. Perhaps these are the thoughts that darken your mood?"

"Aye," Gregory agreed, even though the statement was only half true. "It's been on me mind some."

"You have more thoughts that you wish to share with this old Wicasa about the big council?"

"Nay, this old hoss has been holed up in the woods too long. First I heard about a big palaver on Horse Creek was here in your council lodge."

"Many of our people are tempted by the *wasicu*'s promises of gifts and trinkets. I fear these gifts are like the flick of a rattlesnake's tongue—hypnotizing one, making one forget the hidden fangs."

"Aye. Any way ye lay your sights, trailing your people to Horse Creek is a risky thing to do."

"This Broken Hand—he can be trusted?"

"Fitzpatrick? Oh, you can trust him. He ain't a crawly one, and he damn sure knows which way the stick floats. Question is, can he trust *his* big chiefs?"

"Broken Hand invites all my people's *tokas* to this powwow on Horse Creek. The Kangis. The Susunis. The Palanis. All of them. Are we expected to trust them as well?"

"Ye sure as hell didn't trust the Arikara back in Twenty-three, up on the Missouri, did ye? Ye just about got your hump ribs tickled by an Arikara's tomahawk, if I recollect right."

"But instead, the Palanis felt the sting of Naked Warrior's sword. And that was not the only coup counted by my friend that day."

"Aye, and you and the rest of the Sioux counted many coup, as well."

"But the soldiers," said Sunstone, shaking his head, "they fought like dogs. Cowering and whimpering—afraid of the puny Palanis." Sunstone made a gesture of disgust with his hand. "I am not sure it is wise to trust men who act like dogs."

Camp murmurs filtered in under the tipi's open door flap. Brown-skinned children, some naked, some wearing breech-cloths, scampered between the lodges. Three galloped by on make-believe horses, spearing a rolling hoop with whittled spears. A little farther, near the lodges of the Muddy Water camp, Gregory watched four girls entice a smaller boy to stand in the center of a blanket. Once he was there, the girls grabbed the corners of the blanket, pulling it tautly between them, and tossed the boy quickly into the air.

"It is good to be back among our people?" Sunstone asked, pulling Gregory's attention back inside.

"Aye. It is good." He hesitated. "It is also not so good."

"Memories, my son, are like the wind, coming at us from many directions." Sunstone's dark eyes became still, like deep pools of shadowed water. "Sometimes they soothe, like a gentle breeze during the Moon of Strawberries. But sometimes they are not so kind." He stared intently at Gregory. "But memories, like the wind, cannot be turned away. It is not wise to try to outrun them."

Not wise? *Cowardly* might be a better word. Aye, he admitted it. He'd been on the run for more than ten long years. And where had it gotten him? Hadn't brought his wife back, that was damn certain. And he sure as hell didn't know his daughter like a father ought to. All he had to show for it were some dusty old stones. He looked at Skye, who knelt on the far side of the tipi wearing only her shift and holding her soiled dress in her hand.

"Cover yourself with a robe, *takoja*, while I go wash this sorry garment," Turtle Woman said, taking the faded calico from her granddaughter. Then she handed Skye a porcupine-quill hairbrush. "In case you wish to brush the snarls from your hair while I am gone," she suggested subtly.

Kneeling like that, half-naked, with her disheveled hair loose about her shoulders and the soiled bottoms of her bare feet exposed, his daughter looked like an orphan—or worse, a hangabout-the-fort *femme du pays.* Blasted coward! Gregory cursed himself, staring off into the distance. *How long are ye going to make her pay the price for your grief? How many bloody years?*

Grandfather leaned against his backrest, alone with his thoughts, and said nothing as Skye pulled the brush through the snarls in her hair. Father just sat there staring through the open door with a strange expression on his face. In one of his moods again, she supposed. Then, suddenly, his expression changed to one of angry determination. He rose from the willow backrest and went out, nearly colliding with Skye's grandmother, who was just returning from the creek. Turtle Woman lowered her gaze quickly and stepped out of his way. Skye shook her head at her father's abruptness. *Men. Like bulls thrashing through the undergrowth.*

Within minutes, he returned. Skye's breath caught in her throat and her heart quickened, for in his broad callused hands he carried the rawhide pannier that sheltered his kilt and heirloom brooch, his bearskin hat and the long-silent bagpipes. The same pannier in which Mother's things had been so long sequestered.

"Your father is a foolish man," he said to her, giving Skye's grandfather a quick glance before setting the pannier down in front of her. "Ye need not be wearing a faded rag of a dress to the fandango. Everything ye'll be needing is in there." Then, as abruptly as he had entered, he turned, strode out of the tipi, and was gone.

Skye, dumbfounded, stared at the pannier. The moment swelled, pregnant with possibilities—a great eagerness to open the closed pannier, a fear of the symbolic act. As soon as she opened it, she knew, she would no longer be able to blame Father for shutting her away from Mother's memory, could no longer use the locked trunk, and now the pannier, as an excuse not to face her heritage. She turned to Turtle Woman, searching the deep creases of her grandmother's face and her brown, ageless eyes—looking for a sign, a glimmer of herself, perhaps, in the old woman's features.

"Do not fear the power of your mixed bloods, *takoja*." Her grandmother spoke in a low throaty voice that echoed back to Skye from her grief-stricken childhood. "Do not fear the memories, *takoja*." This time, she spoke only the Lakota.

Again, she reads my very thoughts.

Then her grandmother looked at her grandfather and the two exchanged a brief look. Grandmother cleared her throat and discreetly, though not discreetly enough, nodded her head toward the open door flap. Sunstone rose and left the tipi, leaving the women alone.

For a few moments, they said nothing. From outside, Skye could hear the call of a meadowlark. The flutelike notes lit upon the tapered tips of the tipi's lodgepoles and filtered in through the smoke hole, filling the silence between them. She took a deep breath, then spoke.

"Mother once told me," she said to her grandmother, "that the meadowlark speaks the Lakota tongue, and can be understood by all who know how to listen with their hearts."

"*Han*. As I once told her, and as my *unci* once told me."

"I think I have much to learn from the meadowlark," Skye confessed, trying to apologize, for she knew her grandmother sensed her shame. She turned to face the pannier and finally, with trembling hands, undid the leather strap that held it closed, freeing the memories that had been locked away for ten long years.

The sun completed its arc across the great expanse of open sky, leaving frothy streaks of purple and orange in its wake. Nestled in the shadows of the mountains, the camp of the Oglalas welcomed the coolness of dusk.

The young people, dressed in their finest clothing and painted and adorned for the occasion, milled anxiously around the perimeter of the central tipi. This lodge, with its hide coverings rolled more than halfway up, resembled a pavilion, and would provide protection for the dancers while at the same time opening the ceremonies to view.

A few bold women, parading about in dresses adorned with dentalium shells and trade trinkets, cast brief flirtatious looks at the ornately dressed bachelor warriors who passed by.

"See the dreaming women," one maiden whispered to another, pointing at Doublewoman Dreamer and Black Tail. "They dress like *wikoskalas*, yet hide half their wrinkled faces behind shawls."

The women had indeed cloaked their old, bent bodies in dresses of the finest deerskin, embroidered with exquisite quillwork. But loosely woven shawls, draped over their heads like hoods, hid half their faces from view. They wandered about, pointing at and taunting unwary victims.

"See how they've painted their eyes, trying to look beautiful? And powdered their cheeks . . ."

"*Welo*, too beautiful to recognize!"

The two young maidens giggled, hiding their own faces behind their hands. Then Doublewoman Dreamer and Black Tail pointed at a would-be warrior, embarrassing the boy. "He is the one!" they yelled, laughing. "He is the one!"

"*Haye*, look—that poor boy doesn't know which way to run!"

"*Ai-i-i-i!*" the maidens exclaimed. "Let's move away before the *witko* women point at us." The girls slipped quickly into the crowd, leaving the boy to fend for himself.

On the outskirts of the camp circle, Gregory Macdonald was surveying the scene like a renegade wolf. He spotted the young scout, the one who had accompanied Wolfskin Necklace to his cabin in the Medicine Bows, standing beside a wickiup. "Mahto," he recalled, speaking the warrior's name aloud. The scout wandered toward the ceremonial lodge, where a fire, visible through the lodge's raised sides, already burned.

The Kiyuksa scout cut a more impressive figure than Gregory had remembered. He walked boldly up to the central lodge, the bear claws slung about his neck like a sword upon the hip. Coup feathers sprouted from his dark head like eagle wings. He would make a worthy opponent. *Or a worthy ally.*

The unmarried lasses stole flirtatious glances at Mahto as he walked by, hoping, Gregory assumed, for a chance to capture the scout's attention. Breathcatcher had once looked at Gregory that way—shyly, teasingly. Looks that had captured his passion, and his heart. He knew about Night Dances. Remembered how, once her father had finally accepted his offer of marriage, they had danced their own night dance, celebrated in their own earthly fashion. *God, how he had loved her womanly ways.*

The half-bitten moon, just beginning to show itself, hung low above the chalk-white cliffs. Gregory shook the memories from his mind. Scanning the rest of the scene, he searched the lodges of the Muddy Water camp for Caws Like Magpie, but did not find him. "Macdonald," he warned himself, staring into dimness, "ye had better be watching your backside this dark night, lest that cowardly brown-skin has more than dancing on his mind."

He turned his gaze back to the cliffs and thought of his sheathed claymore, and for a moment was tempted to don his Highland kilt—to unearth his sword and his dismembered bagpipes as he had finally unearthed for Skye her mother's things. Would not that be a sight to rile his enemy, to turn away even the foulest of Droch Shuils?

"If you're keeping to the dark on purpose, Magpie," he said into the graying dusk, "with hair-raising on your mind, I can surely flush ye out, make wolf meat of your cowardly carcass."

Aye, after all these years, the thought was tempting indeed.

20

THE NIGHT DANCE BEGINS

Turtle Woman stood within the ceremonial lodge, supervising the young women who had carried the cooking pots to the central fire.

"*Hiya*, not there," she said as two clumsy girls nearly upset one of the hot pots. "Over there, near the fire." Foolish girls, acting like heat-struck does under the spell of a rutting moon.

She had tried to trade Doublewoman a *pte* robe for the two puppies, but the old hag had only shaken her finger at her. "My *sunkas* are worth more than the scraggly robe of an old *tatanka*," she had complained. "Besides, they are gifts—from the Dreamer to the grandmother of the *wasicu* girl. Ha!"

It had galled Turtle Woman to accept the gifts. The puppies were not gifts at all, of course, but tools with which the dreaming woman could weave her foul deeds. The question remained, what foul deeds this time?

She dismissed the girls with a nod of her head, glancing at the kettles and the rich broth full of tender puppy flesh. *At least the old woman raises sweet meat*, she thought as she headed back to her own lodge to see why her *takoja* still kept herself hidden.

* * *

Mahto held back from entering the tipi with the other dancers, his dark, almond-shaped eyes scanning the pretty *wikoskalas* who already lined the south side of the lodge. He lifted a hand to his throat and touched the turtle shell. The shell was warm to the touch, smooth and round. The light-skinned granddaughter of Turtle Woman was nowhere to be seen.

"*Hau*, cousin!" His friend, True Dog, jostled him from behind. "*Hiyu wo*. Come," he said, pushing Mahto through the doorway. "Howls at Moon must dance tonight."

His friend, also a respected scout, called him by his second name—a name earned last winter when the two of them had returned to camp after successfully leading many hunters to a herd of wandering elk. They had both howled wildly that night as the hungry people feasted on fresh meat, praising the two scouts with exaggerated gestures of grandness and gifts of gratitude.

True Dog pulled him into the tipi, where they stood at the end of the line of young male dancers. "Howls at Moon wishes to impress someone tonight? My friend is gaily dressed."

"And so are you, True Dog. I see you have borrowed some of my coup feathers."

"No, but I'll borrow a handful now!" True Dog teased back, pretending to grab the eagle feathers from Mahto's scalp lock. The two men sparred good-naturedly until they heard the music commence, a signal to the nervous young women to begin.

The females approached the line of men, each choosing a partner by shyly kicking at his moccasins. A round-faced *wikoskala* from the Night Cloud Band giggled at True Dog, then kicked at his moccasin but missed, nearly hitting him in the shin instead.

"Go!" Mahto called after his friend. "Go dance with the pretty shin-kicker!"

Within seconds another *wikoskala* approached Mahto—Lost Morning, the daughter of Dark Cloud, a Big Belly. A pretty, strong-limbed girl, she was coveted by many of the warriors. He soon found himself facing her, standing in the dance line. Mahto kept his smile to himself and, grasping her by the belt, waited for the dancing to begin.

Each couple, their fingers hooked in each other's belts, two-stepped around the fire and the simmering pots of puppy stew to the beat of the pounding drums, the music's rhythm vibrating up their bent knees as they danced sunwise within the huge tipi. On-lookers, watching through the raised sides of the lodge, moved their own bodies up and down to the beat of the drums and the cadence of the song, enjoying the Night Dance, one of the rare occasions when young men and women were permitted to dance together.

Mahto looked the girl in the eyes, his boldness embarrassing her. Then he let his gaze search the crowd. Sunstone and Wolf-skin Necklace were standing near the entrance of the tipi, deep in conversation.

The circle of dancers continued, stopping briefly when the singing paused, then beginning again. Then, after the fourth pause, the dancers returned to their separate places. Mahto looked away, allowing his modest dancing partner to pass by before walking back to the north side of the lodge.

"How was Shin-Kicker?" he teased True Dog. "Did you tread on her moccasins with your webbed feet?"

"You lucky blunt-horn, you." True Dog poked Mahto in the ribs with a bent elbow. "Every warrior here was hoping the daughter of Dark Cloud would choose him, and she chooses to dance with one who howls at the moon!"

"Lost Morning has her father's good sense."

"But not his speed," True Dog said jokingly, "for she waited too long to ask me, and so another chose me first!"

Mahto laughed, trying to act interested in his friend's light-hearted banter, but his mind was far away, the sound of the drums reminding him of how fiercely his own heart had beaten that morning. As he recalled the Light-skinned One—naked beneath the cottonwood tree—he felt his chest begin to pound again. But as he thought of the rearing seed-horse, thrashing at the empty air above the mare's back, he could only clench his jaw, feeling the scar tissue that cut across his face begin to harden into a long, furrowed ridge.

The rolled-up sides of the large lodge allowed Skye to peek, unnoticed, at the dancers. She would have recognized Mahto immediately even if he had not been wearing the superb bear claw necklace or the same black-tipped eagle-wing feathers in his hair. Even the ornately quilled armlet on his upper arm was familiar. But he looked taller in the fringed leggings than she recalled. Perhaps it was the fancy moccasins, sewn with what seemed like thousands of tiny seed beads. Or the furred and quilled breastplate, with the tail of a fox hanging from the strip of leather around Mahto's waist. He looked so tall—much taller than the six feet Skye guessed him to be.

She drew in her breath. He was magnificent. More magnificent than she had dared to remember.

She watched him circle the dance lodge with the young Oglala woman, a striking dark-haired beauty whose long braids hung nearly to her slender waist. They two-stepped around the center fire, their bodies moving with the fluidity of a mountain stream. Skye felt herself begin to retreat, small steps carrying her away from the circle. *I will never be one of them.*

She fought the urge to run—to flee to her grandmother's tipi, or better yet, to saddle Duncan and head back to the Medicine Bows, where all was familiar, where no strange, unbidden urges caused her hands to tremble and her blood to race. But then, as she watched the two of them complete the circle—a magnificently handsome Indian couple, regal in their ceremonial plumage—a new feeling, a twinge of jealous rivalry, stirred her blood even more. *Coward*, she chastised herself. *Be bold.*

Skye let her hands fall to her sides, caressing the skirt of soft doeskin. She was no longer clad in a tattered and faded calico dress; she wore, instead, a dress as fine as any other Indian maiden wore tonight—finer, perhaps. It was, after all, her mother's wedding dress. She fondled the smooth, ivory elk teeth that adorned the bodice of the dress, then looked down to marvel again at her mother's moccasins. Hundreds of brightly colored beads formed the five-pointed star and comet. The heirloom design strengthened her. *You have nothing to fear.* She repeated the words to herself, once in English, then again in Lakota. *Walitakya. Walitakya.* With a deep breath she lifted her chin, straightened her shoulders, and faced the crowd.

Moving through the throng of onlookers encircling the large tipi, she worked her way toward her grandfather, trying to ignore the stares and whispers that followed. But before she reached him, she felt a gnarled hand grasp her by the shoulder. She turned to find two women facing her, holding shawls over their heads, hiding half of their painted faces.

"We meet again, *takoja*," said the nearest woman, digging sharp nails into Skye's shoulder. The woman was dressed in maiden fashion, like the young women inside the tipi, yet seemed much older. Her face, or what Skye could see of it, was heavily caked with powder to appear flawless, possibly even handsome from a distance. Bold lines of charcoal enlarged the woman's eyes, or rather, the one eye not hidden by the shawl. There was something familiar, something eerie, about the woman's piercing half-gaze. For what reason did she hide her face?

"The young *wasicu* dresses like one of the People this night. That is good. Then she can partake in *all* of the People's festivities." The woman's voice became thin and high-pitched. "Be prepared to bite the knife, two-tone girl."

Skye pulled away from the woman's grasp, her skin beginning to crawl at the familiar, yet unfamiliar, voice. Twice now she had heard mention of a knife-biting ceremony. The image sent a chill up her spine. Perhaps her grandmother would explain this thing to her. But, for the moment, her grandfather had seen her and was beckoning her to join the other dancers within the large tipi.

Fixing her sights on the blazing ceremonial fire, whose flames cast long, spiraling shadows onto the upraised walls of the lodge, she approached her grandfather, stepping from the darkness of evening into the flickering light.

"*Hiyu wo*, step forward, you cowardly coyote," True Dog teased Mahto. "The drums signal the brave warriors to now choose their partners."

Percussive drumbeats and the tremolo of many voices undulated through the large tipi, signaling that the dance had begun again. As the milling dancers formed their separate lines, Mahto once more searched the impressive crowd of young people, frowning. Where was the granddaughter of Sunstone?

"Shin-Kicker casts her eyes upon you." He elbowed True Dog. "You go—pick the bold one who awaits you."

"*Hiya*, I had another in mind." True Dog looked at his friend. "You have not yet stood beneath the courting robe with the daughter of the Big Belly? Nor played the music of the flute for her to hear?"

"No, I have not *yet* done these things with Dark Cloud's daughter." Mahto poked a teasing finger at his comrade's chest.

"What if True Dog wishes to dance with Lost Morning? Does Howls at Moon object?"

"*Hiya*, I do not object. And if I did, you would dance with her anyway."

"Ha! It is true. Ho! I am ready, then."

"Soon," Mahto called after him, "I will have to give you a new name—Son of a Big Belly!"

Mahto glanced at the line of girls, watching as True Dog made his way over to the pretty *wikoskala*. Only a fool would not yet have stood with her beneath the blanket—a fool thinking foolish thoughts about the woman they called Light-skinned One. He could feel the beat of the drum reverberating within his chest, could even feel the drums vibrating the bear claws that dangled on his breast. He touched the leather thong that held the turtle shell. *Fool!* he scorned himself. *You should not even be here. Take your half-breed thoughts and gò!*

Spinning suddenly on his fancy moccasin heels, his thoughts swirling like a whirlwind upon the prairie, he turned and came face-to-face—bear claws and turtle shell to elk-teeth bodice—with the very *wikoskala* from whose image he fled.

All of Skye's casual, well-rehearsed words of greeting turned into a heated flush of embarrassment as Mahto turned to face her. *The turtle-shell necklace! He's wearing the turtle-shell necklace. It was he this morning, riding horseback through the woods!* The blush crawled up her chest, tinting her slender throat and soft cheeks a deep pink—and she was helpless to stop it.

"*Hau!*" Mahto exclaimed, caught off guard. He took half a step backward and let the turtle shell fall from his grasp. He was, Skye realized, as startled as she.

Skye stared at *her* turtle-shell necklace.

"You . . . you . . ." she stammered, "you have my necklace."

"This is true. It was lost. And now it has been found." He seemed to have regained some of his composure.

"Do you make a habit of spying on young women?"

"I make it a habit to go for early rides," he said, his voice rising above the beating of the drums and the voices of the singers. "And I make it a habit, before the sun has risen in the morning sky, to check for thieves among my people's horses."

"Aye, it was you, then, after all." The hot flush of embarrassment seized her again. This was not how she had envisioned renewing the Kiyuksa's acquaintance!

Mahto smiled, a slow pleased smile that bent the thin scar below his brow into a curve. This *wikoskala* was no deceiver of men. The bad medicine of the Bone Keepers had nothing to do with her, or with them. The doubts themselves were bad medicine. The words to the song of his Tokala suddenly became part of his thoughts. *If there is anything difficult, if there is anything dangerous, that is mine to do.*

In a heartbeat, his eyes took in every detail—neatly braided hair that glistened like fox fur, eyes the color of ripening

chokecherries, a well-rounded bodice under the elk teeth, muscled curves beneath soft doeskin, long legs leading to ornately
beaded moccasins, the heated flush. His eyes missed nothing.
Han, she was worth it!

"Aye," he said, testing the feel of the strange word upon his
tongue, "it was me, then, after all."

The circle of dancers had begun their rotation around the ceremonial fire, and from across the breadth of the tipi Mahto could
see True Dog two-stepping with the daughter of Dark Cloud.
There had been enough talking for a while, more than enough.
He wiped the half-smile from his face.

"We have both come to dance, *han?* The daughter of the red-
haired Naked Warrior will dance with the son of the great Bear
Warrior."

Without waiting for her reply, without seeking her permission, Mahto took Skye's hands and placed them upon his belt.
Then, bending his knees slightly, he tucked his fingers into the
leather tie at her waist, pulled her firmly with him into the circle
of dancers, and into the flickering shadows of flame.

Skye could not be sure, for Mahto allowed no outward sign
to reveal his inner mood, but she thought she detected a faint,
amused glint in his eyes as he spoke her father's nickname. *Naked
Warrior, indeed. This young scout takes a great deal for granted.*
Then, suddenly, the name conjured up a whole new image.
Naked Warrior? The heat of the fire became almost too much to
handle.

21

THE OFFERING

Caws Like Magpie stood in the shadows outside the ceremonial lodge. He lifted an iridescent feather to his nose and, with its hard hollow tip, scratched an annoying itch. Barbs of envy, as pointed as fresh porcupine quills, stabbed into his shriveled heart as he watched Breathcatcher's daughter dance around the fire.

Past winters of hungry moons and cold lodges, summer moons of tall grass and parched throats, all faded into the flames as he imagined himself a young man again, one whose heart still held hope for the many moons yet to come. He imagined his own hands upon Breathcatcher's slender waist as they circled the fire, remembered chasing her through the wildflowers when they were both young pups, remembered her the summer their two camps had joined for the Sun Dance, when she had grown from a gangly pup into a sleek she-dog.

Life then had been good. There had been no sickness, no *wasicu* diseases, no fur trappers to rob the singing waters of their fine-haired creatures—the swims-carrying-stick and the snow-skin and the white-chin. There had been no red-haired *wasicu* waving the sword-of-two-edges in the air like a *witko* man, no mysterious bag of wind breathing loud bellows into the sky like a rutting *tatanka*, driving the young cows into a frenzy.

"Au!" he cried out. The vivid memories themselves had pierced his blackened soul. *Fool. Self-pitying worm. Only the soft are vulnerable. Harden yourself. No Naca allows himself to wallow in the past.*

He stamped his feet, straightening his long, bony legs. The silver trade discs that hung down his back clicked together, sounding like the crickets that hid in the prairie grasses beyond the lodges. He scanned the perimeter of the camp circle, his gaze drawn to the red-haired Scotsman who stood just beyond the outskirts of camp. "Mac-don-ald." The word oozed from Magpie's mouth like mud.

Magpie returned his gaze to the dancers. The *wasicu's* daughter had tucked her fingers into the cord of the Kiyuksa's leggings, only a hairsbreadth from his manhood. "A spike-horn," Magpie sneered to himself. "No match for a proven cracked-horn who has fought many battles, bred many females." He spat bitterly into the dirt, ignoring the other onlookers nearby just outside the ceremonial tipi.

The drums vibrated the night air, the voices of the singers penetrating the growing darkness. The dancers two-stepped sunwise within the great lodge; they formed lines and pivoted around the fire and the simmering stew. Sweat glistened on their high-spirited faces—while Magpie seethed, and schemed.

Magpie could not see inside the steaming paunches from a distance, but he knew what they contained. He had kicked the sniveling black-and-white *sunkas* often enough, when they had wandered away from the safety of their mother into striking distance. He recalled the pungent odor of burning hair and singed hide, and his mouth salivated at the thought of tender, sweet meat. Yet he knew that neither he nor any of the other onlookers would be served the ceremonial stew. Only the young dancers would be so lucky.

Near the entrance of the tipi stood the sponsors of the feast, Sunstone and Turtle Woman. The only elders who stood within the lodge, they remained quiet, allowing the young ones their celebration. Magpie watched them with a sneer on his face—the one-time Shirt Wearer and his One-Only-One wife. *Always the place of honor.*

Inside the tipi, the dancers had begun the teasing rituals of temptation that preceded the ceremonial feast. Two *wikoskalas*—

Lost Morning, the daughter of the Big Belly, and her cousin, Red Grass—each took a wooden bowl filled with puppy stew. Magpie watched as they danced suggestively toward the men, choosing for themselves two worthy partners. Nudging the Kiyuksa gently on the foot, the daughter of Dark Cloud then pivoted and danced away in the direction from which she had just come. Mahto and his cocky friend True Dog, who had also been chosen, followed the two maidens, reaching for the bowls as they danced. The girls turned and pretended to offer them the food, then teasingly withdrew again. Back and forth they went, the girls tantalizing the men with the tempting bowls, the men feigning disappointment when they were snatched from their grasps: *Worthy? I doubt it. The Kiyuksas have more than puppy stew on their minds.*

On the fourth try, Mahto and True Dog were finally allowed to take the prized bowls of simmering stew. Magpie grunted. *Only fools would be so patient.*

He had not missed the look that passed between Mahto and Breathcatcher's daughter as she watched the young scout dance seductively around the fire with Lost Morning. He had not missed the flush of excitement that colored the light skin of the half-blood. Macdonald's daughter. A rancid taste filled Magpie's mouth.

The servers, all *wikoskalas*, had soon distributed small portions of stew to all the bachelors within the huge lodge. Then, in turn, the men approached the young women, teasing and tempting them. True Dog offered his bowl to Lost Morning, then snatched it from her before she could grasp it. Mahto danced up to the Light-skinned One, pulling her from the spectators with his teasing behavior. *The spike-horn has no nerves; he quivers like the skin of a drum.*

Breathcatcher's daughter hung back for a moment, then let the Kiyuksa draw her into the courtship dance. *She moves like a newborn foal, pretending to be shy and unsure of herself. Ha! See, she forgets herself in the frenzy of the drums and moves like a woman.*

She is not so innocent. Magpie remembered the Light-skinned One on the path only that morning—carrying half her clothes— Mahto entering the camp only a short time later, riding in from the direction of the rising sun and the running waters. *You are not so innocent, my pretty wikoskala; the dance of give-and-take is not so new to you.*

"Ha!" cackled Doublewoman through the veil of shawl. "Too bad my Naca son has grown too old for the Night Dance." Sympathy oozed sarcastically from her lips. "This is your favorite part. I see the young Kiyuksa scout is one of the chosen warriors."

Magpie flinched at the sound of his mother's voice. *A tongue as sharp as the burnt end of a lance, digging into old wounds.* "Old woman, you speak words that make me think that you do not wish to get any older."

"Ha! My winters will outnumber yours. You will wander the Land of Many Lodges long before my spirit has left the flesh."

"You, my mother, are fleshless. Spiritless, as well."

"*Ey-ee!* You are a pitiful son." Doublewoman pulled the shawl down more tightly over the hidden side of her face. "And to think I came to watch the dancing with you."

"Then watch, Anog Ite, watch." Magpie turned from his mother and peered into the ceremonial tipi, ignoring her. He pretended to be distracted by the faraway cries of the coyotes. The wind twisted their voices into strange, bellowing howls. *Do the wandering sunkas wish to join the celebration?* Ha! They would soon find themselves sacrificed, as well.

Four warriors had been chosen to sit in the center of the lodge. The firelight radiated off their sweat-glistened faces in flickering movements that seemed to emulate the beating of the drums and the cadence of the songs. Lost Morning and Red Grass approached the simmering paunch kettles, which were now only half-full. Dipping a ladle into the hot liquid, Red Grass fished around until she found the flesh-covered skull that had been carefully saved. She placed the head in a clean bowl, spooning fragrant broth over it, then carried it to Sunstone and Turtle Woman, who stood near the entrance, their feet gently tapping the dirt in rhythm to the music.

"*Pilamaya,*" she said to them. "I thank you, all of us thank you for this feast." Sunstone and Turtle Woman nodded, taking the bowl from her.

Then Dark Cloud's daughter, bending gracefully, placed four bowls on the ground and, swirling the spoon in the stew, found the second puppy's head. This she ladled into one of the bowls. The puppy's forefeet went into the next bowl, his hind feet in the third, and the tender, flavorful tail into the last bowl. She picked up the bowl containing the second head and approached Mahto. With downcast eyes, she placed the bowl of honor before him.

"The choicest portion," taunted Doublewoman from outside the tipi, jabbing at her son with a bony finger.

"*Han*, Mother. The choicest portion." Caws Like Magpie let his scaly tongue run over the surface of his fleshy lips, then scratched his nose again with the quill of the black feather, listening to the sound of the strange, distant howls. He shifted his gaze from the center of the ceremonial lodge to its perimeter, where the daughter of Breathcatcher stood transfixed, never taking her eyes from the Kiyuksa.

"But not served by the choicest maiden," he said, cruelty tainting his voice. "At least—not yet."

Skye felt as if all the rivers of the Medicine Bows surged within her, coursing through her veins, their rampant waters cutting new banks, shifting the sands of her shores in strange and wonderful ways. For a moment, she thought she heard the lonely bellows of her father's pipes, but then the pounding drums drowned out everything, even the sound of her own heartbeat, until she thought they were one and the same. She watched the beautiful young woman flaunt herself before Mahto and became suddenly enraged; she imagined herself undulating before him as well, like a wild river—a creature she did not know or recognize. Her thundering emotions were as stormy as a tempest.

Mahto lifted the puppy's head to his mouth and nibbled at the tender flesh, then slurped the greasy broth from the wooden bowl. Skye lifted her own bowl to her mouth and thirstily drank. The broth was rich and sweet. The four chosen warriors put down their bowls and rose from the fire, walking among the waiting maidens. Trembling, she took a deep breath as Mahto approached her, not daring to exhale, until he walked past her, choosing the daughter of the Big Belly for the final dance. The river inside her churned.

The four couples came together, then parted and danced backward, then came together again. As the dancers moved forward, joining at the center, they sang, and Skye could discern Mahto's resonant voice among the others. Four times they repeated the pattern. Then, as quickly as it had begun, the music ceased, and an unearthly silence filled the great ceremonial lodge.

Mahto made a gesture to the drummer, who pounded on the stretched hide one final time. The reverberation echoed within the raised walls of the tipi, then faded into silence. Mahto gestured again, this time to the second-chosen warrior. All eyes moved from Mahto to the young man, all ears tuned to the story he was about to tell—the story of a brave act committed, a coup counted on the enemy.

"The great warhorse stood tethered to his owner's tipi," the young man bragged, waving his arms. "The sun stood high in the sky."

"*Han!*" the crowd murmured. "During the light of day!"

"The spirit of the cloud-bird was with me, so bold was I."

"*Han!*" the crowd murmured again, eager to hear the well-known story one more time.

"Like the great eagle, I struck! Walking boldly into the enemy camp."

"*Han! Han!*"

"I even took my own jaw rope to place in the mouth of the enemy's sacred-dog!"

"*Han*—his own rope!"

"I painted my mark upon the enemy's horse!"

"*Han!* His own mark!"

"But then I decided to leave the horse standing, still tethered to the enemy's lodge—so that all would know that this Lakota had been to the enemy camp!"

"*Han! Han!*" the crowd cheered, pleased with the warrior's boastful storytelling. "*Ho he, ho he!* It is so! It is so!"

Mahto waited while two more warriors recounted their brave

deeds, while two more gave gifts of special significance to desirable *wikoskalas* waiting hopefully in the hushed crowd. Then finally he began his own story.

"*Hye!*" he began, thanking the spirits. "*Hye!*" His voice was strong and true, filled with confidence in his own exploits, as the other voices had been, as Skye knew all Lakota warriors must be.

"When I had seen but fifteen winters, when the winter-count paintings show our warriors going to move the arrows against the enemy Scilis, that is when I fought the fearsome Long-Claw, the Four-legged Warrior."

"*Han!*" the crowd murmured. "The humpback!"

Mahto paused, strutted to the edge of the fire, and stared for a moment at someone standing just beyond the tipi's circle of light. Skye thought she recognized Magpie's dark silhouette hovering at the edge of the crowd, and she heard again a faint howl coming from outside—the wind, perhaps, echoing from the white cliffs.

"I had not yet proven myself as a man, and so was doing a boy's task, alone, guarding the horses of our warriors near the camp of our *tokas*.

"*Ho he!* It is so, they camped near the Scilis!"

"That is when the humpbacked grizzly attacked the horses. That is when I battled the fearless *mato!*" With an exaggerated swipe of his hand, he pretended to slash at his own cheek, allowing one fingernail to scrape across the scar on his face.

"*Han! Han!* With his bare hands!"

He sprang forward, vaulting over the fire and landing with his feet planted firmly in the dirt. "*Hokahe!*" he yelled into the night, his words aimed at Magpie's dark shadow. "*Hokahe!* Howls at Moon is not afraid!"

"*Han! Han!*"

Even as Skye searched in vain for Magpie, he had disappeared from the gathering. She gasped, drawing in her breath. So that was how Mahto came by the scar! A grizzly! But only one scar? Could not the grizzly have killed him? And how did the story end? She waited for Mahto to continue, but he said nothing more.

The crowd voiced their approval, then grew quiet, as if the story's ending was already known to them. Their faces grew somber. Did the story have a sorrowful ending? Was the ending too *wakan* to be spoken aloud? Skye could only guess. But then Mahto began striding around in a circle, surveying the crowd as if looking for someone.

Skye watched, mesmerized, wondering if he, too, would bestow a gift upon some young maiden, Dark Cloud's daughter perhaps?

Mahto walked slowly toward Skye until his face was but a whisper away from hers; then he stopped. She held her breath as he reached up to his muscled neck and lifted the turtle-shell necklace from the bear claws and slipped it off.

In front of Skye's grandparents, in front of Lost Morning, in front of everyone, he slowly lowered the leather thong over her head, gently lifting her braids until the necklace rested on the soft bodice of her doeskin dress.

"Ahh-h," she heard the people exclaim. "Ahh-h . . ."

Magpie had turned away, tired of the bragging and boasting, tired of the crowd's foolishness. He ran a nervous finger up the side of his face and absentmindedly traced the path of the black *akicita* stripe that he had painstakingly repainted that morning. *The spike-horn stares at me like a young* tatanka *on the prod, leaping across the fire like a crazy man, expecting me to wait around for more of his coup stories. Not afraid, he says? Not afraid of this old, but young-enough, cracked-horn? Ha! We will see about that.*

None of the dancers or onlookers noticed the lone figure silhouetted against the moonlight high on the crest of the limestone cliffs. Only *igmu'tanka*, and the other four-leggeds, noticed the Scotsman. The cougar had moved beyond the camp of the two-leggeds—beyond sight, but not beyond sound.

She hesitated, one paw in midair, listening to the strange sounds carried on the wind. The cry of an injured four-legged? A wounded creature about to die? She searched the sky for the hook-billed winged ones who preyed on the flesh of the weak and dying, but saw nothing in the darkness. Her keen hearing detected no wing beats, no scavenging sounds. Again, the wind carried the strange noise to her. Her tongue flicked across her nostrils. She blinked her eyes, then lowered her paw and moved north, into the night.

The horses also heard the distant notes of the ancient wind instrument. They turned their heads and flicked their ears forward, all but the old roan mare whose hearing had begun to fail. She lay dozing on her side with her front legs folded under her, but the bellowing sound made the other horses uneasy, and she sensed their nervousness. Instinct, and caution, made her rise to her feet. And then finally, the mysterious music penetrated her deafness.

The shrill, angry notes rose from the tartan-covered leather bag, to the tarnished pipes, and ultimately into the great expanse of sky—notes that began as the challenge of one warrior to another, then faded into an acceptance of grief, melancholy notes that pierced the darkness, enveloping the stars in a symphony of long-sequestered sorrow.

Many moments passed before the night again grew quiet, except for the sounds that drifted from the large ceremonial lodge. The other horses returned to their grazing and dozing. The old roan mare tested the wind, then settled herself back down onto the cool earth and closed her eyes.

22

BITING THE KNIFE

"Haye! **Do you** see this?" Turtle Woman shook the chastity belt at Sunstone, holding a piece in each clenched hand. "It's been cut. Slit with a knife."

"What is it?" Sunstone squinted, stirring the embers of the low-burning fire so that they would cast more light into the dark lodge.

"A virgin's belt—on your *takoja*'s sleeping robe."

"Skye's? It is hers?"

"Hiya! She brought no such thing with her!"

Sunstone took a piece of the belt in his leathery hand and examined the smooth cut edge. "Someone's idea of a prank?"

"No joke, my husband. A warning. The work of that trouble-maker Doublewoman, no doubt. She is up to something—scheming and plotting." Turtle Woman cut her words off as their son-in-law appeared suddenly in the door of the tipi, his bent figure blocking the faint moonlight.

"Naked Warrior," Sunstone said, "we did not see you at the ceremony."

"No, ye did not," Gregory answered in a low tone, half in and half out of the tipi. "I had no hankering for the foolishness of a fandango tonight."

"You do not need to crouch in the door like a stranger." Sunstone gestured for his son-in-law to enter. As the Scotsman approached the fire a moody scowl clouded his ruddy face. He clutched the old wind bag to his side, as if attempting to shield the pipes from view with his broad torso. Perhaps it had not been the distant howling of wandering dogs, after all, above the sound of the drums.

"I have not heard you blow into the music-maker for many winters," Sunstone said.

"Nary a soul has heard me pipes for many a long winter," Gregory answered, placing the pipes carefully back into the leather pannier. "They have been silent since . . ." He let the sentence hang half-finished. "They've been silent for over a bloody decade, until this night."

Sunstone refrained from asking any questions, sensing that the pipes were not the only things to have been silent for many long winters. Much had changed about his son-in-law; once he had been like the bird-who-knocks-on-wood—announcing his presence to all in camp, giving many gifts, telling big stories, filling the night air with bellowing shrieks from the music-maker. Now he behaved more like the kingbird, riding the back of a ghost-enemy, haunted by the past.

Sunstone handed his wife the piece of cut leather, indicating with a nod of his head that she should discreetly dispose of it. Just then, they heard a scratching at the door.

"Turtle Woman, oh, great seer," a cackling voice called out. "I have a message for you from Doublewoman Dreamer."

"I am here," answered Turtle Woman. She rose and poked her head through the door. "What message do you bring?"

"There is to be a virtue gathering tonight. You, and all of the other One-Only-One women, are invited to come." It was the voice of Black Tail, the other *witko* woman.

"It is late."

"The wife of Dark Cloud has soiled the reputation of Doublewoman Dreamer. She must uphold her virtue."

"It is still late. And Doublewoman does not need Walks Ahead to soil her reputation—she soils it herself often enough."

"Ahh-h! Does Turtle Woman, who claims to be the most virtuous among us, fear the virtue gathering?"

"I claim nothing. I also fear nothing."

Sunstone watched as his wife ducked under the raised flap. *She may no longer move like a young woman*, he thought, *but despite the brittle bones, I would wager my best horse that she stares this moment at the crazy dreamer with cool, challenging eyes—still the woman warrior, still a woman worth envying.* It was no wonder the two *witko* women were jealous of his wife. To be a woman who had had only one man, who had been loyal for a lifetime of winters, was truly to be a woman of virtue. And the fact that she could once draw a bow as well as any brave, as well as Woman Chief of the Kangis was rumored to, didn't hurt either. His wife responded to the taunt as he knew she would.

"Tell Doublewoman I will be there."

"*Waste.* That is good," the other woman answered. "For your granddaughter is already among us—learning a few needed lessons."

"My *takoja*'s virtue is not in doubt—nor does she need to be taught any lessons!" Turtle Woman grabbed at the door flap, angrily shaking her fist as she reentered the tipi. Then she turned and thrust herself back through the open door, the two strips of leather in her hand lashing out, whipping the empty night air.

"And tell Doublewoman," she yelled after the departing messenger, "that my *takoja* needs no belt to insure her chastity!"

"Do not be so sure," the woman yelled back. "Did you not notice the way she flicked her tail at the young Kiyuksa scout? And *he* may as well have brought his courting blanket to the ceremony—behaving like the grass-bird, strutting and pruning his feathers! Perhaps it is already too late for the belt!" Her insinuating words hovered between them, like smoke from a smoldering fire.

"Vultures!" Turtle Woman spat in disgust as she reentered the tipi. "Those two women scavenge for gossip like a pair of redheaded hook-beaks!" Sunstone met his wife's anger with a look of self-disciplined restraint, and with a slight nod of his head to remind her of their son-in-law's presence. She lowered her eyes, realizing she had said too much.

"A chastity belt?" Gregory questioned Sunstone, frowning.

"And what did the old woman mean, 'flicking her tail at the young Kiyuksa'?"

"It was nothing. A harmless prank, a meddling tongue."

"A prank? Perhaps. But harmless?" Gregory moved toward his mother-in-law, then took the two pieces of leather from her hand. He rubbed his fingers across their cut edges.

"Harmless? Not by a long chalk," Gregory murmured.

"Hiyu po! Come forward!" the painted woman with the shawled head shrieked into the crowd of men who had gathered with their wives in the large ceremonial lodge.

Who is she, that she tries to look so beautiful? Skye glanced nervously about, relieved when she saw Sunstone and her father push their way into the throng of men. Then her grandmother, walking alone, entered the tipi and began working her way toward Skye.

"Hiyu po!" the shawled woman yelled again. "Any man who has ever lain beneath the robes with me, come forward!" The woman edged nearer.

Two women standing to Skye's right whispered to each other. "No man, no matter how much the heat of the rut was upon him, would lie with the *witko* woman."

"It is said she started the rumor herself."

"Hiya! Herself?"

"She hopes to disgrace the wife of Sunstone—to flush an old lover from the brush."

"Ama! It will never happen." The two women inched away, moving toward the center of the crowd.

Unci? With an old lover? The idea seemed ludicrous. Skye peered across the blazing fire, scanning the men, hoping to see Mahto among the onlookers. She spied her grandfather's adopted son, Wolfskin Necklace, standing at the entrance, and a few paces away from him the young scout. Skye's pulse raced, then slowed to a leaden crawl, sending a shiver up her spine, when she spotted Caws Like Magpie leaning against a blackened lodgepole.

"Hiyu po!" the woman with the shawl-covered face again de-

manded, gesturing at the crowd with a sweep of her arm. "No man dares step forward? No man backs up Walks Ahead who claims I dishonored my husband's memory?"

The men shifted nervously, their eyes scanning the other males for a hesitant movement of bold admittance. The married women eyed the crowd, looking for signs of adultery among the men, some snatching brief, suspicious glances at their own husbands. Many of the furtive looks were cast at a woman standing beside Skye, arms folded in displeasure.

"Ha! It is as I said." The shawled woman moved closer, pulling the shawl tightly over the side of her face. Thick powder made her skin look flawless, her eye painted large and dark. She pointed a finger at the woman beside Skye. "The wife of Dark Cloud speaks with words of smoke—flimsy smoke that comes from a fire that does not burn. A pile of smoldering buffalo dung! I wrapped my legs around no man."

"I did not speak against you. I did not speak at all," the Big Belly's wife defended herself, stepping forward. "It is your words which rise from a dung heap." Walks Ahead spat defiantly in the dirt and the shawled woman moved even closer, so close that Skye could smell her foul breath.

"A dung heap?" The woman's gnarled hands worked ceaselessly in her shawl.

"*Han.* A very old dung heap—not to be disguised by a layer of clay on the face and lines of charcoal about the eyes."

"Ha! As old as the sun! As old as the moon! Older even than Yata, the Wind—as old as Anog Ite, the Two-faced Woman!" With a flourish, eerie laughter coming from her shriveled throat, the shawled woman flung the covering from her head and bared her full face to Skye.

"*Hinu!*" Skye gasped, terrified, the Lakota word rising effortlessly from deep within. "Doublewoman!" She jumped backward, stepping away in horror as she finally realized what the others had already known.

Doublewoman was like a woman split in two—one beautiful, the other grotesque. One eye, small and beady. Half her thin lips curled over worn-down teeth, half blackened with tar. Pockmarks scarring her horrible skin, framed by strands of oily gray hair. Skye's blood curdled; her spine grew rigid. Never before had she understood Father's fear of the Droch Shuil. *This woman came from the Otherworld!*

"*Han*, the light-skinned granddaughter was fooled!" More cackles erupted from Doublewoman's throat. "Let that be a lesson to you, *takoja*—we all have two faces. Even you!" She pointed a bent finger at Skye, and Skye felt the color drain from her cheeks. Then Doublewoman pivoted away and swung her arm in a circle that encompassed all in the crowd.

"And you!" She pointed at the two women who had been standing near Skye, whispering under their breaths about the *witko* woman.

"And you as well!" She pointed at her own son, who had crept forward and was now standing near the fire. Then, swinging her arm in a half-circle, she let her gaze come to rest upon Turtle Woman, who stood between Sunstone and Skye's father near the still-burning ceremonial fire. *Surely she dares not challenge Unci?*

"And even you, One-Only-One woman! Who among our gray-haired warriors has bent his back beneath the robes with Turtle Woman? Surely the great Sunstone was not the only one. Step forward—if your weak memories do not fail you!"

Skye watched her grandmother, wondering how she would handle the affront, wondering how she would redeem her honor. But no redemption proved necessary, for no gray-haired man stepped forward to challenge her membership in the One-Only-Ones circle of women—no man stepped forward, that is, except Sunstone, who moved up to the edge of the fire and, in an act that defied tradition, gave his wife a long, admiring look. *Grandfather. Tunkasila.* Relief washed over Skye like a welcome rain.

"Ha!" Disgust flashed across Doublewoman's face as she dismissed the two with a wave of her hand.

"Perhaps the memories of our younger men are not clouded by so many harsh winters," she continued. "Do any of our *wikoskalas* have the courage to come forward and bite the knife? To prove they have yet to spread their legs for a man?" Doublewoman took a shiny, two-edged knife from her belt and with its sharp tip began digging a hole in the dirt near the fire, looking around as she did so. But no one stepped forward. Disdainfully, she said, "In my grandmother's day, the women did not bite a pitiful knife. They bit the fanged ones! Are all you *wikoskalas* cowards?"

Dark Cloud, his face flushed with anger, stepped forward. "Dreamer," he said, his deep voice hushing the murmuring crowd, "the people fear you because when you were young you dreamt of the Double Woman. But your dreams have made you selfish and vain, like Anog Ite. You chose the *witko* life, and you abuse your power. Your barbs are sharp, like the porcupine quills with which you embroider. My daughter will bite the knife, but she does so to honor the importance of virtue among our women, not because she fears your barbs. Like the *wikoskalas* of the olden days who dared to bite the fanged ones, my daughter will bite the knife."

So this is what it means to bite the knife, Skye surmised. *A way of avowing one's virginity? And the women, in the olden days, had the courage to bite a real snake? Perhaps too many of them died, virgins or no. Perhaps the snakes did not understand the rules.*

Dark Cloud folded his arms across his chest, signaling with a jerk of his head for his daughter to walk to the center of the lodge.

"Ah, the beautiful daughter of the Big Belly," said Double-woman, carefully wiping the honed edges of the blade on her sleeve, then placing the knife, tip up, into the deep, narrow hole. "It is good that such a *wikoskala* avows her chastity."

Lost Morning, looking even more beautiful than earlier in the evening, came near the fire. Turning to face the crowd, she began to follow the sun path, walking a slow, careful circle until she reached the shadowed hole. Kneeling beside it, her long braids nearly skimming the ground, she uttered a prayer that Skye could not hear, then thrust her fist into the pretend den. When she removed her hand, her palm was wrapped around the double-edged blade of the weapon. With her other hand, she grasped the handle of the knife, then placed the blade between her teeth, biting down. Two thin red lines appeared on the palm of her hand.

"Our daughter"—Dark Cloud shared a triumphant look with Walks Ahead—"our daughter pulls the snake from his den and places the fanged one in her mouth!" He scanned the waiting crowd, then said triumphantly, "No warrior challenges her claim!"

"*Hoye! Hoye!*" the crowd yelled in agreement, their enthusiasm growing as they witnessed the symbolic display of courage. *Did the Lakotas of long ago really believe that no snake would sink his fangs into the flesh of a virgin? And what will the Lakotas of today do, if Lost Morning's virtue is challenged?* Skye sucked in her breath.

"Who else is willing to come forth? Are there no other chaste ones among us?" provoked Doublewoman.

Next came Red Grass, who had also danced the dance of temptation as the half-bitten moon rose in the night sky, luring True Dog with the symbolic bowl of boiled puppy. She, too, "bit the snake," passing the knife onto the next young virgin who came forward.

Most of the young women filtered from the crowd, stepping small and soft upon the dirt floor of the ceremonial lodge. The young men stood erect, chins lifted, arms folded. Skye glanced at Mahto. The light of the flames shone in his eyes. He clenched his jaw and cast a troubled look at Caws Like Magpie, who stood fingering the two black feathers that hung about his neck. She noticed that Father, too, stared at Caws Like Magpie, the weight of his burly body balanced on the balls of his feet, tense, agitated, ready. A sudden bolt of dark fear sliced into her, reminding her of the night her mother's lifeblood had seeped onto the snow-covered ground, the eerie yowl of the cougar filling the forested darkness.

Turtle Woman, too, saw the blood on Lost Morning's hand, the thin lines of redness. She remembered another time, long ago, when the *wikoskalas* bit the knife—only then the knife had fangs and a rattling tail, and she and Doublewoman were two of the *wikoskalas*.

Never, not even when she had swung the war club at Wasp Man's oily skull, had she ever needed more courage, or been so frightened. To plunge one's hand into a hole, knowing that the venomed one waited within? *A-i-i-i!* Even now, the memory caused the sweat to run down her back. But she had done it! She had grasped the crawling one behind the head and had drawn him from the hole, his body writhing, his tail rattling. She had bitten the rattles from his tail and spat them in the dirt!

Doublewoman—Whistling Bird they had called her then— had not been so lucky. Barely sixteen winters old, she had not wanted to attend the ceremony. Her parents had forced her, afraid that her absence would provide fuel for the gossiping old women. Her hand had trembled like a quaking leaf, her eyes wide with fear, when she thrust it into the hole. And then the awful silence, Whistling Bird's mouth open in a silent scream, as she jerked her hand from the hole—the venomed one clinging to her, his fangs buried deep in her flesh.

She had lived—barely. And seven months later, with no lodge yet to call her own, no husband by her side, she had given birth to twin boys. One born dead. One born nearly dead. *E-i-i-i.* Turtle Woman shook her head. *The ways of Taku Skanskan are truly mysterious.*

Her *takoja* stood near the fire, watching each girl as she bit the knife, her own hands clenching and unclenching. Shadows played across her face as the flames flickered in the night air. Turtle Woman's eyes began to water as she stared at Skye. *What thoughts swirl within the mind of this half-blooded grandchild of mine?* Half-blooded? Lakota blood? Scottish blood? Kangi blood? Even Breathcatcher had not known about the five-pointed star etched in the cliffs at the Medicine Wheel. Turtle Woman had not even shown Little Badger.

She smiled, thinking of Little Badger. The Hewaktoka would have eagerly bitten the knife! *Han*—she would have even bitten the snake! Surely Little Badger and this Kangi Woman Chief were the same person.

Skye had turned her gaze from the *wikoskalas* to the Scotsman. Turtle Woman studied her son-in-law. He, too, clenched and unclenched his fist. But he stared not at the *wikoskalas*, but at Caws Like Magpie. And they both looked as dangerous as the fanged ones.

* * *

Of all the *wikoskalas* who walked to the center of the lodge and plunged a fist into the hole in the ground, not one was challenged by a man reputing the young woman's virginity. Not one had dirt thrown in her face, or was called a liar in front of the entire assembly. The crowd shunned no one.

But Caws Like Magpie was interested only in Skye, the light-skinned daughter of Breathcatcher, the daughter of the red-haired *wasicu*. What of her? What of the young, but old enough, one? His mother's discordant voice pierced his thoughts.

"There is one *wikoskala* among us who has not yet come forward." She pointed her long, bony finger accusingly at Breathcatcher's daughter. "Do you fear biting the knife, *takoja?*"

The half-blood stiffened, her eyes widening, her shapely mouth falling open.

Waste, Magpie thought to himself, the brazen *wikoskala* flinches like a cornered colt. Let all see her guilty face, let all know of her early-morning rutting with the too-proud scout. He bent and quickly snatched a fistful of dirt from the ground. *Do it! Dare to bite the knife!*

He watched as she struggled to force the flush of embarrassment from her cheeks. *Han, young curly-coat, move forward into the light, let all see your shame.* He remembered the way she had looked that morning, walking barefoot up the running-waters path, half her clothes tucked beneath her arm. He shifted his gaze and looked at the surly Kiyuksa, remembering the stealthy young scout riding into camp. *Bite the knife, Breathcatcher! Do it!*

Caws Like Magpie did not realize that it was the name of Skye's mother that rose, bent and bruised, from his bitter heart. Like his own mother, he did not realize that he still had a heart which remembered.

Skye searched her grandmother's weathered face for an indication of what she should do. *Show them you have courage*, the old woman's eyes seemed to say. *Show them you are the granddaughter of Turtle Woman, the great-granddaughter of Shifting Star. Show them you have the spirit of a warrior!*

Skye stepped forward. She shifted her gaze to her father. Their eyes met, his an intense lichen green. She thought of the passionate, booming notes of his bagpipes and found courage in the memory. She smiled at him, then squared her shoulders and stood tall. *I will not be intimidated!* The crowd looked on, whispering, waiting. She turned and faced Doublewoman, then spoke in a voice loud enough for all to hear.

"The granddaughter of Turtle Woman, the daughter of the Scotsman, does not fear the bite of the snake."

She started to kneel, to plunge her hand into the hole as she had seen the others do, but the *witko* woman stopped her.

"*Takoja,*" she said, her voice high and excited, "I have dug for you a special hole, here, close to the sacred fire." She pointed to one of the hot stones encircling the fire, then rolled it quickly over with her foot. A black hole gaped at them.

"Here, *wasicu*, is *your* hole."

Uneasiness filled Skye. This two-faced woman could not be trusted.

Doublewoman laughed, then turned the smooth, powdered side of her face to the crowd. "Ha! I knew it. The half-blood is afraid."

Skye stared at the dark hole, then looked again at her grandmother. *Unci? What does this mean?* She fought the uneasiness, let her temper begin to flare as she thought of the *witko* woman's words. Afraid? Not she!

She plunged her hand into the hole, felt the heat of the fire, heard her grandmother yell a warning, all in the split second before she felt the long, lean body of the snake.

Fear rooted her to the ground, kept her hand deep in the hole. The crowd grew deathly quiet. Then her grandmother's voice, calm now, floated above the crowd. Her words reached out to Skye like spiraling tendrils of wisdom. "The crawling one is not your enemy . . ." The snake writhed slowly in the heated darkness. Would movement cause him to strike? Her grandmother repeated herself, slowly and calmly. "The crawling one is not your enemy . . ."

The snake was warm and soft, his long-muscled body relaxed. Skye inched her hand up the length of the reptile. He did not move. She felt his body narrow slightly, then grow wide again as her fingers touched the hinges of his powerful jaw. She gripped him, just behind the head, immobilizing him. Still he did not move. Her panic drained away.

Skye drew the snake, head first, slowly from the hole.

The crowd gasped. "*Haho!*" they pointed, as the tail appeared. "Look! Six rattles at least! So big!"

The snake hung like a limp rope. Then Doublewoman's crude laughter broke the silence. "The fanged one sleeps!" she cackled, pointing at the snake.

A twinge of compassion tugged at Skye as she held the heat-tortured snake. It was obviously near death.

Then Doublewoman waved her arm at the crowd and, bending to retrieve her knife from the other hole, tossed it at Skye. "Here," she said, laughing, "kill the fanged one before he kills you!"

Skye kept her eye on the handle of the knife, closing her fist around it as it dropped into her grasp. She lowered the snake slowly to the ground. Just then, a gravelly voice, spilling from fleshy lips, cut through the throng of people.

"This ceremony is not for a *wikoskala* who has already known the prod of a blunt-horn!"

Skye recognized the hateful voice of Caws Like Magpie before she turned to face him, before the handful of dirt struck her face. She saw victory flash in his eyes, a split second before it turned to shock as her father's fist smashed into the black *akicita* stripe painted down Magpie's jaw.

Aye, Magpie, the time has come! Gregory welcomed the pain that shot up his hand as he struck his old rival. The Naca reeled from the blow, then regained his balance and, spinning, kicked Gregory in the ribs. Like two enraged humpbacked grizzlies, the men tore into their battle, hurling their bodies at one another, scattering the crowd and the burning embers of the ceremonial fire, treading on the near-dead snake.

Ye bloody brown-skin, lecherous, bloody brown-skin—daring to throw dirt in me daughter's face! Rage coursed through Gregory, a torrent of pent-up anger as he smashed his other fist into Magpie's gut. He forgot about the rheumatism that stiffened his bones, forgot about the years that slowed his feet. Another kick pummeled his side, and a fist glanced off his thick beard. He grabbed at Magpie's leg, felt the skeletal limb slide from his grasp, then spun and dug a bent elbow into the back of Magpie's spiny, short-waisted torso, tearing the band of silver trade disks from Magpie's hair.

Winded, the Naca from the Muddy Water camp staggered away from the Scotsman, his dentalium-shell earrings clinking in the momentary silence. He reached toward his waist, wrapping long bony fingers around the knife handle tucked into his belt, and pulled the blade free, waving it through the air.

"An he!" Magpie's battle cry rang out, blood from a split lip spattering his beaded Naca shirt. Knife raised, he lunged at Gregory.

The blade cut through the fringed sleeve of Gregory's leather shirt, slicing into his thick upper arm. *Me sword arm!* The thought flashed, as quickly as the blade, through Gregory's mind. *Damn! Where in the bloody hell is me sword?*

Skye gasped in horror as Caws Like Magpie lunged at her father with the knife. Shifting Doublewoman's knife in her hands, she gripped its sharp tip between her thumb and forefinger, judged the balance and weight of the weapon, then, with a snap of her wrist, hurled the knife across the dying embers of the fire, straight toward the two iridescent feathers that hung from the throat of Caws Like Magpie.

Caws Like Magpie caught her movement just as the Scotsman knocked Magpie's own knife from his grasp. In an attempt to deflect Skye's hurtling weapon, the Naca jerked up his hand, crow-skin badge dangling from his wrist. Skye's blade struck the crow skin, slid along its brittleness, then leapt up the side of Magpie's face, along the path of the black *akicita* stripe. Red blood seeped from the open gash.

"*Ey-ee!*" Doublewoman cried out, her voice rising above the murmurs of the startled crowd.

"*Au!*" Magpie jerked his hand to his face, then stared at his red fingers. He looked at Skye, a look poisoned with hatred as deadly as the venom of the rattlesnake.

Gregory leapt, retrieving both knives from the ground while Caws Like Magpie, stunned, stood still before the people.

"When last we met, Magpie," Gregory said, "I warned ye that the next time ye loosed your tongue upon me ears, I would take me claymore to it. Beware!" He squeezed his arm to stanch the bleeding.

"*Wasicu,*" Magpie spat from his blood-encrusted lips, "your foolish daughter tries to walk the trail of the warrior. Soon she will also learn the trail of vengeance. When last we met, I swore to the thunder and lightning that your lifeblood would seep into the earth. Beware, *wasicu!* The sun will soon rise upon that day!"

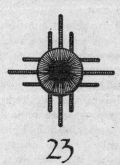

23

THE PRECIPICE

Sunstone's sinewy legs ached from climbing the steep trail that wound its way up the ancient cliff. He sighed; his strong warrior days were gone. He leaned into the weathered rock face, moving slowly and deliberately up the incline, his body hardly visible among the boulders and overhanging ledges.

The winters leave their mark upon me, just as the rains and winds have left traces of their passing on the face of this mountain. My bones grow old and tired. Even my spirit walks with heavy steps.

Sunstone paused in his upward trek, inhaling deeply, then purging his lungs of air. Below him, the smoke from many cook fires spiraled into the dusk-filled quiet, enveloping the entire Oglala camp in a thin gray haze. He pushed on, digging his moccasins into the limestone path, grabbing at a low-growing shrub with hardened hands. The half-circle tracks that he passed on the path led toward camp, not away from it—the tracks of two horses and a long-eared mule.

Much had happened in only four sleeps. His *takoja* had appeared like an immature flutter-wing, emerging from a cocoon that had both ensnared and protected her—and sprouted bold-colored wings of courage. She was changing from bashful-girl to brave-woman before his very eyes, from spotted-fawn to whistling-doe. And he had watched his own wife grow young again, watched her step lighten and her smile widen as hope swelled her withered heart.

But bad feelings also flowed into their lodge, like the bad blood from the gash in his son-in-law's arm. The knife wound had turned angry. Bad blood from bad blood. The two *tokas*, Magpie and Naked Warrior, should have faced each other long ago. Instead, their hatred had had many summers to fester into poison.

Sunstone paused again, breathing deeply. Ahead, less than the distance of a strong warrior's lance throw, the steep path leveled, easing onto an overhanging plateau. There, with the star-filled heaven for his bed robe, he would spend the night. He would watch the sun seek its rest in the western sky; he would listen for the voice of ancient thunder. He wanted answers for the questions that plagued him, the problems that faced his people. The hatred between Caws Like Magpie and his son-in-law was more than bitter rivalry—it was hatred that drew its power from the war between the Lakota and the *wasicus*, hatred that burned in the bellies of all those who fought against the encroaching *wasicus*, whether or not they poisoned themselves with the *wasicu's* drink. It was hatred that threatened to consume his *takoja*.

He reached toward the limb of a young pine, its roots clinging stubbornly to the shallow soil of the steep-sided mountain. Scratch marks had torn the bark from the young tree, as if a four-legged had sharpened her claws on the tender trunk. *Igmu'tanka*, he whispered to himself as his fingers found a faint imprint in the dirt. He traced the track with his finger, outlining the large paw print, following the curve of the padded foot, tracing the four teardrop toe marks. *Igmu'tanka*, he whispered again, *Great Lion. Your call pierces the night like the cry of a grief-stricken woman.*

"Go, *takoja*. Go!" Turtle Woman waved her hand in a shooing-away gesture. "The wound in your *ate*'s arm will not heal just because you stand by his side. It needs the medicine of the lodgepole tree. Go! Fetch me the bark of a young pine before darkness falls upon the cliff trail. I will watch your *ate*."

"Do as your grandmother bids ye, Skye. It'll take more than the bite of a knife to put me under."

Skye looked at her father, at his fever-flushed cheeks and his ugly wound, red streaks of infection inching their way toward his shoulder.

"I'll ride like the deer run, Ate. Ye won't even know I've been gone." She leaned over him, brushing her lips against his beard, then turned and ducked under the open door flap of the tipi.

The day's heat was gone, replaced by a cool breeze that smelled of creek and willow. The tethered horses greeted Skye with low whinnies and impatient pawing; her grandmother's red roan, untethered, nickered softly. "No, this trip is not for you," she whispered to the mare. "Besides, you never stray far from Unci anyway, do you?" She walked to Duncan and untied him, slipping the lead rope over his neck and knotting the end of it to the halter ring. Then, not bothering to bridle or saddle him, Skye flung the empty saddlebags over his withers, hoisted herself onto his bare back, and urged him on, pointing him toward the cliff.

She raised a hand to shield her eyes from the glare of the descending sun. The closest pine trees, a few tenacious stragglers, grew at the top of the limestone cliffs a short ride away. She kicked

Duncan into a fast lope and headed for the steep, serpentine trail. *I am a different girl now than the one who rode down this same trail only four days ago—different, yet not different. Like the wild plum, turned inside out. The seed, the flesh, the toughening skin—all, turned inside out.* She tightened her grip on the rough lead rope, thinking back to last night, remembering the feel of the snake in the dark hole, the coldness of the knife blade as she hurled it at Caws Like Magpie. A shiver went up her spine. *As warm as blood, as hard as death.*

Magpie knelt and dipped his hands into the frigid creek. The running waters eased the raw sting of the open cut on his face, but they did nothing to ease the humiliation that lay in his gut like a decaying carcass. Humiliation, and dishonor. A Naca wounded by a sniveling *wikoskala*, a sniveling *half-blood!* He had been dishonored in front of the whole village, dishonored and shamed—yet none of them had heard his vow of vengeance. Only the thunder and lightning had been witness to his promise.

And now the *wikoskala* rode foolishly alone up the cliff trail, away from the safety of her grandmother's lodge, away from the safety of her mother's people and her father's long-knife.

In the flash of a jumping river trout, the flick of a coiled snake's tongue—hoh! his mother was truly *witko* to have placed the fanged one in the hole!—he knew what he needed to do, what must be done, what he had wanted to do since the first dizzying, man-woman thoughts of Breathcatcher had stirred his groin.

Sucking at the creek water, he drank, then rose and shook the remaining moisture from his long fingers. He tugged on his gaudy belt, hiking up his leggings while settling his roused self into his breechcloth. Turning his back on the sun, he stepped into the lengthening shadows of dusk and strode, like a fast-moving cloud, toward his lodge and his long-toothed warhorse.

Sunstone took a small pinch of *cansasa* between his thumb and forefinger. Then he tossed it into the breeze, watching as the scattered sumac leaves and willow bark drifted to earth. A second pinch went into the small bowl of his pipe, and from the tip of a worn *pte* horn he withdrew a tiny, glowing ember.

"*Hye! Hye!* Wakan Tanka. This old Shirt Wearer gives thanks for the *Peta-oihankesni*, the flame of our ancestors, the flame of the Seven Sacred Council Fires of the Lakotas. *Hye!*" As Sunstone drew on the pipe, the tobacco hissed, red as the glowing ember. His prayers were the sacred prayers of one who prays not for himself but for others, for all the people of his nation.

"This earth man, this wild man of the Ikce Oyate, has a heart heavy with troubled thoughts. I fear our people forget the sacred ways—they forget the ways of humility and sacrifice, the ways of respect and kindliness that mark a truly human life." He lifted the pipe to the Sky, then lowered it to the Earth, then honored each of the Four Directions. He drew again on the pipe, watching the spiraling smoke rise into the air. The breath of Wakan Tanka.

His heart grew quiet and solemn, too solemn for voice, too quiet, even, for song. His quietness mirrored the stillness of dusk, paying homage to the sun as it moved beneath the earth, and to the moon as it revealed its shadowed self. The eternal cycle, the transition from light to dark, from dark to light, encircled the high cliff with its overpowering presence. All became silent—the winged-ones, the crawling-ones, the four-leggeds, the standing-people, even the running-waters. For one eternal and sacred moment, silence reigned.

Then the sound of a discordant human voice, low and threatening, dispelled the quiet—a sacrilege against sanctity. Louder the voice grew, guttural and angry. Sunstone rose slowly, easing himself from one reality into the next. He let the dark ominous sound draw him away from the eternal flame, out of the light and into the oppressive shadows.

He followed them: a male voice, low and threatening, a female's, frightened and angry. And then he came upon them near the edge of the cliff.

His back to Sunstone, the Naca from the Muddy Water camp—the one known by all as the tail-tier, the one who never killed his own *pte* but tied his tag to someone else's kill, the one known as Little Husband because he had never outgrown the need for his own mother's suckling, the one who had once asked Breathcatcher to stand beneath the courting robe—this man had pinned Sunstone's only *takoja* against the barren trunk of a dead pine, clinging to her like a leech upon tender flesh.

"Once away from the herd," Magpie taunted Skye, "you are not so brave, eh, young curly-coat?"

Sunstone stepped forward.

"She has not wandered as far from the herd as you might believe, Magpie."

Startled, the Naca jerked his head back to look over his shoulder. But he did not release Sunstone's granddaughter, nor move his body away from hers. He twisted his face into a sneer.

"Old man, you belong in your tipi, where your old woman can bring you broth to sip through your toothless gums. Go back down the mountain."

"I belong where Taku Skanskan, the Spirit of All Movement, has placed me. I belong by my *takoja*'s side." Sunstone eased closer, eyes unblinking.

"Old man, I warn you."

A rush of anger stirred Sunstone's blood, heightening his vision, his hearing, his sense of smell. The eyes of his *takoja* stared back at him, outraged and indignant; she was immobilized, unable to fight back. But her eyes told him that she had not yet given in to paralyzing fear. Warrior eyes stared back at him—familiar eyes.

Her gaze cut through the present moment, through the winters of Sunstone's lifetime, to when he had been a fearless warrior, fighting the Palanis and the Kangis and the Susunis, and saw the same look in Naked Warrior's eyes as he plunged his long-knife into the ribs of a Palani warrior; saw, even, the same warrior look in Turtle Woman's eyes so many winters past, when he had ridden into the camp of the Kangis—the victory in her eyes as she crushed the skull of the man who had abused Little Badger, the Hewaktoka, the man who had kicked the life from his son.

"*Huka hey!*" Sunstone sprang, every muscle and sinew remembering, every cell imprinted with long-ago battle cries, every drop of blood racing with youth. His rangy old body struck Caws Like Magpie to his knees, precariously close to the rim of the ledge.

The two tribesmen—one toughened by many summers of brave deeds and grieving-heart moons, the other by winters of dark, soul-shriveling bitterness—thrashed and grappled on the high cliff while Skye frantically clutched at her belt, searching for a knife she did not have, a blade she could not find.

Sunstone scrambled for a foothold on the limestone surface of the clifftop. The strong-heart song that pounded in his head gave him strength, but not enough to withstand Magpie. The Naca's relentless onslaught brought him within a hairbreadth of the rim—within a defiant gasp of the edge of life itself.

With one final thrust, like the last percussive strike upon a sacred drumskin, Magpie pushed Sunstone over the cliff. The strong-heart pounding found a new cadence, a new rhythm—becoming a death song that filled Sunstone's being with lightness, even as his old and rangy body tumbled toward the Earth Mother. *Wolfskin Necklace, son of my heart, use your wisdom to guide our people. Honor my wife, my forever-mate, as you have always done. Breathcatcher, child of my flesh, mother of my takoja, cast your light upon the path that I may find my way to the Land of Many Lodges. Greet this old tatanka with a never-ending high-grassed prairie beneath the eternal blue of Father Sky. And Mitawicu, my One-Only-One . . .*

Sunstone's arms flailed at the empty air, instinct stronger, for a brief moment, than courageous acceptance. He clutched at his medicine bag, felt the golden nuggets, round and smooth, beneath the worn leather, remembered the sacred Black Hills of his birth. He thought, again, of Turtle Woman and smiled.

Taku Skanskan, lift me—like the winged one, like the sacred cloudbird, lift me into the Great Mystery . . .

And then, time no longer mattered. Time was no more.

Skye stood transfixed, the reality too terrible to grasp. Her grandfather, the honored Shirt Wearer of the Oglalas, hung in midair for one breathless moment, then vanished from view, leaving the stunned Caws Like Magpie alone on the precipice, his angry lust turning pale and withered beneath the weight of the act he had just committed.

Two swallows flew from the ledge, their alarmed *keer! keer!* piercing the silence. The harsh cries propelled Skye forward, pulling her toward the edge of the cliff. Beneath her, death clung to the sheer limestone walls, like the gossamer web of a widow spider. Far below, on hard ground, lay her grandfather's body.

She stepped away. Inch by inch, her feet retraced their steps, away from the shocked Caws Like Magpie, away from the abyss of tragic loss. Away from the vision of her grandfather's body, lying motionless, broken: away from the memory of Ina lying lifeless in bloodred snow.

As if in a dream, she retrieved her saddlebag and flung it over her shoulder, not realizing that half of the gathered bark spilled down her back, tangling in her hair, falling to the ground like ash. Caws Like Magpie backed away from the cliff, then turned and moved into the graying dusk, up the path, away from camp.

She found Duncan and began to follow him down the steep trail, sensing that her life had taken an irreversible, tragic turn, as twisted as the path on which she now trod, as unpredictable as the tumultuous emotions that gathered like storm clouds within her.

24

THE CRY OF WOMAN

Mahto fought the queasiness that had sickened his gut all day— pent-up anger roiling his insides, rendering his restless muscles useless, like the pathetic, limp snake Skye had pulled from the hole.

"The Light-skinned One did what someone should have done

long ago," he said to True Dog, "only she should have slit Magpie's throat, instead of his cowardly face." Mahto jabbed his heels into the sides of his tobiano gelding, keeping abreast of the red horse that True Dog rode.

"The fight was not our fight, my *kola*," said True Dog. "It was not for any of us to interfere."

"*Hiya!* Someone should have interfered with that Naca long before now."

True Dog gave his friend a knowing look. "I think anger is not the only thing that stirs your blood. You've had more than scouting on your mind this day."

His friend's words were true. A question had been haunting him since Doublewoman Dreamer had tricked Skye into the knife-biting ceremony, had kept his eyes wide open long after yesterday's moon had risen to rule the night. *Why*, he wanted to ask the Light-skinned One, *why did Caws Like Magpie challenge your virtue? Does he know something I do not? Has he seen you with someone?* They were questions he knew he would never ask.

The two Kiyuksas urged their mounts onward, toward the white cliffs flanking the western curve of the camp. They had traveled a great distance that day, crossing the Shell River to avoid the soldiers and the rolling-wood trains of immigrants whose animals devoured the prairie lands. They returned disheartened, having found no long-grassed meadows to which they could move the Kiyuksas' herd of hungry horses. Mahto scanned the horizon, his eyes straining in the dusk.

"*Haho*, look, at the foot of the cliff." He pointed, directing True Dog's gaze.

"A woman? Away from camp, so late, when the moon has nearly risen in the night sky?"

Mahto peered into the twilight as they rode closer, barely able to distinguish the woman's shape from the silhouetted horse by her side. She was kneeling beside a dark shadowed object, but made no move as they approached.

"*Hau*," he called out, "are you hunting trouble, that you are not already within the circle of lodges like the other women?" She did not look up. Her horse whinnied, but the Lakota ponies did not answer, acting as if the horse were a stranger to them. Mahto nudged the tobiano closer.

"*Hau*," he called out again, in a softer voice this time, for he had nearly reached the woman, and he recognized the lighter hair, the shape of her shoulders and the tilt of her head.

A last glint of sunlight flashed across the land and illuminated the downcast face of the Light-skinned One, shining on the single tear that slid down her cheek, illuminating on the ground beside her the face of her grandfather's broken body.

Sunstone. The Shirt Wearer. Respected elder. Disbelief paralyzed Mahto, keeping him rooted to the back of his horse.

He could see now that Skye had been struggling to move her grandfather's body, dragging him across the hard ground, leaving a trail of swept earth behind her.

"*Hau*, my friend," Mahto said again, his voice reaching out to touch her, to ease her grief-stricken daze.

She lifted her head to look at them.

"Tell us," said True Dog, stepping off his horse, "tell us what terrible thing has happened."

Mahto listened as the story spilled forth, searched the cliff trail with narrowed eyes for the lustful Caws Like Magpie. *Hiya! The Naca should die!* To behave like a rutting bull with the granddaughter of the Shirt Wearer—to try to force himself upon her! Even the rutting bull knew better. And to cause the death of the honored *wicasa!* Truly, these were offenses worthy of death.

Mahto barely trusted his own voice to speak. "True Dog will help you to take your grandfather back to the village," he said, trying with great difficulty to keep his emotions hidden. But the pained emptiness in Skye's eyes only stirred his anger more.

He dismounted and helped True Dog lift the body of the Shirt Wearer onto the back of the red horse. The loose, crooked feel of the broken bones filled him with a lethal determination. The death of such a man was a terrible sacrilege, a violation of all that was sacred, of everything *wakan*. A grandfather did not deserve to die at the hands of one of his own people.

The Light-skinned One stood watching them, her dazed face pale and drawn. Had they been alone, away from everyone, he would have broken all traditions and reached out to her, would have shown her that for every great tragedy, there is, in turn, a re-birth—a way to recommit oneself to the passion of life. But they were not alone. For now, she needed to grieve, needed to honor the spirit of her grandfather.

But Mahto feared, as he watched the Light-skinned One stare blankly at the body, that she did not know how to show her grief, did not realize that her own spirit needed to be set free, just as the spirit of the Shirt Wearer needed to be set free. The vacant look in her eyes made him uneasy.

Kneeling, he gathered a small handful of red earth. Then he took a pinch between his fingers and held it up, offering it to the first of the Four Winds. He repeated this for each of the sacred directions, for the Sky above, and for the Earth below. Then he sprinkled the red earth down the center part of the Light-skinned One's hair, rubbing the last remaining bit on her motionless hands. *Taku Skanskan, energy that moves all that moves, stir back to life the spirit of the Light-skinned One.*

He could do no more.

He slid onto the back of the tobiano and turned him toward True Dog. "I will go after Caws Like Magpie," he said, his voice now hard and cold.

"Remember, my *kola*," True Dog cautioned, "the Naca must answer to *all* those who sit in the council lodge, not only to you. Do not trouble their minds with a second killing."

A second killing? Or a coup counted on a true toka, *a half-man whose black ways had darkened the skies above the camps of the Oglalas for too many winters?* Mahto acknowledged his friend's warning with a nod, then spun the tobiano around and urged him into a lope. *I am a fox; I am supposed to die. If there is anything difficult, if there is anything dangerous, that is mine to do.*

Cursing her weakening eyes, Doublewoman Dreamer flicked her finger at the crow perched on her shoulder, tugged a strand of her gray hair from his beak, then ducked under the door flap and entered her own dim lodge.

"*Itka sapa!*" she swore, glancing at her son's empty backrest. *His father's ways, his father's seed—never around, never here to ease the loneliness of an old woman.* She stirred the dying embers of the fire, adding several pieces of kindling to the coals. The crow cawed, dug his claws into her shoulder, and leaned as far away from the fire as he could stretch.

"You fear the flames, winged-one?" she cackled, retrieving a piece of burning kindling from the coals and lifting it into the air, watching the red-orange flames crawl toward her hand.

"I'll tell you a secret, black bag of feathers." She brought the burning stick closer, close enough to feel the heat upon her scarred face. "Everyone fears the fire," she whispered, "the great *wanbli*, the fork-tailed bird who makes his home in the cliffs, the fanged-one. Even that foolish, braggart son of mine."

She tossed the kindling back onto the fire and leaned into Magpie's backrest, dropping her arms to her sides. Her hand fell upon the small leather pouch that held Magpie's paint.

"No need to paint your injured face this morning, eh, my son?" Empty silence echoed back. She opened the pouch, wet the tip of a gnarled finger with her tongue, then dipped her nail into the pigment. Curious, the crow pecked at her bent knuckle.

Holding a piece of broken mirror before her, she drew a jagged black line from the corner of her eye, down her cheekbone, to the corner of her mouth—a bolt of lightning from the land of the Thunderbirds.

"Born during the Moon of the Terrible, eh, my son? Forced from the womb of Anog Ite, the Woman-with-Two-Faces, when Yata's icy breath caused the ravens to fall like frozen dung upon the tipis." She dipped her finger in the black pigment again, painted a jagged line down the other side of her face, then resumed her monologue.

"What you don't know, my son, is that there were two of you born that terrible, frozen night. Two brothers. One who entered this world already dead, with a stillborn heart and unseeing eyes. The other entered this world with no heart at all . . ."

She stared at the fire, tossing a scrap of discarded fat into the flames. The fire hissed and flared as the fat melted. Then she wet her fingers in her mouth and reached quickly into the red-orangeness, retrieving the sizzling scrap. "Here, black one," she said to the crow, "an offering for the winged-one." The crow snatched the hot tidbit from her fingers, then dropped it suddenly into the dirt.

"Wahn! Wahn!" The camp crier's alarm sounded, calling all to come. Doublewoman pushed the bird from her shoulder and rose stiffly into a standing position, then poked her head outside. Two horses, one ridden, one being led, were entering the circle of tipis near the lodges of the Standing People. Overhead, the yelping call of a golden *wanbli* could be heard. The image of the fork-tailed bird being snatched from the sky flashed through Doublewoman Dreamer's mind, and her blood ran cold.

Turtle Woman glanced at her feverish son-in-law, who turned and moaned on his sleeping robe, then returned to her sewing, pushing the bone awl through the elk skin to secure the last quill. The medicine wheel design was complete: the center cairn, the spokes, the circle. Just as she remembered. The tunic remained otherwise unadorned. No five-pointed star, no shooting star. No longer would this heirloom design decorate her belongings, or those to be given to her *takoja*. Not until she was able to return to the Medicine Wheel and once again see for herself. She would pretend no more.

She would tell Skye again about Little Badger. Tell her what she knew of Woman Chief, remind her of the Kangi holy man's prophecy. She had wanted to ease into this thought-sharing, gently, like a new husband should with a shy, quivering wife. But time seemed to be rushing by, out of control.

The empty space at the back of the lodge filled her with uneasiness. Many times before, Sunstone had gone to be alone with his troubled thoughts, to lift his heavy heart unto Wakan Tanka. Always, he had returned cleansed, uplifted. Why, this time, had her fingers trembled as she sewed?

She sighed, then rose and held the dress up to her shoulders, appraising its width and length. "Just right for my *takoja*," she whispered to herself, "not too large, not too small." Satisfied with all but the design, she laid the supple garment on Skye's bed robe and walked over to her son-in-law.

Fever had crept into his brain. "Magpie," he groaned, his words thickly slurred, "ye bloody coward!" He thrashed about, moaning as he twisted his wounded arm. She wiped the sweat from Gregory's brow with a cool, damp piece of rabbit hide. His flesh was warm to the touch, the red snake-of-infection crawling up his skin even closer to the shoulder. Why did it not surprise her that a weapon used by Caws Like Magpie would rot the flesh— would poison like the venomous bite of a rattler? Ah, how proud she had been of her *takoja!*

Turtle Woman needed the pine bark to draw the poison from the knife wound before the infection grew serious. She walked to the door of the lodge. Her granddaughter should have returned long ago, before the sun had slipped from the sky, before the half-bitten moon had risen. Twilight had come and gone; the dusk grazers had left the meadows, retreating from the night hunters who stalked the prairie. Perhaps she should send a few of the *akicitas* out to look for Skye.

Then the dogs began to bark, and the camp crier's call cut through the dusk. *"Wahn! Wahn!"* The call grew louder, closer. Turtle Woman ducked under her open door flap and peered into the dimness. Her hands began to tremble as the shadowy shapes approaching her took form—her granddaughter, horseback; True Dog, walking slowly into the circle of light cast by the lodge fires, leading his horse, a motionless something draped across the sacred-dog's back.

She walked out to True Dog. He took the heavy, limp bundle in his arms and placed it slowly on the ground before her. She stared, unbelieving, at Sunstone.

Tunkasila, onsimala ye! Great Spirit, have pity on me! Have pity on me! Her husband, her forever-mate—he did not move, did not breathe. She knelt and placed her finger on his bloody face, then touched his broken and battered body with her hands—his neck, his ribs, his arms. But when she saw that he clutched his sacred *wotawe* pouch in his hand, the medicine bag that contained his most intimate and sacred objects, she could stand it no longer. *"Yun! Yun! Yun!"* she began to wail, baring her heart, her very soul, to the world.

Sunstone. Elk Man. One-Only-One.

Turtle Woman's cry of anguish swept the circle of lodges, pierced the darkness and echoed from the chalky white cliffs and the towering mountains, until it rose like a soaring cloud-bird to become part of the great expanse of sky.

25

BANISHMENT

Turtle Woman's keening wails forced their way into Gregory's fever-ridden dreams.

The body of his grandfather lay stretched on a board in the middle of a small room, a lantern burning beside it. Winter's damp chill had invaded the room, for no peat fire smoldered in the hearth. It was a house of death, his grandfather's death, and he was just a boy, unused to corpses, or spirits, or mourners.

He wanted to peek beneath the coarse linen burial sheet covering his grandfather, but he knew 'twould only be a moment afore neighbor Mackinnon returned. How long, after all, did it take to get rid of a bit of ale? Aye, Mackinnon would be back to guard the body soon enough.

Gregory licked his small finger and dipped it into the wee mound of salt lying upon his grandfather's chest, then dipped his finger into the little mound of earth next to the salt and tasted it, too. "Graundaddie?" he whispered. "Graundaddie? Why have ye left me? Can ye say nothing to me?"

Fiddle music filtered into the room, the bow scraping, the notes plaintive like cats whining in the night, the sounds of the late-wake, laments and revelry—all coming together, filling the stone house. Gregory hated the noise. Did the dead hear nothing, he wondered?

Durst he peek beneath the linen?

He lifted the sheet and stared at his grandfather's face. Then he touched the pewter brooch affixed to his grandfather's tartan, running his finger across its raised heather design. He peeked behind him. No one. He unclasped the pin and slid it into his pocket.

"Mind yourself, lad! Your grandfather's spirit hovers near!"

God help me! Mackinnon wavered ghostlike near the open doorway, barking at him in a shrill voice.

"And keep your bloody hands away! Do ye want to become like him—like a pile of dirt? Mind the spirits, lad! For once the body rots, nothing else remains—just the salt of the sinner's soul! Beware the devil dogs!"

The crofter's shadowy form shrunk from the doorway and Gregory found himself back in a corner of the main room, next to the fiddler, who stood tapping his boot and drawing his bow, the music loud and frightening.

More neighbors flocked in from outside, crowding against the walls and milling about, disappearing for a moment into the cold darkness where his grandfather lay, floating in and out.

Now a piper stood near the open door, his ancient pipes wailing a mournful tune. Behind him, with a keening lament of her own, danced Graunie Maggie.

Barefoot, her tangled red hair loose, a black robe swirling around her legs, she danced and wept, twirled and howled, while the fiddle and the pipes wailed, louder and louder. Gregory turned away from the sight of his grandmother, clasping his hands to his ears to shut out the wails, crying out as a pain stabbed his injured arm.

Turtle Woman. It was *her* anguished voice he heard. Graunie Maggie faded away.

He struggled against the fevered dreams, forcing himself to sit up, and then to stand. He held on to a smoke-darkened lodgepole for support and worked his way gingerly toward the door flap, easing through the opening and into the night.

Near Wolfskin Necklace, True Dog stood over the body of Sunstone, and Lost Morning was helping Skye from her horse. Turtle Woman raised her arms toward the heavens before falling on her knees to the ground.

He saw Doublewoman Dreamer, black jagged lines painted on her face, as she edged near, slinking around like a furtive camp dog. Then the veil of fever once again ensnared him in a web of darkness; he had not seen Caws Like Magpie or Mahto, the Kiyuksa scout.

Wolfskin Necklace looked around at the others gathered within the council lodge, their leathery faces furrowed by shame and anger.

His own spirit withered; his heart cooled like the rounded stones that lived beneath the running-waters. His second father, his mentor, his *hunka*. Dead. Bruised and broken. *Sunstone*. Soon to go beyond the Path of the Winds, beyond the pines, where the shadows of the dead danced in the Land of Shades. His name would now be only a memory—rarely spoken, no longer uttered in greeting, or in sorrow.

The Ones Who Decide had come together to gather truth, to find the way of justice, to lead their kinsmen once again down the honorable path of the Real People. Yet High Bear, the healer, was the only one not allowing anger to stand in his way.

"From this Square of Mellowed Earth," began High Bear, raising the sacred pipe, "we offer prayers to the Ones Above." His words echoed the words of Sunstone, so often heard within the council lodge. Wolfskin Necklace's blood raced.

"Two great tragedies have befallen our people."

Two? Of what did he speak?

"A great Shirt Wearer, an honored leader and warrior, has been taken from us." High Bear turned his head in Wolfskin Necklace's direction. "His absence leaves a chasm in our souls, and anger in our hearts. This is our first, and greatest, tragedy."

"*Hecetu yelo.*" The other men nodded their heads in solemn assent. Wolfskin waited.

"Our second tragedy is like a poison, like a sickness that kills from the inside out. Caws Like Magpie has had this sickness for all the winters of his life. Even as a child. The people saw it, but could do nothing, for one cannot draw one's bow against an enemy of the spirit. Envy was Caws Like Magpie's enemy. It ate away at him like the maggot eats on rotting flesh. And now it has become our enemy."

High Bear's words puzzled Wolfskin Necklace. They did not fit together easily, did not fit his need for quick revenge.

High Bear gestured to Dark Cloud to lift the lodge's door flap. "Let True Dog and the granddaughter of Turtle Woman enter."

True Dog came in first, his eyes downcast, his rounded face devoid of all humor. Skye, her large eyes wary, came in next, led by Dark Cloud's daughter, Lost Morning. A small piece of bark clung to Skye's hair.

"Tell us, *takoja,* how it came to be that your grandfather fell from the cliffs," High Bear asked gently.

Skye's words unfolded, darkening the lodge with their story. Wolfskin Necklace grew hot with anger. The Naca from Muddy Water camp attacking the granddaughter of his *hunka,* his chosen father? *Hiya!*

"Caws Like Magpie insulted Grandfather," continued Skye, "told him to go back down the mountain. But he wouldn't go— wouldn't leave me." She covered her face with her hands, hiding her tears. Then she straightened her shoulders, wiping her cheeks dry. Lost Morning kept her eyes lowered.

"He was strong! And I had no knife—nothing to fight back with! He said I had shamed him by cutting his face. I spat in his face! He said he would teach me the *true* ways of a warrior."

"That coward knows nothing of a warrior's ways!" Wolfskin Necklace said.

"He shames himself. He shames all Lakota warriors," spoke up Dark Cloud. High Bear nodded his head.

"Grandfather jumped at him, pulled him off me, knocked him

down. They fought, close to the edge, wrestling like bears. Then Magpie pushed him—over the edge, off the cliff . . ." Skye hid her face in her hands again, looking very small within the huge dark tipi. The little fire that burned in the center of the lodge cast but a pale light upon any of them.

High Bear turned his gaze to the scout. "Tell us, True Dog, how you came to be there."

"Mahto and I had ridden far in search of fresh tall grass. But we could find none along the shores of the running waters of the Shell. All had been eaten, devoured by the four-legged creatures of the *wasicus*."

"*Yelo*," the men agreed.

"They are like locusts upon the plains," Dark Cloud said.

"We hunted furtively, for the tracks of the *wasicus* were fresh upon the ground."

"And when did you come upon Skye?" Wolfskin Necklace asked impatiently.

"We found her below the white cliffs." True Dog hung his head. "Struggling to lift the body of our honored Shirt Wearer."

High Bear's face was impassive, but sorrow, deep as the ancient bowels of the earth, darkened his eyes. High Bear also had been Sunstone's friend, his comrade. He had spent many winters seated by the fire in Turtle Woman's lodge, teaching her the healing sacred medicine, contemplating with her husband the loss of the old ways.

Wolfskin Necklace looked around at the elders gathered within the council lodge. All had been Sunstone's friends. Surely all felt the urge for vengeance, knowing that their own desires must not come before the good of the people.

High Bear spoke. "The death of the Shirt Wearer is a great tragedy—the greatest to befall our people since the death of Bull Bear—because he died by the hands of one of our own people." He paused. "The Ikce Oyate do not kill one another." He paused again, then held his own hands up to the dim firelight. "When poison invades the body, it must be cut out. Caws Like Magpie must be banished from the tribe. Exiled. Severed like a gangrenous limb. He is no longer one of the Ikce Oyate. He is no longer Lakota. This is the second tragedy. This day, two men are lost to us."

No longer one of the People? This was to be his punishment? Mere deprivation? Wolfskin Necklace knew the healer possessed far greater wisdom than he. Still. Banishment? Wolfskin's heart wanted blood.

"And what if"—all eyes turned to the Light-skinned One, amazed that she would be so daring as to question High Bear— "and what if my *ate* dies? How many men will you have lost then? Or does he not matter?" Tears threatened to drown her boldness.

Macdonald. Nearly forgotten.

"Your *ate*," High Bear answered in a tone that both acknowledged and admonished, "will not die. His wound will heal."

So. Sunstone's granddaughter had her own vengeful desires.

The other men voiced their concerns, some agreeing, some disagreeing. All knew the choice was theirs, the punishment a matter of individual decision. No elder, no matter how high his rank, would choose to speak for the entire group. But in the end, all agreed with High Bear. Caws Like Magpie should be forever cast out from the tribe.

The council ended. True Dog lifted the door flap and went out, followed by Lost Morning and Skye. The men filtered out, one by one, until only High Bear and Wolfskin Necklace remained inside the lodge.

"Leave your anger, my friend," said High Bear to him, "do not let it become a poison inside of you, as Caws Like Magpie allowed envy to do. Do not let it destroy you."

Not so long ago Wolfskin Necklace had said the same thing to Mahto, back in the Medicine Bows, in Macdonald's cabin. *Leave your anger, and bring the gift to me.* Those had been his words. He had said what he knew Sunstone would have said in his place. *Leave your anger.*

High Bear cleared his throat, then spoke. "Mahto has gone to find Caws Like Magpie. When he returns with him, then you must decide which path you will walk."

"And if Mahto returns to tell us Caws Like Magpie no longer lives?"

High Bear contemplated the dying embers of the fire, rubbing his chin. He obviously knew sparks flew between Mahto and Skye, knew the scout had his own desire for revenge.

"And if Mahto returns alone?" Wolfskin Necklace asked again.

"Then a third tragedy will have befallen our people."

26

THE ENEMY WITHIN

Banished! **It could** not be. Banish her son, the Naca? Never. They would not dare.

Doublewoman Dreamer scurried away from where she'd crouched outside the Red Council Lodge, running in the shadows of darkness until she reached her own tipi. The Shirt Wearer dead. At Magpie's hand. And the Light-skinned One? Ha! The half-caste had probably lured her son, shaken her tail at him like a cow elk during the rutting moon.

And what of Turtle Woman? The One-Only-One's husband dead, and the Scotsman lying wounded in her tipi. Magpie should have spilled that one's lifeblood when he had the chance—slit his throat, not his arm.

Doublewoman stirred her fire's embers, adding a few small pieces of kindling. She lifted the broken mirror to her face and stared at her reflection. Magpie. Little Raven, she used to call him, long ago, when he was but a babe suckling at her breast, when her bones still had flesh on them, her skin still felt smooth and soft.

In some ways, the death of Little Raven's twin brother had

been a blessing from Wakan Tanka—for no mother deserved more than one vile son to rob her of her sanity.

"*E-i-i-i!*" she moaned. To kill the Shirt Wearer! "*E-i-i-i!*"

She stared into the growing flames, adding more deadfall. *Moon Time,* she thought, *the third of the Four Worlds of Creation. Better, perhaps, than this world. Anog Ite. Two-Faced Woman of the Moon Time. Woman who lives with the wood spirits. No one understands you, Anog Ite, not now, not even in the days of long ago. Being a mother is not always easy, is it, Anog Ite? Sometimes devotion rips at our innards—like a hard birth. Yet sometimes it is all a mother has.*

Turtle Woman's blood-encrusted arms and long stringy hair made Skye wince. "Unci," she said softly, "you must eat." Her grandmother did not answer, but sat in the shadows and rocked back and forth.

For nearly four days she had stared at her husband's shroud-covered body, leaving only once each day to disappear into the trees for a few moments. She had not eaten; she had slept only a few hours. She did not answer the nickering calls of the old roan mare.

Turtle Woman had sat thus when the other women came to dress Sunstone, clothing him in his finest regalia and laying his weapons by his side. They braided his hair and wrapped it in otter skins, smoothing the eagle feathers in his scalp lock and combing the hair locks on his ceremonial shirt. "Ahh-h," they had exclaimed to themselves, "such a great leader." They put fringed, ceremonial leggings upon his legs and beaded spirit-moccasins upon his feet. But when they began to straighten the leather thong of Sunstone's medicine pouch, Turtle Woman cried out, "*Hiya!*" and rose from her grieving trance to arrange the *wotawe* herself.

Skye had watched the women, wanting to help, to do something besides bathe Ate's wound with the poultices that High Bear brought, waiting for the days to end. Then, on the third day, slowly, little by little, the infection withdrew its lethal grip from Ate's arm. Today he grew stronger, and she remembered to thank High Bear for the healing poultices. Her own spirit began to lighten.

"Eat, Unci," she pleaded gently, offering her grandmother the bowl of warm broth one last time.

"Ye might as well give up, lass. She's not going to eat until she's good and ready." Ate got up and paced back and forth, restless, then sat back down and leaned into the willow backrest. "Might decide never to eat, ye know. Mourning is a powerful thing for Indians."

A powerful thing only for *Indians?* Skye challenged him with a sideways look. She envied their keening, their wailing, their grief-purging passion. She even envied the scarring slashes upon her grandmother's flesh, the spilling of blood for a loved one. Their grief healed better than her father's brooding silence, and they were cleansed of it, comforted. Yet more powerful? She did not know. A dark power had taken hold of Ate ten years ago, of that she was sure.

The mourning of the women left her more an outsider now than ever. She handed the bowl of untouched broth to her father and watched him drink it down in one gulp.

"Ate"—she looked away from him—"how do the Highlanders mourn their dead?"

"How? What do ye mean?"

"How? Do they cut their hair and black their faces? Do they carry on, or sit solemn and dab at their tears with bits of hankie? How do they mourn?" she repeated.

"They keep guard over the restless spirit of the departed," he answered, not looking at her but vigorously rotating his injured arm.

"Careful," she warned, "you'll start it bleeding again."

He continued to exercise the limb, staring out through the open lodge flap as he spoke. "They keep watch over the restless spirit, and they dance and sing during the late-wake."

"Late-wake?"

"Aye. Following a person's death. The hired *bean tuirim*, the weeping woman, comes to sing songs about the great deeds of the departed. The widow woman dances while the piper plays. They do carry on a mite, ye could say. Now move aside, lass." He ended the conversation, standing again, this time pulling on his boots.

"I'll go plumb daft if I have to stay another minute inside this hovel."

"Caws Like Magpie returns!" The words bounced off tongues, skittered between lodges, flew from feathered lance to painted shield.

People gathered at the edge of camp, angry scowls upon their blackened, accusing faces. But no one, Wolfskin Necklace noticed, no one stood beside the disheveled figure of the *witko* woman. Nor did anyone stand beside the Scotsman and the Light-skinned One, who waited alone near Turtle Woman's lodge.

Wolfskin Necklace fought his own desire for blood, quelled the snarling wolverine raging inside him, sought the patience of the cloud-bird.

Magpie rode into camp alone as Mahto, the Kiyuksa scout, reined in his tobiano and waited on the ridgetop beyond. *The scout allows the Naca to live. This is good. And he allows him to enter camp by himself; the scout is wiser than I thought.*

Magpie rode haughtily, with chin high and shoulders straight. But the shell decorations no longer hung from his ears, and his ornately quilled shirt was gone. He rode in bare-chested and bareheaded, his coup feathers gone, nothing left but the silver trade disks. His arrogance was but a pretense, for red welts covered his flesh.

The crowd stood back, making room as High Bear and the other elders appeared. High Bear signaled with his eyes for Wolfskin Necklace to stand beside him. Together, they approached the mounted Caws Like Magpie.

"Do you wish to tell the people anything?" High Bear asked, his voice restrained.

"The old man thought he was young again. He was a fool."

My hunka, a fool? Wolfskin Necklace lunged at Caws Like Magpie, wrestling him to the ground. He lifted his fist to strike. *Does anger rule you as well?* A voice in his head whispered the question. He jerked the Naca to his feet and stepped back.

High Bear took hold of the horse's bridle. Magpie grabbed the reins from the dirt. Wolfskin Necklace braced himself. For a long, silent moment, no one moved.

Then High Bear spoke. "You allowed your lust and wrath to harm a tribesman. Because of you, our honored Shirt Wearer is dead."

Magpie did not meet the holy man's eyes, nor Wolfskin Necklace's, nor did he humbly look down. Instead, he stared out across the crowd.

High Bear spoke again. "The Ones Who Decide have banished you. You are to leave. You are no longer one of the Ikce Oyate. In the minds of the scattered ones, you no longer exist. If we look upon you again, after this day has ended, we will see only a *toka*—an enemy to be slain. Go. Be gone from this place."

High Bear let go of Magpie's horse, turned, and strode away. He did not wait for the Naca to answer, for Wolfskin Necklace or the other elders to speak. Nothing, really, remained to be said.

I should have struck him. Killed him.

Wolfskin Necklace watched as Magpie led his horse away, watched until he was nearly at the tipis of the Muddy Water camp. Then he turned away. All turned their blackened faces from Magpie. They, too, fought the snarling wolverine within, hid the wish that someday Magpie would return . . . a *toka* to be slain.

The men raised their lances to the sun as they departed for their tipis—silent war cries honoring the Shirt Wearer, filling the emptiness. The women raised keening voices in Sunstone's memory as they turned their backs. The children kicked dirt on the horse Magpie led, and then, wriggling like pups, snuck up behind Doublewoman Dreamer and made water on her moccasins.

27

THE ENEMY WITHOUT

"Move yourself over, lass."

"Ate, I beg of you, do not do this." Skye shielded the pannier with her body.

"I should've done it long afore now. Out of me way, lass."

"Ate, you're not well enough—your arm's barely had time to heal."

"Out of me way!"

Gregory, ignoring the ache in his arm, pushed his daughter aside. His heart was enraged, yet stone cold, all at once. He felt nothing, yet he felt everything. Hate. Anger. Bitterness. Protectiveness. And love. Dreaded, agonizing love. *How he hated to remember.*

Sunstone's death must be avenged and his daughter's honor upheld, and he must rid himself of the agony that tore at his soul. He opened the pannier and withdrew his kilt and saffron shirt, the tasseled pouch, bearskin hat, and heirloom brooch. Turning away from Skye, who stood beside her silent grandmother, he stripped and donned the long shirt of the Highland Warrior, then began gathering his kilt into the great folds of tartan tradition.

A deadly acceptance filled Skye, aging her beyond her years, beyond even her own comprehension. Nothing now would stop her father, or prevent the coming battle. This moment had been written on the pages of history long before, as had been her mother's death, and her grandfather's death. The cougar. The cliff. Yes, even her own birth, even the comet shooting across the sky the night she left the safety of her mother's womb—all had been pre-ordained, predestined.

She walked toward Father, remembering the feel of the knife blade between her fingers as she flung it at Caws Like Magpie, recognizing the same determination in her father's lichen-green eyes. Unyielding. Unswerving. All things became possible—hurling a knife at the heart of a man, hurling your heart into the unknown future.

Taking the brooch from her father's hand, she helped him drape the final fold of pleated tartan over his shoulder, then fastened it with the pin that bore the Macdonald badge.

"For the heather, Ate," she whispered, their eyes meeting, "for the heather."

"Aye, my child," he answered, his voice barely a murmur, "for the heather, and for the Highlands."

They turned toward the light that filtered in under the open door flap of the lodge. A shadow crossed in front of Sunstone's body—Turtle Woman, moving deliberately across the breadth of the tipi. In her outstretched hands, she held up the naked claymore, offering the double-edged sword to her son-in-law.

Mahto's tobiano had pawed the ridgetop impatiently, eager to join the other ponies grazing just beyond camp. Mahto had watched Caws Like Magpie ride into the circle of lodges, carrying his vile head high, like a warrior returning with many coups. Mahto wished Wolfskin Necklace had drawn blood from the coward. Mahto wished *he* had drawn blood from the coward yesterday—*heart* blood. Not just blood from the Naca's sniveling nose.

The temptation to kill Caws Like Magpie had been great, almost more than Mahto could resist. Especially when the Naca came at him in the dark of night, creeping across the ground like a spider. Mahto had welcomed the challenge, had hoped for it, had even been surprised by the strength of the Naca. But he had not killed the man from the Muddy Water camp.

Mahto had watched as Caws Like Magpie picked himself up out of the dirt, dusting himself off. High Bear had spoken, holding Magpie's horse, no doubt telling him the decision of the Ones Who Decide, then turned him loose and walked away in disgust.

The blackened faces of the people, too, had turned away, their weapons raised to the sky, their keening voices floating, like smoke, beyond the camp of the Oglalas. The children had taunted the *witko* woman, no longer afraid of her dreaming powers. They kicked dirt at Magpie as he led his horse toward the lodges of the Muddy Water people, and spat at his retreating figure.

At first, Mahto did not see the Light-skinned One. Then he found her standing beside the Scotsman, off to the side, away from the crowd. The hair of the *wasicu* caught the sun, and the sun flashed from it like fire. Skye's hair looked dark beside her father's, her braids long and pleasing.

Mahto did not hurry to leave the ridge. He sat astride the tobiano, watching Doublewoman Dreamer begin to strike her lodge. She pulled the wooden stakes from the dirt, struggling under the weight of the heavy hides. No other women came to help her. Magpie, dishonored and disrobed, gathered together his arrows and quiver, his bow and war club and shield.

The tobiano pawed at the earth again, then lifted his head and whinnied; his call carried down to the camp. The old roan mare belonging to Turtle Woman saw him, and lifting her head answered with a nicker.

The Light-skinned One and her father retreated into Turtle Woman's tipi. Mahto gave his horse a gentle nudge with his heels, urging him slowly off the ridge. He had much to tell True Dog—and much to tell High Bear, Dark Cloud, and the other elders. There were Kangis crossing the river, with a strange warrior leading them.

Easing down the hill, he heard the old roan mare nicker again. His pony flicked his ears forward and snorted. From a distance, Mahto glanced at Sunstone's lodge, imagined the willow backrest empty, the place of honor unoccupied. Never again would the great Shirt Wearer step from the darkness of his tipi into the brightness of day. The loss to their people overwhelmed him.

He pulled back on the reins and the tobiano impatiently tossed his head, prancing in place. Mahto stared at the tipi's shadowed doorway, hoping to see the Light-skinned One come into the open again. Instead, out stepped the Scotsman, the warrior-skirt wrapped around his burly torso, the long-knife in his hand. He stood for a moment, sniffing the air, then lifted his long-knife over his head and strode toward the Muddy Water camp.

Mahto dropped slack into his reins and kicked the tobiano into a run.

Gregory heard the pipe music as plainly as if he'd been playing it himself. 'Twas a war song—"big music" they called it in the High-lands—and it bellowed within his mind like a bull. His feet struck the packed earth in cadence with the booming notes, air swirling around his bare legs. Sun glinted from the blade of the sword. Shining times, for certain, *shining fighting times*—made the blood race and the heart pound, like a buffler bull's in spring. He was a hard case, and he knew it. Caws Like Magpie would crowd him no longer. If he caught the coward moving for deep water, he'd wade into his liver, make wolf meat out of him! He feared no evil eye this day, no Droch Shuil of the black art.

Skye ducked through the door of the tipi, squinting at the bright sun. Father's long strides carried him quickly toward the Muddy Water camp. She hurried after him, noticing that she did not hear the footsteps of her grandmother behind her.

Wolfskin Necklace saw them pass, saw the Scotsman's many-colored skirt, the sword-with-two-edges flashing against the blue, cloudless sky. The air became motionless, as if the thunder-beings were about to speak. His skin tightened, and a shiver ran up his spine.

True Dog, about to enter his wickiup, paused when he heard the hoofbeats of the galloping tobiano. High Bear and Dark Cloud, talking near the council lodge, turned their heads at the sound. Lost Morning looked at her mother and together they shook their heads as the Scotsman went marching by, chanting his war song. The women did not understand the Gaelic words, but they recognized the chant as a strong-heart song, sung to strengthen the spirit before battle.

The instinct for survival that all two-leggeds share caused Doublewoman Dreamer to straighten from her work. Her gnarled hand flew to her mouth. "A-i-i-i!" she cried, knowing that the inevitable had finally come to pass, understanding how the forked-tail bird felt just before the eagle snatched him from the sky. She opened her mouth to cry out again, but terror had stolen her voice from her.

Caws Like Magpie closed the rawhide case, then, swatting a fly away from his face, scratched at his tender cheek. He was finished with this place, with Bull Bear's followers, with all of them. They were like bones picked clean; nothing remained for him. He would go north, find the Smoke People, join the council of their leader, Bad Face. Surely they knew the value of a Naca.

He set his quiver down next to the case, then picked up his stone-headed war club, testing the balance of the weapon, remembering the feeling of power it used to give him. *Hokahe!* The old war cry echoed in his mind. *Hoppo!* Then, unconcerned, he turned at a slight noise behind him. The war club suddenly weighed heavy in his hand. Staring back at him was the grinning, red-haired *wasicu*.

"I'm glad to see that ye've got your weapon ready, Magpie, for the sun has risen upon your final day." The Scotsman shifted the massive long-knife from one hand to the other. "Come hither, Caws Like Magpie, for I aim to cut out your tongue with me claymore! Then I figure to tickle your hump ribs with the tip of me sword!"

Magpie looked around. The bent figure of his mother stood openmouthed beside the crumpled tipi, the half-blood girl waited behind the Scotsman, hoofbeats pounded upon the ground, his still-bridled horse lifted his head from the grass. Only one recourse remained.

"*Hokahe!*" he yelled out as he dashed for his horse, leaping onto the animal's back. "*Hokahe!*" But the last war cry came out choked and small, for he didn't even have enough saliva to spit. It did not matter, he told himself—he would do his talking with his war club.

Gregory smiled.

Aye, shining times for certain! No more waiting. No more putting off what should've been done long afore. 'Twas a grand day to be tying up loose ends, to be hauling in your trap lines and counting your plews. Caws Like Magpie leapt on his horse, looking small-chested with nary a fancy shirt on. A fella could easily run his sword through such a chest.

Magpie charged, his horse rearing, then plunging forward. He came at Gregory, covering the short distance between them in less than three strides. Gregory grasped his claymore with both hands and lifted it high into the air. He dodged the stone head of Magpie's club as it came whirling at him, then swung at Magpie's back as he ran by. The tip of the sword missed the man, but severed the strip of silver trade disks that hung down Magpie's back, and they fell jangling to the ground along with a strand of his coarse black hair.

Gregory twirled to meet the second charge. Magpie spun his horse around and came at him again, his war club raised, his elbows flailing at the air. This time Gregory timed his swing more carefully, lifting the heavy sword over his right shoulder, bringing it down with lethal force, ignoring the tearing pain in his arm.

The stone head of the war club smashed against the double-edged blade, nearly knocking the weapons from both men's grasps. Magpie clutched at his horse's mane to right himself, then spun around. Gregory, knocked to his knees, sprang up and shifted to the left, facing the charging horse from the opposite side. This time, his sword would be aimed at his enemy's heart, not his back.

Magpie shifted his war club to his right hand and lunged forward again. At the last moment, he jerked his horse's head in front of Gregory, forcing Gregory off balance. The war club caught him in the wounded arm, breaking open the fresh scar. Blood reddened his saffron shirt.

"Wagh!" Gregory yelled, rage coursing through his veins. He met the next charge running, dodging, jumping from one foot to the next. His sword met Caws like Magpie full in the chest, but a well-placed blow with the stone club caused the claymore to twist in Gregory's hand, so only the flat side of the sword struck the Naca. No blood spilled, but the sound of cracking ribs brought another smile to Gregory's face.

Magpie, in a fit of violent anger as he was almost unseated, brought the war club down upon his own horse's flank, and the horse, frightened and in pain, reared. Gregory, despite his weakening arm, lifted the broadsword once more and threw himself at Magpie. The horse reared again, lethal hooves striking at the man before him, catching Gregory on the temple.

The ground came up to meet him, and everything went dark. He cursed himself for getting in the way of the hooves, groped in vain for his grandfather's claymore. He tried to stand, tried to force the light to enter the murkiness, but the earth held him like a mother clutching her sleeping babe. A fleeting image of Breathcatcher came to him in the darkness—Breathcatcher holding their newborn daughter to her breast. He tried to utter her name, tried to will his body to move, but the image faded into near darkness, and another image took its place—his graunie Maggie standing in a field of heather, beckoning to him. Odd, he could almost see through her . . .

Mahto leapt from the still-moving tobiano, hitting the ground running. He saw it all—saw Magpie's horse rear, saw the Light-skinned One's father crash to the earth like a cracked-horn shot through the heart, saw the Naca slide from his horse and press his skinning knife against the scalp of the Scotsman. But Wolfskin Necklace darted to Macdonald's side before Mahto, drawing his own knife against the Naca.

"*Toka*, enemy of the people," Wolfskin Necklace snarled. He grabbed Caws Like Magpie's hair and held his knife to the Naca's scalp. The Naca loosened but did not relinquish his grip on Macdonald.

"*Toka*, to honor Turtle Woman with your scalp would give me great pleasure. To see her dance around the fire with your hair hanging from the Shirt Wearer's lance! *Han!*"

"*Yun! Yuuuun!*" cried Doublewoman Dreamer in fear, holding her hands to her gaping mouth.

The Light-skinned One, already at her father's side, pushed away Magpie's hand, her eyes filled with a hatred so intense that even Magpie stepped back. Then she knelt down, cradling the Scotsman's head in her lap. "No, Ate," she pleaded, "no, no . . ."

Wolfskin Necklace reached past the two black feathers dangling on Caws Like Magpie's chest and pulled taut the leather thong around his neck. Magpie gasped for breath, dropping his knife and clutching at his throat. Wolfskin Necklace gave the thong a final twist, then, nicking Magpie's neck with the tip of the blade, cut the leather.

"You are not worthy to be scalped," he spat at Caws Like Magpie, throwing the feathers to the ground. "You sicken me." He pushed Magpie further away from the grieving girl, then turned and took a step. Like an angry *tatanka*, he suddenly pivoted. Quicker than a colt, he kicked the Naca in the face. Blood spurted from his nose. Then Wolfskin Necklace turned and left, brushing past High Bear and Dark Cloud, leaving the camp's *akicitas* to further deal with the exile.

Mahto stared at Skye. First her grandfather, now her father. He knew her grief, remembered his own father's death at the hands of the Susunis. The forever-pain never left him, never ceased to ache in his heart. To comfort her now would do no good. The Light-skinned One must learn to tame the anguish on her own.

He knelt beside her, letting their arms touch. Then he worked his hands beneath the dead man's body and lifted it from the ground.

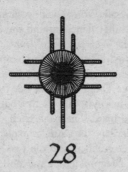

28

STRONG-BACKED WOMEN

O Death, the poor man's dearest friend, the kindest and the best! Thou lingering star, with lessening ray, that lov'st to greet the early morn . . .
— Robert Burns

Skye closed Graunie Maggie's book of verse and held it in her hands, caressing the worn leather cover, wondering if she had the courage to read the words aloud. What else was she to do? Certainly they expected something from her, some sort of ceremony. *Ceremonies.* She shuddered as she thought of the tortured rattlesnake. Was she to slash her flesh? Cut the hair from her head? Kill Roy, as they would soon kill Sunstone's warhorse?

Only one death scaffold, a bed made of sturdy branches held above the ground by four forked tree limbs, stood on the cliff top. High Bear had come to her, asked her about the important customs of her father's people. She had been watching Caws Like Magpie disappear into the dusk, with the crow clinging to his shoulder, the *witko* woman scuttling behind him, a dog slinking alongside, tail tucked. Important customs? What did she know about Ate's people? She answered High Bear lamely, "Someone, I think, usually plays a fiddle, or the pipes. Perhaps there is singing."

"The music-maker—the wind bag?" he asked her.

"Aye, and there is usually someone dancing," she added non-committally, staring at the outcasts as they disappeared into the distance. She had wanted to follow Magpie, to finish what her father had started.

"It is not your custom," High Bear asked, "to allow the sun to rise four times before a burial?"

Oh, God. Another four-day death vigil? She shook her head. "No."

"I have seen the graves of the *wasicus.*" He hesitated, then continued. "Do you wish for your *ate* to have this grave beneath the earth?"

She did not remember nodding, but she must have. For True Dog and Mahto, along with a few other young men, had dug a hole beside her grandfather's scaffold. The mourners waited there for them now, on the white cliffs, small wooden skewers driven through their flesh, ash blackening their faces, keening voices lacing together like a veil of grief.

"*Takoja*, we must go."

Skye barely recognized Unci's voice, for days had passed since last she spoke. A new strength could be heard. Her grandmother's voice lifted Skye, propping her up, giving substance to her own deflated spirit. And as always, Unci knew Skye's thoughts.

"You, *mitakoja* of the sky, are also a child of the earth."

Tears flooded Skye's eyes, threatening to flow down her cheeks. Until now she had been able to keep her emotions in check, because no one, other than High Bear, had spoken directly to her. But Unci's kind words, the tone of her voice, tore at the thin callused layer protecting Skye's heart.

"It is all right for the body of your *ate* to lie in the earth."

"I wish . . ." She faltered, not wanting to think about her father. "I wish I were not alone." The tears escaped.

"You are not alone," Unci said softly, placing a hand upon Skye's cheek, wiping away the wetness. "Your ancestors are my ancestors. And our ancestors of long ago, even before the time of First Man, came from beneath the earth. Our customs are not so different."

But I don't know what my customs are. Can't you see that?

"Come, *takoja*. Together we will honor our men. We will honor the Four Winds; we will honor the Sky above, and the Earth below. Come."

Skye clasped the book of verse to her breast as they stepped from the tipi. Unci walked over to the roan mare and, closing her eyes, placed her cheek against the horse's neck. The horse lowered her head and pressed it gently against the old woman. They stood thus for a full minute. Then Turtle Woman turned toward Skye and the two began their long walk up the trail.

Though Sunstone had been a great warrior and respected elder, his few belongings, set at the foot of the scaffold, were unremarkable. Not much remained to be given away, for, in the way of a true and honorable Lakota, Sunstone had acquired little wealth. Oh, he had once had many horses, many supple robes, many finely crafted weapons and pipes and saddles and blankets. But just as quickly as he acquired them, he gave them away. He had been a true Oglala, a true Lakota, one of the Ikce Oyate: brave, wise, strong-hearted, and generous.

Wolfskin Necklace followed behind four clanswomen who pulled the two travois bearing the robe-enwrapped bodies of the men. As he led his *hunka*'s favorite horse up the ridge, he reexamined the painted red spots that adorned the animal. He had known, even as he had painted them, that they were an inadequate tribute to his second father. Perhaps the other horses that he led, taken from his own herd to be given as gifts, would help pay homage to his *hunka*'s memory. Perhaps giving away his own blankets and robes and finely quilled clothing, piled upon the backs of the horses, would ease the sadness.

Turtle Woman and her granddaughter followed the small procession; their grief shadowed every step Wolfskin Necklace took, accentuated each twist of the wooden skewers as they pulled at his flesh. But he welcomed the pain—it forced him to turn his mind away from the body and toward the spirit.

The entire camp—the Kiyuksas of the Bear Den, the Muddy

Water clan, the Standing People—all stood gathered at the burial site. A gentle southern breeze stirred the air. The women walked sunwise around the empty scaffold, wailing and singing of grief. Black bands decorated the four forked poles of the scaffold, symbolic of the many coups earned by the great leader, and from the poles hung his shield and lance.

Pride rose in the heart of Wolfskin Necklace at the traditional ceremony. The Standing People, and those of the Bear Den and Muddy Water clans who camped with them, unlike folk in many other Oglala camps, remained strong in the old ways. Their braves had not yet succumbed to the fire-in-the-belly drink of the *wasicus*, and their leaders stayed far from the rutted trails of rolling-wood wagons and the trading posts.

The elders had not yet sold their tongues to the *wasicus*, and they resisted going to this "big council" of which Broken Hand spoke. Wolfskin Necklace agreed with the hesitation. To take their women and children to Horse Creek—within range of the sharpened arrows of the red *tokas*, the poisoned drink of the white *tokas*—*han*, it was a foolish thing to do.

And Sunstone? Wolfskin Necklace no longer had his *hunka's* wisdom to guide him. Yet now was not a time for decision-making, but a time for the heart to grow strong with remembering.

Near the scaffold, with a mound of gravelly gray dirt piled beside it, gaped the hole into which the Scotsman's body would be placed. No belongings flanked it, no mourners encircled it. The only sign of ceremony was a wooden cross, fashioned by High Bear from the branches of a young bitter cottonwood, which was lying upon the mound of dirt. How strange that Naked Warrior— the *wasicula* from across the great waters—would end his earthly days here, alongside his friend, the great Shirt Wearer of the Oglalas.

Turtle Woman, her heart heavy with grief, could not help but smile, for the spirit of her husband caused a happy thought to grow within her—the two of them love-wrestling beneath their robes. Elk Man. Her only-man. Her forever-man. She would hold on to this thought, use it like a salve to ease the raw stinging of an open wound, use it to strengthen her own spirit.

She readied herself to face the death of Sunstone's warhorse. His death would force the reality of Sunstone's death upon her, as the pain of childbirth forces the infant from the womb. Her husband would have his old friend to ride upon in the Land of Many Lodges, and this thought also gladdened her.

Turtle Woman looked around her at the many friends gathered about the scaffold, as many as would fill two council lodges—friends who had shared cold, starving winters, times of fresh meat and tall grass. These *kolas* lifted her husband's body upon the scaffold, fastened eagle feathers to the poles, cried with her, and with Wolfskin Necklace, as the great warhorse sank to his knees.

Then she heard the singing, the clear notes of a strong, deep male voice rise above the keening. The voice came from the direction of the South Wind—home of the Falling Star, of flute music and sweetgrass. The song lifted her cries and carried them into the great beyond. She breathed deeply, cleansing her lungs, trying to purge herself of the tiny seed of sickness that had begun to grow within her.

Seemingly borne along by the gentle breeze, his face lifted to the sky, came Mahto. Music flowed from him, a ballad full of grief, and hope. The keening grew quiet as his singing reached the mourners. All watched as the scout drew nearer, watched him approach the Light-skinned One, watched her eyes grow wide and her heart grow big.

Mahto's voice filled Skye with wonder, working its way into the deep hollow ache inside her. It recalled the music of Ate's bagpipes, and her father's presence engulfed her; she could almost feel his big burly arms around her, hear the love in his voice as he shared with her the tales of the homeland.

Then the crowd parted, and Lost Morning stepped forward.

Slowly, the young woman began a delicate soft-footed dance, circling the mound of dirt and the open grave. As Mahto sang and Lost Morning danced, Dark Cloud and Wolfskin Necklace placed Ate's body in the hole. Tears streamed down Skye's face. She could not contain them, could not contain the sorrow—and joy—that welled up inside her.

Dark Cloud walked toward the grave, carrying the bagpipes. He held them out to Skye, gesturing toward the hole. She nodded. He knelt and placed the pipes beside the body. Skye imagined Ate in his kilt and sporran, smiled at the memory of the bearskin hat and kilt garters. *Oh, why didn't I retrieve the heirloom brooch from his tartan before the women wrapped him in the leather robe? What a keepsake it would be!*

Then Walks Ahead, Dark Cloud's wife, approached Skye and took her hands, placing the treasured brooch alongside Graunie Maggie's book. They had known. *They understood.*

True Dog came up to her next, her father's claymore in his arms, and this he laid beside her on the ground. Then, as Mahto continued to sing, and as Lost Morning danced, the others began to fill the open grave.

Skye looked at the book, remembering the well-loved verses. But she did not open it, did not read from it. Instead, in words that called out to her from a decade past, words once spoken with a child's voice, she began to recite:

> "He makes me down to lie
> In pastures green: he leadeth me
> the quiet waters by . . ."

As night fell, a layer of mist draped itself upon the camp of the Oglalas. The old roan mare lifted her head and peered into the damp dusk.

No more sounds came from the ridge, no more mourners came walking down the trail toward camp. But the old mare continued to stare at the horizon, and at the two women silhouetted against the deepening night.

One stood beside the wooden scaffold, arms raised to the sky, head uplifted. The other knelt beside a wooden cross, head bowed, hands clasped. Above them, riding the currents of an updraft, two cloud-birds flew in silent sacred circles.

The mist hung heavy, hemmed in by the chalk cliffs. Eventually, it would rise as all mist rises, to be absorbed into the depths of the Great Spirit.

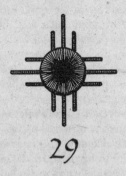

29

FIRE, WATER, EARTH, AND AIR

"**This war party** that you saw, Mahto, they were Kangi warriors?" Dark Cloud narrowed his eyes as he spoke.

"*Han.* They were Kangis. Traveling west. I watched as they crested the far ridge, led by the woman."

"A woman wearing the leathers of a warrior?"

"*Hiya.* Hers was the dress of a woman. But she carried a lance and had a quiver and bow hanging from her back."

"And the others followed her?"

"*Han,* they followed and she led. In the direction of the setting sun. Their horses stopped long to air their lungs, as if they had been traveling at great speeds."

"None remained behind?"

"*Hiya,*" Mahto said. "None remained. All followed the woman."

"And from what direction did they appear?" Dark Cloud asked, still scowling—angry, Mahto assumed, at the thought of Kangi warriors invading Lakota territory. It angered Mahto as well.

"They came from the Medicine Mountains, carrying wood, perhaps *wakan* wood for the making of bows. They moved in the direction of the Shell River, skirting the trail made by the wagons of the *wasicus*."

"Only a handful of men?"

"No more. A handful, plus the woman."

Dark Cloud squatted beside the fire, holding his hands up to the flames although the evening was balmy. Mahto knelt beside him, unwilling to stand when Dark Cloud, an elder, did not. Then Mahto ventured forth a guess.

"Woman Chief, the Hewaktoka?"

Dark Cloud nodded, rubbed his hands together, and stood up. "Stories of her warrior deeds fly from lodge to lodge, from village to village." He gazed into the distance. "It would be a good thing to sharpen our eyes and our ears. The Kangi's thirst for Lakota blood has never been quenched."

Mahto nodded, then stood. "True Dog and I will lift our noses to the wind. No *toka* will approach unnoticed."

"These rocks," queried Turtle Woman, "were important to your *ate?*" The two women stood outside the lodge, bending over one of the open panniers.

"Aye. He hunted rocks as some men hunt meat. When the cougar . . . After Ina . . ." Skye fumbled her words. "It was all he cared to do, though I didn't realize he'd packed some of them along. *Haye*, look," she said, picking a fossilized footprint from the collection. "Ate once told me that fairies had etched their stories into these rocks. Like winter counts painted upon the hides."

"Ah, the fairies again." Her grandmother grinned.

"You know of the little people from the Otherworld? The elfins?" A favorite verse of hers, sung by Father when she was but a child, popped into Skye's head. " 'Up the piney mountain,' Ate used to sing, 'down the open glen. / We daren't go a-hunting, for fear of little men!' "

"*Hoh!*" Turtle Woman laughed. "Sometime you must teach me that song." She traced the footprint with her finger, and Skye tried not to grimace at the sight of her newly maimed hand. "We call them footprints of the ancient ones," Turtle Woman said, "creatures, and rooted beings, which lived in the world of long ago. To us, they are *wakan*, as all rocks are *wakan*. They were sacred to your *ate* also?"

"Sacred?" The thought had never occurred to Skye. "Ate said there were more rocks in the Medicine Bows than in all of Scotland, some of which he'd never seen the likes of. Rocks and bones and all sorts of strange things. He said a person could learn about these things at the universities."

"Universities?"

"Aye. Schools where they teach about such things."

"He went to this school?"

"No, Unci, he went to no school."

"Nor I." Turtle Woman laughed. "Yet we still learn. The ancient ones teach us, do they not?"

Turtle Woman picked up another stone, this one with a leaf imprinted into its surface. The old scar on her knuckle looked almost graceful next to the two swollen, red fingers now missing their tips—a finger shortened for each life ended.

"As a child," she said, "I, too, gathered rocks. Each one told me a story, spoke to me of long-ago places, long-ago times. Then, for a while, I forgot my rocks. Until the Kangis took me to the Medicine Wheel. There, the medicine stones—stones which point the way to the stars—there they whispered to me once again."

"The Kangis—they were good to you?"

"All but one. And he did not kill me, at least."

"You were married?"

"Married, and with child."

"Ina? You were pregnant with my mother?" Skye had heard Breathcatcher speak of the time the Kangis captured Turtle Woman, had heard the story of the young Hewaktoka also captured, though during an earlier raid farther to the north.

"*Hiya*, not your mother. My first child, but no one knew, not even your *tunka* . . ."

A pain tugged at Skye's heart as the word withered on her grandmother's tongue.

"In many ways, you remind me of the young Hewaktoka," Turtle Woman said, redirecting the conversation. "And you have learned to judge the feel of a knife just as well, *han?* Even though I wasn't there to teach you?"

How Skye wished the knife had penetrated Magpie's heart! "Tell me again about Little Badger," she said.

"Little Badger was strong and persistent, determined to have the keenest eye, the strongest arm, the surest aim—even though she was barely a *wikoskala.*" Turtle Woman put the rock back in the pannier and leaned toward Skye. "It would not surprise me," she whispered, "if she is the one they call Woman Chief." Then she straightened and stared into the distance for a moment. "Did your *ina* ever tell you of the prophecy?"

"The shooting-star prophecy? You yourself told me of it, when I was a child."

"I told you only a part of it, for I did not know that the legacy was many-sided, belonging not only to the Standing People. Nor did I ever share with you the words spoken by the shaman high upon the mountain—in the land of the sacred-stone Medicine Wheel."

Unci was whispering again.

"The turtle is like a stone," she said, reaching up and gently taking Skye's pendant in her swollen fingers. "Ancient, like the great land upon which we live. The time has come for you to listen to the stones. The time has come for you to visit the steam lodge, the place of our most ancient of all ceremonies—the place of fire and water, air and earth."

Turtle Woman could feel the grief that anchored her heart turn to sickness within her, a heaviness of breath and weakness of spirit. The cleansing ritual—an *inipi*—would be good. It would strengthen the body and rid it of hurtful things, and the stones would help her to understand the recurring dream that had come to her in the darkness. It would be good to share an *inipi* with her *takoja*. The sweat would purge Skye's hurt from her own grief-stricken body. And, perhaps, even give Turtle Woman the courage to share with her *takoja* the secret of the Kangi grand-mother.

"I have asked Walks Ahead and Lost Morning to come to the steam lodge with us. They will meet us by the running-waters." Turtle Woman gave Skye a glance, then left the tipi. Skye hurried behind her. "We must cut sixteen saplings to build the steam lodge—four for each direction."

"We are going to build the steam lodge?"

"*You* are going to build the steam lodge." Turtle Woman slowed her pace, already out of breath. She and Skye passed behind the tipis and moved down the path leading to the fast-moving creek. The air smelled of willow and cottonwood, of wet rocks and damp grass. She breathed it all in; the musky air smelled of life. Suddenly, more guilt tugged at her. Life. So fleeting. Like the hummingbird.

"*Hau*," Walks Ahead called out, "we are here, near the water."

"*Hau, maske*, you greet the morning before even the sun has risen," Turtle Woman answered.

"It is a good day for *inipi*—too good to be spent in a dark lodge listening to one's sleeping husband snort like a den bear. I have listened to Dark Cloud's snoring enough for this day!"

Walks Ahead's banter brought a grin to Turtle Woman's face. She liked this good woman, this loyal friend.

Lost Morning greeted Turtle Woman with a smile, and a timid "*hau*" cast in Skye's direction. Skye's own hello was soft-spoken, shy.

"It is good of you to *inipi* with us," Turtle Woman said.

Walks Ahead smiled. "It takes much work to build the steam lodge. It is good to have help."

Turtle Woman had a question she must ask her granddaughter, but how to do so without offending Lost Morning and Skye both? She had not spoken of the alone-tipi with Skye, of the place a woman went when her body cleansed itself, when she made a blood offering to each new moon. All women, during this powerful time, stayed in the alone-tipi. None went to the steam lodge during this time. After, yes. But during? No.

"The *wikoskalas,*" she posed the question to both girls, "have no need to visit the alone-tipi?"

Lost Morning gave Turtle Woman a perplexed look, then shook her head. "It is not my time."

"And you?" Turtle Woman looked at Skye. Had her *takoja* been taught this necessary custom? By her *ate?* By anyone?

"My *ina,*" Skye began, slightly taken aback, "would do her quilling during her alone-time. Even then, I understood the need. No," she said, shaking her head, "it is not *my* time either."

"*Waste,* good." Turtle Woman tried to act as if the question were normal, as if all Lakota girls would be asked this question, as if they might not know better. But her words had not fooled Skye. *A-i-i-i, it is not easy to walk with your moccasins upon these different paths.*

Skye secured the last hide over the dome-shaped framework of willows, wiping the sweat from her brow. The day had grown hot; dusk would be a welcome friend.

Lost Morning had helped her to construct the steam lodge, had shown her where to place the saplings, how to bend them, how to secure them with strips of leather. Together they had dug the center pit.

"It must be perfectly round," Lost Morning had said, "like the sun." Skye had watched as Lost Morning sprinkled the dirt from the pit in a line leading away from the small hut. "The sacred path," Lost Morning said, "leading to the *unci,* the grandmother." And then she formed a small mound with what remained of the dirt. "Here," she said, pointing a few feet to the east, "here we will build the fireplace, the Fire Without End."

Skye did not relish the idea of a fire. A cool dip in the creek perhaps, but not a fire.

She gathered up a handful of sage and followed Lost Morning into the hut. They had gathered enough sage to carpet the floor of the steam lodge, covering every bit of bare ground. A pungent aroma began to fill the small, dark enclosure.

Lost Morning turned to Skye, kneeling in the sage. "I liked," she said softly, staring at the ground, "how you drew the snake from the hole. And to throw the knife at the Naca? *Hoye!* How brave!"

Skye lifted a stalk of sage to her nose, unsure of what to say. "I liked the way you danced," she finally answered, pushing away her twinge of jealousy.

Lost Morning lifted her gaze to Skye's, and then a smile came to her face. "One does not wear clothing during *inipi*," she whispered. "One must be naked, like the newborn. That," she giggled, "is my favorite part."

Skye crawled after her, following her back outside, happy for the friendship that seemed to be growing between them—in her life, the first friend of any sort.

Walks Ahead and Turtle Woman stood several paces away, at the cleared area Lost Morning had called the fireplace, solemnly layering sticks of wood in a sort of pattern. Beside them crouched a wizened old man whom Skye had not seen before. He appeared as old as the earth itself. Deep furrows marked his skin, thin silver hair hung down his back, clothes hung in great folds from his emaciated and crooked figure.

"He's the Keeper of the Fire," whispered Lost Morning, "the oldest man of the Oglalas. His memory has left him—he remembers nothing, except to tend the coals."

The old man held a hollowed-out buffalo horn up to the sun and chanted a few words, then, using a small forked stick, reached into the horn and withdrew a red-hot ember.

"It is the *Peta-oihankesni*. They say it has been burning since the time of White Buffalo Calf Woman, many generations past. Hurry," she continued, "the stones must be placed upon the wood before he lights it. Sometimes he forgets and lights the branches too soon. Then the wood burns up before the stones are hot."

Lost Morning hefted a large stone from a substantial pile of heavy, rounded rocks and placed it carefully upon the layered sticks. "Come on," she urged, bending for a second rock, "there's plenty more to go."

* * *

Energy, Turtle Woman reminded herself, is finite. Only so much is put upon the earth by the Great Mystery. Energy does not die, it does not go away. It simply changes form. From the earth, to the sky, to the waters, and back to the earth once again. *Taku Skan-skan*. The spirit that moves all that moves.

And so it is with good and evil.

She ladled water onto the seven white-hot stones in the center of the steam lodge. Steam filled the darkness, and her grand-daughter gasped as it engulfed her. Sounds of cautious breathing came from Walks Ahead and Lost Morning. Turtle Woman poured another ladle of water upon the stones. Another gasp came from Skye.

"Grandfathers, grandmothers, we thank you." Turtle Woman lifted her bare arms toward the heavens. "We sit here, pitiful and weak, in this lodge of the wind, so that we might feel your sacred breath." The rocks hissed and more steam rose.

"We sit within the universe itself."

Turtle Woman paused. The heat took her breath away. It scalded her lungs. It stung her flesh. *Sacred breath. Cleansing breath.*

"We see your energy. It glows from the sacred rocks. It glows with the goodness of Wakan Tanka."

She became silent, letting everyone listen to the sound of the rising mist and watch the light emanating from the stones, the red eyes peering from beneath the ash. For one brief instant, the courage needed to tell Skye about the Kangi grandmother and the five-pointed star at the Medicine Wheel flared within her. Ah, to unburden herself of this secret. But would she only be passing this burden on to her *takoja?* She reached down at her side, found the small ceremonial drum, and passed it to Walks Ahead.

Skye knew the heat would kill her. Walks Ahead's prayers droned endlessly on, the drum pounded mercilessly, but Skye had been submerged in a pool of scalding water and could think of nothing else. Then Walks Ahead stopped talking and Turtle Woman opened the door flap and a gust of cool air penetrated the sweat lodge, and never before had anything been so wonderful. But the heavenly reprieve did not last. Turtle Woman signaled to High Bear's wife, Little Moon, who had offered to tend the rocks, and one by one seven more were brought in.

This is bloody torture! I'll never last!

But she did. The drum passed on to Lost Morning, who spoke her words in a voice so soft and quick that even had it not been for the pounding in her head, Skye doubted she would have understood all of the Lakota. Sweat dripped from her nose. It ran between her breasts and down the small of her back; it ran between her thighs and down her calves. She stared back at the red-eyed stones. They hissed as Unci ladled more water onto their glowing surfaces.

"The spirit of the water," Lost Morning was saying, "is set free by the heat of the rocks. O Wakan Tanka, help the spirit of the water to cleanse from me all that is not good, all that is harmful."

Skye took a tentative breath, to let only a little steam enter her lungs. Her hand brushed against Lost Morning's and she realized, as her grandmother signaled for more stones to be brought in, that her turn with the drum had come.

At first she thought the moisture running down her cheeks was sweat. Then it dawned on her, as her thumbs began to beat a lonely rhythm on the taut skin of the drum, that she was crying.

Ate, dead. Grandfather, dead. Like Ina. Never again would their voices soothe her, their arms protect her.

She continued to tap on the drumskin, but with all of her fingers now. She closed her eyes. The beat grew louder, faster, the hollow thumping crying out in anger at these unfair tragedies. The vibrations traveled from her fingertips to her hands, up her arms, to deep within. The beating engulfed her, drowned out her own heartbeat. Her very soul vibrated.

Then the rhythm began to ebb, slowly.

The anger and tears became like great rivers of acceptance. Tears that now stemmed not from grief but from relief—for a healing had begun, a restoration of wholeness.

A strength grew inside her, a picture of herself grown and womanly. She had choices before her: she could return to the cabin; she could stay here, among the bands of the Oglalas; or she could even venture far across the ocean, see the Highlands for herself, perhaps meet Graunie Maggie.

She pictured Mahto, remembering his eyes as he lifted the turtle-shell necklace from his own chest and placed it upon hers. She wiped the wetness from her face, then ran her hands down her slick breasts and across her stomach. She took a deep, cleansing breath.

"*Pilamaya,*" she said, searching out Unci's face in the near darkness. "Thank you, Unci." Then, saying no more, she passed the drum to her grandmother.

Turtle Woman gently took the drum from Skye. She had not expected her *takoja* to speak, not during her first *inipi*. The words mattered little. The cleansing held the power—and the drum.

Turtle Woman ladled more water on the hot stones, then sprinkled an offering of *cansasa* in the center of the fire. She, too, began to tap the surface of the drum with her fingers, very slowly, listening for the rhythm of the fire, trying to see the stones not with her flesh-and-blood eyes but with the *cante ista*, the eye of her heart.

Gradually, the rhythm grew stronger, Skye's energy still alive within the drum. The sound reverberated within the small, hide-covered dome until the skins themselves began to vibrate. Turtle Woman knew that it was the heartbeat of all creation: the grieving heartbeat of her *takoja*, the heartbeat of the great bison, and of all the creatures who crawled upon, or walked upon, or burrowed in the Earth Mother. The heartbeat of all winged-ones who soared above her, and all swimming-ones who lived beneath her waters, all rooted-ones. The heartbeat of the turtle—beating long after the spirit had left the flesh—a creature of both earth and water, the feminine powers of creation. Maka, the earth, provider of all, grandmother of all. Wohpe, shooting star who fell from the heavens in the long-ago days of creation. Wohpe and Maka—they were as one.

And then there lived Inyan, the Rock, grandfather of all, ancestor primeval. With two sons born—one possessing wisdom, the other evil. Only the prayers of the people could sway the powers in the direction of the firstborn, in the direction of wisdom.

That was why so much sacredness surrounded the steam lodge, for it represented the universe. The rocks, the water, the sacred pipe, the breath of the Great Mystery. All were contained within the steam lodge.

Energy incarnate, the fire that burned within the hearts of the stones became the intermediary between earth and sky, darkness and light, life and death. The fire in the rocks released the spirit of the water, and the spirit of the water cleansed all who breathed her within them. Cleansed their bodies, and their minds. Purged the sickness from the flesh, raised clear thoughts to the surface. Gave direction to one's life. *Gave courage to one's heart.*

The beating of the drum stopped. Turtle Woman took a slow breath and set the drum down beside her. She knew what she must do.

Balance no longer ruled the world. Bad energy had overcome the good energy of Wakan Tanka—disease, killing, hate, greed. Even some of the Lakotas allowed greed to overcome them—slaughtering the cracked-horns for a swallow of the *wasicu*'s drink. Thousands of *pte* lay on the prairie to rot, only their tongues and hides taken.

The words of the Kangi shaman echoed in her memory. *"Here, at the Medicine Wheel, the power of prayer is seven times a holy man's."* She must go once again to the Shining Mountains, not only to shake this doubt and guilt from her own mind, but for the future of all the people. To finish the prayers Sunstone had begun.

Skye, with her mixed blood, represented the world of tomorrow, the old and new. In her blood lay the power of the Shifting Stars—not only Lakota power, and perhaps Kangi power, but the power of the grandmother from across the great waters. Skye, too, must go to the Medicine Wheel, and they *both* must pray for the destiny of *all* the people.

30

THE PILGRIMAGE BEGINS

Though Turtle Woman's spirit grew stronger, the death of the Shirt Wearer had weakened her body. Wolfskin Necklace could see it in her stance, in her thinning flesh, and in her faltering stride as she walked across her tipi.

"The journey is a long one, Second Mother. And a dangerous one."

"*Han*. Perhaps."

"Only a few days ago, Mahto saw a party of Kangis crossing the waters of the Shell, heading for the Rattlesnake Hills." Wolfskin Necklace paced back and forth.

"*Waste*, this is good. For I do not intend to go into the Rattlesnake Hills. We will cross the Shell, and head north, into the grasslands."

"There are many rolling-wood wagons. There are *wasicus* who behave foolishly in their rush to cross our lands in search of the yellow stone. You would be in danger."

"There are foolish *wasicus* everywhere—foolish red men, too."

Wolfskin Necklace pounded his forehead with his fist in frustration, wishing for the guidance of his *hunka*. Two women, alone, crossing the grasslands, heading into the heart of Kangi country! *Hoh!* A foolish idea.

"My son." Turtle Woman placed her right hand upon his shoulder. "My son, we *are* going to go to the sacred Medicine

Wheel. Two will not be noticed so easily as an entire band. No harm will come to us."

"You travel into the very heart of the Kangis."

"We travel to the doorway of the sun—to the eye of the universe. On a prayerful mission." She lifted her left hand and placed it on his other shoulder. "Our path will be a peaceful one."

Wolfskin Necklace could see that his second mother was not going to change her mind. Like a *pte winyela* hurrying to her calf—there would be no deterring her.

"Why must you do this thing alone?" he pleaded.

"My son, you are needed here. All our men are needed here. The time for decision-making is upon us. The Ones Who Decide will meet again soon to talk of this big meeting to be held during the Moon of Yellow Leaves. It is a time of thought-gathering, and to make such a decision without the wisdom of *your* thoughts—now *that* would be a dangerous thing."

He took her weathered face in his hands, something he had never before done in all these winters. The love of a true son welled up inside him. He spoke low, his concern deep and genuine.

"There is another *toka* who concerns me."

Turtle Woman placed her hands over his. "Caws Like Magpie need not worry you. He is no match for a stubborn woman." Then she forced a chuckle from her lips. "He is no match for *two* stubborn women!"

Wolfskin Necklace shook his head and turned away. The Naca might have been banished, but he would return, like the coyote to a kill. *Ama*, maybe their leaving for a while was not such a bad idea after all. For when he did return, Turtle Woman and the Light-skinned One would be many sleeps away.

"*Hau*, Tunkasila." Turtle Women spoke softly, shaking High Bear's door rattles slightly. "Grandfather, it is I."

Something rustled within the lodge. Then Little Moon stuck her head through the opening.

"*Hau, maske*," she said, clutching a prairie turnip in one hand while holding the door flap open with the other. "Welcome."

Turtle Woman stepped into the shadowed tipi. "The roots are large after last winter's snows, *han?*" she asked.

"Large and tough to chew." Little Moon fetched her water paunch from the pole where it hung, then grinned her near-toothless grin. "Of course, everything for me is tough to chew." She laughed. "I must fetch fresh water. We will share some strawberry tea," she said, then ducked out through the door.

High Bear, seated at the rear of the lodge opposite the door, reclined against his backrest.

"It is too warm to heat water for the brewing of leaves," he said.

"And you have no lodge fire," Turtle Woman answered.

"Little Moon goes to fetch water she does not need, so that you and I can have the alone-time we do need," said High Bear, motioning her closer.

"Your sits-beside-you wife is a good woman," Turtle Woman said, kneeling on a robe beside High Bear, grateful to Little Moon for her perceptiveness. "I need your guidance, honored Tunkasila."

High Bear sat up, crossed his legs, and placed his hands upon his knees. He took a long, slow breath, then closed his eyes. Turtle Woman waited. Finally, he spoke.

"Your granddaughter is a messenger," he said, opening his eyes, "like the long-necked goose who returns to tell us that the cold moons of winter are gone. She brings with her a new knowledge, a new direction."

"And this message . . . it is a good one, like the coming of spring?"

"It is as unstoppable as the coming of winter. Like all things in life, it is good and bad."

"There seems to be much that is bad in the lives of our people lately, and little that is good. Not just what the *wasicu* brings—the diseases and the fire-in-the-belly drink—but among the Lakota themselves. My spirit grieves when I think of these things."

"Your spirit has had much to grieve about," said High Bear, "yet it does not surprise me that your grief is not for yourself, but for your people."

High Bear flattered her. The *real* grief inside her, the forever-grief, had little to do with her people, and everything to do with her One-Only-One man. The power of *that* grief had yet to surface.

"Some grief is easier to bear than others," she said modestly.

"But you did not come here to talk about your grief, nor the prairie root, nor to share a drink of tea."

"*Hiya*, Tunkasila. I did not. I came to ask for your guidance, and for your prayers of protection."

"For the great journey which you are about to begin?"

Turtle Woman looked at High Bear, surprised yet not surprised that he already knew about her intended journey to the Medicine Wheel.

"You know of my wish to return to the Medicine Wheel?" she asked.

"I have known for many winters, my daughter, that you would go back to this place high in the Shining Mountains. And I have known that you would take your granddaughter with you."

High Bear truly was a man of vision, a man so spirit-filled that he could walk away from his own shadow. Turtle Woman had witnessed this phenomenon once, when she was a young woman. He had simply left his shadow behind.

High Bear had honored her many times by sharing small kernels of knowledge with her. He had shown her the healing powers of the herbs, helped her to learn the secrets hidden within all of the Great Mystery's creations. Yet she knew that the gift of seeing, this power to look beyond, could not be shared, but must be earned—silently, soulfully, prayerfully. Someday, perhaps she, too, would be wise enough, and humble enough, to leave her own shadow behind.

"Do not forget, my daughter, that a journey does not become great only because of what lies at the journey's end. The journey itself, each step that you take, offers the opportunity for greatness. For none of us, not even those who see beyond, truly know where one journey ends and another begins."

"I will step lightly upon the path, Tunkasila."

"Use the journey to teach your granddaughter the history of

her people. Tell her the stories of long, long ago so that she may learn the ways of the Ikce Oyate. For like the long-necked goose who brings news of spring, your granddaughter must bear witness to the goodness of her people. Yet she cannot do so if she becomes lost in the ways of winter. Help her to step forth into the light, help her to see with the *cante ista*, the eye of the heart.

"And do not forget, my daughter, that a heart which grows heavy with secrecy is a heart which cannot soar. All things must change. It is the way of Wakan Tanka. It is the energy of Taku Skanskan."

Skye, busy securing the halters on Duncan and Roy, had not heard the soft footsteps of Lost Morning behind her, nor did she realize that the young woman stood quietly waiting for Skye to sense her presence. Skye, ready to lead the horses back to camp, turned and jumped at the sight of Lost Morning, her figure grayed by the dim light of predawn.

"Lost Morning, you are up early."

"Mother tells me your journey begins today."

"Unci says we must leave before the sun has climbed into the afternoon sky."

"I have brought pemmican for your journey. It will fill your bellies and keep you strong."

Lost Morning held out a rawhide parfleche with bright geometrical designs painted on its flaps. She patted its sides. "There are dried turnips, too, and buffalo fat, and dried gooseberries for mush."

"We will eat like warriors!"

"Father says if you are to walk the warrior path, you must eat the warrior food. Give them much pemmican, he says, for they must have the strength of the *pte* nation within them!"

Skye laughed. "Unci says we are to follow the path of prayer, but I think it is wise to prepare for the path of war. And it is more exciting, is it not? Aye, your father is correct, though, for despite which path we take, the Medicine Wheel is still more than a fortnight away—more than ten sleeps."

"You are very brave," Lost Morning said, taking Duncan's reins. "I would not have the courage."

Skye looked at her friend as they led the horses through the short-cropped grasses where the herd had been grazing. The young girl was strong and lithe, used to walking great distances and carrying heavy loads. Her black hair hung in long neat braids, framing a smooth sun-darkened complexion unmarred by small-pox.

"You have more courage than I," Skye answered, envying the ease with which Lost Morning moved, secure in her own tribe. "You have the courage of a Lakota." A fleeting image of Mahto and Lost Morning dancing together caused her heart to pound. They had looked so *right* together. "A *full-blood* Lakota," she added.

Lost Morning glanced at Skye but said nothing. Finally, when they arrived at Turtle Woman's lodge, she spoke, her voice almost a whisper.

"They have given your father a new name, a Lakota courage-name," she said, turning toward Skye. "They are calling him Cante Tanka—Heart of Greatness."

Mahto's pulse raced as it did when he thrust his lance into the heart of a stampeding cracked-horn. Never before had such anxiety risen within him, not even when they moved the arrows against the enemy Susuni people. How could the sight of a *wikoskala* cause him to quaver like a piece of fresh boneless meat? Of course, he had never before painted vermilion on his cheeks, or hung shells from his ears, or draped a red courting blanket over his shoulder. At least True Dog had not seen him as he headed down the running-waters path!

He watched as the Light-skinned One, carrying two of her grandmother's waterskins, grew nearer. Two paunches, one for each traveler. *A-i-i-i!* What would he say?

The early morning run had not helped, though he had winded himself just as he always winded his warhorse before battle—to bring on that second wind, the stamina needed to run farther and faster. And now he shook like a piece of dead flesh.

Fearless one, he ridiculed himself. *Do it now, before it is too late!*

"*Wikoskala*," he said, stepping onto the path in front of Skye. "You fetch water for your grandmother?" What a lame thing to say. Of course she fetched water for her grandmother. "You fetch water for your journey?" he corrected himself, trying to recoup. Skye lowered the waterskins to the ground and nodded, a blush coming to her cheeks. The flush of embarrassment appealed to him, made him remember the Night Dance and the feel of his hands upon her waist as they circled the fire. Then, he had not been sure whether the pounding in his chest came from his heart or the beating of the drums. This time, he knew the tremors came from within.

"It is not a good thing for you to go," he blurted out, taking hold of her elbow and pulling her gently off the busy path.

"The choice is not mine to make," she answered, lowering her eyes. "It has already been decided."

"The Shining Mountains are many sleeps away, far from the safety of the camp circle."

"Unci is determined to do this thing," Skye said, lifting her gaze. "I have tried to dissuade her, but it does no good."

The nearness of the Light-skinned One made Mahto's thoughts flee, like deer from an open meadow. He wanted to touch her again, but instead he reached out and touched the turtle shell suspended from her neck. "It was tangled on a gooseberry bush when I found it," he said, his thoughts wandering dangerously, "the leather still wet from the running-waters." He pictured her leaning against the cottonwood, remembered the arched neck of the seed-horse and the lifted tail of the mare.

Skye's blush deepened. She lowered her eyes again—eyes as bright as the swiftest fox, as warm as the sun. Then he dropped the delicate weight of his red blanket softly over her, and his arms pulled her to him.

Mahto held the curves of her softness against him, felt her hair brush against his cheek as he inhaled her scent. He pressed his mouth against her tender temples, touched her closed eyes, bent his head and brushed his lips across the nape of her neck. With one hand he held the blanket over them, with the other he caressed the small of her back and the curve of her hip. He lifted her chin and placed his mouth on hers, gently for a moment, probing and exploring as the passion within them grew. She tasted of desire—of hunger and heat and longing.

Then the blanket slipped from his grasp and fell quietly to the ground. The stark light of day shone down upon them. Voices could be heard coming down the path, laughing and joking. Mahto pulled away and opened his eyes. Two young girls, giggling, walked by. He picked up the blanket and tossed it over his shoulder. Skye had turned her back to him and stood leaning against a tree.

"You must not go," he said.

"I must," she answered, her voice hushed, like the stillness which comes just before the great winds.

"Then I will go with you."

"This is something I must do without you," she said, facing him, the warmth gone from her eyes. "This is something Unci must do."

"You will return from this quest?" he asked.

"We will return," she answered, bending to retrieve her waterskins. "We will return before the fall hunt, before the big council on Horse Creek."

"You are foolish to do this alone." He jerked his head angrily, pushing his long, loose hair away from his face.

"Aye, and you are foolish to try to stop me," she retaliated, her eyes flashing.

Pride rose up in him. He stood tall and erect, the quavering feeling gone. He was a warrior—the tribe's most able scout. He was Lakota. He was Mahto—the One Who Fights the Bear.

"Before the leaves cover the earth, then," he said, "we will perhaps see each other again. Unless the Kiyuksas choose *not* to be a part of this powwow, and strike their lodges early." He looked past her, into the trees. Then he pivoted and strode away, wiping the vermilion from his cheeks as he disappeared into the willows.

* * *

Wolfskin Necklace let no trace of sadness touch the features of his face as he watched Turtle Woman climb onto the Scotsman's red horse. It took her a moment to get her foot into the saddle's stirrup, and even longer to lift her leg over the saddle's high-bowed cantle. *She will never make the journey. The way is too far, the Shining Mountains too steep.* He resisted the urge to help, knowing by the dignified pride on her face that she would resent his offer. He resigned himself to the inevitable.

If Wakan Tanka so desires it, it will be. Then again, if Turtle Woman so desires it, it might also be. Even now, after all these winters, after a stillborn son, after the death of a daughter and now the death of the Shirt Wearer, she still possessed a fierce determination. *Perhaps, if her flesh fails her, her spirit shall give her the strength to carry on. Perhaps Wakan Tanka shall give her the strength to carry on.*

"Avoid the rolling-wood wagons," he reminded them. "And the soldiers. And those who chase the yellow stone."

"We will travel the paths of the four-leggeds," his second mother answered, "not the paths of the *wasicus.*"

"If the leaves begin to turn brown and you have not yet returned, I shall come to find you."

"Do not come looking. We will return."

"And if the camp is gone? If we strike our lodges and go to this big council of Broken Hand's?"

"Then we will find you at Horse Creek."

"Waste," he said, his throat suddenly tight and dry. "Then we will see you."

"Han, my son. *Toksa.* We will see you."

He watched them as they rode off, the granddaughter mounted on the nut-brown horse, the long-knife strapped to her saddle, Turtle Woman on the red gelding. The long-eared mule, not needed, stayed behind with the other horses. The two women took little extra with them on their journey—no tipi, no lodgepoles, no cooking pots or extra robes—only a few saddlebags and the rawhide case. Nothing that would slow them down in the dangerous land of the Kangis.

The old roan mare, her black mane and tail glistening in the sun, lifted her head and pawed at the ground. Wolfskin Necklace patted her on the neck.

"So you shall miss your old *kola*, too, eh, scorched horse? And we shall miss the Light-skinned One as well. *Han*. We shall miss them both."

The mare whinnied again and Turtle Woman turned in her saddle, holding up her hand to shade her eyes from the midday sun. "*Maske*," she called out to the horse, "you are too long in the tooth to make this journey." But at the old woman's familiar voice the mare pricked her ears forward, tossed her head, and, snorting, ran to catch up.

"*Toksa!*" Wolfskin Necklace smiled, calling after them one last time. "We will see you *all!*" Then he turned and headed for the path leading to the top of the cliffs, for the scaffold of Sunstone and the grave of the Scotsman. From the top of the ridge, he could open his heart. He could look to the Spirit of the West, which presided over evening and the coming darkness, and to the Spirit of the East, which presided over the new day.

31

THE COYOTES

"**I am going** after the Naca," Mahto told True Dog, "to make sure that he does not try to return. I will follow him—see that he keeps the nose of his pony pointed away from our people."

True Dog knew this was only a half-truth. Even though Mahto tried to convince them both that he did not leave camp to follow the Light-skinned One, he fooled neither of them.

Mahto did not like or understand Turtle Woman's need to make this mysterious journey alone with her granddaughter. Still, he would not allow the Light-skinned One to ride out of his life, nor would he let her ride into the talons of Caws Like Magpie.

He had seen no sign of the Naca within the territory of the camp, could find no tracks of the Naca or his mother anywhere near the tracks of Turtle Woman and her granddaughter. The camp gossips believed that Magpie headed northeast, toward the grasslands of the White Earth country. If so, then he would cross the waters of the Shell to the east, before the river began its journey into the land of the Scilis.

Skye and her grandmother would cross the waters of the Shell where the river made a great arc around the Black Mountains, far to the north of Magpie and, Mahto hoped, far east of where the *wasicus* gathered like ants to take their wagons across the river. Then they would veer northwest, away from the rolling-wood wagon trail and into buffalo north, into the grasslands that led to the Shining Mountains.

Mahto rode the high ridges of the eastern slope of the Black Mountains, following an old buffalo trail, but found no tracks belonging to a banished Oglala and his mother, no tracks of a camp dog. He dropped down into the valley after a long line of wagons had crossed, following the trail to the shores of the east-running Shell River.

The tobiano lowered his muzzle into the water and drank deeply. Slipping from the horse's back, Mahto knelt and splashed the wetness on his face and neck, washing the trail dust from his skin. He stared up and down the river, wondering where the Naca would have chosen to cross—wondering *if* he had chosen to cross.

But all he could find were the tracks of mules, oxen, and shod horses; wagon ruts cutting deeply into the earth; land trodden bare of grass, grazed to nothingness. Discouraged, he decided to follow the river west, into the descending sun.

* * *

Doublewoman Dreamer's horse had gone lame; the animal was as useless as a pierced waterskin. "Why must you scurry across the ground like a scaly one rushing to shade?" she complained, pulling her horse behind her. "At this pace, I'll be as lame as this brute."

"Why don't you ride the *sunka?*" Magpie kicked his horse into a faster walk. "That *sunka* is nothing but wolf bait anyway. Like you, black winged-one." He flicked a finger at the crow perched on his shoulder.

"We are all wolf bait—no more welcome at the lodge fires of Smoke's people than in the tipis of our own camp."

"I am an honored Naca. They will welcome a warrior into their midst."

"Why is the early sun at our backs, and not in our eyes," Doublewoman dared to ask, "if we travel to the camp of the Smoke people?"

Magpie threw her a look of warning as his only answer.

"And an old woman?" she ventured. "Will they welcome an old woman into their midst as well?"

"An old woman dreamer who reminds them of Anog Ite? They will welcome you out of fear—as long as *I* do not tell them that your dreams are as shriveled as your skin."

Pain grabbed at Doublewoman's heart. No matter how often her son had vilified her, over a lifetime of winters, she had never grown callused to his cruelty. Yet he spoke the truth. Her dreaming power had disappeared long before the death of her husband.

"As the flesh grows older, the dreams grow stronger," she lied. "Beware you do not push me too far, my son. I shall not be mocked."

The black crow let out a shrill *caw! caw!*

"I do not need to mock you, Mother. The bird does it for me!" Laughing, he pulled ahead, leaving her to plod along on foot.

The temptation to turn around and go back, to face the disdain and ridicule, nagged at her. She tried to think of even one person who would welcome her, offer her the "old woman's place" near the door of their lodge. But even her friend, Black Tail, had turned away from her upon the death of the Shirt Wearer. *Not one would welcome me back.*

"*Wey, wey,*" she called to the dog, stooping to pet the animal's head. *Not even one.*

The world smelled of dust.

"Unci," Skye gasped, staring down at the hazy valley floor, "there are hundreds of them, following each other like ants."

"Your grandfather warned me, but I thought he exaggerated." Turtle Woman shook her head in disbelief.

"How will we ever cross?"

"We will cross before dawn, before the sun begins its path across the sky and after the night moon has faded."

"And if we crossed now? What harm could come to us? Ate would not have waited."

"Your *ate* was a *wasicu.* Look at yourself, *takoja.* Do you look like a white woman? You wear skins, you braid your hair, you wear moccasins upon your feet. They would treat you as an Indian."

Skye inspected her clothing. True, she wore Indian leathers, but her skin was light, her hair brown, not black, and her eyes not nearly as dark as Unci's.

"They would know as soon as I spoke."

"*Han,* they would know as soon as you spoke. And then what?" Turtle Woman's question hung in the air like smoke from the old plains rifle.

And then I would meet someone. Perhaps a wikoskala *my own age. Perhaps a woman Ina's age. Perhaps someone who spoke with a bit of the brogue, who told stories of the Highlands and could quote a bit of verse. Perhaps . . .* Skye shook the thoughts from her mind. Grandmother was right. They would treat her as an Indian. Or worse: a half-breed.

"It will be good for you to rest, Unci," she said. Her grandmother's body became thinner each day; her maimed fingers healed slowly, the scars red and swollen. But her grandmother's indignant grunt made her amend her comment. "It will be good for the horses to rest, Unci."

"No fire must burn this night," Turtle Woman warned. "No firelight by which to show ourselves."

* * *

Skye stared into the darkness, trying to concentrate on the stars. They flickered like sunlight upon crystals of newly fallen snow. Lifting her fingertips to her mouth, she touched where Mahto had boldly placed his lips. She had tasted his eagerness, his manliness, even her own womanliness. The sensation left her nervous, like a cornered colt.

She listened to Unci's soft sleeping sounds and closed her own eyes, trying to sleep herself. But the sounds of the wagon train found their way up to the quiet camp and a restlessness took hold of Skye—a curiosity and yearning that she could not resist. Someone down there had coaxed a mouth harp to life.

She rose noiselessly from her blanket and fumbled in the dark for Duncan's bridle. The ride down the hill would take barely a few moments, and she promised herself she would be back at Unci's side long before midnight. She wanted only to see the wagons, to listen to the music, perhaps hear the sound of English upon some pioneer's tongue.

Turtle Woman heard Skye rise, heard the horse's hooves upon the earth and the soft nicker of the old mare. She wanted to cry out to Skye not to go but bit down upon her tongue and silenced herself.

There would always be this dichotomy within her *takoja*'s blood, the call of two, *a-i-i*, three worlds—the call of the long-ago grandmothers, the call of the shifting-star legacy, the legacy of which her granddaughter knew almost nothing yet that still called out to her. Turtle Woman accepted it, as she accepted all things. She knew the torn-in-half feeling. She settled herself to wait patiently for her granddaughter to return. *Wakan Tanka, creator of the sacred energy which moves all that moves, she will return!*

Skye tied Duncan's reins around the branches of a clump of snakeweed, then tiptoed toward the river, letting the melody guide her. Near the water's edge, and a fair distance from the tail end of the great wagon train and the last posted guard, she could make out a slender figure kneeling on a large, flat boulder. She tiptoed nearer.

"Boyo, isn't this 'ere moonlight somethin'!" The shadowy figure spoke to itself while sloshing something in the water. The voice was too high for a man, too low for a woman.

"Never would you see a sky like this, goin' down in a Welshy mine." Slosh. Slosh.

"Scrubbing dirties 'appy-like, a wilderness moon shinin' above—imagine it, would you?" Rinse. Rinse. Whistle. Whistle.

Skye crept closer, close enough to almost reach out and touch the figure. The constant chatter and the sounds of scrubbing kept her from being detected. The figure leaned forward, reaching into the water. Skye suppressed a giggle. Naked skin shone in the moonlight. The outline of two small breasts told her that the rough voice belonged to a young woman.

"Gold." The woman whistled softly, then began singing a short tune. "You'll get rich quick, they says, by pickin' up a chunk what's as big as a brick!" She wrung out a small piece of clothing and laid it on the rock. "Won't mind pannin' for gold, 'cause won't be nothing like goin' down the mine, coughing and hacking and such. Be nothing like that, see."

Skye crept toward a bush growing at the water's edge. Reaching out to step onto a boulder, her moccasin slipped on the stone's wet surface. Panicked, she grabbed at the bush, but the willowy branches slipped through her grasp. SPLASH! She plunged into the river.

"Look you, who the 'ell's out there?"

Skye fought to swim, but scraped her elbows on the gravelly bottom. Lifting herself up, she sputtered an answer.

"*Hau*, it is only I, Skye Macdonald."

"And who, look you, might Skye Macdonald be, anyways?"

Skye stepped to the shore, shaking the water from the fringes of her doeskin dress.

"Well, I'll be damned! An Indian you are!"

The young Welsh woman had scrambled for her clothing, and was pulling on a pair of boy's trousers and a homespun shirt that hung nearly to her knees. A wide-brimmed hat quickly covered her short-cropped hair.

"Look you, what you doing like that, sneaking around?"

"I wasn't sneaking exactly."

"The 'ell you wasn't. Indian you don't sound. Come closer. Can't hardly see nothing in the dark."

"My father was Scottish."

"Scottish? You don't say. And your mum?"

"Oglala, of the Lakota."

"Sioux, is it? Them is troublemakers."

"I make no trouble."

"That's 'cause you isn't all Sioux."

"I am Scottish, *and* Lakota."

"A half-breed! I'll be damned. Them is the worst, they say. How come you was sneaking around, anyway?"

"I heard the music."

"What—me mouth harp?"

"The sound carried, even up the hill."

"Say you now. Didn't know I 'ad that much lung. S'pose you heard them coyotes howling, too?"

"The coyotes always howl."

"I've noticed. Scares the pants right off a' me."

"So that's how you lost your pants." Skye laughed. She had been unable to resist the impulse to tease the young woman. The immigrant slapped her knee and let out a hoot, then held a finger up to her lips.

"Shh," she whispered. "Isn't nobody supposed to know I isn't a boy."

"Why do you want to be a boy?"

"Now there's a stupid question! 'Cause girls can't pan for gold, that's why! Hell, you hears of lots a' women heading to Sacramento, but isn't none of 'em going to the mining camps, that's for damn sure!"

"What about the Welsh mines?"

"I 'aven't never worked in no Welsh mines."

"But you said—"

"Didn't say nothing 'bout me. My father, he worked 'isself

to death in them coal mines. Died in Cardiff."

"What about your mother?"

"Isn't *no* mum. Isn't no family."

Skye shivered in her damp leathers, despite the warm, balmy evening.

The young woman sat down, leaning back on her bare heels. "And your folk?" she asked. "What about them?"

Skye could only shake her head.

"Isn't no family for you, too? Well, see, isn't bad so much. Person gets along—just sometimes tougher, that's all."

"I've got a grandmother—two grandmothers."

"Say you now. One Indian, t'other Scottish, I s'pose. So what's you doing here?"

"Traveling," Skye answered shortly. She sat down beside the Welsh girl. "Tell me," she said, inching closer, "tell me about the wagon train, about the places you've seen. What's it like, to travel so far?"

"What's it like? Why, it's the craziest thing you'd ever imagine—men pushing wheelbarrows across the plains, or harnessed up to drays like so many oxen. A fancy fellow from Hungary—calls hisself an 'equestrian,' wearin' an ostrich feather in 'is hat! Thinks he's quite a horseman riding that fool mule. Missourians and desperadoes, too. As far as these pilgrims are concerned, yours truly 'ere's a desperado.

"And women! Women toting feather mattresses across the country. A little lace bonnet I spied one wearing—scuttle-shaped, with a real pretty face wreath of pink rosebuds. Look you, del—wearing pink rosebuds and shaking her apron at a herd of stampeding buffalo! Who'd 'ave believed it! A drove of cattle passed one day through the train. Never did get all the dust out of me mouth." She wiped a finger across the surface of her teeth, which shone white in the moonlight.

"You never did tell me, anyways," she said, turning to Skye, "what's a half-breed like you doin' sneaking around in the middle of the night, out in the middle of nowhere. Sure as 'ell isn't just me harp playing." The howl of a coyote echoed off a distant ridge, and the young woman scooted even closer.

Skye eased deeper into the soft sand at the water's edge, pulling her knees up to her chest and wrapping her arms around her legs. *What's a half-breed like me doing out in the middle of nowhere?* She wished she knew.

Skye turned her face toward the young woman. The woman's hat was tilted back and her eyes shone in the moonlight, the boyishness gone. Skye looked away, scraping at the sand with her finger. "Have you ever . . ." She hesitated. It was the question she had wanted to ask Lost Morning. "Have you ever been in love?"

Turtle Woman watched the stars shift in the black sky as night moved on, wondering how long it had been since the soft music had drifted up the hill. Too long. The music had ended shortly after her *takoja* had left. She wanted to follow, to cling, as the web of a spider to a winged-one. But she also wanted, like a river stone tumbling downstream, to allow the water to cut its own banks, forge its own path.

The words of High Bear came to her as she stared into the darkness. *"None of us, not even those who see beyond, truly know where one journey ends and another begins."* Did the journey, then, end here? *"Each step that you take offers the opportunity for greatness."* Where, in this moment of aloneness, did the greatness hide itself?

She started to rise, nearly crying out as she put weight on her throbbing fingers. But she ignored the pain and thought about her granddaughter. Was this wagon train of *wasicus* a cruel joke of Iktomi, once wise but now the imp of mischief? Spinning a web of delusion? She settled back on the hard ground.

The river stone does not fight the power of the water but, instead, allows the water to round its edges and smooth its surface. It becomes sacred, like the stones of the inipi *ceremony.* Again, High Bear's wisdom spoke to her.

"Do not forget, my daughter, that all things change. It is the way of Wakan Tanka."

She would wait. The stars would shift in the night sky, and she would wait. *But there are some things,* she reassured herself, *like the rising of the sun, like the beckoning call of the coyote, that do not change.*

* * *

Mahto had been following the river west now for two sleeps, staying near the shoreline except when he caught up with the tail end of a wagon train. Then he disappeared into the draws and rolling hills, traveling faster than the *wasicus* with their horses and mules and oxen. The gaunt animals plodded slowly across the land, like shadows that grew smaller beneath each high sun. Shallow burial mounds—the dung piles of a new age—marked their passing.

Far ahead of the rolling-wood wagons he returned to the banks of the river, and once again he and the tobiano drank from its murky waters, then followed the Shell west. A cloudburst the night before had smoothed the sands, and the shore glistened, damp and glossy.

Here and there the tracks of small animals could be seen near the water—winged killdeers and painted turtles. Even the wandering-dog. But as Mahto dismounted and knelt to examine a set of dawn-fresh tracks, he knew that they had come from no crawling one, no winged creature.

He ran his fingers over the rounded indentations. Four toe marks in a half-circle, spread as if running. Too large for a coyote, too small for a wolf. No claw marks either, such as would have been left by the wandering-dog, or the fierce true-dog. *Igmu'tanka,* he whispered to himself. Not coming to drink, but to cross, for the tracks emerged from the running-waters and disappeared north, into the grasslands. A cat venturing across the river? At a near run? And limping? *The energy of Taku Skanskan is with you. May you reach your destination, four-legged one. May the wind carry you there!*

He rose and moved upstream. Occasional floating debris caught his eye—a dead fish, the wilted flower from a prickly pear, the sodden bonnet of a white woman. He mounted the tobiano and moved on, riding into the fading light, on the lookout—always—for the *wasicus.*

Then, just past a bend in the river where the waters widened and grew shallow, he found the tracks of two unshod horses—one in front, the other limping behind. Fresher than the tracks of the great cat, their edges still sharp and well-defined. Indian pony tracks. Dismounting, he knelt and studied the impressions, reading their sign as one would read a winter count.

The small party had forded the river while the sun still hung high overhead, long after *igmu'tanka* had emerged. The cat had crossed the running-waters at dawn, before the horses, before the tracks of the woman who walked behind, before the camp dog who trotted alongside. Even before the bird who had left his coiled, half-white droppings in the sand near the dung left by one of the ponies.

Mahto poked at the horse manure with a twig, turning over in his mind the story revealed by the tracks. He dug the blossom of a partially digested fireweed from the still-moist pile and frowned. Caws Like Magpie and Doublewoman Dreamer? Who else would travel with a dog and a bird? But northwest? Why not to the land of the White Earth River, where Smoke's people of the Oglalas had fled trying to outrun the dreaded cholera? What would cause Magpie to venture into the land of the Kangis, unless he believed that the Smoke People now pitched their tipis on the banks of the Shifting Sands River? True Dog had heard rumors that some of the Oglalas were moving farther west. Perhaps Magpie, too, heard these rumors.

Hiya! The Naca traveling in the same direction as the Light-skinned One and her grandmother? It made his skin crawl and his nostrils flare. He swung his leg over the back of the tobiano and headed away from the murky Shell, away from the trail of the rolling-wood wagons and the abandoned graves of the not-so-lucky *wasicus*. He headed northwest, allowing his own tracks to obliterate the tracks of the Naca as he rode, enjoying the sound of the tobiano's hooves striking the earth.

Had Mahto ventured upstream a little farther, perhaps the distance of two well-drawn arrows, he would have come upon the day-old tracks of a small Kangi war party, five men and one woman. He would have seen, also, the naked and disfigured body of a *wasicu* who had dared to gallop across the prairie, challenging the Kangi warriors, the fancy plume of his foolish hat fluttering in the wind.

32

DREAMING

The dream returned once again to Turtle Woman: a Kangi woman standing before her, tall and handsome, a quiver of arrows and a well-strung bow over her shoulder, a war club and enemy scalp hanging from her waist. The face of the woman has been toughened by the snows of many winters, furrowed by the laughter and tears of a lifetime. Yet her warrior eyes sparkle with the spirit of a young girl. With one arm raised, she points toward the path leading to the Medicine Wheel.

"Stand at the heart of the Medicine Wheel," she says. "Face the morning sun, and begin your true journey." Then the dirt path turns into the luminous tail of a comet, strewing silver stars across the deep purple heavens. A gust of wind ruffles the single eagle feather in the woman's hair, and the vision fades, evaporating into the night like vapor rising from the stones of a deserted steam lodge.

"Little Badger," Turtle Woman called out, "Little Badger . . ." Her voice faded, and she awoke in darkness.

A horse crested the hill, and the roan mare and sorrel nickered softly. Ah . . . *takoja*, you return. Turtle Woman almost nickered herself. From down in the valley, the music of a mouth harp once again rose on the breeze.

Turtle Woman's heart swelled with relief. She listened as her granddaughter slid from the gelding and secured a pair of leather hobbles to the horse's front feet, then took the bridle from the horse's mouth. Skye eased beneath the blanket that lay crumpled next to her, then lay motionless, despite breathing that remained shallow and fast. Turtle Woman waited for the deep breaths to come, for her *takoja*'s body to grow soft upon the earthen bed. Finally, she sensed the change.

Then a funny notion came into Turtle Woman's head, so funny that she lost her solemn mood, forgot the serious thoughts within her mind. Forgot even, for the moment, the dream. She could not help but laugh aloud.

"Unci, you are awake?" Skye whispered.

"*Takoja*, a very funny thought has just popped into my old and feeble brain."

"What is that, Unci?"

Turtle Woman laughed again at the foolishness of the situation, at life's trickster ways and the joke being played upon her by the trickster spirit.

"I do not even know how to *get* to the Medicine Wheel!" she blurted out, her thin belly tightening as the laughter rose within her.

The roan mare trailed behind, in dire need of water. For nearly three days they had been cutting across the open grasslands, baking under the hot white disk overhead, herds of pronghorns their constant guides. Fleeing always before them, the antelope led the two women onward—away from the wagon trains, away from the immigrants, away from Lizzy, the frisky young Welsh woman. A sense of loss took hold of Skye as the distance between them grew, adding a new layer of melancholy to her already grieving soul.

Finding the Shining Mountains posed no challenge, for they stood before Skye like giant sentinels, the snow-covered spine of the mountain range long and curving like a serpent's. But once in the folds of the great mountains, then where? She feared they wandered not only into the heart of the unknown, but into its ravenous jaws as well.

No moisture remained in the air of the sagebrush basin across which they rode; it had already fallen as rain far to the west. Turtle Woman and Skye rode in the land of rain shadows, the desert land of thirst lying low between the great mountains.

Duncan sidestepped, shying at a clump of sage. A rattlesnake slithered from the shade beneath the plant and moved silently away. Skye felt barely a tremor of fear at the sudden memory; as much as she had tried to hate the *witko* woman, she could muster up only pity.

Skye's own parched throat begged for a drink of water, yet the guilt of quenching her thirst when the animals could not kept her from lifting the waterskin to her mouth. But guilt or no, melancholy or no, she was about to succumb.

"Unci, how long since you've taken a drink?"

"Not so long—but my thirst is nothing compared to the thirst of the grasses upon which we tread. They wait patiently for the winds to bring clouds, for a brief rain to dampen the hard earth."

"They are better suited to the desert than you, or me. I am finding it harder and harder to ignore my thirst."

"Do not try to ignore it, *takoja*. Acknowledge it. Here," Turtle Woman said, stopping her horse. "Ask the stones to help you." She stepped slowly to the ground, working the stiffness from her limbs, then rummaged around in the gravelly soil beneath a clump of rabbitbrush. She returned with two small round pebbles.

"Put one in your mouth. It will moisten your throat."

Skye took a pebble from her grandmother's outstretched hand. "How will a stone help to quench my thirst?"

"The stone works many miracles," Turtle Woman said, getting back on Roy. "It is the mystery of the elements—fire, water, earth, and air. Each comes from the other. They are as one."

Never before had Skye experienced real, unslakable thirst, not even when crossing the Red Desert en route to Fort Bridger, not even—a lifetime ago—when she and Ate had crossed the wide basin between the Medicine Bows and the Black Mountains.

Skye put the cool stone in her mouth and tasted dust. Then, as the stone began to warm, her mouth brought moisture to her parched throat.

"Water from a rock," she said, tucking the pebble between her cheek and tooth. "It's a miracle indeed."

"The yellow flowers of the rabbitbrush are pleasing to the eyes, are they not?"

"They remind me of the glaring sun."

Turtle Woman laughed. "Everything at the moment reminds you of the sun. You must make the sun your friend."

"I would rather befriend a rain cloud." Skye waved a pesky fly away from her nose.

"Tell me more about this strange young woman you met by the river."

"Lizzy? She came from across the Atlantic Ocean, from a place called Wales, south of Scotland."

"And she came all this way alone?"

"Aye. Her father died just before they were to leave, so she came without him."

"And she has dressed as a boy ever since she left this land?"

"The whole journey, all the way from Wales."

"Except when bathing in the running-waters by the light of the moon," Turtle Woman said, laughing.

"Except then," Skye chuckled. "No one gave her any trouble that way, she said. Kept the men away!"

"Her journey makes ours seem not so long. Her reasons for traveling across the great waters, and clear across the great Turtle continent, must be very strong. Perhaps she has her own *wakan* journey to complete?"

"No mysterious journey, Unci. Gold fever."

"The yellow stone? I do not understand this need for the yellow stone—unless the stone is *wotawe*, has been made sacred by the holy man. But even then, one or two stones would do. What is the need for so many?"

"The more gold, Lizzy said, the more money. Said when she gets rich, she's going to travel all over the country, maybe even the world. She said the great waters back east are much grander than the Shell could ever hope to be, with huge steamboats churning through them, immense paddle wheels turning round and round."

"Still," Turtle Woman said, "I think more than the yellow stone caused her to come here; one does not leave her birth land for so plain a reason. I think it is like the great waters this Lizzy crossed—hidden beneath them is much we do not understand."

Skye held her breath, fighting the urge to speak her mind. Then she exhaled, slowly and forcefully.

"Yet you are leaving the place of your birth," she said, "for a reason *I* do not understand. We travel to a mysterious place—a place you are not even sure how to find—and for what? Not even gold lies at the end of our journey."

The question that really irked Skye hid like a wayward child. *Why must I be forced to follow your dream?*

Turtle Woman kept her eyes forward. She was not leaving the place of her birth. She was born not in the Black Mountains to the south, but to the east, near the sacred Black Hills of her people. At least, that was where her mother had always told her she had been born.

In the distance, a dark green line stretched before them. Treetops. The waters of the Shifting Sands River were not far, near enough for those long of tooth and short of breath. She turned her *takoja*'s words over and over in her mind. The horses trudged past several clumps of sagebrush before she answered her granddaughter.

"Often those places in our memory, or in the memories of our ancestors, are the most important places of all. And I am not leaving the land of my birth. This entire land, this great Turtle continent, is the land of my birth. They tell me I was born near the headwaters of the Bad River. My mother, your great-grandmother, was born . . ." She hesitated, not trusting her words to be true. "She was born between the waters of the Big Muddy and the Dakotah."

"The grandmother of whom you speak"—Skye's tone had softened—"she is Shifting Star?"

"*Han*. And your grandfather, Sun Dog, of Standing Bull's band—he was a great warrior. Your great-grandfather went with Standing Bull on their first journey into the Black Hills. And your great-grandmother, Shifting Star, she belonged to the canoeing people, to the camp of the Strong-backed Women. That was long before we had the sacred-dog," she said, patting the sorrel horse on the neck, "to do our work for us." She pulled on her reins and slowed the sorrel, allowing the old mare to catch up.

"It is said," she continued, "that I was conceived on the shores of Antelope Creek. My mother used to giggle as she told me the story. A painted turtle crawled out of the waters, ambling right across my father's foot. They stopped their rutting for a moment and watched as the turtle dug a hole in the sand and laid four tiny eggs in the hole. They decided then that their first child would be called Little Turtle. They prayed for me to have a strong heart like the shelled one, and a peaceful spirit like the pronghorn."

Turtle Woman thumped her hand upon her chest. "My heart is still beating, so it must be strong, though I do not think I was given the peaceful spirit of the antelope."

"Tell me again the story about Shifting Star," Skye asked, pulling her horse alongside.

Turtle Woman had lied; her heart no longer had the strength of a turtle's, and her *takoja*'s question made it flutter like a nervous butterfly. Had she the courage to share all the shifting-star legacies? To tempt Skye with the glory of the warrior trail? *Hoh!*

"The old ones say, *mitakoja*, that a proper moment exists for the birth of each story." Time and distance stretched before Turtle Woman. She rode on in silence, High Bear's words echoing in her mind. *"The journey itself, each step that you take, offers the opportunity for greatness."* She listened to the horses' hooves dig into the parched earth. Despite their heaviness, they walked with grace upon the Earth Mother.

Maka, the earth. Wohpe, shooting star who fell from the heavens in the long-ago days of creation. Wohpe and Maka. They were as one.

She would tell her granddaughter the creation stories of the Oglalas. She would tell her the fourth-world story of Wohpe, the White Buffalo Calf Woman who came to earth, reminding the Lakota people of the great power and dignity inherent in all women. She would explain the prayer power of the Medicine Wheel and the prophetic words of the Kangi shaman. And, *han*, she would even explain how the shifting-stars births of both Skye's great-grandmothers bequeathed her a great warrior spirit. After that, Skye would have to decide herself whether or not to follow the warrior path, and it would be up to Wakan Tanka to guide her.

But not until they arrived at the Medicine Wheel—if she found the five-pointed star still etched in the rock wall—not until then would she tell her of the Kangi grandmother.

"*Ehaaaaanni*," Turtle Woman began, turning toward her granddaughter and taking a deep breath, "once, long, long ago . . ."

Travel at a snail's pace infuriated Caws Like Magpie. Another sun would rise before they saw sign of the Shifting Sands River, let alone camped beneath her meager shade trees. Another day of thirst, another day of his mother's nasal whines. He took the tethered crow from his shoulder and flung the bird in the air. Hopeful, the bird flapped his wings, flew ten paces, hit the end of the rawhide cord, hung suspended for a split second, then fell to the ground in front of the horse. The horse sidestepped, and Caws Like Magpie retrieved the disheveled bird.

"He never learns, does he," Magpie laughed, setting the bird back on his shoulder.

"And you never tire of torturing him."

"Well, I'm tired now."

"It is a tiring journey."

"Ride, then. The horse has rested long enough."

Doublewoman lifted her horse's front foot, inspected the tender bottom of the hoof, then pulled herself onto the horse's back.

"You remind me of the ancient woman in the cave," he said. "You remember, the old tale you used to tell me when I was a boy. She was so crippled she could barely move. Ha! A soothing bedtime story for your son."

"It was a tale told me by my grandmother, a tale told to her by her grandmother, and so on, and so on."

"Well, then, tell it to me again. I am bored with this journey." He scratched his nose with the tip of one of the black feathers hanging from his neck.

"Some stories are meant to be told during the moons of winter, when the days are short and the nights are long. When the spirit is willing."

"Then I'll tell you the story of Iktomi and the strawberry patch and the pretty *wikoskalas*. He is always willing!"

"*Hiya!* You tell so many stories of Iktomi that I am surprised you have not worn him out."

"I have heard you tell your share about the spider man."

"Since when do you hang around with the women and listen to our stories? Very well, then. I will tell you the story of the old woman in the cave."

"In the Bad Lands."

"*Han.* Where the spirits of ancient monsters from long-ago times roam the gigantic buttes and lonesome valleys." Double-woman stretched her back and yawned, then began. "Hidden near there, in a cave, lives an ancient woman, her face as gnarled and shriveled as the land itself."

"I told you this story reminded me of you."

"You are a vile son."

"Go on, go on. I will keep my thoughts to myself."

"Her dress is old and tattered, the leather stretched to fit her bent and bony body. She has been sitting there for more than a thousand winters, more than a thousand summers, quilling on a blanket strip that she sews for her buffalo robe. Sitting beside her is a huge black *sunka*."

"No kin to your scrawny *sunka*," said Magpie, unable to resist goading his mother again.

She cast him an exasperated look, then continued. "*Sunka* stares at the old woman, his eyes never blinking, never moving. She pulls porcupine quills through her teeth, and her teeth are flat and worn, her hands bent and twisted.

"A fire burns near the old woman, a huge fire which has been burning for as long as the woman has been quilling. Suspended over the flames is a clay cooking pot filled with boiling soup. The berry stew is thick and red and sweet like honey. The old woman begins to rise to go and stir the soup, but her bones are stiff as winter-dried branches and she moves achingly slow."

"Ha! The woman really does remind me of you."

His mother ignored him and went on. "The moment

the woman turns her back to the *sunka*, he grabs the blanket strip with his teeth and yanks out the quillwork.

"The old woman stirs the stew, then hobbles back to her sewing. It is no closer to being finished than it was when the sun fell from the sky the day before, or the day before that, or the day before that.

"The old ones say that if she is ever allowed to finish the blanket strip, then the world will come to an end."

Magpie waited for her to finish, but she yawned again, then grew silent and stared off at a distant herd of pronghorns.

"That's it? The world and the story come to an end, just like that?"

"*Han.* Just like that."

"It is a stupid story. I do not remember it being such a stupid story."

"Sometimes the world is a stupid place. We feed our feeble bodies so that they will live, and we live only to feed our feeble bodies. What else do we accomplish? Nothing."

Caws Like Magpie tried to gather spittle but his mouth had no moisture, no saliva to spare. *Aaagg!* The heat ate away at him, like a wolf gnawing on the still-live body of a cracked-horn. The end of the world—all because an old woman was allowed to finish her quilling. Stupid!

"So what does the story make of the *sunka?*" he demanded to know.

"The *sunka?*"

"*Han,* the foolish brute."

"Perhaps the four-legged is nothing more than a four-legged."

"Perhaps we are all nothing more than brutes," he said, lifting the crow from his shoulder one more time. "With no more sense than this bird. We dream of flying but have nowhere to go."

He cast a sideways glance at his mother. She did not believe, as he did, that Smoke's people now camped by the Shifting Sands River, that they had moved their camps far from the stench of the *wasicus* and the *wasicu* trails that carried death and disease.

His mother's pockmarked face reminded him every time he looked at her of the *wasicus*' sickness that had killed his father and both Magpie's wives, pocked the faces of so many of the Lakotas.

Perhaps Smoke's People would be different. Perhaps the huge black beast of the Lakotas would rise up to rip out the roads and trails of the *wasicus*, and *their* world would come to an end.

Magpie lifted the crow up against the blueness of the sky. The crow struggled to free his feet from Magpie's grip, then flexed his wings as if to fly.

And where would you go, winged-one, if you could fly? Where would you go?

Skye tiptoed through the pines with Unci, both bent on flushing dinner out into the open. She exaggerated her stalking, imagined hunting a ferocious grizzly instead of a puny squirrel, or counting coup on an enemy warrior.

The warrior way had been Ate's way, and her grandfather's way. And it was the way of the Kiyuksa scout who filled her dreams with wanting. But would it also become her way? Did the wrath of a warrior simmer deep in her bones? She did not think so.

Something different caused her blood to race and her heart to pound. She touched her fingers to her mouth, as she had done so often in the last week. Lizzy, too, had once been in love. The young woman had told Skye amazing things, man-woman things.

Mahto. His name filled Skye with mysterious urges, but a desire to fight was not one of them.

She took a deep breath and smelled the pine forest. Gone was the scent of sage, the scent of rabbitbrush and alkaline soil. Once again, familiar woodland scents and sounds enveloped her—the cawing of blue jays, the chattering of squirrels. Squirrels. Damn, she was hungry!

Unci held a warning finger up to her lips, and pointed to the gangly limb of a nearby pine. A squirrel perched on a branch, motionless, his dark beady eyes fixed on them. Very slowly, Turtle Woman drew her knife from her waist cord, raised her still-strong arm above her head, and flung the knife with such fluid speed that Skye barely saw it.

The squirrel emitted a single, high-pitched squeak, then fell to the ground in a furry heap, impaled—*hiya*, nearly cut in two—by Turtle Woman's knife.

"Unci, you have not lost your skill," marveled Skȳe. She retrieved the rodent from beneath the tree.

"The hunger in my belly remembers the feel of the knife, and my poor teeth seek something soft to chew. Boiled squirrel and acorn mush shall slide easily down this old woman's gullet."

"Still, you moved like a striking snake, so fast did you flick your wrist."

"The wrist simply follows what the mind already sees. Now if you could only cook it as quickly. My belly gnaws like a teething pup."

Skye's stomach also growled with hunger. But despite the gnawing pangs, being back in the mountains made her feel invincible, able to survive anything.

"When you were younger, Unci, when you still played the war games with boys, did you wish to become a warrior?"

"I wished to shoot straight and far, to ride like the wind, but I did not dream of the war path."

"Nor did your grandmother?"

"I have known only one female who dreamt of the warrior path. The one I called Little Badger."

"And you taught this young Hewaktoka to throw the knife and draw the bow?"

"At first. Then the others began to show her, once they saw that her moccasins did not walk the path of the woman."

"She had the warrior spirit?"

"Even as a child," said Turtle Woman, stripping the hide from the squirrel, "but she carried a woman's vengeance in her young heart."

Vengeance, thought Skye—every time Caws Like Magpie came to mind, every time she remembered the feel of his hot breath and the grip of grasping hands, the awful silence as her grandfather's body fell from the cliff, or the dull, muffled sound of the horse's hoof striking Ate's head. Vengeance. She prayed, to all the spirits she could name, that the Naca would meet with a slow and painful death on the barren plains.

33

BRITTLE BONES

Mahto's plan slipped through his hands like sand. He had intended to follow the Light-skinned One and her grandmother across the lands of buffalo north, not the Naca and the *witko* dreaming woman. But Caws Like Magpie had veered northwest, across the arid basin and toward the Shining Mountains, forcing Mahto to trail him.

Half the camp gossips spoke the truth, the other half foolishness: the Naca had no intention of traveling to the country of the White Earth River. Did the Naca believe the Smoke People had moved their camp to the shores of the Shifting Sands? Or did he hunt the Light-skinned One? Had he learned of Turtle Woman's quest through some mysterious power of Doublewoman Dreamer? Mahto dared not leave the Naca's trail until he knew for sure.

The banished pair had traveled slowly, the *witko* woman's pony lame and weak. Mahto now rode even with them, separated only by an expanse of sagebrush and cactus. Turtle Woman and Skye still rode ahead, probably already camped at the headwaters of the Shifting Sands, deep into the first folds of the Shining Mountains and the hunting grounds of the Kangis. Each journey the sun made across the sky lessened Mahto's chance of tracking the Light-skinned One—not on rock and stone, trails churned with the tracks of Kangi ponies. *A-i-i-i!* So many dangers for two Lakota women far from their people.

The tobiano lifted his nose, flaring his nostrils: the scent of the river. With a high-pitched whinny he leaned into his bridle, eager at the nearness of water. Mahto glanced across at the stretch of prairie separating him from the slow-moving Naca. Time enough. He let the tobiano break into a lope, moving ahead of the Naca.

They reached the wide, shallow river long before the final descent of the sun into the land of the thunder-beings. The Naca, he surmised, would not arrive to quench his own thirst until well after dark.

Little food remained in Mahto's saddlebags—a few strips of jerked meat, a few pieces of dried fruit, a bit of *wasna*. He gave thanks for the running waters and rejoiced at the cool wetness, but his body hungered for fresh meat. He tested the point of an arrow. Soon, he would hunt.

Traveling upriver, allowing the running waters to wash away all sign of his passage, he reached a fork where a stream flowing down out of the foothills joined the lowland waters of the Shifting Sands. Old tracks of many horses stamped the dirt near the water's edge—Kangi ponies perhaps, or Susuni. Or even the ponies of the Sahiyelas. He followed the fork south for a short distance, then, finding nothing of interest, doubled back and continued upstream.

Soon, another stream joined the river, this one from the north, flowing down from the tail end of the mountain's curved spine. He steered the tobiano closer to the bank. *Han! I am one lucky scout!*

Tied to the top of a wooden stake plunged in the bank perched the shoulder blade of a buffalo, with Smoke's picture-name painted boldly upon it, along with pictures of hoofprints and a travois. The camp-moving sign displayed itself like a sharp-tailed ground bird on the strut. Disgust tainted the victorious moment. Bull Bear, honored leader, had died at the hands of these traitors.

The parched bone pointed downriver, toward the widening body of the Shifting Sands and away from the Shining Mountains. A few of the gossips had spoken the truth, after all. Smoke's people had moved their camp to the shores of the Shifting Sands River, and if Mahto judged the Naca's course correctly, he would approach the river here, near the north fork. The camp sign would lead him downriver, to the east. *If,* that is, Caws Like Magpie truly sought the Smoke People, and not the Light-skinned One. Mahto shook his head. Surely the dreaming woman did not have all-seeing power. Caws Like Magpie would follow the sign downriver.

Mahto, on the other hand, did not desire to travel east, nor north, where Yata's icy breath and frigid touch froze all who ventured too far. But Long Chin, the elder scout of the Kiyuksas, had told him that the path to the Medicine Wheel climbed north, up this fork of the running waters. As if daring Mahto to go on, a brisk gust smelling of snow and mountain blew down upon him. He turned the tobiano into the wind, wading upstream through the fast-moving waters, until the wind quit suddenly, no longer disguising the tobiano's splashing gait.

"Shh," Mahto whispered to his faithful friend, "step lightly. For we enter the land of the *tokas.*"

A hearty laugh rose from Woman Chief's stout frame. Despite her many exploits, she knew that she reminded men more of a curly-horn buffalo kicking up his hooves than a fierce humpback roaring and batting his massive paws. Her courage, however, matched that of any grizzly, and no man lived long who dared to underestimate her.

"Red Horn," she said as she and five other mounted Crow warriors approached the running-waters, "Red Horn, that white man's feathered hat would look better on his long-eared horse than on your foolish head."

"He was the foolish one." Red Horn grinned. "Swinging his long-knife from the back of his mule as if he had an entire war party with him."

"Yip! Yip! Yip!" No Toe ran his pony in circles around Red Horn, whooping and grabbing at the dead immigrant's hat, the feather torn and tattered.

"I offered him a good trade," said Red Horn, ducking his head. "His fancy hat for the right to pass through our land. Too bad he wanted to fight instead."

Woman Chief shook her head at the younger warrior's eagerness. They were all eager at this age—full of foolish bravery and foolish deeds.

The next time No Toe tried to snatch the hat from Red Horn, Red Horn reached up and grabbed No Toe's outstretched hand, and both men fell from their horses, landing on a steep sandy bank at the water's edge. Woman Chief laughed with the rest of them, then looked away and scanned the shores of the river.

She envied them. Wished she could, just once, relax. But always, this burning inside. This restlessness. A desire to return to the land of her childhood? She shook her head. She had had no childhood.

On the opposite side, where another stream joined the main river, a large black-and-white bird strutted up and down the sand, occasionally poking his long beak at a bit of shoreline debris. Disgruntled by the riders, the bird let out a harsh carping sound, then rose from the sand and flew a short distance away. Woman Chief squinted at where the bird had landed, then urged her horse into the shallow river. Burning Hair followed her across, leading behind him the immigrant's mule, now laden with medicine wood for the making of bows. The others eased their horses into the running-waters, laughing as the steep bank gave way beneath Red Horn and No Toe, plunging the wrestlers into the river.

The bird left his perch and flew to a nearby cottonwood. Woman Chief sat back in her saddle and stretched her legs, pondering the bird's perch—an old and brittle bone bearing the picture-name of the enemy Smoke People. So, they camped downriver, and bravely—or stupidly—left their mark for all to see. Did these Smoke expect so many other Titonwans to follow that they pointed the way? How far would the Titonwans push?

"Prairie people," grunted Burning Hair.

"So it seems," she answered. "Moving their camp to the land along the Shifting Sands."

Red Horn and No Toe climbed onto their horses' backs and raced across the river to rejoin the others. Water dripping from their bare legs, they pushed their way into the small circle of warriors. "What have you found?" queried No Toe, the feathered hat now on his head.

"A moving-camp sign," answered Burning Hair.

Red Horn raised his eyebrows. "From Smoke's people of the Titonwan?" He slid from his pony's back and touched the painted bone. "Downstream."

"We do not have to allow this Titonwan sign at the foot of our mountains," said No Toe, suddenly riled. "I will rip it out!"

"Too late, my friend!" Red Horn jerked the stick out of the ground and started to toss it into the river.

"Wait!"

A sly, cunning grin replaced the anger on No Toe's face, a grin Woman Chief had seen many times before when a prankish idea snuck into the young warrior's mind.

"What would be more fun," he asked Red Horn, "to toss the sign into the running-waters, or to play a joke on our enemies from the prairie?"

"A joke?"

"Point the sign up, into the mountains, instead of downriver."

Red Horn visibly turned the idea over in his mind. Then an equally cunning grin spread across his face.

"This is a clever idea, my friend, very clever."

"Careful you are not so clever that you invite the whole Titonwan to our doorsteps," said Woman Chief.

No Toe laughed off the warning. "They shall not find us. We shall find them!"

"We shall not destroy the sign of the Titonwans," Red Horn said. "We shall leave it *almost* as we found it."

"Almost," chuckled No Toe, "only with one small difference." He jabbed the stick back into the ground, pointing the narrow end of the scapula up the small stream that fed into the Shifting Sands.

"It appears as if the Smoke People have moved their camp up the north fork, into the hunting grounds of the Crow." Red Horn laughed. "How foolish of them."

"Ha! A good joke!"

The men slapped their thighs and laughed as No Toe got back on his horse. "Yes, a very good joke!"

A-i-i-i. Woman Chief only hoped that the trick was not on the mischievous young warriors, and thus on them all. She shook her head.

But she was not yet ready to head north, into the high country. She turned her horse along the main river and headed downstream. No Toe and Red Horn followed, racing past her, their ponies sinking into the soft shoreline. The others trotted along behind. The black-and-white bird, who had returned to his perch on the buffalo bone, carped loudly at them, flapping his wings.

Truly the messenger of the north, just as the stories of the Titonwans said. Woman Chief had to shake her head again. She did not fully approve of the prank, but the irony did add a nice touch. The magpie, the prairie people's own messenger, would lead the Titonwans into the hands of their enemy.

Mahto eyed the trail for recently broken twigs or bent grasses. He listened to the warning calls of the winged-ones and to the tree-top chattering of the small four-leggeds, and searched for stones with fresh earth still clinging to them, dislodged from where they had nestled in the ground. He listened for the enemy hoot of night owls during the light of day, and the caws of mountain jays during the dark of night. He ignored the gnawing in his belly and let the blacktail deer disappear safely into the trees.

"Fool!" True Dog would have chided him. "Her trail is cold. Not even the best Oglala scout could expect to find the Light-skinned One, not even Howls at Moon!"

He rode on.

Then, as he stood beside the tobiano making water on the stem of a stalk of horsemint, he found it, tangled in the plant's purple blossom. A long strand of red hair from the tail of a sorrel pony. He twisted the strand between his fingers. *Many horses have manes and tails colored like the red fox. Many horses. Kangi ponies. Susuni ponies. Even Lakota ponies. Many. Not just the horse which Turtle Woman rides, the horse belonging to the Light-skinned One.*

He tied the hair around his wrist and searched on hands and knees for tracks, but found none on the rocky trail. So he turned away from the path and headed into the trees, into the protection they offered two women traveling alone.

He found no visible signs of their passing. He sensed her lingering presence—in the air he breathed, in the noises he heard. He imagined her just ahead, imagined that her last breath became his next. Still, he found no more sign of the Light-skinned One.

He began walking, leading the tobiano behind him. He pushed all hunger from his mind, all expectations. He quit looking for what did not belong, and began looking, instead, at what did belong. An ant perched on the tip of a blade of grass. A beetle scurrying at the vibration of his step. Berrywood picked clean by the winged-ones. The steady tap-tap-tap of the bird-who-knocks-on-wood. Browsing marks upon the ends of the red-grass. The split-hoof mark of an antlered creature. The rounded mark of a horse's hoof left on the burrow of a yellow-bellied marmot . . .

For a split second, Mahto quit breathing. He knelt and examined the clearly visible track—the mark of an unshod horse carrying no rider. Mahto ran his finger over it, tracing the curved outer edge, stopping when his finger came to the unusually straight-edged inner hoof, which left a deeper imprint in the damp ground. A horse with a front foot bent slightly inward like a duck's would leave a mark such as this, a horse who walked with her weight on the inside of the foot. He knew of one horse, especially, who left such a mark upon the earth. The old roan mare of Turtle Woman's.

Caws Like Magpie squatted by the stream, splashing water on his face and neck. What difference did one more sleep make? he grumbled. They traveled at a snail's pace anyway. He would camp here, on the south fork, and when dawn came he would travel the short distance to the Shifting Sands River. There he could begin to look for signs of the Smoke People.

He splashed more water on his face, and his grumbling turned to sardonic laughter. They were a pathetic lot: two gaunt horses, one lame, sucking the creek down their scrawny throats; a half-starved mongrel bitch dragging her pup-heavy belly through the water; a scraggly crow, missing half his tail feathers, floating downstream. The crow! Caws Like Magpie pulled on the tether and drew the sputtering bird through the water like a piece of driftwood.

His mother, bent like the twisted roots of an upturned tree, made her own sucking noises as she drank. The sight hurt his eyes. "You sound like a toothless horse," he said to her.

She ignored his jab. "Why do you keep that bird, anyway?" she asked.

"I am doing him a favor."

"You do him no favors. You torture him. He is miserable."

"His life is better than most. Not every bird gets juicy scraps fed to him by such a beautiful *wikoskala.*"

Doublewoman gave him a look of disgust. "Perhaps one day I will roast him, and you will be glad for all those juicy scraps that put meat on his bones. We will probably have to eat him, anyway, so that we do not starve, wandering around like fools. Admit it. You do not know where we are going."

"Ina"—the word rattled sarcastically from his throat—"do you doubt me? Turn back, if you would rather. Go. The foolish Ones Who Decide did not banish you, only your Naca son."

Doublewoman Dreamer did not answer, but knelt at the water's edge and rubbed at her skin with wet sand, cleansing the trail dust from her hands and face. Her silence annoyed him, just as the painful gash on his cheek annoyed him—more than annoyed, the gash enraged him. Every time he touched the tender red scar where the girl had cut him, he became inflamed at his own impotence. He had done nothing, could do nothing. Even the death of Macdonald gave him no satisfaction, for the horse, not he, had dealt the killing blow. He turned back to his mother.

"The sand cannot rub the marks of the *wasicu*'s disease from your face," he said, wanting her to give him another hateful stare.

She said nothing. Then, finally, she looked up. "I go where you go, my heartless son."

A surprising barb of guilt, or hurt, stabbed at him. Heartless, she said. The woman never had understood him, even if she was his mother. She was also, he acknowledged, his only ally, his only remaining family. But he shook the guilt from his conscience and plucked the hurt from his thick skin. Family. What good were they? Their spirits left the flesh, wandering the path of the dead, while you remained alone to wander the barren desert.

Doublewoman peered at her reflection in the water. *Where does the evil come from? From my seed? From his father's seed? From the venom of the fanged-one?* The water, murky from the horse's hooves, gave forth no answer. She picked a pebble from the creek bed and rolled it between her fingers, fingers almost too stiff and sore to work again the awl and sinew. Would she even have the strength to hang the old tipi hides from the lodgepoles her lame horse dragged behind them? And who, in a camp of strangers, would offer to help? She tossed the pebble back into the running-waters and, not waiting for her son, led her horse across to the stream's opposite shore.

"You know the way, old woman, that you lead?" Caws Like Magpie yelled after her.

"What is to know?"

"What is to know?" he mimicked her.

Behind her, she could hear his horse splashing through the water. She forded the creek, then sought a young rustling-tree and eased her aching bones down, leaning against its still-smooth bark. The sky had begun to turn a pale pink, the color of the night-blooming rose. She watched for the moment of redness to come, for the sky to catch fire as the sun sank to earth, for the shiver of fear to run through her as it always did when she saw the power of fire, the danger of flame. Like the wandering-dog drawn to the warmth of the campfire, she could not look away.

"Do you know enough to gather wood, old woman, or do you plan for me to do this thing?"

The moment of fire did not come. The sky faded from pale pink to dismal gray. Doublewoman rolled over to her knees, then pushed herself up.

"Itka Sapa," she swore at her son, "and where is the fresh meat to cook once I have gathered wood? Or do you really want me to roast that black bird of yours?"

The raucous call of a noisy-winged bird woke Caws Like Magpie. Ha! He sat up and rubbed his eyes. The large bird hopped from the back of Doublewoman's pony to the ground and stepped onto the top of a hardened pile of horse manure, his black feathers iridescent in the sun. *Aag! Aag!* the wild bird called out, defending his territory against the intruders.

Magpie's tethered crow strained against his cord, pacing back and forth, flapping his wings and rising a few feet off the ground. *Kahr! Kahr!* he cawed back. The dog, no longer sleeping, lifted her head.

"You would lose the fight, my friend," said Caws Like Magpie to the bird, rolling up his robe. "The wild one would peck your eyes out." He threw a chunk of *wasna* at the pet, then bit off a piece for himself, ignoring the dog's whining.

"Rise, Ina." He poked at his mother with the toe of his moccasin. "Rise. We must go."

He saddled both horses, bit off another chunk of *wasna*, then mounted his pony and watched Doublewoman Dreamer attach the travois poles to her saddle. It took her three tries to lift her foot to the stirrup. Magpie shook his head. Too many winters.

Traveling down the south fork, they reached the Shifting Sands River before the morning star had faded from the sky. A cool breeze blew down from the snow-covered mountains that rose before them like giant sandhills. In the distance, but a short ride away, another tributary from the north flowed down out of the foothills. He kicked his pony in the ribs and began trotting up the shoreline, shutting out the dragging sound of his mother's travois-laden horse behind him.

Here! A sign—directly in their path! Caws Like Magpie could not have done better had he been riding the very tails of the Oglalas.

"Ha! And you doubted me. Where are your doubts now,

Mother? Is that not the mark of Smoke upon that sign?"

"*Han*, it is the mark of Smoke. But why would they move their camp so far up into the land of the Kangis? Why would they not camp near the Shifting Sands waters?"

"You expect me to know everything?"

"I expect you to know nothing."

Magpie did not allow his mother's cynicism to spoil the moment. Only one thing would make it sweeter—to know that he left no unfinished business behind him. But he was a patient man. After he joined the Red Council Lodge of the Smoke People, he would return to the camp of the Standing People; the wait would make his revenge only that much finer.

A sudden image of Breathcatcher flashed into his mind. He forced the image from him and focused, instead, on the Scotsman's daughter. *She wants to walk the warrior path? Ha! Let her feel the warrior's lance.*

"*Hoppo!*" he commanded his mother. "As long as it took you to travel across the prairie, it will take you until the next full moon to climb the steep mountain trail. Let's go!"

When the sun had risen overhead, and their shadows had all but disappeared, then began to lengthen again, Caws Like Magpie and Doublewoman Dreamer had traveled deep into the Shining Mountains. They passed from sagebrush grasslands and quaking aspens into rocky snow-covered peaks and pinnacles of stone. Magpie did not recognize the steep angles and bare rock faces, or the dark mountain caverns whose mouths gaped at him like creatures from the First World of long-ago times.

Never before had he ventured this far into the land of the Kangis, and he did not like it. He looked down over the side of the trail and saw charred trees and blackened earth, remnants of an earlier forest fire. The rock-strewn path they followed grew more narrow, more perilous. And Doublewoman's horse lagged behind, lame-footed and sore-legged, knocking rocks from the trail to ricochet off the steep walls into the charred desolation below.

"You should be riding a mountain goat instead of that worthless brute," he said to her.

"I should be walking," Doublewoman said. "The weight is too much for him."

"You weigh no more than that scrawny *sunka* of yours. It would make no difference."

She did not listen to him. She pulled her horse up and started to dismount, easing her thin leg over the saddle's cantle, her weight in the downhill stirrup, but her leg caught on the travois pole. At that instant, the horse tried to back up, then lunged forward. As his rear hoof slid from the path, he scrambled for a foothold, Doublewoman hanging precariously from his side; then the travois jackknifed and slipped over the edge. The horse pawed frantically at the stones and gravel, but the heavy load pulled him toward the ravine.

The horse rolled on top of Doublewoman, slid down the granite wall, then crashed against the blackened trunk of a spruce several paces downhill of where she lay. *Foolish woman!* Magpie dismounted, slowly and cautiously, on the uphill side where he could cling to the face of the mountain if need be. Should the beast fall, at least he would do so alone! Looping the crow's tether around the horse's neck, he inched past the animal.

"Mother!" She lay less than a short toss away. "Get up if you can!"

"The pain is too great."

"Try," he said, easing his way down to her sprawled figure.

"The horse? How is the horse?"

"The stupid animal has broken his back, and the travois is useless. Can you stand?"

"I don't think so. I fear my hip is crushed, like the pit of a chokecherry."

"*Hoh!*" The situation was disgusting. Broken and useless—the brittle bones of an old woman took forever to heal.

"You cannot travel?" It was a statement more than a question.

"I cannot travel," she answered slowly.

Doublewoman read the look in her son's eyes, knew his thoughts as intimately as she knew her own. But this look surprised her; this thought sank lower than she would have believed. *Born with a frozen heart.* She had never before realized just *how* frozen.

"You are going to leave me, aren't you?"

He looked away.

"You are going to leave me." She wanted to hear him say it, wanted to force him to admit his cowardice.

"You're going to leave me! Aren't you!" she screamed.

Finally, he looked at her.

"Old woman, you give me no choice. You cannot walk. You cannot ride."

"There is always choice. It is the Lakota way." She gritted her teeth against the pain, watching as the dog picked her way toward them down the steep rock-strewn hillside.

"Then choose to walk."

She stared at him. Did no seed of compassion lie within his tortured soul? Had all the goodness within her womb been buried along with the stillborn body of his twin brother? *A-i-i-i!* To enter the world with no heart—truly, a fate worse than not entering the world at all.

Her *son*—the word stabbed at her heart with a pain worse than the crushed hip—her flesh-and-blood son retrieved the rawhide case and waterskin from the shattered travois and tossed them beside her, throwing her saddlebags over his shoulder.

"The *sunka* will keep you company."

"Do this thing, leave me here to die, and my *nagi* will haunt you for an eternity."

"You haunt me now. What's the difference?"

"I will starve."

As if an afterthought, he said, "I will send someone for you, once I have found where the Smoke People camp."

"I will starve before then."

"Then eat the horse."

"The horse will bring the wolves."

"Then eat the wolves!"

He turned his back on her, crawled up to the trail, and rode away. Just like that. Rode away.

Eat the wolves. She looked around her. Huge granite peaks tow-

ered overhead, charred and blackened trees pointed their jagged
trunks at her from below, a cold wind blew down from the north.

The *sunka* whined and pushed her nose under Doublewoman's
arm. Doublewoman ran her hand down the animal's slick head
and along the thin backbone. The bitch's stomach, heavy with
pups, protruded on both sides in gross contrast to the animal's
gaunt frame. Doublewoman tried to move her hips, to slide down
the hill toward the groaning horse, but the pain robbed her of her
breath.

*My son, you had it wrong. The wolves shall eat me. Or did you know
that all along?*

34

MOUNTAIN MUSIC

Mahto's tobiano blended invisibly into the steep granite side of
the gray mountain, whose snow-covered tip disappeared as a procession of dark clouds stampeded across the sky like a herd of restless buffalo.

Even Wi, the great sun, grew weak as he struggled to rise
above this mountain. His rays had not power enough to melt the
snow clinging to the rocky peak.

The moon had risen in the sky many times since the Light-
skinned One and her grandmother had left the safety of the camp
circle. And for too many of those nights Mahto had been forced
to follow the Naca, to travel like the coward's shadow. But no
longer.

From his elevated vantage point, Mahto could see all who approached the summit on horse. Only the foolhardy attempted to scale the peak from the east, where jagged black walls guarded the mountain with bared teeth. But more importantly, he could see all who entered the gentle meadow below. He slid from his horse and waited.

Han! His hunch proved true! A wide grin spread across his face. *True Dog, if only you were here to see this with your own eyes. Howls at Moon is one damn good scout!* He watched as the Light-skinned One and her grandmother rode into the clearing, followed by the old mare.

The tobiano started to nicker. Mahto quickly closed his hand over the horse's muzzle to silence him, for as much as he wanted to ride into the clearing, to stand once again beneath the blanket with Skye, he must resist. She must not know he had followed her. He wanted her to worry, to think perhaps that she would never see him again. He wanted her to want him, to thirst for him as he thirsted for her. And never again would he be disturbed by two giggling girls wandering the water path.

The sun cast long shadows across the meadow; little daylight remained. The meadow would make a fine camp, sheltered from the wind and lush with grasses for the horses. If True Dog were here, he'd bet him his best saddle blanket that the women would stop, hobble their horses for the night, and unroll their sleeping robes. *Han!* He should have bet his horse! The women did not even ride to the far end of the clearing, but made camp where they stood.

His stomach rumbled. He would find his own camp, then prepare to hunt. But first he would make an offering of flute music to the spirits of the forest. In long-ago times, the South Wind had honored Wohpe, the Falling Star, by wooing her with flute music. His songs, too, would rise to honor the Falling Star. And his arrow would fly to pierce the heart of an antlered-one. Then he would bed down with a belly full of roasted meat, and with visions of the Light-skinned One running naked through the woods like a shifting star falling through the night sky.

*   *   *

Skye hated to admit it, but each hour they rode, each new turn, brought an even more breathtaking view than the last: sharp summits and glacier-cut valleys, alpine meadows rich with mountain wildlife—red-breasted nuthatches and twittering chickadees, porcupines and bighorn sheep. She loved the mountains, loved their immenseness, their mystery and grandeur, their pungent pine smells and crystal-clear lakes where moraine dammed the summer thaw. How she wished she could share this with her father. Once he had shown her a rock that he had found while trapping in the Shining Mountains, the picture of a fish, armored and jawless, drawn into it. Was it, perhaps, still in his collection? Ate. How she hated Caws Like Magpie!

Unci had been right to bring her along, and she better understood, now, the power of the shifting-star legacy.

A great woman warrior will be conceived within the womb of the Titonwan. She will spill from the heavens like a thousand stars. Were the shaman's words true? Would her prayers, when uttered at the Medicine Wheel, really be seven times more powerful than a holy man's?

A shudder traveled up Skye's spine. Unci expected her to pray for the Lakotas, indeed, for all the people of the world. The responsibility was awesome. Overwhelming. Was she expected to pray for Caws Like Magpie? For Ate's enemies? For her grandfather's enemies—the Susunis, the Scilis, even the Kangis? *Hiya!* She did not think so!

Still, she now better understood the depth of her grandmother's urge to return to the Medicine Wheel. Unci's purpose transcended personal need; the calling rose from the anguish of the entire Indian nation.

Guilt tugged at Skye. White men, half her people, swarmed over the Indian lands, following the trails mapped by the mountain men, by trappers like Ate. They came to conquer. Another twinge of guilt. But Lizzy had not come to conquer. Despite the Welsh girl's bravado, she was an orphan, escaping a grueling life. Nor, Skye realized, had her father come to conquer. He had been forced from his homeland, had watched his home and the crofts of other Highlanders torched and destroyed by the rich landlords—

absentee owners answering to the needs of England. Och, Father had said 'twas terrible. Hundreds murdered, young people turned into slaves by the thousands and shipped abroad.

The guilt caused Skye's head to ache. It was all so confusing. *For whom was she to pray? The conquerors, or the conquered?*

There was something about the shaman, though, that Unci had not told her. Some other reason, perhaps more urgent, for their journey to the Medicine Wheel. Skye could see it in Unci's eyes, in the way she held back a little when answering Skye's questions. *What other reason*, Skye wondered, *could there be?*

Skye and Turtle Woman avoided the main trails, well marked with abundant signs of Kangi passage. Luckily, the plentiful streams and small lakes meant they could also avoid the more popular watering places. Skye was glad to see the sheltered meadow. They all needed rest, and the horses needed good forage—sweet meadow grasses. The journey had taken its toll on Unci; she looked as stiff and gaunt as the old mare. A long rest would do them all good.

"You have chosen a good camp, Unci," Skye said, unrolling their robes. "Shelter from the wind, wood for the fire, and grass for the ponies." She led the horses a short distance away.

"And a soft robe for my creaking carcass to lie upon. I need only one other small thing."

"What is that?"

"The hump of a *pte* to roast in the fire."

"You call that a small thing?" said Skye, laughing. "Unci, we have seen no buffalo. Besides, you have not yet taught me to hunt the *pte.*"

"Ha! You think it is so easy? To hunt the *pte* takes great courage. Your grandfather was a brave hunter. They used to pester him about the many meat racks that surrounded our tipi. 'Are you going to feed the entire nation?' they teased."

"Well, there are no meat racks in this camp. Would you settle for the tender flesh of a mountain trout?"

"Two, at least!"

"Very well, Unci, two trout, then. With wild onions."

"I will gather the onions, while you follow the creek up-stream."

"You rest. I shall gather the onions, and the fish."

"*Han.* You gather the onions, then. I will count the clouds as they roar past. But hurry, I fear the thunder-beings are sending a storm our way. And *takoja*, wait until you return to do your day-dreaming about the Kiyuksa."

The Kiyuksa? She knows? A-i-i-i, when will I learn?

"Don't worry about my daydreaming, Unci. Just count the clouds and wait for me to return with enough fish for a dozen bel-lies!"

Duncan did not want to leave the meadow, despite Skye's re-assurance that they would soon be back. She urged him on, tuck-ing a bone hook and long line of sinew into her saddlebag. He heeded her gentle prodding and they trotted across the clearing, leaving Turtle Woman already stretched out on her robe and nearly asleep.

A blood feeling had begun to stir in Skye, a feeling she had not had since Ina's death, since Ate had closed the trunk and turned the key, locking away her ancestry, her memories. A sense of kin-ship had sprouted within her from the seed of the great Lakotas. The proud feeling excited her.

And there was no denying it, Mahto's caresses had stirred the Lakota blood in her as well. Even the Gaelic sap in her veins ran hot.

She loved hearing the stories Unci told, but she welcomed the alone-time, the chance to daydream. For only then could she once again imagine herself with Mahto, imagine the man-woman things. She closed her eyes, letting Duncan find his way upstream. She imagined the soft dusky-rose light beneath the red blanket, Mahto's hand upon the small of her back, gentle yet forceful, pulling her hips into him, leaving no space between them. Would she ever see him again, in this huge country, with its mountains and prairies and rivers? And if so, what then? She opened her eyes. What could one embrace mean to a Kiyuksa scout?

She nudged Duncan on, watching for the stream to widen into a good fishing hole—ahead, perhaps, where another small clearing opened up. She heard the sweet song of a finch, then saw a bright yellow evening grosbeak perched on the limb of a pine. He sang out, his notes ringing clear and true. Another finch answered him. Then, farther upstream, a different song, more melodic, more soulful. She followed the bend in the creek and found herself on the fringe of the clearing—and in a near panic pulled Duncan up short.

On the far side of the small meadow grazed a hobbled horse.

She backed up into the trees, slid off, and looped her reins over a high branch, then crept back to the near edge of the clearing. Tobiano markings colored the horse—a white back and rump, a dark belly.

She heard the melodic song again and her knees weakened as her heart began to pound. No bird sang so sweetly, so soulfully. She took off her moccasins and walked as Ina had taught her as a child: toes down first, weight on the heels, holding her breath. She moved noiselessly through the trees, guided by the music and by an unrealistic yet thrilling hope.

The late afternoon sun cast soft rays of light upon Mahto's kneeling and near-naked body. He faced away from her, the flute raised to his mouth, the magnificent necklace draping from his neck. Mahto! Here?

So, it is my turn to spy upon him! The scout was not the only one able to glide unnoticed through the forest. Slowly, like a tuft-eared cat stalking her prey, Skye circled him, her steps as graceful and lilting as the flute music. Twice, when he lowered the flute, she stopped, not daring to breathe, not daring to blink an eye. Then he lifted the cedar instrument to his mouth again and began playing, his hands moving softly up and down the flute, as if caressing the carved wood. The motion mesmerized her, hypnotized her, drew her to him. She could not take her eyes from his sun-darkened skin or his powerful muscles. She could not stop thinking about kissing him.

Two more steps, Mahto guessed, and she would be directly behind him. Two more steps, soft, but not quite soft enough. And the pretty *wikoskala* thought she could fool him! He had been a fool, though, to openly kneel in enemy land and make music. He should have known better.

One more step. There. He lowered the flute. Her breath, as faint as the flutter of a butterfly's wings, stirred the air. Did the Light-skinned One wish him to chase her, as the seed-horse had chased the mare? Or did she desire, simply, to be caught?

In one fluid motion, he turned, grabbed her around the waist, and pulled her to the ground.

"*Hau, wikoskala.* You would toy with me like the wildcat with a mouse? Only now, who is the mouse?" She struggled to sit up but he pinned her beneath him.

"I am no mouse!" She laughed. "And you are certainly no wildcat!"

"We are both *wild* cats, Light-skinned One, trying very hard not to be."

A blush came to her cheeks but she said nothing, simply squirmed halfheartedly beneath him. The squirming made it even more difficult for him to try to tame the wildness within him—difficult if not impossible. Like telling the sun not to rise. He gently pressed her back into the long meadow grasses, then, with both knees on the ground, straddled her and sat up, pinning her arms with his hands.

"You followed us," she accused him.

"I followed Caws Like Magpie."

She trembled at the mention of the Naca's name. "Caws Like Magpie? He is here?"

"Not here. Down below. He follows the Shifting Sands River in search of the Smoke People."

"The Smoke People? Oglalas?"

"*Han.* Lakotas. Split from Bull Bear's people many winters past. Caws Like Magpie must hope to join their camp. He has nowhere else to go."

"And they would allow him to do this?" She struggled again to sit up, more determined this time, but he held her down. He liked the feeling of her moving beneath him. *Beneath, or on top . . .* The quick and pleasing thought brought a smile to his face.

"You think it is a joke?"

"*Hiya,*" he said, unable to wipe away the grin.

"You think it is funny that they allow this vile man to walk about freely while Ate lies in his grave? While Unci mourns? You think this is something to smile about?"

Suddenly, she jabbed a knee into his back and twisted over on her side, pulling an arm free. With hands clenched, she swung a fist at him before he could stop her, catching him on his lower jaw. *Hoh!* His jaw stung.

"Easy!" he pulled her back over, pinning her down again. "You have the temper of a bearcat."

"That man goes where he pleases while Ate and Grandfather can go nowhere."

"*Hecitu yelo,* this is true." He forced the smile from his face. "I do not laugh at this tragedy. I, too, mourn the death of the Shirt Wearer, and mourn, for you, the loss of your *ate.*"

"Then let me up."

"You might hit me again."

"I might."

"You have the temper of a bearcat, and the strength of one, too. I think you are able to get up"—he lowered his mouth to her neck—"only you don't want to." He took in her scent, remembering the taste of her, the wetness of her mouth, the hunger, the heat. He touched his lips to her skin and kissed her throat. Then, fighting every instinct that urged him to do otherwise, he freed her arms and sat upright.

She did not move, only writhed a little under him while stroking his forearms with her fingertips. *E-i-i-i,* the virtue of a Lakota woman was a sacred thing. *A tribe whose women are honorable will be an honorable nation.* So the old ones said. The hearts of the women were to be revered, as was the heart of the sacred *pte.* It was the lesson taught by White Buffalo Calf Woman. A nation with strong-hearted women would always be a nation of strength. To resist was harder than fighting a thousand Kangi warriors!

He moved off her and knelt in the grass beside her. She sat forward, then reached up and touched his bear-claw necklace, fingering each claw, each bead. *E-i-i-i! She makes this difficult.*

"Your *unci*," he asked, "she is strong?"

Skye dropped her hand. "She tires easily. But she does not give in to her weakness."

"Grief and old age are a dangerous pair. It is easy for an old one to grow tired of this earth, to want to follow their loved ones up the star path."

"She is determined to go to this Medicine Wheel. The desire gives her the strength she needs."

"Still, her body needs rest, and fresh meat."

The Light-skinned One laughed and tossed her head. *Eyes as bright as the swiftest fox, hair the color of ripening chokecherries.*

"Today Unci asked for the juicy hump of a *pte* to roast upon the fire!"

"I will bring you meat—maybe not the *pte*, but the antlered-one at least." He would not ask, again, to travel with them to the Medicine Wheel. Skye tilted her head, turning the idea over in her mind.

"Meat, for Unci? Aye, that would be good."

"*Waste.* Before the sun next sets, I shall bring you meat. Then I shall leave you and your *unci* to finish your journey."

"Fish!" she shouted, jumping up and laughing. "First, you must help me catch fish! Two, at least!"

Skye sat beside Mahto as he cleaned the fish, one hand upon his thigh. She had loosened her hair and it draped her shoulders, veiling her throat.

"You are a better fisherman than I," he said, holding up a spotted trout as long as his forearm.

"I caught all five." She laughed. "You caught nothing!"

"I caught what I was after," he teased, wondering if he had the courage to answer the question she had, only moments before, asked him. He had spoken to no one about his father for a long, long time, not even True Dog. To speak about the dead required great caution, a special reason. This day he had already shared much about himself with the Light-skinned One, more than he could believe. He had told her of Sun Dance Mountain where he was born, of his mother's death five summers past.

He cleaned the last fish and set it on the grassy bank next to the others, then washed his hands in the cold stream. A deep sigh escaped him.

"Tell me about the fight with the Susunis," she asked, softly touching the scar on his jaw with her fingertip.

"I had pleaded with my father to let me go with him to move the arrows against the Susunis, but he refused."

"You were only a boy?"

"Nine winters, nearly ten."

"So young. I do not blame him for wanting you to stay with your mother."

"I was old enough to kill. I had already hunted my first *tatanka*—a huge bull, enough meat for two families."

"Still, to kill a man must be a very different thing."

They were both silent for a moment. Then Skye spoke. "Ina taught me how to hunt the gray hare, and how to find the burrows of the fox, and the nests of the ground birds. How to tell the call of the red-headed woodpecker from the red wingfeather. Even," she smiled, "how to use the bone hook to catch fish."

He wanted to touch her just then, stroke her skin and feel the curves of her womanhood. Again, he resisted.

"She was beautiful," Mahto said, "like you."

A faint blush came to the Light-skinned One's throat. "You knew her?"

"*Han.* Everyone spoke of the beautiful *wikoskala* from the camp of the Standing People. Everyone knew of her. Even the young boys."

"And my *ate?*"

"The young boys, especially, liked your *ate*. He made us all feel good, with his dancing and bag-of-wind music. 'The hairy-faced *wasicula*,' we used to call him."

"Hairy-faced!" Skye laughed and the sunlight flickered in her eyes. It was good to see her happy, the cloud of sorrow lifting slowly from her heart. But Mahto knew that grief could not, should not, be rushed. The memory of her, so willing to avow her virtue, bending and pulling the fanged one from the hole, flashed in his mind.

He strung a line of sinew through the fish and lifted them from the grass, then stood.

"Your *unci* must be starved," he said, handing the fish to her. "You must go." Turning, he started to walk away. Then he walked back. "I will bring you both meat." He brushed her hair away from her neck and, bending slightly, kissed her on the throat. *"Toksa,"* he whispered, "until later."

35

VISIONS FROM THE PAST

Turtle Woman woke from her nap to an unnatural silence. She lay perfectly still, not even blinking an eye. She listened for the sounds of squirrels chattering, or chickadees whistling, or even the soft *whee-ah* of the gray jay, but she heard nothing. The sky had grown quiet, the wind slept, the crawling-ones did not stir. She opened one eye. Lying on her back, she saw only a patch of dusky sky. She opened the other eye. A larger patch. Day would soon give way to night. Slowly, one wrinkle at a time, she rolled over onto her side.

The sorrel horse, hobbled, had managed to hop halfway across the meadow and grazed with head lowered and tail swishing. The roan mare had stayed nearby and grazed in the shadow of a large rock formation off to Turtle Woman's side. What had awakened her?

Grrrrrr.

A growl, so close.

Grrrrrr.

Too close. As slowly as an aging tree grows, she eased herself into a sitting position, then turned and looked over her shoulder. *Igmu'tanka!* Crouching on the huge rock, about to pounce on the back of the old mare! *A-i-i-i!* What a coward to prey on the near-fleshless carcass of an old and helpless horse. It angered her! She reached for her skinning knife, then stood and strutted toward the great cat.

Grrrrrr. Yeooowl!

The growl turned into a warning yowl at Turtle Woman's approach. She reached the rock, then stopped, her feet slightly apart and her hands on her hips, the knife secure in her grip. They faced each other at eye level, close enough to see the hairs on each other's head. Amber eyes flashed at her; the long tail flicked back and forth. Turtle Woman squinted. The scar of an old injury ran down the cat's forehead, a scar that stirred Turtle Woman's memories. She had seen this scarred face before—in the flames of a smoke-filled vision, ten long winters past. *Ah, Taku Skanskan, spirit that moves all that moves. You bring the* igmu'tanka *to me here, now?*

Grrrrrr.

"Great cat of my visions," she bellowed, "if you must rob an old soul of her body, leave the mare alone and take me instead. You prefer the two-leggeds, do you not?"

The cat's tail stopped flicking.

"Where is your courage? Why do you not hunt the antlered-one—something with a little more meat on its bones?"

The cat blinked, then sat on her haunches. The pads of her feet had left faint traces of blood on the rock.

"You, too, have traveled many sleeps to reach the Shining Mountains, *han?* Your old body is as worn out as mine." Indeed, the lion's gaunt and sagging frame revealed a lifetime of cold winters fighting the moons of hunger.

"You spilled my daughter's lifeblood. I should kill you!" Turtle Woman slashed at the air with her knife. The cougar gave her one final look, then raised her haunches, stood, turned away, and jumped from the rock, limping off into the trees.

"Ha! Just as I thought—no courage!" Turtle Woman yelled at the retreating cat. "What would I do with your moth-eaten hide, anyway? You will die soon enough." She tucked the knife into the cord at her waist, turned, and walked over to the roan mare. "You are deaf, eh, *maske?* Old and deaf!" she hollered.

Startled, the mare jerked her head up.

"*Igmu'tanka* so close," Turtle Woman scolded, "and you do not smell her? Or hear her? You are lucky to be alive." She swatted the horse on the rear, then returned to her sleeping robe.

"Wakan Tanka," she said, stretching her tired bones, "the cat did not come to kill. What message is there in this? What meaning? Is it the circle of life? Like the Medicine Wheel? All spokes leading back to a single center? Ah, it is no use. I hunt thoughts while my belly grumbles. Where is *mitakoja?*"

Turtle Woman picked her teeth clean with a fish bone, tossing the rest of the scraps into the dying fire. A great horned owl hooted in the dark, and Skye hugged her robe around her against the cold mountain night.

"Is it true, Unci? Does an owl's hoot really mean someone is going to die?"

"It is said that when one hears the *hoo-hoo* of the night-bird, someone's *nagi* hovers near."

"And do you believe that?"

"I believe that the night-bird can see in the dark. Perhaps he sees what we cannot."

Skye stirred the embers with a stick, waiting for her grandmother to continue.

Turtle Woman said, "High Bear taught me never to harm the owl, and never to forget the power of one's dreams. For dreams that come at night give us a certain sight, an ability to see into our lives, just as the owl peers into his world of darkness."

"I dreamt last night of Scotland. It was just as Ate had always described—heather-covered hills, the misty floor of the Great Glen, thatched houses made of stone."

"And did you dream of your Scottish grandmother?"

"*Hiya*. Only the countryside."

"But this night," Turtle Woman said, snuggling down under her robe, "this night my *takoja* will dream of a young man, *han?*"

Dream, and imagine, and long for. Yes, this night, as with all nights of late, Skye would think of Mahto. She would relive their meeting in the meadow, their time by the creek—every moment, every word, every touch. Oh, how she wished he had kissed her full on the mouth. This time she had been ready for it, had hungered for it.

"And you, Unci, will you dream?"

"We will both have our dreams this night, *takoja*. I shall dream about what has already been, and you shall dream of what is yet to come."

Turtle Woman again woke from a sound sleep. But not this time to silence. Owls hooted and wolves howled. Bats swooped and darted, snatching bugs from the air. Tree-eaters gnawed half-circles through sticky pine bark.

She sat up on her elbow, glancing at Skye's sleeping figure. Then she lay on her back and stared upward. Night had chased the clouds from the sky, revealing immense heavens, and silver light from the Stars of the Seven Tribes pricked the darkness. Some people believed the stars to be evil, because they hid from the sun, but Turtle Woman did not believe this. Some believed the stars to be evil because Iktomi had once lived among them, but, becoming too clever, allowed knowledge to make him vain and self-centered. The Star Council banished him to earth, where he became Trickster, and Bear inherited the spirit of wisdom. This part she believed.

But the stars had not awakened her. Perhaps her old-woman's bladder had not wanted to wait until morning. *Aaarg*, she grumbled, *the young should be plagued with these inconveniences, not the old. The old should spend their time contemplating the mysteries of Wakan Tanka, or some such thing.* Anything besides rising in the dark of night to expose one's flesh to the bite of the wind.

She picked her way through the darkness, glad for the full moon and the dimly glowing fire. She did not let the wind bite too long by dawdling. Collecting a few pieces of deadfall as she walked, she tossed the sticks on the embers when she returned, then gathered her robe around her and studied the burgeoning flames as they illuminated the small camp.

"Hau, maske," said a voice coming from the darkness.

Turtle Woman's heart leapt to her throat as a woman's figure emerged from the trees. "Who's there?" she demanded. "What stranger is this?"

"I am not a stranger to you," said the woman, moving into the light of the fire. She was cloaked in Kangi dress with a quiver and bow slung over her shoulder, scalps and a few hides hanging from her waist. She was tall, treelike, her back broad and her limbs strong.

"Not a stranger? Who are you, then?" Turtle Woman asked, even as awareness deep within her grew that she knew this handsome woman—recognized her to be the woman in her dreams.

"You used to call me Little Badger," the newcomer answered.

"A-i-i-i! It is you?" Turtle Woman peered across the flames at the woman's face. A single eagle feather jutted up from her scalp lock.

"Han, it is I. Many winters have passed since last you rode with your husband like a whirlwind from the camp of the Kangis."

Turtle Woman stared with disbelief. *An apparition?* She rubbed her eyes. Perhaps she imagined this. Perhaps the *igmu'tanka,* too, had been an apparition. Perhaps her aging mind played many tricks on her.

Turtle Woman moved closer to study the woman. The smoothness of youth was gone. Carved into her face now—by a lifetime of brave acts, as the swift-running river carves canyons into the mountain's heart—were deep furrows. But the compassionate, familiar eyes of Little Badger stared back at Turtle Woman.

"It is really you," Turtle Woman said, sinking to her knees.

"And it is really you," Little Badger answered, sitting down next to her, "just as the shaman predicted."

Turtle Woman placed her hands on her cheeks, shaking her head back and forth, then looked at Skye's sleeping figure, wondering if she should awaken her granddaughter.

Little Badger read her thoughts. "Let the girl sleep."

"The shaman, he still lives?"

"He still draws breath, though he has become as blind as a mole."

"Yet the power of prophecy has not left him?"

"No. He knew you would return to the land of the Medicine Wheel."

"*Han.* I return. I have only one small problem."

"And what is that?"

"I am lost! But you have come to show me the way."

"You do not remember the trail?" Little Badger laughed.

"It is a good joke on me, ha! Lost, at my age!"

"The way is simple. I will draw the trails for you in the dirt. But I think you are not as lost as you pretend."

"It is just the opposite. We all pretend to know where we are going, yet we are all lost."

"Even the girl?" Little Badger looked in the direction of the sleeping form. "She is the one born beneath the shifting stars, is she not?"

"*Han*, with two great-grandmothers also born on a night the stars moved around. A legacy coming to her from her father's blood and her mother's blood. *Ama*, it is too much."

"The warrior power is strong within her, then?"

"I do not wish this thing for her. Even the prayer power is almost too much."

"The warrior path is a difficult one to follow. But for some of us, it is the only path."

"For you, *han*. For me? Well, I feared I did not have the strength."

"Do you not remember teaching me that warrior strength comes not just from being fierce, like the humpback, but from being determined, like the crawling ant?"

"And like the badger?" Turtle Woman chuckled. "How could I forget this?"

"Like the badger!" she said, jumping to her feet. "Watch." She pulled a hide from her belt, wrapped it around a stick, then laid it on the ground. Quick as the flick of a rattlesnake's tongue, she leapt on the skin. The stick snapped, like a spine breaking in two.

"*Han!* I always knew you would be faster than me!" cheered Turtle Woman.

"And you taught me how to draw on the power of the four-leggeds, and the winged-ones and the crawling-ones."

"On their power"—Turtle Woman shifted her gaze and looked Little Badger directly in the eyes—"and on their wisdom."

"Yes. Knowing *when* to throw the knife, you taught me, is even more important than knowing *how* to throw the knife. Learn from the fanged-one, you used to say, who knows enough not to waste his venom."

"I spoke to you of these things, and many others. I am glad that you listened, and that you understood."

"I understood, my old friend," said Little Badger. "And now, it is my turn to pass on what I have learned. Take this eagle feather," she said, removing it from her scalp lock, "and give it to your granddaughter."

Turtle Woman took the sacred feather and held it up to the firelight.

"Remind her of the first thing you taught me—that the cloud-bird is able to see all because he remembers to soar in a sacred circle. It is because of the sacred circle that his vision is great. Tell her if she remembers this, her strength shall never fail her. Her aim shall be as true as the cloud-bird's; no prey shall escape her, no purpose be left unfulfilled."

"It seems as if there is much that I am to tell *mitakoja* on this journey."

"There is one more thing."

"One more thing?"

"The shaman told me: purify her father's sword in the sacred smoke of the silver sage. He also said to beware of the noisy-winged-one."

"The noisy-winged-one?" No bird had a more raucous and irritating nature than the magpie, not even the jay. Many people joked that the Naca had been given the most fitting name in camp. *The Naca!* Turtle Woman shivered beneath her robe.

"These things he told me to tell you."

A-i-i-i! "The shaman may be blind as a mole, but he still sees plenty."

Little Badger stood as if to go. "Each warrior," she said, "whether man or woman, whether young or old, must travel the path of the shifting stars. This I have learned from you, wise grandmother. But the holy man says you must now begin your true journey. Go to the Medicine Wheel. Pray for the people. Share your knowledge, *all* your knowledge, with your granddaughter. Then place yourself at the heart of the Medicine Wheel and wait for the sun to rise.

"Oh, one final thing, grandmother. Do not fear the Kangis. There are many fine and worthy people among us. Even old grandmothers, so old they themselves remember when their own grandmothers walked with them around the sacred Medicine Wheel."

Turtle Woman studied the fire, contemplating the words of Little Badger. Old grandmothers? How old? Old enough to have carved a five-pointed star into a rock face? She shook her head at the mystery.

Would her *takoja* choose to set her feet upon the path of the shifting stars? Was the choice Skye's to make? And what did Little Badger mean, her own true journey—had it not begun long ago? Surely she neared the end of her journey, not the beginning. She did not wait for the sun to rise, but to set. She touched the tip of the feather to her cheek, then scratched at the map in the dirt. The flames began to die down; the firelight grew dim.

"Little Badger," she said, "tell the holy man this old woman thanks him . . ." But her old friend had disappeared. She peered into the darkness surrounding the small camp and saw only the deep of night. No movement came from her sleeping granddaughter. No sound came from the forest, except for the soft *hoo-hoo* of the round-eyed night-bird.

"Tell the shaman I will burn the silver sage," she whispered into the emptiness. "Tell him I will heed his warnings." Then she walked over to Skye and tucked the eagle feather in her *takoja*'s hair.

36

WARRIOR BLOOD

Skye's hand trembled in the gray dawn as she wrapped the eagle feather next to Ate's brooch in the soft cloth.

"I still think you should wear it," said Unci, placing a hot coal in the fire horn.

"It is a coup feather. Only a true warrior should wear the feather of the great eagle."

"True, it is not wise to bellow like a bull when one is only a calf. But nor is it wise to flee like a deer when there is wolverine blood in your veins."

"I flee nowhere!"

"Little Badger wanted you to wear the feather."

"Was it really Woman Chief? Here?" Skye slid the bundle into her saddlebag behind Graunie Maggie's journal. "And to think I slept through the whole thing."

"You saw the trails she drew."

The Kangi woman, sitting by their campfire in the middle of the night? Perhaps Unci had imagined it. The eagle feather could have fallen from the sky.

"What do you think, *takoja*—that the feather fell from the sky? That it appeared out of nowhere?"

Will I never learn?

"It's just difficult to believe that I slept through the whole thing."

"If I dreamt of the Kiyuksa," said her grandmother, stomping out the last few live coals, "I would not want to awaken either."

"Unci!" Skye blushed. In her dreams, the fish had not been the only things to writhe upon the shore. She gave the saddle cinch a final tug, then looped the latigo through the cinch ring. Lifting the claymore, she tied the scabbard to the side of her saddle.

Suddenly Duncan jerked his nose into the air and flicked his ears backward, his profile a dark silhouette in the dawn. A frightened, tingling sensation traveled up Skye's spine.

"Unci, Mahto will bring us fresh meat," she started to say, turning back around.

"The surly scout will bring you nothing!"

Caws Like Magpie! Where in God's name—"Let my grandmother go!"

"She is not so uppity now, are you, old woman?" Caws Like Magpie pinned Turtle Woman's arms behind her.

"Let her go!" *Where did he come from?*

Unci's face paled as the Naca pulled her arms backward.

My God, he's going to break them!

He flung Turtle Woman into the ash pit. "Cook me something good, old woman. My belly grumbles like a starving bear." He walked toward Skye. "I see the half-breed still has no manners."

Skye's blood curdled at his bitter voice. Still touching the scabbard, she eased her hand up the sword's sheath as her grandmother rolled out of the fire. What did he mean, "The surly scout will bring you nothing"?

"This Naca is hungry. Like the hibernating bear, I go too long without many things. *Ha!* Many things!" He had nearly reached her.

Skye curved her hand around the broadsword's grip. "Most snakes," she said, "know enough to stay in their dens." The words rolled forth from deep within.

"Snakes, eh? Like that pathetic thing you pulled from the

hole? Put the weapon down, *wikoskala*. You would not know a snake from a worm."

In an obscene gesture he placed his hand on the crotch of his leather breechcloth and began to rub himself, closing the distance between them. "I will show you the difference, *wikoskala*, while the old woman cooks."

Skye closed her other hand around the heavy sword and pulled it free. She gritted her teeth and sucked in her belly, centering her weight. *Feel the earth beneath your feet* . . . She lifted the claymore above her head and with a whoosh sliced the great sword through the air.

An astonished look of disbelief wiped the sardonic grin from Magpie's face a split second before the claymore swung violently down, severing his hand from his forearm. Blood gushed forth.

Magpie lunged toward Skye, clawing at her neck, his handless arm raised grotesquely in the air. He smelled rank, his breath like a maggot-infested corpse. Blood from his wrist spewed everywhere.

Turtle Woman finished getting to her feet. Her hand went automatically to the butchering knife at her waist and tightened around it, pulling it from its sheath. *Let your thoughts form a trail to the heart of the enemy.* Her eyes bored into the back of Caws Like Magpie, searching for the soul of a warrior, the love of a husband, the loyalty of a son. She found nothing.

She raised the bronze blade to eye level. With a snap of her wrist, she hurled it through the tense air. The knife sliced into Magpie, cutting through flesh and bone, impaling itself in the blood-filled cavity of his heart.

"*Au!*" he cried out, his fingers sliding from Skye's neck, trailing red claw marks down her dress.

The earth sucked him down. He could not rise. Death had him tethered and staked. The air weighted him down from above, the ground pushed up at him from below. He thought he heard the crow cawing, flapping his wings and cawing. It occurred to him that if he could get to his horse, he would cut the crow's tether. Lift this horrible weight from his back. Then he heard himself asking the crow, "And where would you go, winged-one, if you could fly? Where would you go?" But the crow never answered.

Turtle Woman fell to the ground. Skye dropped the sword and rushed over to her. "Unci," she pleaded, "Unci, are you all right?"

Her grandmother's eyes fluttered open. "Is he dead?"

"*Han*. Very dead."

"*Waste!* He was an evil man."

"A very evil man. Are you all right, Unci?"

"*Han*. Just help me sit up. I don't know what happened to me."

"You fainted. That is all."

"Fainted? How disgusting. Like a weak-hearted rabbit."

"You are anything but weak-hearted, Unci."

"Look at you. There's blood all over your new dress."

"We'll make another dress, Unci. You can teach me, show me how to quill with the porcupine needles."

"Quilling is hard, sacred work. It takes much, much time."

"When we get back from the Medicine Wheel, then you can teach me."

"*A-i-i-i!* There is something we must do!" Unci gripped Skye's arm, pulling herself up to her feet.

"Careful, Unci. Not so fast. You'll faint again."

"Ha! Never. Quickly, *takoja*, you must gather some sage— silver sage."

"Sage? For what?"

"We must purify the long-knife. Did I not tell you? The shaman said we must purify the long-knife in the sacred smoke. Hurry!"

"And the Naca?"

"The Naca will have to purify himself."

Skye forced herself to look at Caws Like Magpie. Shock had twisted his face into an ugly sneer; his fixed eyes gazed into noth-ingness. She jerked her grandmother's knife from his back, then took hold of him by his moccasins and inched his heavy corpse across the ground, pulling him slowly into the trees.

She tried to muster even a pittance of compassion, but none surfaced. She dropped his legs and left him where he lay. Then she headed out into the open, where stalks of sage grew among the bunch grasses. His bragging words, so cocksure and arrogant, robbed her of any sense of relief. *"The scout will bring you nothing!"* Where was Mahto? She peered into the grayness. The sun had yet to show itself. *Where was he?*

Mahto toyed with the broken arrow shaft, inspecting it again as he had done so often during the last three days. It was good to be on horseback again.

The arrow had whizzed down from the jagged black walls that guarded the mountain's back. Only the foolhardy would attempt to scale the peak from the east, he had told himself. *Hoh!* And now he had an arrow wound in his leg. The arrow had flown with such force that it went right through his leg. Had it not then impaled the deer's carcass, slung over the tobiano's back, it would have pierced the horse as well. He patted the tobiano on the neck. Kola, *you were the lucky one,* han?

He did not recognize this arrow as being Kangi, or Susuni, but at least no more flew down upon him. He cursed the lost days spent nursing his wound in a deep, narrow cavern hidden in the mountain's side. Stronger now, after eating much of the meat intended for the women, he followed the trail he believed would lead him to the Medicine Wheel, and to the Light-skinned One.

"One hell of a scout, eh, True Dog?" he mumbled to himself, disgusted. "With not even enough fresh meat left for a *sunka.*"

The word conjured up a pathetic image of Doublewoman's dog. He turned the arrow in his hand. It could have been Lakota, could have been fashioned by the bitter and twisted Naca. Three days lost. Who, Mahto wondered, now trailed whom?

Women, he decided, made fools of men. Made them stalk the grasslands like coyotes, sit in the open like a duck in water, wander the woods like a rutting elk. And bare their souls while pulling

fish from a mountain stream. Had he been a fool to walk away
from her? To not have stroked her skin and felt the curves of her
womanhood. Perhaps he had been a fool—for who but a fool
would resist such an impulse? Certainly not Caws Like Magpie.
Another image came to mind, one that caused him to grit his teeth
and clench his jaw. The scar on his face hardened into a thin ridge.

He tossed the broken arrow to the ground and kicked the tobiano into a lope, up the trail.

Woman Chief peered over the edge of the narrow path to the
charred trees below. A movement caught her eyes; then a groan
reached her ears.

"No Toe, did you hear that?"

"It looks like a dead horse, there against the blackened
trunks."

"Where?" said Red Horn. "I see nothing."

"The feathered hat covers your eyes. Give it back to me and
maybe your eyes will work better."

"Ha! The white man's hat is mine."

Burning Hair pulled up behind them, leading the immigrant's
mule. "Start wrestling over that hat again, and you'll both be over
the edge."

"Hush!" Woman Chief commanded. "Listen—do you hear
that?"

They waited. A breeze fluttered the ragged plume on the immigrant's hat. A cluster of mountain chickadees skittered from one
burnt tree to another. But no human sound climbed the granite
wall to the rock-strewn trail. Still, Woman Chief did not doubt
her ears. She had heard a woman groaning.

"The wind plays tricks with us, yes?" said Black Tail.

"No Toe is right. That's a dead pony against that tree. I'm
going down there." Woman Chief climbed off her horse, eased
along the narrow trail, then worked her way down the steep slope.
Two of the men followed behind her.

The horse's belly swelled with the death of at least three or four sleeps. His jugular had been cut, his hind quarters gnawed on. A bridle still looped over his muzzle and an ornately quilled chest blanket covered his forefront. Woman Chief hunted the ground for sign, let her eyes follow a faint trail leading away from the horse to a tall, rounded boulder. She pulled her knife from its sheath and stepped behind the rock.

A ribby black-and-white dog, tail tucked, turned, ran a few steps away, then came back, cowering and whining.

"A camp dog," she said to herself, "but where is the camp?" She knelt and called the dog—a female, judging by her swollen sides. The dog came, slinking along the ground. Woman Chief rubbed her ears.

The dog sat up and yipped. And a woman groaned.

She lay between two boulders, an empty waterskin at her feet, an open rawhide case by her head. Woman Chief scanned the area but saw no one else.

"Red Horn, No Toe, look around. Make sure she is alone."

She knelt, scrutinizing the old woman—her hair, her pock-marked face, her finely quilled clothing. *"Hau,"* she said in the language of the Titonwans. The woman's eyelids fluttered. *"Hau,"* she said again. "Are you alive, old woman?"

The woman's eyes jerked open and her hand flew to her mouth. She struggled to sit up, but could only lean forward on one arm. *"Yun!"* she cried out in fear.

"I will not hurt you, old woman." Woman Chief slid her knife back in its sheath. The dog moved between them and lay down by the old woman's side.

"Where are you hurt?"

The woman said nothing.

"Your back? Your legs?"

Still the woman said nothing.

"She is alone," No Toe said, returning.

"She is Titonwan," Red Horn snarled, sending a wad of spittle into the scorched dirt.

"Who left you here to die?" Woman Chief asked. "Have you no family?"

A barely perceptible whisper came from the woman's throat.

"Burning Hair," Woman Chief yelled up to the trail, "bring me some water."

The quillwork on the old woman's clothing was precise and flawless, more so, even, than the work done by the women of her own lodge. Woman Chief herself never did any woman's work; she supplied the meat and hides, and the rest was up to the others.

Something about the old woman stirred Woman Chief's compassion. Maybe it was the cowering dog—used to being beaten, no doubt. But by whom? Surely not this one.

Burning Hair appeared with the water.

"She is Titonwan," he said. "Why do you pamper her?"

Woman Chief bent and held the waterskin up to the old woman's parched lips. She clutched frantically at the bag, spilling the water down her chin. "Easy, old woman." Woman Chief pulled the bag away. "Only a little at first."

Red Horn spoke up. "Kill her, and let's be on our way."

Woman Chief silenced him with her eyes.

"Can you travel, old woman?" she asked.

"*Han,*" the woman answered, her voice feeble and weak.

"Did you hand embroider the dress?"

The woman nodded her head.

"And the horse blanket?"

The woman nodded her head again.

"Can you still sew?"

The woman held out her gnarled hands and made fast flicking movements with her fingers.

"That quick, eh, grandmother?" Woman Chief laughed.

"*Han.*"

Woman Chief stood and scratched her head. It had taken many buffalo hides to form the covering for her large tipi. Yet only five of them slept within its shelter, herself and four other women, and not one of them slept near the door, to tend the flap.

"No Toe," she said to the young warrior, "help me to repair that travois. I am taking her home with me."

37

THE MEDICINE WHEEL

The old cougar flinched as a lone bolt of lightning flashed across the sky above the mountain. Then all grew quiet again. She limped around the circle of stones, sniffing at the old kinnikinnick scattered about. Only a faint oily scent remained from the two-leggeds who had once visited the barren plateau. She stepped over the circle, then followed a row of stones until it led her to the center. There, a black-horned skull from a shaggy four-legged rested on top of a pile of rocks. She sniffed at the buffalo skull, then batted it with her forepaw. No flesh and blood odor remained. Nothing to chew on—no leg bones, no ribs, no entrails. But it did not matter, for the urge to hunt, even the urge to move on, had left her. She desired, simply, to sleep.

She walked to the edge of the high plateau and lifted her nose to the brewing storm. The earth dropped off sharply below her, breaking into pinnacles of rock where few but the winged-ones would venture to go.

Lifting a paw to her mouth, she licked at the bleeding pads. In the distance, an elk moved through the pine trees, a young calf at her side. The sight did not stir the cat's blood. She blinked her round, amber eyes and moved on, hunting the shadowed opening of a mountain cave where she could rest. A ground squirrel scurried across her path, but she ignored him, not even bothering to sniff at the trail he left.

She retraced her steps back across the plateau to the other side of the mountain, where the sides angled gently away, leading to open meadows and stands of pine trees growing tall and straight. Energy from the pent-up storm caused the hair on her thin back to rise and her long, dark-tipped tail to bush out. She moved nervously down the slope, into the shade of the pines. Thunder rumbled overhead, close and threatening. She jerked her head up.

A second bolt of lightning, drawn to the timbered slopes, flashed like a sword through the sky. A shattering CRACK split the air. The cougar froze, not knowing which way to flee. In less than a heartbeat, a giant pine groaned and crashed toward the earth, crushing everything in its path.

Within moments, all was still again, except for the faint wisps of smoke rising from the newly fallen tree, and the last audible breath of an old, majestic cat.

The damp smell of yesterday's storm clung to the air. Turtle Woman blinked the tears from her eyes and lifted her head. The mountain was just as she remembered: beautiful on one side, sloping down into smooth-needled trees, and jagged and rocky on the other side, where the mountain had worn away. But she no longer feared the crags as she had long ago, when she thought the shaman had intended to push her over the side. This time, she would embrace the mountain as a loving child does her mother.

The well-worn trail disappeared as the crest of the mountain opened up into a broad plateau. No trees grew on this wind-blown top—no shaggy-leaf trees or rustling-trees or sagebrush or sumac. From the top of this high place, the Earth Mother opened herself to Father Sky, spreading herself beneath a great expanse of blue. And the Sky reached down, touching the Earth with his clouds and his winds and his sunlight. An eagle flew between the Earth and Sky, reminding them both of their connection to Wakan Tanka, the great father of them all.

Finally, Turtle Woman had the strength to face her husband's death, and the truth awaiting her, whatever it might be.

The rocks of the Medicine Wheel lay upon the ground like a

skeleton from the long-ago days of creation—an ancient fossil embedded in the heart of the earth. From the center cairn, upon which some worshipper had placed a parched buffalo skull, radiated the spokes of the wheel, formed from thousands of pieces of limestone—each rock like the remains of a loved one.

The forever-grief welled up inside her. The earth became the barren plateau, and the barren plateau became Sunstone, fleshless and bloodless. The wind blew at Turtle Woman's desolation, emptying her of all need. She no longer had to yearn for the old life. Spirit had replaced it, and memory would sustain her. For what were memories, but Spirit's way of greeting? And what was the Medicine Wheel, but the door to Spirit's home?

Slow, faltering steps took Turtle Woman from the gently sloping side of the mountain, across the barren crest where the Medicine Wheel lay, to its rugged edge. She reached out for Skye, steadying herself with her *takoja*'s arm.

"The air is thin," she said, "too thin for the frail lungs of an old woman." Her heart fluttered like a bird's.

"We are nearly as high as the *wanblis*, Unci. Look, you can see far beyond that great basin—clear to the next range of mountains."

"Finally, *takoja*, I am learning to look no farther than my own nose. It happens, you know, when the eyes begin to cloud from the smoke of too many winters."

"Your vision is still as sharp as a hawk's."

"Come, I want to show you something."

"Unci, it's too steep! You'll fall."

"*Hiya*, we won't fall. Come on, step lightly."

Limestone flakes fell from the edge of the mountain as they eased their way down into the towering crags, tiptoeing along a narrow trail that wound its way in and out. Finally, Turtle Woman stopped. She steadied herself, bracing her hand against the cool face of a rock. She ran her fingers over the stone, searching. She moved a few feet farther, all the time running her hands across the surface of the rock. Nothing. She could find nothing!

"Unci, do you look for something?"

"An etching, carved into the stone."

"A carving? Of what?"

"Like the design on my moccasins, *takoja*, my moccasins." She pointed to her feet. "Look for the star."

Skye, too, ran her hands over the face of the rock. "I see nothing, Unci."

"Keep looking, *takoja*. It's got to be here somewhere."

"*Haye*, Unci, here, what is this?" Skye brushed powdery dust from a small raised area near a crevice in the stone.

Turtle Woman pushed her granddaughter's hand away and stepped closer, peering at the rock, her nose only inches from it. She wet her fingers with her tongue and darkened the stone. A faint, weather-beaten image began to appear.

"What is it, Unci?"

Turtle Woman stared at the etching, trying to make the lines of a five-pointed star appear, yet at the same time not wanting them to—hoping that her memory had, indeed, failed her. "*The mark is Kangi*," the shaman had said. "*You have the blood of a Kangi.*"

But no five-pointed star appeared. No comet shooting through its center. Instead, a turtle appeared, with four legs and a tail and a head. A simple turtle. Such as anyone might carve. A Lakota, or a Susuni, or a Scili, or a Sahiyela, or a Kangi—or even a *wasicu*. A simple turtle, like one would find anywhere.

Turtle Woman felt dizzy. She put a hand to her head and leaned against the cool stone.

"Unci, are you all right?"

She waved her *takoja* away. "I am fine." She closed her eyes. *What, Great Mystery, is the meaning of this?* She listened for an answer. A fly buzzed by her ear. *Is the meaning as plain as that, as simple as a fly on my nose?* She waited. She listened to the wind as it blew through the shaggy-leaf trees below.

She opened her eyes and contemplated the turtle. She thought about all that she knew of this simple creature: how a turtle had ambled across her father's leg while her parents were making love, laying her eggs in the sand beside them; how the shell of a turtle was as hard as stone, yet the flesh was soft as a child's; how the people turned the shell upside down to hold their paints; how they made bowls and plates from it, even spoons. She closed her eyes again.

She thought of the great mythical turtle who rose from the depths of the vast waters of the world to create this land, an island of immense plains and snow-covered peaks. The turtle, whose heart continued to beat long after the spirit left the flesh.

The turtle. Of the earth, and of the water. A feminine force, the guardian of life. Yet with an image so universal, it could have been carved by anyone.

By anyone? Kangi, Lakota, wasicu? Is that my lesson, Wakan Tanka? That it does not matter who my grandmothers were, as long as their hearts continue to beat within me? As long as I carry as a part of me their strength, and their tenderness? Do you wish for me to rise from the depths of my fear?

Turtle Woman had to smile at the irony. Were not these the very lessons she had been trying to teach Skye? She had been blind, seeing through the eye of fear instead of the eye of the heart. She had betrayed Sunstone's love by not trusting him with her secret. And all along, a lifetime of winters, there had been no Kangi blood in her veins.

She opened her eyes and ran her fingers one last time across the cool stone image of the turtle. Truth. Finally, so simple.

Turtle Woman had waited a long time to return to the Medicine Wheel, to watch Father Sun lower himself from the Sky, to feel the last rays of warmth light upon Mother Earth. Slowly, she started back up the narrow trail, beckoning to her granddaughter.

Skye followed Turtle Woman across the plateau of the mountain. They stepped lightly over the outer stone rim of the Medicine Wheel, then walked softly upon the sacred ground until they reached the center cairn.

"You remember the *Peta-oihankesni, takoja,*" Unci asked, "the Fire Without End?"

"Aye, I remember."

"They say it has been burning since White Buffalo Calf Woman came to our people, long ago."

"I remember. Lost Morning told me the story."

"Lost Morning is a true Oglala. She will be a good friend to you."

Skye smiled. "What about the fire, Unci?"

"It is not really the same fire, is it, *takoja*, as the fire that burned when White Buffalo Calf Woman came?"

"Part of it, perhaps. If the Keepers of the Flame never allowed it to go out."

"Ah, you are wise enough to understand, then."

"Understand what?"

"You have been called a half-blood by some, *han?*"

Skye turned her head away.

"*Takoja*, do not be ashamed. Your blood is like the Fire Without End. And the blood of your children will be like this sacred fire, for no matter how diluted the blood of your descendants becomes, the sacred fire will always burn within their souls. You, my *takoja*, have become the Keeper of the Flame."

Deep inside, in the dark recesses of Skye's heart, a tiny light began to burn. The light grew brighter, and its warmth caused tears to come to her eyes. Her heritage need not cleave her in two, but could become a beacon to guide her. Keeper of the Flame. She wiped the tears from her face and smiled, then leaned over to kiss her grandmother's cheek.

"Thank you, Unci. I will try to make my prayers worthy."

Her grandmother placed her hands on Skye's shoulders, then nodded to the buffalo skull resting on top of the center cairn. "This *pte* skull is like the heart of the Great Creator. And these rock spokes"—she made a wide sweeping motion with her arm—"are like the spines of all the tribes of the world. Now let me be, *takoja*, for I must spend the night in prayer."

Unci walked back to the outer edge of the wheel, then began to follow the circle of stones, stopping at every spoke to lift her hands in supplication. Then she returned to the center and, taking the buffalo skull in her lap, lowered herself onto the cairn. Skye walked back to the horses and loosened her grandmother's bed robe from the back of her saddle, then returned to the wheel. She draped the robe over Turtle Woman's shoulders.

"Is there nothing else you need, Unci?"

"*Hiya*, nothing else, *mitakoja*. But perhaps to look at you once more."

Skye knelt in front of her. Taking a deep breath, she took her grandmother's gnarled and maimed hand between hers and caressed it. "I will be here in the morning, Unci."

"*Han*, Daughter of the Sky, you will be here in the morning."

Nightmares haunted Skye—Caws Like Magpie clutching at her throat, blood dripping down her dress, Mahto lying dead, the Naca's arrow in his heart. Finally the first rays of sun illuminated the plateau. She rose from her sleeping robe as the morning star faded from the dawn sky, letting the dark dreams fade with the night.

Skye hoped to entice her grandmother with some soft gooseberry mush, for Unci had eaten nothing in three days, not even a bite of pemmican. She had plucked savory grasses for the old roan mare to eat, but would eat nothing herself. Skye worried about them both, about their gaunt frames and the long journey home.

Unci had remained at the Medicine Wheel all night. She sat there now, the robe over her shoulders, her head bent in prayer. A beam of sunlight, like a bridge between heaven and earth, reached out to her. Skye smiled; she would wait a while longer before disturbing her.

The horses had wandered down the gently sloping side of the mountain during the night. At Skye's approach, Roy and Duncan, still hobbled, lifted their heads. The old mare kept her nose to the grass. Skye eased up to her from the side, whistling to her. Finally, she lifted her head and nickered a greeting.

It would not take long to gather firewood, for a recent lightning strike had felled a pine and it lay charred and shattered upon the ground. Skye stepped over the trunk, picking up broken limbs and twigs. Something out of place caught her eye—tan with a dark tip. A tail. She pushed the branches aside: huge paws, their pads split, the nails worn; lean ribs, crushed; the stomach gaunt, the nipples hard and dry. A dead mountain lion, an old female. Her shoulders lay trapped beneath the tree. Skye put her firewood down and worked her way around to the other side. Blood had trickled from the cat's nose and mouth. More leaked from an ear. A twinge of unexplained sadness caused Skye to pause. She touched the broad, heart-shaped nose, then scratched the cougar between the eyes, rubbing her forehead where an old scar marred the fur. She tried to lift the tree, but it would not budge.

Suddenly, she missed her father—missed his strength, his hearty voice, even his stubbornness.

She retrieved her firewood and headed back up to where she had unsaddled the horses the evening before, wondering if the cougar perhaps had had a den somewhere in the limestone crags on the other side of the mountain. She dug a small pit, then arranged the twigs in tipi fashion. Within minutes, a fire snapped and crackled. She filled their only cooking pot with a small amount of water from the waterskin, then added dried gooseberries and marrow fat. The pot hung securely over the fire on a makeshift tripod of stout green willows.

Skye rummaged around in her saddlebag, looking for Graunie Maggie's journal. She found, instead, the three pewter mugs. Och, she had meant to give Unci the other mug long before now. Still rummaging, she found the journal. Walking back to the fire, she settled down to wait for the mush to cook. Gently she turned the yellowed pages. She reread several verses, then, toward the back of the book, came across an entry she had not seen before—not a poem, but a brief diary entry in her great-grandmother's faded cursive. *"The dreaded Clearances continue,"* she had written. *"I fear for me grandson's life . . ."*

Skye closed the journal. The words awed her, made her feel as if she had stepped back through time into another world. Oh, how she missed Ate. And how Graunie Maggie must have missed him—he had not been much older than Skye when he left home.

Heart of Greatness was the courage-name the people had given him. *Heart of Greatness.* The name caused her own heart to swell with pride.

The mush had begun to simmer. She stood and walked back over to the saddles, tucking the journal into her bag. A cloud drifted across the early sun, shutting off its warmth, and a wind began to stir the tops of the pines. She set the pot on a flat stone near the flames, then added more kindling. She would encourage Unci to come eat by the warmth of the fire.

"*Hau*, Unci, good morning."

The robed figure did not move.

"Unci," Skye repeated, "come warm yourself by the fire."

Still the robed figure did not move.

"Grandmother." Skye gently shook her shoulder. Nothing. The cloud passed and a shaft of sunlight beamed down upon them both, casting Skye's shadow onto the ground. Suddenly, feeling very alone, she stepped away, her shadow following her. She stared at Unci's bent figure. No shadow darkened the earth beside it. Just the beam of sunlight, casting a golden glow.

Skye looked again at her own early morning shadow, watching it disappear as another storm cloud obscured the sun. Still there was no movement, save the wind ruffling the silver hairs on her grandmother's head and the dark fur on her robe.

"Unci?" The word came out a sorrowful whisper.

She uncurled her grandmother's gnarled hands from the buffalo skull and set the sacred object upon the earth. Then she knelt and gathered her grandmother's body in her arms, lifting her slowly from the pile of stones. She expected to stagger beneath the weight, but she did not, for her *unci*, the One-Only-One woman of the Oglalas, was spirit-light.

Mahto arrived at the Medicine Wheel as the thunderclouds from another summer storm began to gather above the Shining Mountains. Skye's bay horse and the Scotsman's red gelding whinnied as he approached, tossing their heads in greeting. He did not see the old mare.

He slid from the tobiano, swinging his injured leg over the fresh deer meat draped across the horse's back. Holding his hand to his forehead, he shielded his eyes from the late afternoon sun and scanned the plateau. At the far edge, its four poles silhouetted against the horizon, gaped an empty burial scaffold, a bundle stretched out beneath it on the ground. Beside it stood a horse, and the figure of a female. *A-i-i-i, Wakan Tanka, let it be the Light-skinned One.* Mahto dropped the tobiano's rein, drew a blanket from his saddlebag, and hurried toward the woman. A drop of rain fell, dampening his cheek.

The woman's hair shone in the fleeting sun, the warm wind blowing through it like a breeze rustling red willows. Mahto's heart skipped a beat. The body on the ground was Turtle Woman's.

Sorrow, and relief, rose up in him—sorrow for the old woman, sorrow for the Light-skinned One, sorrow for the people. Three deaths in less than one moon—an ultimate test of courage, for only the most courageous spirit could survive such grief.

Skye watched the man stride across the ground, skirting the border of the Medicine Wheel. She sucked in her breath. Even from a distance, and despite the limp, she recognized the proud step. But she did not begin to breathe again until she could count the bear claws upon Mahto's chest, until she reached her hand up to his handsome face and stroked the scarred jaw.

"You are alive," she whispered.

"*You* are alive," he answered.

Together, their eyes went to the robe-wrapped body of her grandmother, and then to the empty scaffold standing like a barren womb. Together they knelt and lifted the body, raising it up, placing it above them on the wooden frame. A distant memory, *the tinkling of bells*, floated through Skye's mind. She unwrapped a small cloth bundle and withdrew from it the single eagle feather which had been Woman Chief's. From another bundle she withdrew the extra pewter mug and the heather brooch that had been Ate's. She hung the mug from one of the four sapling poles, then tied Woman Chief's feather to another pole, letting the breeze lift and twirl it.

"She was the true warrior," Skye said, starting to pin Ate's brooch to the buffalo robe.

But Mahto gently took it from her. "The Scotsman would want his strong-spirited daughter to keep the *wotawe*," he said, pinning the brooch to her dress instead.

She touched her finger to the heather design, the war crest of the Macdonalds. To have a warrior spirit, she was beginning to realize, did not mean that she must walk the warrior path. The warrior spirit lived within her, as it had lived within Ate, within Ina, within Unci. And aye, it must have lived within Graunie Maggie as well. Lived there even still, perhaps. Destiny's arrows might have pierced Skye's past, but the lance of the future stood within her grasp.

The old roan mare lifted her nose to the wind, smelling the storm. Skye petted the horse's gaunt neck, then ran her hand across the deep sockets above the mare's eyes.

"Your grandmother will need her faithful friend to ride upon down the spirit trail," said Mahto, his words more a question than a statement.

Skye pleaded silently with him, her eyes filling with tears. There had been enough death.

"Perhaps," he said, "your grandfather's warhorse can carry them both to the Land of Many Lodges."

Only one patch of sunlight remained. A jagged spark of lightning flashed from the valley floor. Together, Skye and Mahto walked away from the scaffold, off the high plateau to the sloping hills below. The roan mare did not follow them, but stood beside her old *maske*, her fleeting shadow light and lean upon the earth.

A soft rain began to fall, warm and gentle on Skye's face. She let Mahto lift his blanket over their shoulders and lead them to the shelter of a huge boulder half-buried in the gently sloping hill.

In the distance, somewhere over the great basin, the thunderbeings began to rumble. Skye thought of the cougar, and the charred tree. She closed her eyes and leaned into Mahto. The wind blew warm and tender against Skye's skin, and she let the rain wash the weariness from her soul, let her lungs fill with the cleansing air, remembering the purifying steam of the *inipi*, the moist breath of the hot rocks upon her nakedness.

The satiny rain caressed Skye's face and throat and she gave in to its wetness, letting it lift and carry her as had the waters of the creek a lifetime ago. She became the swiftly moving stream, felt it surge within her, finally let the rampant waters cut new banks, shift the sands of her shores with its fervor. Sparks of lightning crackled across the sky, small shafts of faraway brilliance not yet striking earth.

Mahto watched the storm clouds move across the sky like a band of wild horses wading in summer grass. He heard the thunder approach the Shining Mountains and knew that the thunder-beings were about to unleash a great and awesome tempest. The body of the Light-skinned One grew warm against him, and he remembered the sacred hot springs where he had gone to purify his thoughts, yet had been able to think only of Skye.

As the storm grew, so grew Mahto's need. Thunder shook the earthen valley and caused his heart to tremble. Lightning flashed from the granite mountains and set his passion on fire. He pulled Skye closer to him, saw the eddy of longing deep within her eyes. The rain formed little streams which ran down her throat, and he felt the river of desire rise mightily within her.

The ground became damp and fertile, sating the succulent root tendrils of the grasses and the buried tips of the great trees. High above the earth, waiting for the power of the storm to ebb, the sun and the stars lingered on their coverlet of clouds. The earth lifted her face to the sky, and the sky gazed down upon her. Together, they waited for the vibrant colors of rebirth to paint the horizon— fiery reds and golds and crimsons. And then, as the day ended and the moment of afterglow finally came, a deep calm settled upon the land, and the Shining Mountains rejoiced.

Epilogue

SONG FOR THE SKY

by Gwen Morgan-Jones

The sky is a ribboned dress sewn crookedly,
uneven stripes of pale blue, grey, white.
I imagine putting her on—I am the most beautiful
woman in the world. I dance to the gentle
music of songbirds, schottische to the bagpipes and drum,
yip with the coyote when the Lakota campfires rise.
I could be in the highlands of Scotland or the Medicine Bows
pulling traditional songs from my bosom with laughter.
I touch my sleeves with wind, whirl the hem around
the edges of prairie,
dancing.

THE ISLE OF SKYE, 1855

The old woman, seated within the *tigh-cheilidh*—the gathering place of the small crofting community—dozed in her chair. The past mingled with the present, this day's celebration of Saint

Michael becoming confused in Maggie's mind with all the others.

"Graunie," her graundochter coaxed, setting a plate on her lap, "have a piece of the Michael *struan* I brought for ye."

"Leave her alone, Katie," said Iona. "Canna ye see she's trying to sleep? The cake will keep."

"But she's grown so thin, Mother. There's barely any meat on her bones."

Meat? Maggie smelled the lamb roasting over the central fire in the *tigh-cheilidh*—bramble, oak, and rowan. Sacred woods. She fingered the small, heart-shaped river stone which she held in her hand, then opened her eyes.

"Bring me a morsel or two of the Uan Micheil, lass."

"Och! Ye frightened me, Graunie."

"Bring me some meat, lass." She handed Katie back the plate. She wanted lamb, not cake. "And cut it up good, won't ye?" She put the stone back in her apron pocket, then pulled two letters out. She inspected them both—one yellow and faded, the other a wee bit ragged, having traveled clear from the New Land, but with a postmark on it less than a season old. She returned the faded letter to her pocket, then closed her eyes, cradling in her lap the one that had just arrived.

Saint Michael. The protector, patron saint of sea and horseman. Son of Danu, the great mother goddess. Maggie had no son of her own, just her dochter Iona, Katie's mother. A lone tear escaped her eye.

And now she had no grandson.

Gregory. Dead four summers past according to the letter's sad news, at the age of forty-eight. She had yet to tell his mother Iona, or his sister Katie.

None of them had seen Gregory since the Micheil celebration nearly thirty years past, and only the one letter received from him in all those years. Not since the Micheil race had she spoken to him, when he had raced down the shoreline with the other lads and lassies, whipping their steeds with dried pieces of seaweed, using no saddles or bridles, just flimsy straw harnesses. She had ridden in the race once herself, had even won the race. The smell of the sea, the sand flung high in the air, the horse's muscles moving beneath her legs—aye, she remembered it all.

He had been only eighteen when the great sea carried him away. And Gregory had been one of the lucky lads, leaving of his own accord. *He was the warrior of courage, going on the journey of prophecy.* . . . The incantation washed over her, like the high tide that had washed his tracks from the sand. He had left the very day of the race. Alas! The evil clearances! Surely the work of the Otherworld. Only a handful of the old crofters were left. *And we seem to be withering up, like heather dug from the earth and left to dry.* Even the Celtic ceremonies, all but a few, had vanished like smoke.

And now, her grandson would never return.

Maggie wiped the tear from her cheek and carefully slid the pages of the letter from their envelope, rereading them carefully.

My Dearest Graunie Maggie,

I do not know if this letter will reach you, nor if you are even still alive. I am Skye, your great-granddaughter. My father was Gregory Macdonald. I was born twenty-one winters ago, in the Medicine Bow Mountains of Indian Territory. My mother was Breathcatcher, of the Standing People band of the Oglala Lakotas. She died when I was but seven winters old.

Father used to say that the old times were changed, old manners gone. I am writing to tell you a sad thing. Four winters past, Father died. He, too, is now gone. He is buried in the Black Mountains of America, alongside my Lakota grandfather.

Do you remember the journal you gave him? It is how he taught me to read and write. And to commit to memory the poems of Scott, and Burns, and all the others whom you loved. "O hush thee, my babie, thy sire was a knight, Thy mother a lady, both lovely and bright." Do you remember that one? He used to sing it to me when I was just a lass. And now I sing it to me own daughter—Little Flame we call her. Aye, you are a great-great-grandmother.

My husband is called Mahto, a Kiyuksa of the Oglala Lakotas. He says someday he would like to meet this shifting-star great-grandmother of mine from across the big waters. He wants to know, do you still like to smoke the pipe?

*Soon, I would like to travel to Scotland and meet my High-
land family. I would like Little Flame to see the land of her other
grandfather. And to meet her great-graunie Iona and aunt
Katie. Do they yet live?*

*But first, I must go to the Laramie Fork, for nearly one hun-
dred Brulés from the camp of Little Thunder have just been
killed by a General Harney—over seventy women and children
taken captive. There must be something I can do . . .*

Women and children murdered. Och, was it the same in every
nation of the world? Maggie rested the letter on her lap. She had
grown tired and the writing had begun to blur. She slipped the letter back in her pocket and closed her eyes. She had learned not to
expect too much of her old heart.

Skye. Grown, with a wee lass of her own. After all these years.

Later, alone by the light of her bedroom candle, she would finish reading the letter, tracing the words with her finger until they
were etched into her mind, as were her grandson's words.

"Graunie."

Maggie opened her eyes. Katie held a plate out to her. She
took it, and lifted a piece of tender lamb to her mouth. The Cail-
leach an Dudain was about to begin.

The music enveloped the crowd: the plaintive stringed fiddle,
the ancient wind instrument, with its sad, bellowing notes. Two
dancers, one male, one female, appeared in the center of the
throng of people. The woman wore a loosely woven tunic; he
wore woolen homespuns and a long saffron shirt. The man lifted
a druid wand in the air, waving it above his own head, then the
woman's head. She crumpled in a heap at his feet, as if dead. The
crowd wailed.

His arms rose to the heavens, pleading for his lover's life. The
bagpipes moaned and the fiddle keened. He fell to the ground beside his lover, caressing her face, kissing her hands. The crowd
cried out in mock mourning. Maggie watched with her eyes, but
her mind wandered to long ago.

The man stood and danced around his lover's lifeless body,
tearing at his own clothing, pulling at his hair, scraping his nails

across his flesh. Then he knelt beside her again and once more raised his hands in supplication to the heavens, holding the wand up to the sky. He took one of her hands gently in his own and tapped it with the wand. The hand began to twitch, coming to life. The man rejoiced. The crowd and the music howled. Maggie's own hands twitched in her lap. Never a day went by that she did not think of her husband. *It seemed as if the late-wake had been only yesterday.*

The dancer touched the woman's other hand and it, too, began to move, swaying back and forth, reaching for the man's lips. The man began to dance around her, ecstatic. He touched her left leg with the wand, then her right. She began to stretch, bending her limbs, arching her back. He knelt again and breathed into her mouth, then touched the wand to her heart. *No matter how long Maggie had danced, her husband had never come back to life. And now, all hope of seeing Gregory again, dashed like surf upon the cliffs.*

The crowd went wild. He raised her to her feet and they began to dance around the circle, the woman's long hair flowing behind, the man's arms lifting and twirling her in a celebration of life. A second tear slid from Maggie's eye. *Can it really be? Skye, coming to visit? Will she bring her husband and wee child with her? Och.* Maggie wiped the tear away and placed her hand on her heart.

Hope was such a fleeting thing. So elusive. Yet without it, what was left? She patted her apron pocket and felt the letters, and beneath them, the tiny river stone.

"Born in the wilds of America," Gregory had written. *"We've named her Skye, after your beloved island."* And now, a child named Little Flame.

She hoped her heart would be patient a wee bit longer.

Afterword

The truth is more multi-faceted than we care to believe; written history is not infallible, and has, no doubt, fallen victim on many occasions to the personal bias of the historian.

Scholars would generally agree that the statements written and presented by our historians are, for the most part, accurate. However, oral history often disputes the suppositions of archaeologists and scholars, especially among American Indians and other indigenous peoples whose voices have long been silenced.

Some of the oral histories among the Oglala Lakotas of the western Teton convey a belief that their people originated in the Black Hills (He Sapa) of South Dakota, not in Minnesota near the headwaters of the Mississippi as most historians write. According to Severt Young Bear in *Standing in the Light* (University of Nebraska Press, 1994), "The Oglala are very adventuresome and very spiritual people and very fearless warriors. . . . The oral history I heard said they moved from the Black Hills in all four directions."

To those who appropriately give great credence to oral histories, and who feel that characters such as Turtle Woman and Sunstone would have believed their ancestors to have originated in the Black Hills, and not farther to the east, I apologize.

If we are to understand the wisdom of traditional truths inherent within all cultures then we must begin to weave these truths into our own lives in very intimate and honest ways. We must learn to walk soft-footed around the ceremonial fires of the past, yet we should not fear stepping into the healing light of today's fires. Our lives, if dedicated to truth-seeking, will thus be dedicated to all the peoples of the world.

Shifting Stars, though a work of fiction, seeks to honor this truth-seeking. The lives of the characters spiral closely around historical accounts. Fictive Skye Macdonald is born in 1834 beneath the shifting stars, close to when our own scientific records (and many American Indian winter counts) show Halley's Comet streaking across the sky. Gregory Macdonald bares his fictitious broadsword to reveal the true and tragic history of the Scottish Highlanders. Escaping a nation of conquered clansmen, he finds himself now to be the *wasicu*, the conqueror, playing an integral role in the true and tragic history of his wife's people. Turtle Woman grows old alongside the memory of Woman Chief, a Gros Ventre actually captured by the Crows around 1820 when she was a young girl, while Graunie Maggie lives imaginatively through a period of historic terror.

Mahto grieves for a Lakota father who existed only in the author's mind, while real Oglala tears were shed in 1841 when the Kiyuksa leader, Bull Bear, died at the hands of fellow Oglalas. Doublewoman Dreamer lives in a world of mystical make-believe, haunted by the time-honored creation stories of Anog Ite. Sunstone, respected elder of this fictive world, grieves for the future of a true people, as he debates within the Red Council Lodge the need to go to the historic meeting on Horse Creek where the Fort Laramie Treaty of 1851 will soon be signed. And, yes, according to Iron Shell's winter count (of the Miniconjous and Brulés), a man named Ties His Penis in a Knot really did die in 1832.

Such is the joy and hardship, I am learning, of writing an historical novel of the West—to intertwine the lives of the novel's characters with the lives of history's characters, and to do so with bared soul. The Medicine Wheel exists, first and foremost, in the hearts of those who have been singing songs of prayer and leaving offerings at this sacred place for hundreds of years. Yet, what a joyous feeling when the wisdom of the past, unbeknownst to us, enters the souls of our characters!

It is said that we live in the present, we dream of the future, yet we learn eternal truths from the past. May *Shifting Stars* honor all three—the trilogy from which all sacred stories spring.

Glossary

The Sioux Nation is comprised of the Lakotas (Western Tetons), the Dakotas (Santee Sioux), and the Nakotas (Yankton Sioux). This book concerns itself solely with the Lakota People. The Oglalas (meaning to "Scatter One's Own") are one of the major tribal divisions within the Lakotas, another main tribe being the Sicangu (meaning "Burnt Thighs" but referred to as Brulés). Historically, within the Oglalas existed seven distinct bands, each with their own small camps. Often, the bands would gather together in one large village. The following groups have relevance to this story.

Bear Den Camp A fictitious camp belonging to the Kiyuksa Band of the Oglalas where Mahto lived.

Ghost Heart Band A band within the Oglalas circa 1825 about which little is known, but to which Turtle Woman belonged.

Kiyuksa Band A prominent band within the Oglala division of the Lakota (Western Teton) People. Bull Bear was the Kiyuksa leader until his death in 1841 at the hands of a few Smoke warriors. Known as the Bear People.

Muddy Water Camp A fictitious camp of the Night Cloud Band of the Oglalas (who were also followers of Bull Bear). Caws Like Magpie, Doublewoman Dreamer, and Black Tail belonged to this camp.

Night Cloud Band A little known band of the Oglalas existing circa 1850.

Smoke People A division of the Oglalas named after the leader, Chief Smoke. They separated themselves from the main group of Oglalas in 1841 after a few of their warriors killed the Kiyuksa leader, Bull Bear, causing a rift that split the Oglalas in two.

Standing People Camp   A fictitious camp (with a historical name) belonging to the Ghost Heart Band of the Oglalas. They were followers of the great leader, Bull Bear. Shifting Star, Turtle Woman, Breathcatcher, and thus Skye, belonged to this camp.

a-i-i-i expression of apprehension or anxiety. AH-ee-ee-ee.
akicita tribal police from warrior society. ah-KEE-chee-tah.
ama expression of doubt. ah-mah.
an he! war cry. ah^n-HAY!
Anog Ite vain Double-faced Woman of Lakota creation story. an-U^{N}K ee-TAY.
ate father (also used for paternal uncle). ah-TAY.
aze teats or udder. ah-ZEH
cansasa tobacco (shredded inner bark of red willow). chah^n-SHAH-shah.
cante ista eye of the heart, eye of the soul. chah^n-TAY eesh-TAH.
Cante Tanka Heart of Greatness. chan^n-tay TAH^{n}kah.
ehanni equivalent of "once upon a time," or long time ago. e-HAH^N-ee.
e-i-i-i expression of dismay or regret. AY-ee-ee-ee.

haho interjection of attention, Look here! Also thank you. ha-HOH.

han yes (interjection). Also *to* (tos, feminine). HAH^n.

hau greetings, hello, literally, "I am attentive." HAH-oo, HOW.

hau, kola hello, friend (masculine). HAH-oo KOH-lah.

hau, maske hello, friend (feminine). HAH-oo mah-SHKAY.

haye interjection of attention. Look here (feminine)! hah-YAY.

hecetu yelo male expression of agreement. hay-CHAY-too yay-LOH (way-LOH).

hehaka male elk. hay-HAH-kah.

He Sapa Black Mountains (Black Hills of South Dakota and Wyoming, older term). HAY SAH-pah.

He Ska Big Horn Mountains, Shining Mountains. HAY shkah.

Hewaktoka Gros Ventre (Atsina) tribe of the prairies. hay-WAH-toh-kah.

Hinhan Kaga old woman, Owl Pretender, who guards the Spirit Road. hee^n-HAH^n kah-gah.

hinu, hinu woman's expression of regret or astonishment. hee-NOO.

hiya no. hee-YAH.

hiyu po come forward (to many). hee-YOO-po.

hiyu wo come forward (masculine—to one). hee-YOO-wo.

hoh! interjection of denial. HOH!

ho he, ho he it is so, it is so. hoh-HAY hoh-HAY.

hokahe! a war cry, or "Let's go." HOH-kah-HAY!

hoppo! Let us go! (hopo). HOH-poh!

hosti expression of dismay. HOH-stee.

hoye (hohe) expression of affirmation, agreement, assent. ho-YAY.

huka hey! a war cry. HOH-kah-HAY!

hunka chosen relative. hoo^n-kah.

hye thank you (also *pilamaya*). hee-YAY.

igmu'tanka great cat, cougar, mountain lion. IGMOO-tah^{n}kah.

Ikce Oyate (wicasa) the common people, Real People, first Lakota. The Red Sun People. eek-CHAY oh-YAH-tay.

Iktomi spider, legendary Trickster. eek-TOH-mee.

ina mother. ee-NAH.

inipi steam-lodge ceremony. To be reborn over and over again. ee-NEE-pee.

inyan rock, stone, pebble. ee^n-yah^n.

itka (witka) seed, egg, testicles. eet-KAH.

Kangi Crow Indian. kah^n-GHEE.

Kangi Oyate Crow Nation. kah^n-GHEE oh-YAH-tay.

keya turtle. KAY-yah.

kinnikinnick smoking tobacco, often mixed with sumac, red willow, etc. KIN-ee-kuh-NIK.

Kiyuksas prominent band among the Oglala Lakotas, "cut off" band, Bear People. kee-YOO-s'sahs.

kola friend (masculine). KOH-lah.

Lakotas Western Teton tribe of the Sioux Indians. lah-KO-tahs.

li'la waste very good.

Mahpiyatos Arapahoe tribe (Blue Sky People). MAH-pee-yah-tohs.

Maka Earth. MAH-kah.

maske friend (feminine). mah-SHKAY.

mastincala rabbit. mah-SHTEEN-chah-lah.

mato bear (mahto). mah-TOH.

mitakoja my grandchild. mee-tah-GHO-zhah.

mitakuye oyasin ritualistic ending for speech or prayer, "all my relations." mee-TAH-koo-yeh oi-AH-see^n.

mitawicu my wife. mee-TAH-wee-cu.

naca civil leader, man of prominence in council, "big belly." nah-CAH *(naca ominicias)*.

nagi ghost, soul, spirit. NAH-gee.

Oglalas one of the Seven Council Fires of the Lakotas (Scatter One's Own) oh-GLAH-lahs.

onsimala ye have pity on me. oo^n-shee-mahla-yay.

pahin porcupine. PAH-i^n.

Palanis Arikara tribe. pah-LAH-nees.

Peta-oihankesni Fire Without End. pay-TAH oh-ee-ha^n-gesnee.

pilamaya thank you. pee-LAH-mah-YAH.

pte buffalo. p'TAY. *(Pte Oyate*, Buffalo Nation).

pte winyela buffalo cow. p'TAY win-YAY-lah.

Sahiyelas Cheyenne tribe (northern). shah-HEE-yay-lahs.

sapa black. SAH-pah.

Scilis Pawnee tribe (southern). The Liar People. SHCEE-lees.

Skan supreme judge, Sky, superior God of Lakota creation story. SHKAH^n.

sunka dog. shoo^n-KAH.

Susunis Shoshone tribe, Snake People. SHOO^n-shoo^n-ees.

takoja grandchild. tah-GHO-zhah.

Taku Skanskan spiritual vitality, source of all movement. tah-KOO SHKAH^n SHKAH^n.

tatanka the male buffalo. tah-TAH^n-kah.

tinpsila (timpsila) prairie turnip. TEE-p'see-lah.

Titonwans term used by nontribal members to refer to the Teton nation of Lakotas (lived/born on the plains or prairie country). tee-TOO^n-wah^{n}s.

toka enemy. toh-KAH.

tokahe the first. First Man. toh-KAH-hay.

tokala kit fox, name of warrior lodge. toh-KAH-lah.

toksa later on, expression of good-bye, until we see you again, I will think about it. TOHK-sa.

tonwan spirit, sacred essence, eye of the soul. toh^n-WAH^n.

tunkasila grandfather, or ancestor. Also, loosely, God, or sun. too^n-KAH-shee-lah.

unci (kunsi) grandmother. oo^n-CHEE.

wakan mysterious, holy, sacred. wah-KAH^n.

Wakan Tanka Great Mystery, supreme creator. wah-KAH^n-tah^{n}kah.

walitakya to be brave. wah-LEE-tah-kah-yah.

wanbli eagle, cloud-bird. wah^n-BLEE.

wasicu the white man, sometimes used disparagingly. (*wasicula*, complimentary term). wah-SHEE-choo.

wasna pemmican. wah-SNAH.

waste good. wash-TAY.

welo female term of agreement. way-LOH.

wey, wey sound used by women for calling dog. way-way.

Wi the sun. WEE.

Wicasa Itacan leader of people or nation. wee-CHAH-shah ee-TAH-kan.

wicasa okinihan revered and honored person. wee-CHAH-shah oh-KEE-nee-hah^n.

wikoskala pretty young woman. wee-KOSH-kah-lah.

winyan woman. WEE^n-yah^n.

Winyan Numpa Double Woman (or *numpapika*). WEE^n-yah^n noopah.

witko crazy. weet-KOH.

Wohpe (woope) the Falling Star, White Buffalo Calf Woman, laws or values. WOO-pe.

wotawe a charm relied upon in war, an object made sacred. wo-TAH-way.

Yata North Wind. YAH-tah (or *waziyata*).

yelo male term of agreement. yah-LOH.

yun female cry of pain. YOO^N.